The *Killswitch* Review

from Bestseller
Steven-Elliot Altman

and

Diane DeKelb-Rittenhouse

The Killswitch Review
Steven-Elliot Altman
First Edition Copyright © Steven-Elliot Altman, 2009
Second Edition Copyright © Steven-Elliot Altman, 2016

Published by Yard Dog Press at Create Space

ISBN 978-1-937105-90-7
The Killswitch Review
Second Edition Copyright © Steven-Elliot Altman, 2016

Yard Dog Press
710 W. Redbud Lane
Alma, AR   72921-7247

http://www.yarddogpress.com

Edited by Selina Rosen
Copy Editor Leonard R. Bishop
Technical Editor Lynn Rosen
Cover art by Eran Cantrell

Second Edition June, 2016
Printed in the United States of America
0 9 8 7 6 5 4 3 2 1

Dedicated to the late, great Philip K. Dick.

Special thanks
to Patrick Merla, Hillery Borton and Selina Rosen for their
priceless gifts of editing
to Victoria A. Brownworth for her unfailing
guidance and support
to Barry Gilbert, Dr. Jack Kevorkian, Kurt Cobain, Philip K.
Dick and The Green Hand for their inspirational
arguments which planted the seeds of this novel
to Michael Reaves, Matt Vermoten, Jamie Brashear, Mindy
Yale, Dawn Thorne, Julie Marsh and Dr. Kimberly
Telesh for contributing sparks of insight
and to Chantel Kaufman, Walt Rittenhouse, Josh Schechter,
Marc and Elaine Zicree, Emma Gillings, Scot Lang,
Johanna Shapiro, Alan and Justin Tholl, Lourdes Navarro,
Stephen and Bridget Susco, Rachel Bieber, Paul and Seth
Edelstein, C. B. Spencer and Robert Burdige for their love,
encouragement, notes and the occasional rescue.

In the year 2156...

...stem cell therapy has triumphed over all forms of disease, extending the human lifespan indefinitely. Americans who have been granted Conscientious Citizen status now live healthy, youthful lives well beyond the century mark.

To combat overpopulation and depletion of resources, America has sealed her borders and instituted strict measures of birth and death control. Families are now restricted to one child per couple, and the leading cause of death in the U.S. has become technology-assisted suicide.

BLACK BUTTONS, INC. is the government authority responsible for dispensing Kevorkian units—handheld devices which afford the only legal form of suicide.

An armed "Killswitch" monitors and records a citizen's final moments—up to the point where they press a button and peacefully die.

Post-press review agents— "button collectors"—are dispatched to review and judge these final recordings to rule out foul play.

Chapter One
BLACK BUTTONS, INC.

Haggerty had his finger on the button. The black onyx set in the gunmetal casing felt cool beneath his touch. There were millions of registered buttons just like it, hundreds of millions, in fact. No one knew that better than he did, but this one was his, tailor-made. His name glowed across its base: JASON P. HAGGERTY.

He looked around the living room of his spacious compartment, remembering the pride and excitement with which he had made every acquisition it held. His plasma dome viewscreen cost more than most people made in a decade. The glass-topped bar was stocked with premium liquors, not cheap bar brands. A replitext that could become any book he'd ever read or ever wanted to read rested on an elegant simumarble pedestal. Those were just the most obvious of the niceties of life he had been afforded. He called the outer wall into full transparency mode. It cleared instantly, revealing the cityscape outside: close-packed stalk-like buildings stretching to the blazing blue sky dappled with wisps of clouds above distant snow-capped mountains. That view had been the main reason he chose to live here. All these luxuries, so casually on display, never failed to impress the few friends he kept or the even fewer women he'd brought here since Lorraine had left him. The pain that came with his job had once seemed a small price to pay for such wealth. No longer. The compartment and everything it held was too big, too luxurious. Too empty.

All week long he'd contemplated the act. He planned on pressing around midnight. There was a certain poetry to a midnight press on a Saturday night, a certain feeling of closure, pressing as the week ended, before a new one could start. He'd always been a man who saw things through to the end, no matter how difficult the task. He'd worked to be a true Conscientious Citizen, someone who made a positive contribution to society, who unfailingly honored his commitments, who promptly and thoroughly discharged his obligations, and who brought all his skill and ability to his chosen profession. If he were still that man, he'd be getting into his uniform and preparing for his final shift, making sure that when he pressed, he left no loose ends for someone else to clean up. Instead, his finger was on the button, fifteen hours early.

It would take so little, just a light push, to gain release. Why wait? It was unlikely anything earth-shattering would require his presence at work today. Black Buttons, Inc. could manage without him. Haggerty could barely recall the last time a Kevorkian unit had been tampered with, or a press coerced. These days there were no surprises in the reviews he conducted, rendering them largely a formality. Let his successor deal with the unclosed files in his office. No fortunes would be reversed, no futures altered. The outcome of no case would be affected by his passing.

Nor would any thing outside of work. Or anyone. He had no family left, and most of his friends had drifted away long ago. Only two remained who might regret his passing. Doug, the company doctor, who'd likely be pissed as hell, and Elsa, Haggerty's personal assistant. He didn't know how she would react. He wasn't sure she was capable of comprehending the depth of the loss he'd suffered, or to feel loss herself. Any regrets she had would likely center around not having noticed what he was about to do and not acting to stop him. But Elsa would not wallow in self-recrimination or prolonged grief. Most likely she would pragmatically accept that there was nothing she could do to change things and move on to serve whichever reviewer was next in line for a new assistant. Haggerty had no final words for her or for Doug, nothing that mattered enough to say. All his affairs were in order, and if the only duty left to him was to rubberstamp some paperwork, well, that was one obligation his successor at BBI could discharge.

So easy, he thought. The cool metal drew heat from his finger—that exchange seemed reasonable. He could trade the inertia of routine for the act of pressing, trade the anesthetizing drug of work, duty, and obligation for the anesthetic spray on his thumb, the unfelt injection of tailored toxin that would deaden his pain centers as life drained from his body.

A fine tremor ran through his hands. He sat back, letting go of the unit. He felt old, tired, done.

He reached for his button once more. *Just one push*, he thought, one tiny exertion of pressure and it would be over—

much as his father must have thought a year earlier, Haggerty suspected, as his thumb tensed on the trigger of the registered antique, double-barrel shotgun illegally restored to working order. Haggerty drew a deep breath and flipped the ARM switch.

"Recording," announced the soft feminine electronic voice he'd selected years ago from a dozen options. "Eighth March, Twenty-one-fifty-six, oh-nine twenty-four." The pale amber light he'd chosen came on beneath the button.

It was customary to say something. But nothing came to mind—no *Forgive me* or *Not without you* or *Since I am ruined* or *Just done it all* like he'd seen in so many reviews. So he merely said, "Enough ... it's been enough," wondering who the agency would send to do the post-press, hoping it wasn't Corbin. The Dragon owed him that much, at least.

A bead of sweat made its way through his hairline and down, stinging, into one eye. The climate control system silently switched on, no doubt registering his rise in body temperature, pumping cool air. His compartment was more alive than he was. Haggerty circled the button with the tip of his middle finger with hesitant tenderness, like a man exploring the nipple of a new lover, certain now. He couldn't stand to face another day. He stared at his unit, ready to press.

The phone chimed an incoming call.

"Damn it!" he grunted, laughing mirthlessly. "Answer, visual off!" he barked, and disarmed his KV unit.

A small, clear light appeared in the air a few feet in front of him, began spinning fast, acquiring color, depth, texture, expanding outward until a life-size holographic representation of Elsa floated in the center of his living room.

"I'm downstairs, Jason," she said. "Why is your visual off?"

"I'm naked," Haggerty lied, stowing his KV unit in the drawer of an end table. "Still interested in seeing me?"

"Do you want me to see you?" she asked with polite disinterest.

Elsa was dressed in regulation BBI grays. The jumpsuit, though neither fashionable nor flattering, did little to hide her physical perfection. When she'd first been assigned to him, Haggerty had been married only fifteen years, and Lorraine had teased him, claiming to be jealous of his beautiful, supportive, fiercely loyal assistant. After all, flesh was flesh, and most reviewers did end up taking their assistants to bed, Haggerty included. But that was before Lorraine, and no matter how adult

Elsa looked, she reminded him of a child.

"I thought you might like to ride to work together," she said. Meaning she had concluded that his behavior over the last few days was worrisome, and she wanted to keep an eye on him.

"Go in without me," Haggerty said. "I'm debating calling in sick."

"Are you seriously ill, Jason?" Elsa asked. "What sort of symptoms are you—You'd better let me come up immediately."

"Wait there, I'll be down in five," Haggerty said. He snapped off the connection, glanced at the end table drawer and headed for the master bathroom just off his bedroom. The lights flared awake as he entered. "Cold," he said, and the basin tap came on.

Haggerty popped open his pillcase and extracted a celtrex. The translucent, faint green gelcap sat in the palm of his hand like a drop of seawater. Sometimes he wished it were more than a drop, wished it were enough to drown his sorrows. He reached into a cabinet for a disposable cup. His hand came into contact with something soft. He frowned, pulled out the unexpected object, then froze, staring down at one of the bejeweled fabric ribbons Lorraine had used to tie back her long black hair. How had this one escaped his notice? He'd thought he got rid of them all. Haggerty lifted the ribbon slowly to his face. It was still there, ever so faint, the scent of jasmine and Lorraine.

He gripped the sink, closed his eyes, got himself enough under control to put the scrap of cloth back into the cabinet and grab for a cup. He filled it with water and swallowed the pill, calming instantly—a psychological reaction; it would be three or four minutes before the drug could do the job it was intended for, if not the job he needed done. He bent over the sink, splashed his face, then stared into the mirror and waited for the celtrex to take effect.

The mirror continued to lie, proclaiming him to be exactly as he had appeared on his thirtieth birthday, sixty years ago. His hair was still dark, his chin still cleft, still the most notable feature in what might be called a boyishly attractive face. Only his gray eyes revealed the truth: Haggerty had seen too damned much, too damned often. His eyes would always be haunted.

It appeared that he would be discharging his final obligations, after all. Maybe he should request that as his epitaph: *A Conscientious Citizen to the End*. With another mirthless laugh, Haggerty left the bathroom, pulled on his uniform, slid his pillcase into a pocket, grabbed his com from where he'd left it on the nightstand, and headed out for what he decided would be his last day of work.

Elsa waited patiently in the lobby. She was exquisitely beautiful, in a way that had gone out of fashion at least fifty years before. Petite and curvaceous blue-eyed blondes with what had once been called "classic" features were the goddesses of a bygone day. Now the rage was for cream-skinned brunettes standing a minimum of five-feet-ten, with the lean lines of well-bred greyhounds. Still, of the dozen people passing through the lobby, not one failed to look at Elsa just a bit longer than was polite.

Haggerty suggested they use the Ojai beltway. It took a little longer than the superbelts but was more scenic and a lot less jammed at this hour (which, at this time of day in a city the size of NewVada, simply meant that it wasn't standing-room-only with people packed six deep).

Elsa cocked her head. "Are you sure you wouldn't be more comfortable driving?" she said. "Air quality and visibility are both very good this morning, but the heat index is above normal for this time of year."

"I'm not getting behind the wheel of a car," Haggerty said. "Not today."

"I suppose I can understand that," she conceded. "I am aware of the date, Jason. You shouldn't ..."

"Let it go, Elsa," Haggerty said firmly, knowing she had no choice. Nodding acquiescence, she followed him outside.

Despite the cooling fabric of his regulation grays—a nonthreatening, neutral color meant to reassure adjusters and surviving next of kin present at press sites—the heat of the city slammed into him as soon as the door opened, before he'd crossed the threshold. Used to its impact, Haggerty kept moving. Elsa was enviably unaffected, her smooth skin unmarred by perspiration, her long blonde hair untouched by anything so vulgar as sweat.

The street outside Haggerty's complex was packed with thousands of lower-status citizens on their daily commute, who had to use public transport. Haggerty and Elsa fell in step among them and were jostled along by the slowly moving crowd. In less than ten minutes they reached the silvery column of hypersteel that would transport them to the beltplatform. They tubed up and quickly made their way to the on-loops, moving forward with the crowd to the entrance turnstiles. Most people used their thumbprints for access, though a few individuals scanned voucher strips or identiplates to charge the cost of transportation to a corporation or government agency, rather than to their individual private accounts as happened with thumbprints. Someone had been pulled aside by security, drawing the attention of passers-by; the lines to the turnstiles nearest the altercation slowed as people turned to gawk. A guard frowned intently at the strip of plasticine that a slightly paunchy, gray-haired man had tried to feed into the system. Outside the immigrant enclaves or the Vegas Black Light district, it was rare to see an adult whose true age was so painfully obvious. The man, clearly not a Conscientious Citizen, spoke slowly, his English awkward and not easily intelligible as he tried to convince the guard that his employer had given him the voucher to run an errand. The guard wasn't buying his story.

The line at Turnstile Number Three is moving quickly. Elsa's words projected into Haggerty's mind via a neural transmitter link implanted at the base of his skull. The link, allowing review agents and their assistants to communicate silently within a hundred yards of each other, to hold private conversations in public situations, had once been a closely guarded industry secret, a crucial factor in BBI's, and Haggerty's, success. Now, it mainly helped him avoid traffic jams and social *faux pas*. Elsa sent another message: *There's a pylon obscuring the view of what's going on here, so there's no rubbernecking beyond it.*

Let's go, then, he linked back, moving toward the line Elsa had indicated. He flashed his BBI identiplate at the reader and stepped through the turnstile to the on-loop, Elsa following behind.

The loop fed them quickly onto the Ojai, thousands of feet above ground level, and they were soon being conveyed through the city. The belt was pretty full, but there were a few marginally comfortable bench seats available for those who wanted them. The trip was short enough for Haggerty to prefer standing. Elsa stood quietly beside him as the moving path ushered them along, correctly reading his mood to be that he preferred silence.

Looking over the rail, Haggerty thought he could make out the terminus of the Creutzfeldt-Jakob Building, but it was too far down to see without lenses. He considered what falling from such a great height might feel like, the rough, hot wind on his face. But a last thrill before termination was not for him, even if he could overcome the programmed safeguards and throw himself over the edge. He was simply admiring the view. Tired as he was of his life, he could still be awed by the cityscape of towers rising from the floor of barren desert to challenge the distant mountains for supremacy.

Until the end of the last century, much of NewVada had been part of California. Politics, and the need to build a city that straddled the old state lines, had redrawn the map. Though Haggerty had a distant memory of when this part of the Nevada/California border had been nothing but miles of scrub, sage, and sand, that memory was hard to reconcile with the current reality. Because that memory was the world of his childhood, when the human body was subject to incurable diseases and the encroaching debilitation of old age. Aggressive funding had fueled stem-cell research, and death from age or illness was relegated to the past, until overpopulation became the most pressing concern facing America and every other industrialized country in the world. The increased demand for living space, coupled with the need to conserve land that could be productively farmed, forced governments to carve cities out of terrain previously deemed uninhabitable.

Now, buildings packed tightly together covered the desert, rising into the clouds, interwoven with massive twelve-lane elevated beltways for those rich enough to afford cars, and, a few stories beneath them, pay-as-you-go pedestrian belts for the masses. The higher up you lived and traveled, the higher your status. All belts circled and offered multiple offramps to Downtown, the heart of the city, which housed most of the city's government infrastructure: City Hall, Police Headquarters, Central Morgue, and Haggerty's own agency, BBI. Transfer between belts was possible at any number of junctions, and all of the city's belts converged at four different locations, North, South, East and West, the beltwheels acting as transfer points so that riders could get anywhere in the city, no matter from which belt they started.

NewVada had been one of the first megapolitan cities built, its forty-two-million population crammed into two-thousand square miles of the hottest land on earth. Temperatures in excess of 130 degrees Fahrenheit were common, at least at ground level. But only those with no other option lived and traveled at ground level: immigrants awaiting Provisional Citizen Status; denizens of the Vegas Black Light District; those on the fringes of society. Most NewVadans rarely had to deal with such extremes, and in theory could go from one climate-controlled environment to another—compartments to transportation to offices, hotels, public buildings or private residences and back again—their entire lives spent without ever experiencing the raw power of the untempered heat suffusing the city around them. Even so, some vital system always broke down or wore out, causing people to swelter uncomfortably for an hour or a day or a month until climate control was restored. Like anything else, if you lived in NewVada long enough, you got used to the heat, or at least enough used to it to take the occasional shortcut out of doors. And after tonight, Haggerty thought as they approached their transfer point off the Ojai, there would be one less person putting out heat.

Haggerty and Elsa merged onto the Northside beltwheel, where practically the entire cityscape came into view: the Northside heavenscrapers, home to the uber-rich, where Haggerty lived; the Westside slums, refuge of the ultra-poor; the Southside, an uneasy blend of those who struggled in between. And the Eastside, dominated by Vegas, the world-renowned Black Light District, the place where one's monetary status could change for better or worse with a single roll of dice.

A group of teens sporting garish skinpaint and stickjewel artwork on the visible portions of their bodies sped up on airboards to Haggerty and Elsa, surfing several feet above belt level, the hovering boards the latest end-run by Junior Citizens around the law prohibiting those without full CC status from setting foot on privileged belts during rush hour. Legally, the kids couldn't even apply to be CCs until they were of employment age. Haggerty wasn't sure how they got past the entrance turnstiles, unless they airboarded from the floor of the terminal to the maintenance catwalks, along those to the overpasses, then dropped a hundred feet to belt level. Just the kind of dangerous, brain-dead stunt typical of JCs. They thought they could come away unscathed from any outrageous stunt. He couldn't deny that they *were* skilled as they maneuvered their boards deftly between annoyed CCs without causing accidents. Still, the belt wasn't wide enough to leave much margin for error; Elsa had to step aside quickly to avoid being hit.

"Sorry," one of the teens called back in a voice of indeterminate gender.

"Reckless," Haggerty said as he watched them weave in and

around ducking pedestrians, the stickjeweled words CLONE JESUS! flashing on one JC's bare back.

"What's Clone Jesus?" he asked Elsa, not bothering to link. "A new religious movement?"

After a moment, she answered, "It's a band of musicians. They have the number-one song on the current Indranet download charts. Would you like to hear it?"

"No, thanks," Haggerty said. He didn't like the music popular with JCs these days. He was happy to let Elsa keep track of such cultural trends, along with all the other bits of trivia she tracked as part of her assigned duties.

A buildingboard-sized cityscreen flashed the morning news as they belted along, repeating a story Haggerty had seen last night depicting dozens of illegal ships off the California coast, filled with hopeful immigrants, fired upon relentlessly by the American Coast Guard. Their tiny boats were no match for the gargantuan U.S. gunships. Those that did not capsize fled back toward the free zone, their dreams of the Promised Land never to become reality. There was simply no room for them here.

"Poor bastards," Haggerty said to Elsa. "Do they have enough rations for a return trip, or even homes to go back to?"

Elsa considered his question, then shook her head. "Unlikely," she said softly. "Space is at a premium on the pirate ships smuggling illegals into the country. More cargo means fewer passengers and less profit. When a ship fails to make landfall here, mortality rates increase rapidly after the first few days of the return journey. For those who do make it back to their homelands, there is a very high probability that any property they left behind has already been confiscated."

Haggerty nodded, not really surprised. He knew that for most illegals, the journey was all or nothing. He could only imagine the sufferings they'd face upon return.

"*Keeping America's borders safe for Americans*," the board stated, and then displayed a five-second advertisement from BBI of a smiling man reclining in a hammock with the latest unit model by his side. "*KV. The choice is yours*," the advertisement droned.

Haggerty and Elsa stepped onto the exit belt that would take them to BBI's platform. Haggerty scanned his identiplate at the gate, which obligingly rose out of their way, and they headed toward the building's main entrance.

They heard shouting. Haggerty grimaced. Another protest

must be underway. The Religious Right had more or less set up a permanent camp on the BBI quad. Maybe a hundred people hoisted flashbanners demanding NATURE FIRST and DISARM YOUR SWITCH! And, inevitably, HEAVEN WON'T TAKE THOSE WHO PRESS!

"Do you want to go around back to avoid them?" Elsa asked.

"Tempting," Haggerty admitted. "But I'm already running late. Not like we haven't run the gauntlet before."

It was, in fact, almost a daily occurrence. They pushed past the protesters with practiced ease, but as they reached the marble archway flanked by six bull-faced guards wearing crash gear and holding multi-burst autostuns, a girl with long, sandy-brown hair rushed to block their path.

"Don't go in there and fit for a button," she pleaded. "You don't need a Killswitch. Life and death are decisions meant for God, not for you!"

Her eyes caught Haggerty, their green depths so earnest he couldn't simply walk past, as he had walked past a thousand protesters before her. He allowed himself to be stopped, and returned her intense gaze. Judging anyone's age by physical appearance alone was always dicey. She was wearing the kind of clothing popular among Junior Citizens—loose-fitting pants that started at the hip and ended just below the knee, a half-tee that truncated right beneath her breasts, both in a mossy green that matched her eyes, and the backpack no one but students ever seemed to carry. Skinpainting of a purple iris bloomed on her torso. But Haggerty had long ago trained himself to read more subtle, almost subliminal, signs to figure out how old someone really was. Usually, there were clues—the way people spoke or dressed, the specific films or music or books they enjoyed, the sports playoffs they talked about, the politicians they admired—something that revealed when they'd grown up. No clues were needed now. The girl's unlined face had a rawness that plastiche would have smoothed away, all the more attractive for its lack of perfection. Haggerty was sure that she wasn't much older than the twenty or so she appeared.

"I'll make my own choices, thank you," he said, not unkindly, and tried to move past her. She mirrored his action, continuing to block the path. He sensed Elsa tensing for action, and hastily sent reassurance across their link.

"Pressing is a mistake," the girl said vehemently. "And it's one you can't fix. There are no second thoughts with a Killswitch."

She all but spat out the derogatory slang for the Kevorkian unit.

She was so young, Haggerty thought. Too young for this much intensity. Then again, maybe only the young *could* feel so intensely about life anymore. He guessed she had lost someone recently, maybe a parent, someone she wasn't ready to let go. He might feel pity or compassion, even empathy, for her, but he still had to do his job.

"That's a risk I'm willing to take," he said truthfully. "Now, if you'll excuse us."

She remained in their path. Haggerty tried to force his way past her.

The girl grasped his arm. "Don't do this," she pleaded.

There was nothing particularly aggressive about the way she'd reached for him. If anything, her hold was tentative, a gesture to get his attention, nothing that could really have prevented him from moving. But her effort did not go down well with security. Elsa grabbed the girl by the wrists as the nearby guards swooped in. Exasperated by everyone's overreaction, Haggerty raised a hand.

"It's okay," he said.

The guards lowered their weapons and at Haggerty's linked command, Elsa let the girl go.

Haggerty stared her in the eye. The girl returned his gaze with defiance, even pride. But he had the edge on her, the weight of age and grief and the sheer length of time he'd gone on living enabling him to face her down as long as it might take. After a moment, her gaze faltered. Haggerty gave the girl a grim smile and continued walking. Elsa threw her a disapproving look before falling into step behind him.

As they entered the BBI building, the girl came forward once more. "Go ahead, then," she cried out angrily. "Cough and die if it suits you! Press your Killswitch!"

There was no point in telling her he planned to.

"Haggerty, where ya' been?" Tanner grumbled as they entered the viewing room, looking up from his breakfast. "Diddling your assistant? We had a double press over an hour ago."

Elsa took a seat at the main switchboard and began downloading data, ignoring Tanner's comment. Haggerty envied her ability to remain unmoved. After decades of ignoring it himself, he'd lately found Tanner's habitual, juvenile crudeness unbearably irritating.

If Jason Haggerty tried to live up to the ideal of what a Conscientious Citizen should be, Mitch Tanner seemed intent on living down to the worst excesses associated with the status. Haggerty didn't like Tanner, finding in him the extreme example of everything that was wrong with the majority of people who'd been CCs for more than two decades. He dosed too much in his off time, bitched too much when he was on, and had been campaigning to get Elsa into bed almost from the moment she'd become Haggerty's assistant. He also went in for plastiche to the point of absurdity. Nobody went much past thirty without at least one visit to the best plastiche parlor he or she could afford, but Tanner chose to look like a JC rather than an adult, and acted like he was no older than he looked. He was ninety-two playing at twenty-two, and not very convincingly. But whatever Haggerty thought of Tanner's perpetual adolescence, he had to work with the man, if only for the rest of the day.

A quick look at what Tanner was eating, greasy cubes of cloniform beef from the cafeteria dispensary, was enough to turn Haggerty's stomach. Some of the grease had made a bid for freedom on its way to Tanner's mouth, and got as far as his chest; two small dark spots marked his regulation grays, which the self-cleaning fabric would eliminate within half an hour. At the moment, though, they remained revoltingly visible.

"Do you have a clue how they prepare that stuff?" Haggerty asked, indicating the plate of food.

"Nope," Tanner said. "As long as they're doing the preparing and not me, I don't really care."

"There hasn't been a live cow on the planet for half a century," Haggerty pointed out. "What they call meat in that swill was culled from a one-hundredth generation clone, grown in a nutrient tank, packed in fake gelatin, flavored with synthetics, and then saniwaved"—which was the reason Haggerty, despite his love of rare steaks and thick burgers, reluctantly followed a vegetarian diet.

"Jeez, Haggerty," Tanner said, forking up another mouthful of cloniform beef, "you sound like that Code Six guy who's supposed to be holed up in the desert someplace. What's his name? Cody?" Tanner scrunched up his face in concentration. "Bodey? Brody?"

"Tomas Yosif Svoboda," Elsa supplied.

"Yeah, him," Tanner said. "The back-to-nature nut."

Code Six was one of the "blue codes," police designations for threats to public health and safety that required the intervention of law enforcement officers, in this case designating that the person causing the disturbance appeared to be mentally defective and should be approached with caution. Haggerty dimly remembered headlines from decades ago regarding this man, Svoboda—a physicist who supposedly found God, denounced society and founded a cult of subversives called—what was it—the "Indivisibles?"

Tanner lifted his fork to his mouth and another scrap of breakfast hit his grays, making a third spot bloom on the cloth. Haggerty's mouth tightened. Like so many others, Tanner didn't look deeply into the nature of things, or care about anything unless the telemonitor warned him to. Perhaps Tanner's failure to see below the surface was the reason he was merely a trace and dispatch operator, while Haggerty was a reviewer.

"Who and what?" Haggerty asked now, giving up speculation and turning to the job at hand.

He stepped into the pulpit and powered it on. Elsa's fingers blurred in motion on the transparent board. Data streamed before Haggerty: holo-reps of both pushers, one male, one female, their lives in coded bytes listing below them.

"The dearly departed," Tanner quipped. "His name was Gustavo Nyuga, one hundred and four, and she was Maria-Christina Rosenberg, one hundred and thirty." Tanner smiled nastily. "Guess he liked older women."

To the eye, they both seemed nubile, ageless. The remark was another of Tanner's crudities: with people living well into their second century and no one looking much over thirty, age gaps between couples were commonplace. What did a few decades matter when everyone had so many of them to look forward to?

"He was a retired investment banker; she was his client, then boss, and then lover," Tanner continued.

"When and where?" Haggerty asked, moving into the scaled continuous-update holo-rep of the cityscape.

"Oh-eight forty-two," Tanner read aloud. "The Hodkins Building." An amber pinlight fixed on a Southside compartment. Haggerty knew the building; he'd been assigned there on a number of occasions. "Looks like they pressed together. Very sweet," Tanner said.

Who, what, when, and *where* duly answered, it was Haggerty's job to find out the *why* and make sure it was clean. The *how* he knew all too well.

"Elsa, code us last rites and warrants and get me a thermos of coffee, won't you?" he requested as he returned to the pulpit.

The Southside was thick with buildings, stalk after stalk of hypersteel, plasticine, and permaglass rising in square columns of sandy beige and yellow and tan, as if the desert had merely redistributed itself vertically rather then been swallowed whole by Man. In this desiccated garden, the Hodkins Building was the one notable bloom, an exclusive residence, a superior example of the Karin Li school of architecture that had flourished in the second half of the previous century. The building curved around itself, spiraling upward in a graceful sweep, its permaglass surface gradations of blue, from deepest navy at the base to light aqua that seemed to fade into the sky at the upper reaches. The inside was as elegant as the outside. They entered the tube and Elsa typed the pass code to allow them entry to the floor they needed. As they approached the compartment, Haggerty raised the flashing yellow police tape and they passed beneath. A uniformed officer halted them.

"Sorry folks, this is a press scene."

The man had to be new on the job, not to distinguish between the gray suits of ordinary citizens and their regulation grays. Haggerty flashed his BBI identiplate and the officer, with an embarrassed apology, waved them on.

The door was ajar. Inside they found a well-dressed man seated calmly on an esplanade couch drinking a glass of blue liquid, maybe KeepAwake. Dark-haired, tanned, handsome in that bourgeois way that plastiche seemed to have made everyone's birthright, he placed his drink on a coaster on a delicate antique end table and rose to greet them.

"The name's Primrose," he said. "Haggerty, right?"

Haggerty reached to shake hands. "You're the adjuster? Never seen you before." He'd also never seen anyone who'd chosen to keep his physical appearance at early middle age, though he knew the trend was gaining popularity with some businessmen. Primrose sported a frost of silver at each temple, stark and handsome against his dark hair, and the barest suggestion of lines around his eyes. His athletic build had a hint more solidity than the usual thirty-year-old look. Primrose's look was distinguished, striking, sophisticated, intended to convey authority and experience—invaluable in an adjuster's work, Haggerty thought.

"Just got assigned to NewVada," Primrose said. "Transferred from New York."

"You must be excited," Haggerty said.

Primrose appeared confused.

"The game?" Haggerty added.

"Oh, the Superbowl. I won't be there. I'm not much of a football fan," Primrose said with a self-deprecating smile. "Don't appreciate violent sports."

Haggerty nodded. He had his own reason for not being there, beside the fact that tickets cost a small fortune and were near impossible to come by. He'd shared a love of football with his father, and had painfully let it go in his absence. Pressing the night before the big game would itself be an act of defiance for Haggerty. The fact that NewVada was finally a contender made it all the more ironic.

"Mind showing us the press site?" he asked Primrose.

"This way."

Primrose's swaggering walk suggested confidence, another asset in an adjuster. Who wanted to leave their final affairs in the hands of someone who didn't have absolute faith in what he was doing? But, Haggerty thought, Primrose overdid it a bit. Like Tanner's love affair with puberty, Primrose's idealized middle-aged man rang false. From the clothes he wore and the jewelry he affected, Haggerty read Primrose to be not much older than the appearance he maintained, a youngster of fifty or so. Most likely he was an up-and-comer with great prospects but a minimal track record in his field, for which his appearance was calculated to compensate. He couldn't blame Primrose for trying to gain advantage. Everyone started someplace.

He really is young, Elsa told Haggerty through their link. *I can tell.*

So can I, Haggerty sent back.

Primrose led them into the bedroom, a healthy-sized chamber nearly eight-by-eight, half the size of Haggerty's but still indicative of wealth, as were the room's furnishings. Before he'd pressed, Nyuga had indulged a taste—his or his lover's—for antiques. Real wool carpets covered the floor; bureaus, end tables, and armoires of genuine wood stood against the walls. There were lighting fixtures on tall, elegant poles with fluted crystal glass bowls to deflect the illumination—torch lamps, Haggerty vaguely recalled, his mother had owned one, inherited from a great-aunt. The bed was not the standard platform but a carved fantasy designed to look like a Russian sleigh from at least three centuries back. The wood was natural, though Haggerty couldn't say from what kind of tree, and against the dark frame a set of mauve silk bedclothes had been twisted by passion, not slumber, and heaped together like discarded flower petals. Drool-tinged blood was evident on one pillow, urine and fecal stains on the sheets—typical evidence of a press. One KV unit lay half hidden beneath a coverlet; Primrose pointed out the other one on the floor, under the bed.

Haggerty cleared his throat. "Do you have the DCs?"

"Right here," Primrose said, holding up his com and hitting the recall codes. He withdrew the two strips of plasticine the com disgorged. "Do you have the warrants for the boxes?"

Haggerty nodded, following suit with his own com. The two men exchanged documents that were neatly encoded on plasticine cards. Haggerty scanned the death certificates, observing that they were affixed with the proper coroner's seals, then asked, "How long since the bodies were removed?"

"Half an hour," Primrose said. "They took all the necessary samples. The detective, I believe his name was—"

"Woyzeck, I know him," Haggerty interrupted. "He called it a love-spawned clean double, pending our review."

"His exact words," Primrose said.

"Okay, let's do it," Haggerty said. "Record on."

Elsa leaned against the bedroom door, casually smoothing blonde hair from her face and folding her arms. "Recording," she said.

"Eulogic proceedings for Gustavo Nyuga and Maria-Christina Rosenberg. Jason P. Haggerty, representative for BBI, presiding."

"Oliver Wendell Primrose, adjusting agent for the insurance firm of Cromwell and Sons, prepared to review," Primrose added in a more officious tone.

Haggerty went to the bed, pulling on black duratex gloves. "Elsa," he said, "please note: By the authority vested in me by legal warrant of the State of Nevada, I am taking possession of, and responsibility for, two KV black button units that are, to the best of my judgment, the property of BBI and assumed to be the devices of record assigned to the deceased."

"So noted," Elsa responded.

Haggerty picked the first unit off the bed and read out the serial number engraved on the casing, then got down on his knees, retrieved the second unit, and repeated the process.

"Serial numbers confirmed as those registered to the deceased," Elsa said a few seconds later.

"Units appear fully intact and previously armed," Haggerty continued. "Tabs popped clearly indicate that both buttons have been pressed." He tipped the boxes up for Primrose to inspect.

Keeping a safe distance, Primrose eyed the tabs and called, "In my best judgment, I confirm that both buttons appear to have been pressed."

Post-press, the units were, at least in theory, toxin-free, but Haggerty was careful as he handled them, anyway. BBI protocol required that he not put the theory to the test. He brought them over to Elsa. "Mind closing the curtains?" he said to Primrose, who located the console and dialed them shut.

Elsa stood motionless against the door, waiting for Haggerty to reach her. She gave him a look; he supposed she'd smelled the celtrex lacing the coffee on his breath. As he handed her the first unit, she unfastened the tab at the collar of her jumpsuit and pulled the zipper down to her waist in one smooth motion. Primrose watched with an avidity bordering on the salacious as she pressed her thumb hard against her sternum, snapping open her breastplate and exposing her ported upload center, then deftly inserted the unit.

"Analysis?" he asked.

Elsa was silent a full minute, then, "Serial numbers as previously confirmed. Residue on unit confirmed as a BBI toxin. Prints on unit confirmed via requiem for the registered owner. It is established that this is the device of record for Maria-Christina Rosenberg."

"Play recording with full room projection," Haggerty said. "Adjust for the light."

Behind Elsa's irises, twin beacons whirred into motion, projecting onto Haggerty's face. He stepped aside. A duplicate holo-image overlaid the room, with the notable inclusion of Gustavo Nyuga and Maria-Christina Rosenberg nude in bed, KV units in hand. Hers was armed; tears wet her cheeks as the soft male electronic voice announced, "Recording," and went on to give the date and time. The unit cast a violet light across the couple's bare skins.

Primrose stood mesmerized, as if this were his first post-press viewing. Haggerty had encountered that sort of prurience before. Some adjusters never got tired of the show; it was almost indecent. It seemed to Haggerty that the final moments of the deceased should be observed solemnly, with respect. He turned his attention back to the review.

Gustavo Nyuga took Maria-Christina in his arms, peering over her shoulder as he armed his unit. "Recording," it droned, bathing the curve of her back in pale green light.

"Quickly, Gustavo, before I change my mind," she wept. "I love you forever."

"God, I love you too," he said, and pressed. She moaned when she heard his unit pop. Then hers popped as well.

Her unit continued to record as they crumpled against each other onto the pillows, euphoria in their eyes. Their bodies trembled and gave a final spasm as their hearts seized simultaneously. Looking at them, Haggerty wondered if having someone to press with made it better. Was there comfort in being so close to someone that the decision could be made, and acted upon, jointly?

Primrose stood by the bed, so near he looked comically like a participant in the scene, his hand to his mouth as though holding something back. Nausea? Excitement?

Haggerty didn't want to know. "Judgment," he called.

Primrose took a breath. "Cromwell and Sons declares the cases of Gustavo Nyuga and Maria-Christina Rosenberg to be legitimate presses, their actions apparently the result of joint bankruptcy and inability to secure future income. As neither Mr. Nyuga nor Ms. Rosenberg has any living relatives or heirs, the settlement of their affairs will be posted to the State." After, of course, Cromwell and Sons took their cut, Haggerty thought. Certainly there were enough antiques in the bedroom alone to cover the normal fees, dues, and charges such firms exacted for their services, before the client's creditors and heirs—in this case, the State—got to wrangle over what was left.

Haggerty had listened to Primrose stoically. Properly speaking, they ought to have waited for the second review before signing off on both cases. "In the case of Maria-Christina Rosenberg, death by press judged clean," Haggerty pronounced. "Stop projection."

The couple vanished. Elsa removed the unit, and Haggerty took it from her, handing her Nyuga's, sliding Rosenberg's into a minthizine case for transport back to headquarters. Elsa had already run the analysis, confirming the second unit as Nyuga's device of record, and begun uploading his final recording, when

Primrose spoke.

"Don't see any need to play the other recording," he said, fetching his drink from the end table.

Elsa looked at Haggerty. *I don't understand why adjusters are always so impatient, Jason,* she sent across their link. *Shall I proceed?*

Elsa was right: adjusters never wanted to hang around a press scene once the unit was reviewed. They preferred to have the formalities handled as expeditiously as possible so they could go about the business of securing assets, finalizing arrangements, and determining their percentages. A year ago, Haggerty would have ignored Primrose's comment and told Elsa to proceed with the projection. Adjusters might not like the additional delays and attrition of assets that accompanied the exceedingly rare finding of a criminally manipulated press, but Haggerty had always been scrupulous in carrying out his duties. As a result, he found those exceedingly rare criminal manipulations a less conscientious reviewer would have missed.

But he was a different man today than he had been a year—a lifetime—before. Fewer and fewer manips had been found over the past few decades. These two clients certainly had reason to press and—unless Governor Benfield had suddenly acquired a passion for torch lamps—no heirs to benefit from hurrying them along their way. What was the point of looking further?

It's all right, Elsa, Haggerty sent across their link. *I think the first projection told us everything we need to know.* Aloud, he said, "It's clear what happened. Record epitaph: Regarding the case of Mr. Gustavo Nyuga, one-hundred-four, and Ms. Maria-Christina Rosenberg, one-hundred-thirty, consecutive presses observed and both judged clean. Eulogic proceedings convened on March eighth, Twenty-one-fifty-six, by BBI senior agent Jason P. Haggerty. Life insurance settlement to be placed in trust to the State." Formalities taken care of, he gestured for Elsa to return the second unit. "Go ahead and open the curtains," he told Primrose, and secured the second discharged unit in another minthizine case.

The other man dialed the curtains back open, rubbing his eyes as sunlight flooded the compartment. "Is that all?" he asked Haggerty, pulling out his com and flipping it open to record the BBI agent's verdict in the appropriate files.

"Yes," Haggerty said, concealing his distaste for Primrose's cavalier attitude. "That will be all as far as BBI is concerned."

Primrose closed the com again and put it away. "Nice working with you, Mr. Haggerty." He extended his hand, realized Haggerty was still wearing the duratex gloves, and settled for a nod. "Have a good day."

Primrose left the room.

Haggerty went into the bathroom and ordered the sink, "On, hot." Elsa helped him out of the gloves, which she put in a minthizine biohazard bag, before they began sterilizing their hands as BBI protocol required once discharged units had been contained.

"Jason, I have a question," she said, looking up from her cleaning.

He saw that she was addressing his reflection in the mirror, and found it odd. "What's on your mind?" he said.

"The decision those two people made to press together. It was premeditated, wouldn't you agree?"

Haggerty nodded.

"Please explain to me why two healthy people, in no apparent jeopardy, would decide that they have had enough of life at precisely the same time."

Haggerty stopped scrubbing and looked at her reflection, perplexed. They'd worked together a long time, reviewed hundreds of double presses together. Why this question now? He thought about how to summarize, knowing that inevitably his answer would fall short of acceptable to her logic board. He knew Elsa was perpetually reprogramming herself, to better understand the nature of those she served, but this was a difficult query, perhaps important to her development. He selected his words carefully.

"Two people can grow together, share so much together, have such a commonality, that they begin to make decisions as one," he explained, or hoped he did.

Elsa gazed into the mirror, unblinking. "So if the drive to press is based primarily in despair, I should assume they shared the exact same level of despair?"

Haggerty toweled his hands, aware he was not doing a very good job of explaining. "Sort of," he said. "Let's say they were committed to each other and circumstances led one of them to decide that pressing was the right choice. Even though the other may not have been suffering the same level of despair at that moment, the strength of their commitment, coupled with the fear of being separated from each other, the person who is the main reason and purpose for living, compounds the despair." Haggerty scratched the back of his neck. "That could bring them to a decision to press together."

"Despair by osmosis," Elsa stated flatly.

"Something like that. Does this shed any light on the human condition for you?"

"I'm going to *digest* it," she said, using one of the phrases Haggerty employed in rare moments of uncertainty—or, more usually, to mask defiance toward his superiors. "I'll run it parallel against previous input and observe the variable shift."

Haggerty smiled, ever astonished at her desire to learn, to understand. The bulk of androids produced these days were suited only for the most menial or dangerous work no human wanted to do. Intelligent, intuitive androids like Elsa were few and far between, too expensive to produce in quantity, the jobs they were suited for too badly needed by the burgeoning human population. Haggerty took the extra time and effort with her because she had, in many ways, been raised by him, a standard perk in his department long before the impact of androids in the workforce had become an issue with the unions. Her personality, distinctly machinelike and artificial when she'd arrived to replace the earlier model he'd been assigned, had evolved over time, largely in response to his influence. While she was, perhaps understandably, a little too protective of him and inclined to nag, he was happy to have had a hand in her development.

"You do that," he said.

Tanner gave them the high sign when they got back to BBI, and reminded Haggerty that a staff report was due upstairs. Haggerty looked at the clock and nodded, keying in his pass code to the mausoleum. The meeting was due to start momentarily. He didn't really have time for his planned detour to the men's room to dose a celtrex; lateness was something that was sure to have the Dragon breathing fire at him. Then again, a man about to press didn't have much to fear from those flames. The meeting could start without him. Haggerty stepped forward, allowing the scanner to pan his retinas, and waited as four sets of interlocking gates disengaged and slid back into the floor and ceiling, revealing a permaglass wall with one narrow concave section forming an access port. Once the hypersteel gates had disappeared, Haggerty glanced back at the control panel, stamping his thumbprint against the flatscreen to turn off the remaining electronic wards, before pulling on the pair of black duratex gloves Elsa handed him. When the system sent the green light clearing him for access, Haggerty took the minthizine cases and biohazard bag from her and stood on the pressure plate in front of the access port. There was just enough room for one person to stand within its circumference. Once in place, the concavity slid open around the access port, effectively bringing Haggerty inside the room while ensuring no one else entered with him. The shield's permaglass construction ensured that his actions would be observable by any duly assigned witnesses. Originally, two were mandated, usually the on-duty dispatcher, the reviewer's assistant, or another reviewer. These days, little actual observation was ever done. Tanner didn't even bother to turn his attention from his own console, though Elsa managed to keep Haggerty in her line of sight even as she headed over to a nearby decontamination sink to wash her hands and run the requisite sterilization protocols on her internal systems.

The discharged KV unit storage room was the highest security area in the building; only state-registered review agents could enter. Somewhere in this same facility a similar room held thousands of brand-new, uncalibrated units—Haggerty had been there once, his first day on the job, when he'd signed for his own—boxes without namescreens housing buttons without printscans. But the mausoleum, with its stone floor and vaulted ceilings, held only discharged black boxes: row after row and shelf after shelf of dead units. T. J. Sovereign, the man who'd designed the first box, had suggested they be recycled. This was quickly vetoed on the grounds that no one wanted a device that had been discharged. In order for it to be safe and unthreatening, it had to be clean, untarnished, sterile—and unique.

Haggerty stepped to the console, uttered the command, and waited for the program to identify his vocal pattern. A few seconds later, a pair of narrow panels slid aside, revealing freshly sterilized containment slots. He deposited the units within—evidence in the unlikely event of future challenge—and watched as the panels automatically sealed shut. Most likely, those seals would never be broken, the units' evidence never required.

Haggerty headed for the exit sink and coded open the appropriate secure waste container beside it. He dropped the biohazard bag inside, stripped off his gloves and sent them after, then coded the container closed. Though the minthizine cases and duratex gloves made it virtually impossible for him to have picked up a single spore of contamination, he followed protocol, washing his hands once more, then returned to the access port to leave the mausoleum. He stepped from the pressure plate and the mausoleum's four pairs of gates closed behind him for the last time.

Elsa sat at a console, sorting through data streams. She smiled at him as he made his way out of the storage room.

"I have a staff meeting," he said.

"I'll keep myself busy," she replied.

"Welcome, Mr. Haggerty," said Consuela Pitcairn, the division director, referred to in whispers as the Dragon. The sole person at the table not wearing grays, she was dressed in a stylish business suit of pale gold that featured an elegant straight skirt ending demurely at the knee, over a cream-colored synthesilk blouse. She had been with BBI since before Haggerty, and had to be nearing the century mark, but like almost every one else looked no older than thirty. Right now, she also looked annoyed.

Haggerty didn't bother trying to excuse his lateness. He headed for the only seat available at the large round black onyx table, between Tanner and O'Connell, directly across from the new kid, Corbin, who was chewing one of her irritating cubes of gum. She had been recruited two months ago, after the union complained that three retired agents' positions had gone unfilled far beyond contractual time limits. Management had successfully argued that there wasn't enough work for three new agents, but the arbitrator upheld the union's position that the contract required that at least one job be filled. Thus BBI acquired Corbin to take up the nonexistent slack and Consuela acquired a devoutly loyal agent. Because Corbin was the minimum legal employable age, thirty. This made her two decades younger than the national average for initial employment in any job, let alone this highly sought-after field. No doubt Corbin's loyalty was also due to the fact that the field still skewed heavily toward the male demographic.

Corbin had smooth, clear skin, short dark hair, and piercing blue eyes Haggerty figured were natural. Like every other Conscientious Citizen, she was good-looking—most would probably say beautiful. But something about her left Haggerty slightly repulsed. She was smart-mouthed, certain she knew more than the experienced agents, much like Haggerty when he first joined BBI. But Corbin was hard, smug, unlikable. Her not so subtle hints that BBI would be better off if she were to take over Haggerty's position didn't help to foster a good working relationship, either. Haggerty's biggest gripe was that Corbin acted as if she were doing everyone a favor by being there, that she was just killing time until something more worthy of her talents came along. Even at his most callow, Haggerty had never done that. Corbin was clearly unhappy about having to attend this meeting, her eyes darting from one object to the next; she was barely able to sit still.

"Clean presses, I assume?" Consuela said as Haggerty took his seat.

He nodded.

"Good," she said. "Let's get started then. Most of you know that pressage is markedly down these past few months, following a pattern that's been growing for several years." She smiled provocatively. "Which means some of you may be advantageously positioned for early retirement."

Haggerty could feel Corbin's too-blue eyes burn into his flesh. That meant Haggerty's name was probably on the list. In most industries, the youngest employees were the first to be cut during lean times, but like the police, BBI agents suffered high burnout rates, which worked in favor of younger colleagues. No matter. She could have his job tomorrow.

"With full pension and continued benefits, of course," Consuela went on. "BBI doesn't forget its own."

Tanner leaned in to whisper, "We'd benefit more from *her* early retirement."

"Fat chance," O'Connell whispered back, past Haggerty.

"I realize you're all in perfect physical condition," Consuela said calmly, attributing the murmuring to a mix of excitement and apprehension about her news, "but I'm calling for psychevals on each of you later this afternoon. You'll go down alphabetically."

"So sayeth the Dragon," Tanner echoed, loud enough for Haggerty to overhear. Corbin's eyes continued to target him. Haggerty gave her a thin smile. *Relax, kid, you won't have to wait much longer for my post.*

"Are there any questions? Gupta?" Raj Gupta, the only person with more seniority than Haggerty, shook his head no. "O'Connell?" Another head shake. "What about you, Haggerty?"

"Nothing immediate comes to mind," he said, leaning back in his chair and scratching his neck. "I'll digest what you've told us. Maybe later I'll have questions."

Corbin's eyes narrowed slightly. Was Haggerty willing to fade away quietly, without a fuss? He smiled at her, amused when she scowled back. He was tempted to make up something, just to yank Corbin's chain, but decided it wasn't worth the effort.

No one else had questions. The rest of the meeting was routine reporting of clean presses by mature clients—*mature* being defined as having reached the century mark.

An hour later, Haggerty found himself in a chair under psycheval by someone who probably knew more about him than any test could ever reveal. But conducting the evaluation was part of his job, and Haggerty knew that Doug Zabrowski never slacked off. Though that didn't mean he liked running evaluations on his friends. His incessantly puffing on a cigalite was a clear sign he was distressed. Doug only smoked when something was bothering him.

"In my day, those things would have done serious damage to your lungs, Doug," Haggerty said.

"In your day, anyone taking the equivalent of what you take in celtrex would be on suspension until he'd completed a detox program," Doug retorted.

Doug Zabrowski was living proof that there was only so much plastiche could achieve. He was as good-looking as everyone else, and every bit as youthful, but there was something worn about him, something tired and solemn that caused him to close in on himself, pinching his attractive features and making them ever so slightly less so. The smoking, at least in Haggerty's opinion, didn't help, a fact of which he'd tried to warn his friend, off and on for the past fifty years.

Doug saw it differently. "Cigalites are safe enough for a baby, Jason, and you know it," he said, fiddling with his setup programs.

He was right, of course. Tobacco had been detoxified decades ago, its natural poisons genetically engineered out of existence. And even had they not been, Haggerty understood that the lungs of a fully geno-immunized body could easily tolerate the abuse, and the annual stem-cell therapy all Conscientious Citizens underwent would repair any tissue damage. In the rare instance where deterioration occurred, there was always the option of having an afflicted organ regrown. No one found smoking offensive these days, whereas Haggerty's prescription for celtrex had raised the eyebrow of his pharmacist on more than one occasion—which struck Haggerty as exceedingly unfair.

"It's not as if I'm dosing on something recreational," he said, unpleasant images of Tanner at his worst coming to mind. "Everyone who's had stem therapy takes celtrex."

"Not in the doses you use," Doug said. "It's meant as a telemor maintenance drug, not a sedative."

"I don't use it as a sedative," Haggerty protested. "If anything, just the opposite. It clears my mind, helps me focus, stay keen. It takes the edge off."

"Listen to yourself," Doug said as he adjusted dials with perhaps a shade more vigor than required. "If something is taking the edge off, by definition it's making you *less* keen, not more so. You think you're focusing and clearing your mind, but what you're really doing is pacifying yourself. Your mind doesn't clear, it becomes dull, latching on to the first solution that presents itself and clinging to it, whether it's the best solution or not."

"It helps me get the job done," Haggerty persisted.

"Really? Look, Jason, the fact is we're not designed to live forever. The things we do to ourselves, to extend our lives beyond what our healthiest ancestors could ever have dreamed of, aren't natural. Our bodies know that, try as we might to fool them."

"You've lost me," Haggerty said.

"I may have lost myself," Doug said ruefully. "What I'm getting at is, your reaction to celtrex, the way you're abusing it—" He held up a hand to stop Haggerty's protest. "I think your body may be resisting the artificial attempt to make it live longer. Your need for celtrex may be tied to an instinct to die, to make room for the next generation, continue the life of the species rather than the life of the individual."

Haggerty had never heard this particular theory before.

"You think celtrex is making me suicidal?"

"I think maybe it's exacerbating something in the telemor treatments that your body is rebelling against."

"Is that possible?" Haggerty asked.

"Oh, Jason, my friend," Doug smirked. "The more science learns about the body and the brain, the more we realize we don't know."

Doug grunted satisfaction as the last setup program flashed ready. He threw a switch. An inkblot engulfed the room.

"Tell me what you see in this image."

Haggerty got up and walked around the black, flowing globules.

"This part looks like an old steamship," he observed. "Those globs look like buoys. The centerpiece seems like a giant spider, spinning ..."

Haggerty knew each word was being recorded, analyzed by patterns of semantics and symbol, each syllable and pause and inflection compared to the dozen other times he'd taken this test. There was no way to cheat. The machine would detect that he was stressed. It might even factor in the significance this date held for him. The results would get sent upstairs; he'd never see them.

Apparently, some results didn't take long to analyze. Haggerty watched with interest as Doug consulted his screen and sat back.

"Anything interesting?"

"Nothing I hadn't already figured out," Doug said. "But I had hoped ..."

"What's the bad news, Doc?" Not that it mattered. Haggerty wondered if Doug knew. Maybe that was why he'd invited Haggerty to dinner this evening with himself and Mandy, remembering the anniversary, figuring he'd help Haggerty get through the day. But Haggerty had declined the invitation, and Doug was enough of a friend to understand that some things couldn't be helped—and enough of a friend to dislike his own helplessness.

"You know what the bad news is," Doug said quietly. "I could see it in your eyes when you turned me down for dinner. You used to beg me to invite you over for Mandy's famous cream cheese cakes."

"Doug... ."

"That isn't all," he went on brusquely. "The other bit of bad news the analysis has come up with ..." He looked at the reading again, and Haggerty was surprised to see a smile break out on his face. "Well, maybe it isn't bad news, although I'm sure you'll consider it a disaster."

"What is it?" Haggerty said sourly.

"Your response arc to the celtrex is baseline lethargic."

"What the hell does that mean?"

"It means that your body is no longer responding to the higher dosage. You'd get the same therapeutic effect, as far as telemor maintenance properties go, from a smaller dose."

Haggerty frowned. It didn't matter a damn. But the surest way to rouse Doug's suspicions and subject himself to a well-meaning, futile attempt at intervention was to let this go without protest.

"That can't be right, Doug," he said, making the argument he would have made had he not intended to press. "I feel the difference with the higher dose. I don't know why the analysis says it isn't working. I guarantee that it is."

"Jason, old boy, you are in no condition to guarantee a damned thing. Not according to these readings. Trust me on this." Doug was clearly enjoying himself. "The higher dose isn't helping. It might even be making things worse. I'm decreasing your dosage of celtrex."

Haggerty shook his head. When he recorded his press tonight, he'd have to remember to include an apology to Doug. "Trying to counter my instinct to die?" he said, knowing that in his case, the instinct was too deeply ingrained to be negated.

Doug didn't know that, though. He flashed Haggerty a wicked grin.

"God, I hope so."

Chapter Two
GENERATION ZERO

Haggerty spent the rest of the day behind his desk checking paperwork from cases reviewed by other agents and officially closing the files, grateful that the boards were clear—he couldn't have handled another review. Maria-Christina Rosenberg's soft sobs, the bleak despair in Gustavo Nyuga's voice were still with him. His limit for handling emotional pain—his own and others'—was well and truly exceeded. He could no longer deal with Tanner's obscene glee while recounting the stats of someone who'd pressed. He would hand off any other cases that came in that day, even if it were Corbin who took them.

He reflected on the system and the part he played within it. Did presses really need to be inspected, anymore? When KV units were first introduced, attempts had been made to use them for illegal purposes—fraud, even murder—and review agents were necessary. Haggerty knew this from experience. From the start of his career, he had detected manipulations, including some missed by the initial reviewer, and was proud of his reputation as one of the best in the business. But there had been nothing of importance to detect in a very long time. Second reviews, standard in the initial decades, had been reduced to random samples, then done away with altogether. The kind of paperwork check in which Haggerty was currently engaged involved catching clerical errors or mistakes in protocol. Haggerty had begun to think that meticulously reviewing the recording of every press to uncover criminal intent was a waste of time and resources. Surely a random review system provided whatever safeguards were needed to deter wrongdoers from interfering in a press.

But no one with the power to change the system was in any hurry to do so. The scrupulous reviews, the follow-up reports and analyses, were all expensive components of a lucrative process that benefited a number of parties. As long as there were insurance agencies trying to avoid paying more than they had to for as long as possible, and heirs trying to inherit more than their due, Haggerty's and his colleagues' skills would be required. Death by press might be government-sanctioned and BBI a subsidiary of the state's Department of Public Health, but it was also a business.

Haggerty felt drained when his shift finally ended. He glanced around the room, satisfied that it was ready for whomever the Dragon assigned to take his place. Walking down the familiar corridor a final time, he passed the portrait of T. J. Sovereign, a young man with pale skin, dark eyes, reddish-brown hair, and a look of perpetual sobriety—the inventor of the KV unit. Haggerty had always been curious about him, but found little in the official records beyond statistics—birth date, degrees, marriage, children, employment, and when he'd invented the black box. There was nothing about the man himself, why he'd invented it, how he'd felt about the way it was used. Haggerty knew Sovereign had been one of the original directors of BBI, but he'd resigned after a mere five years, and there was nothing about what happened to him after that. He might have retired and moved to Florida, or died peacefully in his sleep; he might even have used his own invention. It wasn't the most important mystery Haggerty had ever faced, and he was reconciled to leaving it unsolved. He nodded good-bye to old T. J. and made his way toward the exit.

"Good night, Elsa," he called.

She was still sorting data. "Good night, Jason," she said, looking up briefly from her viewscreen and smiling. Haggerty took a last look as she turned back to the data streams. He was going home to a compartment that could easily house two families, while Elsa would tube up to the eightieth floor and a recharging cell which—because it was the size of a coffin, possessed no interior illumination yet provided Elsa with the electrical "sustenance" she needed—the reviewers jokingly referred to as a "womb-box." Haggerty understood that—being a machine—Elsa didn't find such restriction objectionable. But his gut insisted she ought to object to being so confined. As far as he was concerned, Elsa had more humanity in her circuit boards than many of his flesh-and-blood coworkers, clients, and neighbors.

He stood lingering too long. Elsa noticed.

"Is something wrong, Jason?" she asked.

He scratched the back of his neck. "Not really," he said. "Everything checking out with the decedents' records?"

"The Nyuga and Rosenberg remains have been turned over to the mortuary designated in their wills. Their affairs are properly concluded."

"Good work," Haggerty said. "Good night again, Elsa."

"Good night, Jason. See you in the morning."

She might at that, he reflected, if she were sent with the agent conducting his post-press. He wondered if he ought to leave instructions for the Dragon about his assistant's Personal Loyalty Chip, supposedly removed long ago. It occurred to him that, if Elsa were reassigned to Corbin, it would do the brat good to find out the hard way about the chip. Haggerty was mentally going through the short list of reviewers without android assistants, trying to figure the odds on Corbin upgrading to Elsa, when the green-eyed girl who had accosted him earlier once again blocked his path on the quad. Haggerty braced himself for a confrontation, expecting her to rail at him.

Instead, she merely said, "Why didn't you have me arrested this morning?"

"If that's what you want, I still can," Haggerty said, grinning mildly, supposing that she was hoping for media coverage to help spread her message to the uninformed masses. *Splintered* masses would be closer to the mark. Though BBI had been incorporated nearly three quarters of a century before, many citizens, even those with CC status, were on the fence regarding the morality of the right to die. But the girl surprised him again.

"No," she said, almost contritely. "I'm sorry I told you to cough and die."

"It's okay," Haggerty said. "But what exactly does 'cough and die' mean?"

"It's an old-style cracker term for when a computer program unexpectedly crashes," she explained. "When there's no apparent cause, like a virus or a fatal error. If a cracker *makes* a system crash, he'll leave a message saying SCREAM AND DIE."

"Is that the new lingo, 'old-style cracker'?"

She smiled. "It's mine, anyway."

"Well, your apology's accepted," he said. "But you'll have to find someone else to arrest you."

"I saw you go in there twice today. You're a button collector, aren't you?"

The slang term always stuck, Haggerty thought ruefully. In the end he was always a button collector.

"I am," he said. "The polite term is 'post-press review agent' or just 'reviewer.'"

"I didn't realize. I didn't mean to insult you."

"I don't think many people remember our real title anymore," Haggerty reassured her.

The girl wasn't willing to let herself off the hook that easily. "I should have known. I've been researching the issue. I wouldn't fight against something I hadn't tried to understand first."

She stopped. Haggerty studied her as she worried her lower lip, struggling with whatever it was she wanted to tell him. Her hair was sandy brown, her expressive green eyes set above high cheekbones in a classic oval face. Her light golden complexion and pleasantly rounded figure were striking changes from what was now fashionable. Even her height wasn't quite up to par. But Haggerty found her more appealing than any of the women whose images flashed across viewscreens and e-covers everywhere. The thought startled him.

The girl finally began speaking again. "I know this is nervy of me, after what I did today, but would you be willing to talk to me for a few minutes?" she asked, anxiously tugging the straps of the backpack slung over her shoulder.

"I'm sorry," he said. "I'm sort of in a hurry."

"Please," she whispered softly. "I have questions only someone like you can answer."

Maybe it was the sincerity with which she asked, or that she was truly as young as she appeared. Or maybe it was that she looked as tired as Haggerty felt. Whatever the reason, he hesitated. BBI had strict rules. Confrontations with protesters were to be avoided, and a private conversation with one was guaranteed to lead to confrontation. But the girl seemed harmless, and anyway he wouldn't be around long enough for disciplinary charges to be filed against him. He wasn't sure he knew anymore why people pressed, or why someone would make a career of reviewing those presses. Maybe *she* had answers for *him*.

"Sure," he said. "What's your name?"

"Regina," she said, visibly relieved.

He took her to the Java Joint, one of his favorite haunts, an unimposing little cafe not far from BBI headquarters to which he usually came alone. All white plasticine furniture, white tiled floors, and white painted walls, the Java Joint served the best coffee in NewVada—real coffee, made from real coffee beans. Haggerty often wondered where they got the beans from, but had never asked. During his parents' day, beans were imported from places like Costa Rica, Peru, or as far away as Indonesia, but that was before the sanctions had been put in place.

He lifted his cup, savoring the dark, bitter brew. "Tell me why you're protesting against BBI, Regina," he said. "Why do you think we're doing something wrong?"

Her green eyes narrowed. Now that she had him alone, she didn't seem to know what to do with him.

"Tell me honestly," he coaxed her. "I mean, besides the pro-life bit."

"You mean the Sixth Commandment," she said with a grin, taking the sting out of the words. " 'Thou shalt not kill'?" She sipped her coffee, leaving a purple lipstick smudge on the rim of her cup, either not noticing or unimpressed by its quality. "I know that you wouldn't do what you do if you didn't believe it was right. But I believe that suicide is self-murder. It used to be a crime."

"It still is, if you use any method other than the Kevorkian unit." The image of his father's body flashed painfully across Haggerty's mind.

"I know that you're not fitted for a button unless you've already passed a psycheval that proves you can make a rational decision about ending your own life," she said. "But that just gives you a free pass to do away with yourself at any time, without really thinking it through. When they first made suicide legal, you had to give notice of intent and wait a few days, giving you a chance to reconsider. It's not like that anymore."

"That was a very different time. There were so many other ways you could die, and it was certain that you *would* die decades, maybe even a century or two, before natural causes will kill you today. Our lives are so long now, it's inevitable that sometimes people have had enough of living. But you're young; I can understand that it's hard for you to accept that."

She shook her head. "I'm always being told that I'm too young to understand things, too young to make an informed choice, too young to think for myself," she said quietly.

"I don't believe you're too young to think for yourself, just too young to have the experience to see all the aspects of a given situation."

"There are other sources of wisdom, other ways to learn than experience," she said. She leaned forward, her eyes passionate. "Ever read the Bible?"

"Decades ago," Haggerty said. "I prefer the Buddhist approach. Suicide is viewed as a negative act, because it ends life, but in extreme situations it's acceptable, if it ends one's suffering or the suffering of others, which only you can judge."

"I'm not talking about judgment or religious philosophy, I'm talking about overlooked science."

Haggerty arched a brow.

"Got a pen?" Regina asked.

Haggerty pulled one from a pocket and handed it to her. She undid her napkin and sketched a graph, on which she drew a line.

"This is Adam, Old Testament times. Genesis 5:5. The Bible says he lived to be nine-hundred-thirty years old."

She drew another line.

"Over a thousand years later, Lamech lived to be seven-hundred-seventy-seven."

"He would've wanted a button, I'm sure," Haggerty joked.

Regina smiled. "Maybe I can shake up that certainty."

He smiled back. "You're welcome to try."

"Methuselah lived to be nine-hundred-sixty-nine. The Bible doesn't present these numbers as miraculous or extraordinary. They're just stated. It was commonplace to live that long."

"I don't think those numbers are meant to be taken literally," Haggerty said.

Regina nodded emphatically. "As many intellectuals and bagbiters have argued. They suggest that back then each month may have been misinterpreted as a year. Divide by twelve, that'd make Methuselah about eighty-one. That fits nicely, right?"

"Yes," Haggerty said.

"Except that they also recorded that Cainan was seventy when his first son was born. Divide that by twelve and Cainan was about five years old when he became a father. Think that's probable?"

"The Bible was compiled by different writers," Haggerty countered. "Obviously, some used the twelve-month rule and some didn't."

"Convenient theory," Regina said airily. "But wrong." She drew a new line. "Noah lived to be nine-hundred-fifty. Then came the Flood. Noah built the Ark and God did some global sterilization. And before you say the Flood's not accepted fact, ask an archeologist about the layers of clay deposits in what used to be Mesopotamia, or the universality of contemporaneous flood layers around the world."

Haggerty raised his hands in playful acquiescence.

"This is where things drop off considerably," she continued. "By two-thousand B.C., Abraham only lived to be one-hundred-seventy-five, Joseph one-ten."

Haggerty finally caught her meaning. "You're saying the Flood changed something major in our ecosystem."

"It introduced things that were harmful to us by design," Regina said. "Radiation. Bacteria. Viruses. Things that decreased what was once our natural lifespan. David only made it to seventy-one, Solomon to fifty-eight."

Haggerty hadn't heard this analysis before, and doubted Regina had come up with it on her own. She seemed like an enthusiastic student reciting her latest lessons. He'd bet she was regurgitating some more complex oration, but couldn't imagine whose.

"Solomon's lifespan was pretty near the mark for most of recorded history," he pointed out. "It wasn't until the medical advances of the twentieth century that people began to live longer lives, and of course stem cell and telemor research resulted in our current longevity. How does the Biblical trend toward diminished lifespans fit in now?"

"Don't you see," Regina said earnestly, "all medical science has done is give us back what we had before. We're *supposed* to live hundreds of years. Black buttons are just a quick cure for sadness or loneliness, cures that wouldn't be needed if people gave themselves time to work through issues."

Haggerty sipped his coffee, recalling post-press reviews on pushers who'd changed their minds. Abandoned attempts rarely exceeded fifteen minutes of tape, those mysterious "dark zones" where they'd planned to press and succumbed to survival instinct—or maybe an incoming call.

"Before black buttons, suicide wasn't only illegal, it was tough to do, right?" Regina continued. "You had to plan it, find a weapon, pick a building to jump off. It was going to be painful and even messy. BBI took all that away. Someone having a bad day or just a bad moment can make a bad decision and—" She snapped her fingers like a challenge. "By making death so accessible and painless, your company's hijacked the natural barriers most people need to really consider the choice to die. It gives them an instant, selfish escape from responsibility."

"Responsibility to whom?" he asked.

"To God," she said. "Would He have allowed us to find a way to lengthen our lives again if He didn't want us to live those lives fully? And each other. Do people who press stop to think how their friends and families will feel about their deaths? Their children, their partners, their parents? Maybe you don't believe you owe God or your family a thing. But if you're really a Buddhist, don't you have a responsibility to *yourself* to learn as many lessons as you can in this lifetime?

"I say, live and love as long as you can. Make the best of whatever life hands you. Tired of your body? Save to get it retrofit. Bored with your job? Change careers or go back to school and learn something new. Get a hobby. Take a trip. Make new friends. Visit old friends. Whatever. Pressing's not the answer."

"Then what is?" Haggerty said flatly. He was damned sure that the pain that had driven him to decide to press couldn't be assuaged by a world cruise, a year's worth of tango lessons, or all the plastiche money could buy. People who pressed had done what Regina said they should do. They'd lived as long as possible and when they couldn't continue, they had taken the legal, responsible, government-approved way to end their lives. Things seemed so clear to the young; the world was black and white. Haggerty knew that age brought a myriad of gray complexity, of living life and dying from it.

"There's another way to look at this," he said, thinking back to his conversation with Doug. "If God sent the Flood, then He intended the lifespan He initially gave us to be reduced. Maybe it's the way we've gone about lengthening our lives that's the problem, and the Kevorkian unit is really an instrument of Divine Will."

"That's close to blasphemy," Regina said dryly. "The Catholic Church still holds that suicide brings eternal damnation."

"You don't truly believe that if you press you'll end up in hell, do you?" Haggerty asked, unable to keep from smiling.

Regina looked away. Sensing he'd somehow touched a sore spot, Haggerty changed topics.

"Are you still in school, Regina?"

"I was," she said, absentmindedly. "But I dropped out when my mom ..."

There it was, the person she'd lost before she was prepared to let her go, the reason she was so opposed to KV units. Her mother must have pressed recently, and he'd just belittled her memory, smiled at what might be a tremendous, unresolved fear for her daughter.

"I'm sorry," he said. "This must be a difficult time for you. But I can't believe that, if there is a God, He'd sentence us to eternal hellfire for ending our own suffering. Is your father still around?"

"Never was," she said. "I was an accident. Quality byproduct of a one-night-stand."

Haggerty was surprised. Compulsory contraception at puberty insured that there were no accidents, no unplanned pregnancies. Unless ...

"It didn't happen here in the States," she said, answering the unspoken question. "We emigrated when I was a kid." Regina stared at the floor.

What was logic in the face of grief? Haggerty mused. Abandonment must have driven her to seek solace in religious doctrine.

"Why did you quit school, Regina?"

"I saw how useless it was," she said. "You can't be hired full-time before you're thirty, and most people don't get a real job until they're fifty or older. Then, if you're lucky, you get a job that you hate. Any post worth having is already filled by some oldster who's been holding on to it for at least half a century."

Haggerty inwardly winced, although she did not seem to be accusing him. Had his body reflected his true age, she probably would not be with him now.

"Unfortunately, the way your system works, only when someone presses does someone else get a good job."

"Fair enough," Haggerty admitted. "I can understand why a college degree seems like a waste of time, right now. But didn't you just suggest we have a responsibility to ourselves to learn as many lessons as we can in this lifetime? To keep us from giving up and pressing? Trust me, you're going to eventually realize that you need the competitive edge a degree gets you. My advice is to go back to school, when you're ready of course. What were you studying by the way?"

"Programming, like all the other drones. My entire generation is gonna be nothing more than code monkeys and data farmers for yours. Unless you're an athlete, or some trillionaire's brat, ya know? I'm neither, so I'm learning all right. I'm learning to crack." She grinned at him. "You'd arrest me if you saw some of the things I've already done."

"I'm not a police officer," he said mildly. "I'm just the button collector, remember?"

"You don't see the people who use the buttons you collect, do you?"

Haggerty was confused by her question. "You mean, after they're ... ?"

She shook her head no. "I mean, you don't meet them when they sign up?"

"I'm not a sales rep or a fitter," he said. "I guess you might say I sort of meet them after they press."

"You see their final moments, on recordings. How long are they?"

"Sometimes a few seconds, sometimes they go on for hours. The units have several shivabytes of memory. They warn you if you exceed capacity, then disarm."

"Do you save them forever? Are they uploaded? Could I ..."

"Crack into our system and retrieve one?"

Haggerty supposed she thought seeing a recording might help her understand why people pressed. But most likely she would see someone at the last reaches of despair, and he wasn't sure she'd see why the press seemed to be the best answer. It didn't matter. However good a cracker she was, the BBI safeguards were better.

"I doubt you'd be able to pull it off," he told her. "And you'd be guilty of a felony for trying."

"I'm not saying I would."

"I'm not saying you did."

Her lips curved upward. "I bet I could," she said mischievously.

Haggerty laughed.

Suddenly Regina was on her knees on her chair, peering over Haggerty's shoulder. "Oh wow, an Indran," she whispered.

He followed her gaze to the lithe individual making her way into the cafe. The woman's skin was the color of burnt sienna. Dark hair coiled down her back in long, wild ringlets. A simple shroud of white synthesilk neither hid nor revealed her sex. Pure East Indian descent—rare to see and unenhanced by plastiche— was obvious in half the woman's face. Above the eye on the other side, sloping up her forehead and over her ear, a clear prosthetic window revealed a circuit mesh of blinking lights and fiber-optic neural implants inside the woman's skull. Her presence visibly unsettled Haggerty.

"Do you know her?" Regina asked him.

"I've seen her here several times," he said.

"You don't seem too happy about that."

"I'm not," Haggerty said bluntly.

In fact, the woman repulsed him. The Indranet was perhaps the only product, if such a vast information and communication infrastructure could be called a product, for which the US relied on a foreign provider. Indrans were the latest advance of the Net, and nearly two-thirds of India's population was indentured to the United States in this manner. Though the sheer number of Indrans made them a common sight elsewhere in the world, the immigration freeze made their presence within the States uncommon. Many Americans resented them; the popular consensus was that finding an alternate resource might very well determine the future of the current executive branch of the government. Haggerty agreed that having to outsource the Net was detrimental to American interests, but he knew that few citizens would be willing to offer up portions of their own brainspace and endure the surgical procedures this Indian woman had undergone in order to underbid India and source the Net themselves.

The idea that Regina was at odds with KV technology but fascinated by this woman's proudly displayed self-mutilation saddened him. It seemed contradictory. Perhaps Regina was too young to understand the root of the cultural divide on the subject. Though he'd been a teenager himself at the time, Haggerty remembered the riots that ensued when the American Net had been judged so corrupt it was condemned by the United Nations. Even looking back at those days from an adult perspective in his current profession, he still couldn't quite understand why Net system-separation anxiety had fueled such an epidemic of depression and caused so many violent suicides. Personally, he'd never had use for the Net.

"She's a bit on the abrasive side," Haggerty finally told Regina, attempting to downplay his disgust. "She thinks that being part of the Indranet has somehow exalted her. To hear her tell it—and I've heard her tell it more than once—she's over a hundred but has never needed stem or telemor treatments because her elevated neural system is enough to sustain her."

Regina eyed the woman thoughtfully. "And that's abrasive because ... ?"

"It's not," Haggerty admitted, sipping his coffee. "The abrasive part is that she believes that what she proudly calls her 'enhancements' gives her the ability to predict the future, and that this entitles her to let the other patrons know what they're in for, whether or not they want to hear it. Only after she's done haranguing them will she settle at a table and order herself a cup of coffee. But by then the damage has been done."

"I want to hear my future!" Regina exclaimed, and waved the Indran over before Haggerty could interject. Having sternly admonished the woman on multiple occasions, he braced himself for unpleasantness.

But the Indran merely stepped to their booth and smiled. "What a beautiful couple," she said in a soft, tektronically enhanced Indian voice.

As guilty as he felt about what had been done to her and millions of her countrymen in the name of his own countrymen's convenience, Haggerty could not mask his revulsion. "We were just leaving," he told her, hoping she'd move on to other game.

"So brash," she said with a *tsk,* and turned to Regina. "He's going to be very aggressive in bed, little one."

Regina blushed, but seemed delighted by the Indran.

"She's not going to have an opportunity to discover whether you're right about that," Haggerty said.

The Indran continued to stare intently at Regina. "You've got mothering all around you, little one," she said gently. "Not too far off."

"Really?" Regina beamed.

The Indran nodded, then turned to Haggerty, splaying her empty hands out, palms up.

Haggerty reached into his pocket and pulled out five credits. "This is to leave us alone," he said.

She placed her palms together, refusing the offering, and stared into his eyes. He realized how dark hers were. Everything was the same shade of inky black; he couldn't tell where the iris began and the pupil ended. She looked at him, unblinking, her brow furrowed in concentration, the organic and tektronic portions of her brain engaged in a chaotic dance he could not fathom.

"Misfortune coming toward you," she said, saddening.

"Yeah?" he said.

She ignored his sarcastic tone, taking his hand and closing her eyes. Haggerty pulled his hand back. She regarded him gravely, her dark eyes boring into his, her tektronic array alive with flashing diodes. Haggerty felt uneasy.

"You have a difficult night coming," she said. "Difficult, and more important than you realize, with more things ending than you plan, and more things beginning than you dare to dream. I see you inside a morgue, inside a hearse, and coming to rest inside of your family's mausoleum," she said.

Regina tensed. Haggerty attempted to wave the Indran away. But she wasn't finished. She bent low to whisper in his ear.

"I see you pressing a button tonight and harming yourself, and I beg you to refrain."

That caught Haggerty's attention. Could the Indranet actually harbor some sort of intuitive supernatural transcendence after all?

He chastised himself. The Indran's generalizations were tricks only the gullible would fall for. Given the prevalence of pressing, it was more than likely that she would be right at least some of the time. Though he had to admire her daring "tonight."

"Thanks for the warning," Haggerty said dismissively.

The Indran smiled. "Thanks and blessings on both of you," she said, once more the colorful local eccentric, and moved on to the next booth.

Regina seemed upset.

"Come on," Haggerty said. "You don't believe in fortune-telling, do you?"

"No, but the Indranet's gone quantum now and utilizes collective intuition. It can predict with an accuracy that tweaks me. And she's a part of it."

Haggerty had to admit that she'd tweaked him too. While he wasn't an Indranet user like Regina, he knew enough about the evolution of technology to understand how rapidly it advanced. The neural transmitter that allowed him to link with Elsa was one of the most amazing pieces of technology he'd ever encountered, never mind that the science behind it had been evolving since the first thought-wave response computers were developed for paraplegics at the close of the twentieth century. But prophecy? Actually foretelling the future? That was tantamount to saying that God lived on the Indranet.

"I've spent a lot of time jacked in," Regina continued. "I've watched the Net calibrate. It's beautiful. But for her to tell you such awful things ... It's not right. What if it made you nervous and you did something crazy, and then something bad *did* happen to you?"

"I'm not nervous," he said. "And the histrionic ramblings of an Indranet server aren't about to make me so. Forget her. Now tell me, where do you live?"

"*As if* you'd come to the Westside slums to visit," she said lightly. "I live with four other girls in a pairplex. We share bunk beds. Last one in gets the flowmat on the floor and a pushpillow. It's paradise."

Haggerty grinned at her candor.

"I bet you have a nice place," she teased. "With a tremendous view of the city and a god-awful big viewscreen."

"Guilty as charged," he said affably. He glanced at the faux antique clock on the wall a few feet away. They'd been at the Java Joint a bit longer than he'd realized. "Perhaps it's time I got back to it. I don't think I have any more answers for you, Regina, but it's been a pleasure."

"The pleasure doesn't have to be over now, does it?" she protested, managing to look adorable and wounded at the same time.

Haggerty scratched the back of his neck. "It's not that I don't enjoy talking to you. And you've given me some things to think about," he said.

"It's still early," she coaxed, "and our conversation was just getting interesting. Can't we move on, maybe go have some fun someplace?"

Haggerty glanced at the clock again, considering the pros and cons. He could spare Regina a bit more time and still carry out his plan at midnight. He wondered why she was so determined to keep him with her. She wasn't sending out signals that she was interested in pairing. Or was she working up the nerve? No need to worry about that. Perhaps she hadn't yet got the answers she was looking for. He doubted she would, even if he thought he had them to give her, which he didn't. But there was no harm in indulging her a while longer.

"What do you have in mind?" he asked.

She brightened. "How about this. You've shown me one of your places, let me show you one of mine. There's this new club I heard about, but I didn't wanna crash it without a date."

"Date?"

"I didn't mean ... ," She was clearly embarrassed. "I just wanna scope out this place my girlfriends rave about. And it'll give you a glimpse of my world."

Haggerty hesitated. Then: "Why not?" he said, as much to himself as to Regina. "What have I got to lose?"

Night was no cooler in NewVada than the day had been, and the climate control on the crowded beltway wasn't working. It was well past rush hour. While a number of Conscientious Citizens still went about their business, younger, somewhat rowdy JCs were in the majority, taking advantage of the time to legally belt around the city. Too many conversations were going on around them for Haggerty to continue his discussion with Regina, so he sweltered along until she tugged him toward the exit loop that ramped them off at Fremont Boulevard, on the edge of the Vegas Black Light District. When Haggerty queried Regina as to how far they were going, she grinned.

"It's actually pretty far inside," she said as they were deposited onto street level. "Not scared, are you? I promise I'll protect you."

Haggerty shook his head. BBI frowned upon agents openly visiting the area of the city with most of the unlicensed vice dealerships and the least surveillance. What happened in the Black Light typically stayed in the Black Light. The Triads, NewVada's last organized crime leagues, had seen to that with regular police payoffs. Haggerty knew that the platform surveillance scanners prevalent throughout most of NewVada would record his arrival, but given his plans he was not worried about being called in for questioning simply for entering the area.

"Actually, I'm surprised you'd come to Vegas," he told Regina.

"Because they used to call it Sin City?" she said. "I'm not planning to do anything particularly sinful."

"Most folks on the Religious Right feel that even supporting the legitimate businesses in Vegas somehow furthers an immoral agenda."

She surprised him again. "But I'm not on the Religious Right. The two words don't automatically go together."

"That wasn't you at the Ban the Box rally today?"

"That's the only issue I agree with them on. Doesn't mean there are others. For instance, as far as I'm concerned, Conscientious Citizens can do whatever they like in their own bedrooms. Saint Paul said that love is of God, so how can human lawmakers dictate the way people express their God-given love for one another? And when it comes to teaching intelligent design and sex ed, I'm about as far left as you can get. Yes, I believe in God and have strong ideas about His will—for my life and for humankind. And while I may not approve of everything that goes on in Vegas, I understand why people come here. As long as laws aren't being broken, if people need a place where they can party hard to find relief, where's the harm?"

Haggerty drew her attention to a huge pyramid fronted by a replica of the Sphinx. "That place used to be one of the most famous casinos in Vegas, back in the days when the worst you could lose here was your shirt and there were plenty of counselors from Gamblers Anonymous and the like to help minimize the damage. Now it's mainly a residence for people who never got off the strip. This place isn't as harmless as you seem to think. In the new casinos, damage seems to be the whole point.

"Things are difficult for a lot of NewVadans," Haggerty continued. "And the dicier casinos prey on that. People are lured with the promise of dramatically improving their lives by chance, but more often than not, they wind up being driven deeper into poverty. And poverty all too often equals death.

"I had a case here a few years back, involving an unlicensed casino where people could bet their lives for a mere one thousand credits. It's completely illegal, but that didn't stop it from happening. The man involved had been driven to take those odds, and he lost. The establishment called in his debt, and he was *encouraged* to press in front of a paying audience of so-called CCs, who enthusiastically cheered him on. My review led to some arrests—observers whose images were captured on the recording as well as the management of the casino—all of whom got off on a technicality. The man had made his bet of his own free will, and then pressed of his own free will. Aside from a fine for running an unlicensed gambling parlor—the cost of which could be made up in an hour or two of play—no one but the man who pressed and the family he left behind suffered any losses."

"So they got away with it," Regina said glumly.

"I suppose so," Haggerty admitted. "But that case and a few uncovered by other reviewers inspired a number of legislative actions statewide, and got our wonderful City Council off its collective butt long enough to pass an ordinance prohibiting organizing or profiting from a press done as public entertainment."

"That's something, at least."

Gambling was not the only thing for which Vegas was known. Garish signs and glitzy holograph projections boasted an array of services in lurid, multicolored lights as they made their way down the old strip—CHANGE YOUR FACE WITH YOUR MOOD! 30 MINUTE MAKEOVERS! (a plastiche parlor); HIDDEN

SEXCAMS INSIDE THE HOMES OF YOUR FAVORITE CELEBS!
FREE PRIVATE INTERFACE! (a cybercafe)—outrageous promises
of quicker and cheaper diversions than those offered by their
legitimate counterparts outside the Black Light, and less picky
about legalities. Shooting galleries guaranteed their drugs rivaled
the quality of anything offered in Amsterdam, OR YOUR CREDITS
BACK! As if their patrons were in any position to go to Holland
and compare, then file a complaint at home that they'd been
victims of false advertising.

Regina turned off the boulevard, into a dark alley.

Haggerty stopped in his tracks. "Where exactly are you taking
me?" he called after her.

She trotted back. "It's just a few doors down," she said,
playfully taking his hand. "I promise it's safe."

Haggerty considered tapping his com and putting a pulse
out to Elsa, just in case, then decided not to. If Regina meant to
kill and rob him, well death was what he wanted so why did the
how matter? Haggerty relaxed.

Not far into the alley they came to a large hypersteel door set
into a faux concrete wall, the only marking a sprawl of glowfitti
above it that read ORPHANAGE. Barely audible retro-trance
music blasted into a din as Regina pulled open the door. The
sheer volume was enough to make Haggerty wish he'd declined
her invitation. She tugged him down a poorly lit, crusty staircase
lined with faux velvet.

The place was actually an oversized boiler room, packed with
underage Junior Citizens—all beautiful and half-naked, their
flesh and hair stained and stickjeweled in fantastic colors and
patterns, their fists hammering up and down to the backbeat.

"Don't worry," Regina said into his ear, her small hand still
cupped around his. "There's nothing illegal here, no alcohol or
drugs. Even if there were, no one could afford them. Don't sweat
your CC status."

"That's not what makes me sweat," he said. If possible, the
room was hotter than the night outside, where it had to be over a
hundred degrees.

Regina led him across what felt like hard, coarse pavement—
it was too dark and crowded to see the floor beneath them.
Haggerty glimpsed something odd, set up beside the boilers. He
craned his neck to get a better look as Regina pulled him along.
There in an overcrowded basement in the middle of the desert,
a young boy, his golden-orange hair streaked with red and spiked

to resemble a bloody, exploding sun, stoked glowing embers with a hand trough in a makeshift forge, the kind ironworkers used when there was still iron to be worked!

Regina released him as they reached the dance floor, raising her arms and swaying to the music as she led him through the throng of JCs to the bar, such as it was. Looking at the crowd around them, Haggerty realized that a lot of the skinpainted designs weren't at all garish or bright. Many were black, white, or gray deathheads and gargoyles, worms and ravens, rather than Regina's fanciful iris. She leaned across the rough planks that served as the counter and spoke to a shirtless boy with sweat dripping down the spider painted in the center of the web inked across his chest. He reached below and extracted two plastic bottles from a cooler.

Regina turned to Haggerty and called, "Six creds."

Haggerty handed her the credits and accepted one of the bottles. The label read Cafblast, but the liquid inside was clear.

"It's just water," she told him. "They recycle the bottles themselves."

"Tap water?" he asked apprehensively.

"Yeah, don't be such a snob," she teased. "You're fully geno-immunized, I'm sure." Regina unsealed her bottle and took a long pull, then recapped it and licked stray drops of moisture from her lips. "None of us are, and we're drinking it."

Haggerty took a swig. Why should he care about pollutants? The taste was unpleasant, but it soothed the stifling heat, however momentarily.

"Whattaya think about this place?" Regina asked him.

"It's a dump," he said.

"Exactly," she said. "A dump in the worst part of town. And it's the only type of place Gen-Ohs can afford."

"Gen-Ohs?"

"Short for Generation Zero," she said bitterly. "If you do the math on CC status achievement rates and factor population control curbs, it's clear we're gonna be the first American generation that has basically no chance of reproducing ourselves one-for-one."

"And less than one is zero," Haggerty said.

Regina saluted him with her water bottle and took another deep drink. "Add to that the fact that data farmers and code monkeys don't earn a helluva lot, and you wind up with this."

Haggerty recalled a recent viewcast about the aftermath of

birth restrictions in China during the previous century. The circumstances, the narrator reported dispassionately, were of course vastly different in China from anything facing Junior Citizens in present-day America, and such horrors were unlikely to be repeated. Looking at the JCs around him, Haggerty wondered.

"Do you have kids?" Regina asked him. "Frightened they're hanging out in places like this?"

"No," Haggerty answered, scratching the back of his neck before finishing his water.

She gave him a speculative look, and he braced himself for another brazen interrogation. He was about to change the subject when a shrill cry of pain pierced through the roar of the music. His training as an official triggered; he cut a swath through the crowd to investigate, pushing kids out of his way until he arrived at the source of the scream, then stood still, shocked.

A girl several years Regina's junior stood leaning next to the forge, hands splayed against the wall as the orange-haired boy pulled a smoldering branding iron away from the bare flesh of her back, leaving her skin blackened. The acrid stink assaulted Haggerty. The girl moaned, looking behind her with glazed eyes at the boy with the brand, her face dripping sweat. There was no blood loss along the weltmarks left by the iron, the brand having at once caused and cauterized the wound.

Haggerty was about to step forward when Regina caught his arm, moving close and saying, "That's blisterbranding. It's legal. Didn't you know how it was done?"

"Who's next?" the boy said, pointing the brand at Haggerty. "How 'bout you, oldster?"

Kids queued up by the forge. Haggerty suddenly understood why none of the JCs had seemed distressed or tried to intercede. They regarded this spectacle as normal, unremarkable. That some legislative body had actually condoned such a practice appalled Haggerty. He took one more look at the girl's burns, then pushed past Regina and headed for the bathroom he'd noted earlier.

He stood trembling at the sink, grasping the edges, his eyes swimming with silverfish, then twisted the ancient manual faucet marked COLD. A thin stream of lukewarm water trickled into the basin. He splashed water against his face, pale in the pockmarked mirror.

"You okay there?" a voice beside him said. It belonged to a

well-dressed young man with ash-colored hair slicked back off his forehead, who held out a handkerchief to Haggerty.

Haggerty's fingers brushed the edge. The handkerchief didn't have the usual slick synthetic feel. It was soft, with a subtle sheen to the fabric. He took a closer look. It was silk, probably as costly as his viewscreen. He pulled his hand back.

"Go on, take it," the young man urged. "There's no paper in here and the jetdrier's broken. Just trash it when you're through. I've got a drawerful of 'em at home."

The kid appeared whipped on Sky or some similar drug. Haggerty accepted the handkerchief. If the kid's parents could afford to supply him with a drawer full of them, they weren't apt to harangue him if he misplaced one. The silk felt cool and soothing against his face. "Thanks," he said, clearing his mouth with tap water then wiping his face again.

In the mirror he saw the young man relieving himself at the urinal. His clothing set him apart from the other Orphanage patrons half-naked and sweating on the dance floor. He seemed cool, despite the heat of the place and the contemptuous opulence of a jacket made of real leather that ought to have been intolerably warm. If he was in any way uncomfortable, nothing in his manner betrayed it. Perhaps this could be attributed to the Sky, or some similar drug, that Haggerty detected in his eyes. Whatever the reason, he looked almost as out of place here as Haggerty felt.

"Wanna hear a funny story?" the kid asked when he'd finished his business.

"Sure," Haggerty said.

"Once upon a time we were warned that Four Horsemen would deliver the Apocalypse." He counted them on his fingers. "War, Famine, Pestilence, Death. We insulated ourselves from War, then did away with Famine and Pestilence, and that let us get the better of Death—we kicked his ass and made him our bitch. But you know what?"

"What?" Haggerty asked, throwing the ruined piece of silk into the bin.

"I think Death's a sore loser, and he's red as hell, and he's about to get back on that horse—and make everyone *his* bitch," the kid said as he washed his hands in the sink and pulled another bit of silk from his back pocket to dry them with. "And you'll be surprised at how happy we are to have him back."

He smiled a wasted smile and waved as Haggerty pushed

open the door and left the restroom. Haggerty considered the kid's Sky-whipped fantasies as morbid as the death-themed skinpaintings sported by the other JCs and their horrific self-mutilations. He'd had enough of the Orphanage.

Fortunately, Regina was where he'd left her in the dimly lit room. She was talking to a too-thin girl around her own age, who was trying to hand her something. Regina shook her head no, refusing the offering. The other girl shrugged and headed toward a table a few yards away, where someone large and obviously male waited for her, but that was all Haggerty could discern. Regina turned and, seeing Haggerty, smiled, then frowned as she got a closer look at him.

"Are you okay?" she asked.

"I'm leaving, you do as you wish," he said, waving the question aside. "What was that all about?" he asked as she gripped his arm and ushered him back toward the stairs.

"Traci? She's one of my roommates," Regina explained. "Someone's giving away tickets to the game tomorrow, and she thought I should have some plasticine strips.

"Free tickets to the most anticipated Superbowl in years?" Haggerty said skeptically. "They gotta be counterfeit."

"Probably," Regina agreed. "Since Gen-Ohs can't afford the real thing, someone's always producing counterfeits to one event or another. Sometimes they work, sometimes they don't."

They were passing the forge now, where a boy screamed to the kiss of burning metal. Haggerty clenched his teeth and moved away quickly. Up the strip and onto the beltway, he said nothing. He breathed deeply, trying to get the stench of burned meat out of his lungs, to purge it from his mind. Regina respected his silence.

"Why would they brand themselves?" he finally asked.

Regina was thoughtful. "They're fucked, and they know they're fucked," she began. "The odds are against them, for jobs, children, even happiness. That has a sort of numbing effect, ya know?"

Haggerty did know.

"And when you're numb to the world, to yourself, and you're not feeling anything—feeling nothing at all—you go to extremes. You hurt yourself until the pain rushes in and tells you you're alive." Her tone turned flippant. "Besides, it's the latest in celebrity fashion. No more dangerous than getting pierced or tattooed."

He looked at this pretty young stranger beside him who was part of a generation he clearly did not understand. He considered telling her that even oldsters with jobs they'd held for decades, not making way for younger folks, didn't always have it easy. That not everyone gets a break making it possible to afford a huge compartment with a god-awful big viewscreen. That he had only been so rewarded after a long, difficult apprenticeship. But what was the point? She'd find out for herself.

"You haven't—"

"No way," she said. "Skinpainting like this"—she indicated her iris, stickjewels meant to represent dewdrops twinkling in the light— "can be removed with plastiche in less than an hour. But burns that require surgical procedures to repair? No, thanks. My body's a temple."

"Good," he said, unaccountably relieved.

"But I have to say," she went on wistfully, "when done right it looks really cool."

They approached the intersection dividing West. "You'll be safe here," Haggerty said. "It was a pleasure—"

"Can I see your place?" she asked.

"Regina—"

He was wavering, and they both knew it.

"This is the only chance I'll ever get to see how your half lives," she cajoled. "I'll stay five minutes and then you can send me home in a taxi. I promise."

Chapter Three
CLONE JESUS

Haggerty watched from the bathroom door as Regina turned away from his cityscape view and moved to his bar. Streams of alcohol and carbonation flowed into a short glass.

Why had he let this girl distract him?

His experiences with Regina and her unpleasant world where hopeless children tormented their bodies with blisterbrands in order to control something in their lives had done nothing to convince him not to press, especially since that hopelessness seemed to be the only birthright now afforded to the young. There was nothing in his own life left to hope for. Why continue? He would wait for the girl to leave and then fall into the peaceful sea of eternal darkness. He continued to observe her while her attention was directed elsewhere and she was unaware of his regard.

Regina paused at the stand holding his replitext and ran her hand over it almost reverently. He wondered if she'd open it, what book she'd call up if she did. She sighed and withdrew her hand. Holding her wouzeburst, she crossed the room and sank into the form-adjusting esplanade couch, making herself comfortable. With a word she activated the viewscreen.

The Nine O'clock News offered a menu of headlines:

WARPLANES DELIVER OVER MIDDLE EAST; SELECT NOW

UGANDA DEMANDS ACCESS TO STEM THERAPIES; SELECT NOW

NEWVADA BULLS SET TO RUN AGAINST NEW YORK; SELECT NOW

CLONE JESUS PREPARES TO ROCK NEWVADA; SELECT NOW

"Clone Jesus," she said.

A raven-haired viewcaster appeared, standing before a stage where workers were setting up for a concert. Regina leaned forward, enraptured.

Maybe that was it. Regina had stated her anti-BBI sentiments plainly. She was all about living and enjoying life as fully as possible. Perhaps she'd simply wanted to see what might be in store for her when she was an adult with a successful career, and the perquisites that went with it, a hedge against despair. Haggerty didn't know what things she hoped would lead her to success, but she had at least a decade before she could even begin to make her own path. He wished her well, hoped she'd end up with more contentment than he had.

He slid a celtrex from his remaining supply and swallowed it. As he came out of the bathroom, the lights dimmed behind him.

"Not the four-by-four cell you'd wanted?" he said, smiling.

"At least you've got a decent-sized viewscreen," she tossed back, her eyes riveted on the report. She let loose a squeal, frantically waving at the monitor. "That's them! I can actually see them! That's my band!"

"*Your* band?"

"Okay, my *favorite* band," she amended. "You know what I mean."

The screen now showed a crew of bare-chested young men with buzz cuts and blisterbrandings of Asian mandalas on their skin, carrying their instruments past a cheering crowd of young people and boarding a small jetcraft.

"The band Clone Jesus, due to arrive in NewVada in less than two hours to kick off their world tour, will be performing a full concert before a live audience on this very stage," the viewcaster intoned.

Haggerty was surprised that the band was reviving the old custom of world tours. He wondered what something like that must be like. Sure, any Conscientious Citizen could register to leave the United States, but who in their right mind wanted to? Celebrities with a great deal of money to be made, obviously. They were the only ones with enough of it, and enough power behind it, to be granted re-entry.

"I've heard about this band," he said. "Why all the fuss?"

"They're enlightened," Regina said excitedly. "They *grok*!"

He was about to ask what, exactly, it was that they grokked and what sort of enlightenment they'd attained, when the glass in her hands caught his attention. He'd nearly forgotten that detail. The news byte came to an end, and Haggerty ordered the viewscreen to mute.

"You're too young to be drinking," he said.

Regina looked at him quizzically. "I'm old enough to press a button legally and die, but too young to drink?" she said mildly.

"The law says twenty-five to consume."

"And eighteen to press," she said. "I know the law. I also know why the law to raise the drinking age was passed, and it had nothing to do with preventing accidents or lowering crime, or any of the other reasons politicians like to spout. Look at the statistics presented in the debates and you'll see the real reason. The age limit was raised to keep so-called Junior Citizens in line—to reduce our power by infantilizing us. Three hundred years ago, a woman my age who was still unmarried would be considered a hopeless spinster. Two hundred years ago, she'd be pressured by her family to marry, or sent off to college to earn her M-R-S degree. A hundred years ago, women my age had careers, served in the military, ran for public office. There were exceptions, yes. But there are always exceptions. My point is that women my age were considered fully competent adults. Not girls. Not *Junior Citizens*.

"Telling us we're not old enough to drink keeps us children. Letting us press when we're only eighteen gets us out of the way. So before you go all Blue Code on me, let me ask you: Do you agree with the morality behind it? Do you really think it's sensible, or even fair, for the law to say that the decision to drink requires more maturity than the decision to end your own life?"

"It isn't sensible at all," Haggerty acknowledged. "Go ahead, enjoy your drink." One wouzeburst wasn't going to significantly impair her judgment, he decided, but he certainly wouldn't let her have more than that.

She lifted her glass. "You want one?" she asked.

"I don't drink," he said. "I keep it for guests. I'm going to order your cab. There's usually a wait. If I call now, you'll have plenty of time to finish your drink before you leave. I have something important to do, and it's getting late."

"Why do you think your life's so different from mine?" she said unexpectedly.

Haggerty considered. "I'd say the only real differences are communal privileges, a shift in responsibility from yourself to society," he said. "And maybe a sense of security."

"That reminds me," Regina said. She took another sip of her drink, then set the glass aside and rummaged through her backpack, from which she pulled a small gadget that Haggerty did not recognize. "I need to charge this; can I squeeze some of your juice?" She looked around his living space expectantly.

"My juice?" The dots connected. "Over by the desk," he said. "Electricity's free, you know."

"Tell that to the superintendent of my building," she said, fitting the small box into the wall receptacle he'd indicated.

"What is that thing?" he asked. "I've never seen anything like it."

"It's a remote Indranet access terminal," she said. "My friend Joe makes them. He's an Indranet jock who builds bulletproof tek. It's my vice."

She returned to the couch.

"If you say so," Haggerty said. Electric power had to be pretty low on the vice list.

"Can I see yours?" she asked.

"My vice?"

"Your button."

Haggerty hesitated. But the unit couldn't accept her press, even accidentally. It was a harmless request. He reached over to the end table, opened the drawer, pulled out his black box, and joined her on the couch.

Regina's flippancy evaporated in the face of this instrument of mortality.

"Jason P. Haggerty," she said, reading his name on the screen aloud. "I've never held one before. What would happen if I pressed?"

"You could arm it, but you couldn't press," Haggerty assured her. "The button scan needs my print, down to the biometric ridge and pore structure. Scans make zero errors. Even if you *could* press, the toxins in that unit are calibrated to my biological chemistry. Your thresholds are different. It might make you sick, possibly quite ill for a while, but you'd probably survive it."

"What if I forced you to press it?"

"That would be murder—and the unit would record it."

"You probably have to own this hideous thing, don't you?"

"It's company policy."

She tucked her legs beneath her on the couch. "Have you ever...?"

"Considered using it? This morning, as a matter of fact."

Haggerty regretted admitting it even as the words escaped his lips. He did not say that he was only waiting for her departure to do it. That he was probably in the last few moments of his life did not disturb him. He was oddly grateful for her companionship.

Tears welled in Regina's eyes. "Why?" she said quietly.

He found that he couldn't help but tell her the truth, or as much of it as he could bear.

"Tomorrow is the anniversary of my father's death a year ago. It's also ..." Emotion pummeled him. "I had a son, just a few years younger than you. He died in a car accident, exactly a year before that. My wife left me almost immediately afterward. Every day since then has been a struggle."

Regina's cheeks were wet as she leaned over and put her mouth softly yet firmly on his. He resisted a moment, then relented and let her have her way. Her tongue licked the seam of his lips. He opened his mouth for her, twined his tongue with hers, tasting the sticky tang of the wouzeburst and something more, something purely Regina—delicious and sweet enough to break his heart.

But she was so young, so full of hope and committed to life. Haggerty drew back, steeling himself to resist.

"I think it's time to say good night."

She looked him in the eyes. "I'd rather say good morning ... many hours from now." She placed her fingers over his mouth. "Don't talk. Just listen.

"We've agreed I'm mature enough to decide about life and death. This isn't life and death, Jason. I've paired before, more than once, and I want to be with you tonight."

And then she was in his arms, warm and soft and smelling like summer strawberries that he had eaten long ago in his childhood, when such fruits were common and he'd been able to get his fill. She kissed him tenderly at first, and then with open-mouthed hunger, and he found he couldn't quite refuse her. It had been so long. And after all, it was just one night and his KV unit would be there in the morning.

"Lights off," he whispered, and pulled Regina closer in his arms.

Their kisses grew more passionate, more needy, but Haggerty was damned if he was going to make love for the last time in his life on the narrow confines of his couch, form-adjusting or not. He startled Regina by suddenly lifting her up, rising from the couch and carrying her toward the bedroom. She broke the kiss with a laugh.

"The Indran said you'd be aggressive in bed," she teased.

"But I need my backpack."

"No, you don't need your backpack."

"Will you please let me get it? It's just over there."

He carried her the few feet to her backpack. Giggling, she leaned down and scooped up the straps.

Haggerty resumed the pleasant task of kissing her breathless, carrying her to the bedroom and setting her down on the bed. She dropped the backpack to the floor beside it. Fastenings loosened, clothing removed, he bent her backward with a sense of urgency he hadn't felt in years, sighing as her legs came up to hug his hips.

Regina's hair was a tangle, her breasts rising and falling with her gasps for air. The iris undulated on her belly, stickjeweled dewdrops sparkling as she moved. Her lips were kiss-swollen, her green eyes glazed with passion.

She was not Lorraine. Her figure was not as full, her hair not as dark, her skin not as pale. She did not taste like his wife, she did not kiss like her or move like her. The feel of her skin beneath his fingers was different, unknown, new. She was not the one woman who had shared Haggerty's bed for the past half century, but she was beautiful and willing and all that he could desire, right now. Perhaps too much so.

"We need to slow down," he said, attempting to pull back.

"No," she said, sinking her hands in his hair and pulling him closer, devouring his mouth with hungry kisses.

"If we don't, this is going to end much more quickly than you'd like," he warned.

"Don't care," she said, and startled him by taking the lead, rolling them so that she was on top. She sat up with another giggle, leaving him to stare up at her, bemused. "The Indran seems not to have predicted that I'm pretty aggressive myself." She smirked, then leaned over and began rooting for something in her backpack.

"You don't need the damned backpack!" he said half amused, half exasperated.

"Lot you know," she teased.

She sat up with a triumphant cry, holding four simple gray disks in her hands.

Haggerty eyed them dubiously. "What the hell are those?"

She smiled wickedly, green eyes glinting with mischief. "They're nerve impulse transmitters, vaporware," she said. She fixed one of the disks onto each of her temples, then leaned forward and pressed one to each of his.

"And these do what, exactly?" he asked warily.

"Transmit nerve impulses, silly," she said impudently. "Don't be such a neophobe."

He raised a brow.

She leaned over him, small breasts temptingly close. "You'll like them, I promise," she whispered seductively.

"I certainly like *these*," he grinned wickedly, and lifted his head to capture a rosy nipple in his mouth.

Regina hissed in satisfaction.

Haggerty gasped in shock, releasing her. "What the hell ... ?"

"Don't stop, Jason," she urged, drawing his head back to her breast.

Once again the sensation of lips and tongue surrounded his own nipple.

"It transmits nerve impulses," Regina moaned. "You feel what I feel. Go ahead, make me *feel!*"

And so he did.

They began slowly, sharing worshipful kisses, tender tastes, caressing touches, growing hungrier and more demanding. Tentative touches and shy explorations becoming a claiming of flesh. Every touch and taste echoed and re-echoing, spiraling up and up, sensation intensifying, magnifying, building.

And that was only prelude.

The longer he wore the disks, the more in tune he became with what Regina was feeling, the easier it was for the transmitters to convey their electronic messages of stimulus received. There were a few moments of disorientation, when he seemed to be in two places at once—and then he adjusted, transcended, defied the laws of physics. Haggerty was no longer limited to his own body, his own perceptions. He occupied two spaces at once, became two beings at once, experiencing what he did to her as she experienced it, just as she was experiencing what she did to him, their responses predicated upon perfect, immediate comprehension of each other's needs. This was intimacy taken to a new level, communication of the most immediate kind, beyond intuition or sensitivity—a revelation.

She made him feel things he'd long forgotten. Passion and grace and fire. Strawberries in summer and salt spice, hot and humid as the sea beneath a blazing sun. Haggerty lost himself in the sensuous pleasure of her touch, echoing back his own touch upon her flesh. And when they joined, strength and power and deep need. It went on unendingly, or so it seemed, as he drifted on the tides of passion.

Eventually they came to completion. Regina collapsed over him, exhausted. She rolled to his side and pulled off the disks at her temple.

Haggerty felt disoriented. He took a moment to compose himself, to readjust to the limits his own immediate bodily sensations. From a purely physical viewpoint, that had been the most mind-blowing sex of his life. It had not been making love. It had not been what he'd shared with Lorraine. And by that standard, it had not been quite as good. But it hadn't needed to be.

"You kids and your toys," he said teasingly.

"Not bad yourself, old man," she teased back, a sated smile on her face. She settled her head on his chest and stared into his eyes. "If you don't mind, I'm going to watch the Clone Jesus concert. Care to join me?" she added affectionately.

"I think I'll pass," Haggerty said. He wasn't much for the discordant sounds JCs thought of as music, these days. "Enjoy yourself."

"Already did," she smirked, and kissed him lightly.

He watched appreciatively as she disentangled herself from his arms, stood, and stretched, her beautiful breasts rising and falling with each breath, her lips still kiss-swollen. A twinge of regret surprised him as she reached for his undershirt and pulled it on as though she'd done it a thousand times before, the fabric falling to her thighs, as she lazily slumped off to the living room and called on the viewscreen, closing the bedroom door so that he wouldn't be disturbed. He was reminded of how young she was; young enough to be his granddaughter. That intellectual truth didn't register on a visceral level, though. Not anymore. He didn't perceive Regina as a child needing protection, but as a woman with more compelling needs.

Haggerty felt grateful now that he'd been prevented from pressing this morning, happy to be ending his life on this bittersweet note. Tomorrow he would make breakfast for Regina and send her on her way in a cab. Maybe he'd make a slight alteration to his will, leave her a small portion of the wealth he'd accumulated. There was no one else to inherit but a list of charities, and he supposed leaving her enough credits to move out of her pairplex, get started on some of those dreams she had, was as much an act of charity as anything else. Then he'd take out his unit and press—and this time he would turn off the phone.

But for now, he lay reliving their encounter, smiling and content, until he could no longer tell if he were awake or asleep.

"NOOOOOOOO! *No, no, no, no, no!*"

Regina's screams woke him abruptly. Haggerty threw on his robe and rushed into the living room, catching her as her legs began to buckle.

On the viewscreen Haggerty saw a thin-lipped viewcaster in mid-sentence.

"... during a concert where three as yet unidentified teenagers apparently committed simultaneous suicide live on global television."

On the replay, Clone Jesus strummed their guitars and pounded their syncdrums; Haggerty felt he could touch the bass player's branded arm, the definition of the telecast was so real. Fireworks erupted off the stage as the song ended. The lead singer came forward and bowed. He was shirtless and, unlike the rest of the band, his blisterbrands were not limited to his arms. Brands were raised along his chest, his back, and his shoulders, and a single weal curved from just beneath his left eye to the corner of his lip. The singer rose up, spread his arms, and signaled backstage.

Two boys and a girl in Clone Jesus jackets, all teenagers looking younger than Regina, rushed to his side. Staring at him in evident adoration, they pulled out three KV units, armed and flashing, and displayed them proudly.

Haggerty caught his breath as Regina wailed and buried her face against his chest.

The crowd went silent as the youths pressed their black buttons in unison, then crumpled to the stage.

The transmission abruptly cut back to the newscaster.

It's a hoax, Haggerty thought. *Dear God, let it just be a hoax.*

The chime sounded an incoming call.

"Answer, visual off!" Haggerty barked, muting the telemonitor.

Elsa's image appeared. She was still in the BBI viewing room.

"Jason," she said calmly, "we have three lights on board. They appear to originate from the Clone Jesus concert site at Death Valley Commemorative Park."

Regina's screams escalated into uncontrollable sobbing. She collapsed to the floor, hands to her face.

"Jason, who is that with you?" Elsa queried.

"Never mind," he shouted. "Who's the agent on call?"

"Corbin," she said. The last name Haggerty wanted to hear.

It figured the agent with the least experience would be assigned to cover this potential publicity nightmare.

"Connect me to dispatch," Haggerty said.

Tanner came on immediately. "Jeez Haggerty, you see that on the news?"

"Listen Mitch," Haggerty said. "You can't assign this to someone as inexperienced as Corbin. The agency's about to get slammed."

"I was thinking the same thing," Tanner quipped. "You wanna take it? It's in your jurisdiction and you've got seniority. Corbin's on the other line now, requesting assignment and warrants, but I can't reach the Dragon."

Haggerty felt torn. *Why now?* he thought. He glanced at the black box waiting on his coffee table, then down at Regina's crumpled form on the floor, moaning at fever pitch. *Don't do it*, he thought, *pass it on*. But the call to duty roared within him.

"I'm on my way," he said.

But first he had to deal with Regina. Nothing he did or said seemed capable of calming her. She wailed and gasped, struggling for breath. Haggerty managed to get a celtrex down her throat, and carried her back to bed. The drug would soon exhaust her—the enhanced effect on someone who hadn't gone through the therapy. He murmured something soothing, placed a box of tissues within her reach, and fetched a glass of water for the nightstand as her eyelids fluttered shut. It wouldn't be good if she woke up alone and panicked, so he bent over and spoke quietly, his tone reluctant.

"I need to leave ..."

Regina's eyes flew open, all confidence leached from her expression, and she grabbed his arm. "Don't!" she cried.

She looked so pale, so vulnerable, so young.

"Just for a little while," he said soothingly, gently extricating himself. "I shouldn't be more than an hour. Get some rest. I'll be back as soon as I can."

She closed her eyes and turned her face into the pillow as Haggerty backed quietly out of the room, grabbing his uniform on his way.

Regina's renewed sobs echoed in his ears. He hated leaving her alone, although he couldn't imagine why her reaction was so extreme, even given her abhorrence of the black boxes. There had been worse disasters caught on live viewcasts over the years. But if BBI had ever faced a crisis, this was it.

He had to get to the press scene as quickly as possible, and there was only one way to do it. Donning his grays, he ordered his car from the garage.

"I was beginning to wonder if you forgot you owned a car," the valet greeted Haggerty cheerfully as he stepped out of the autolift and handed him a tip. "It's been so long since you've used it, I was thinking of offering to buy it from you."

Apparently he was unaware of the public tragedy that had just unfolded on the airwaves.

"I'll keep that in mind," Haggerty said pleasantly.

He slugged into his vehicle and powered it on. The thrusters engaged. Firing into the long downgrade sloop that fed into the intercity slotway, he punched the comlink to BBI.

"Elsa, please feed me the coordinates of the triple press and give me any pertinent news commentary."

"Coming through to you now, Jason," she said.

"Thanks," he replied. "Now code me warrants for those three units, check status on all related police warrants, and meet me there as soon as you can."

Sirens ablaze, the car shifted into autodrive. Elsa had set its coordinates onto a priority track, past the stopped traffic. Haggerty swiveled his seat to bring up the latest coverage on a small plasma console. The thin-lipped viewcaster offered, "Following the alleged triple suicides, the entire entourage of the chart-topping musical group Clone Jesus, including the band members themselves and their manager, entertainment magnate Shintag Lake, are being held for questioning... ."

Haggerty's car slotted into the exitway for Death Valley Commemorative Park. He saw ambulance lights near the stage, where police forced throngs of spectators away from the press site. The sirens allowed him to park reasonably close by.

Climate control in outdoor venues wasn't impossible but it was costly, and not designed to last more than a few hours. The system was beginning to fail, and the oppressive heat had begun to seep into the area. Haggerty found himself loosening the top of his uniform. The huge field was packed tightly with crying and shouting JCs. Many seemed dazed. Flashing his identiplate, he forced his way through the mob, past security, to the lip of the stage where JCs pushed and shuffled for a better view, and hoisted himself upward with a grunt.

He was unprepared for the sight of the crumpled teens being prepared for transport by gloved Med Techs. Usually by the time he reached a press scene the bodies had been removed. Detective Woyzeck was calling the shots, his badge slung from his neck and a frown on his dark, leathery face. Haggerty had worked with Woyzeck for years, and knew him to be thorough and focused. If anyone could keep this press scene from turning into a circus, it was Woyzeck.

"Fucked up, huh?" the detective said as Haggerty came to his side. Sweat trickled down Woyzeck's face; he mopped it away with a handkerchief already limp with moisture.

Haggerty looked at one of the teens, her blonde curls splayed against the stage, her eyes blank. On her cheek was a small blisterbrand in the shape of a teardrop.

"Have they been certified?" he asked Woyzeck.

"The coroner hasn't arrived yet. But I was told to remove the bodies immediately. Normally I'd make you wait for your boxes, but if you promise to get back to me on the contents over drinks sometime, you can have 'em now. Just wait till the bodies get lifted."

It was a break in procedure to take the boxes prior to certification of death and removal of the bodies. Haggerty knew of cases where reviewers had been docked pay, or worse, for such infractions. But this situation wasn't normal. Haggerty hoped there'd be something on the recordings that would help him make sense of this tragedy.

"Deal," he said.

He gloved up and moved toward the girl as two techs rolled her body onto a stretcher and lifted her in unison, then excused themselves. Haggerty watched them move past him toward the foot of the stage. He knelt down to retrieve her KV unit and stared at the popped tab, then glanced back to where she had fallen and saw that she'd dropped something else—a white plasticine keycard.

Haggerty looked around for Woyzeck, but the detective had gone to speak to one of the cops working crowd control and it would be several minutes before Haggerty could get his attention. He glanced from the keycard to the black box.

The casing of the Kevorkian unit was gouged and abraded where the alphanumeric code should have been, the name and serial number completely scrubbed from the unit.

Haggerty went cold. An unheard-of triple press in a public venue, a higher-up ordering a break in protocol to remove bodies before their deaths could be certified, and now this. The wrongness factor had increased exponentially.

Haggerty had never seen anything like it. The only reason for removing the means of identification was that the unit wasn't hers. But that was impossible. Only the person to whom a unit was registered could successfully press it. If somehow this girl had got hold of someone else's box and broken through the safeguards, the registration files for the unit would be useless. Unless the recordings on the box identified her, or someone who recognized her from the broadcast stepped forward, it could take weeks, even months to determine who she was. The information they could obtain from a thumbprint—largely transit and consumer purchase data—might prove useful. But again it could take months to navigate the maze of constitutional protections and procure a warrant that would allow them to get an ident that way.

The right thing to do was to alert Detective Woyzeck to the problem. Woyzeck had been a by-the-book guy as long as Haggerty had known him. Surely he would tag the keycard as evidence and ensure that it was properly processed. Unless someone ordered him to break protocol on that, too...

Haggerty looked around. Another M.T. headed toward the next body. Heart racing, Haggerty placed his boot over the card, suddenly wary of everyone. He forced himself to follow procedure, concentrating on the need to secure the unit in the minthizine case, to insure against contamination.

"You okay, Haggerty? You look a little tweaked." Detective Woyzeck was beside him again. "Maybe you'd better hang back with me until they clear the bodies."

Woyzeck took Haggerty by the elbow. As Haggerty began to step away, the plasticine card scraped beneath his boot.

"Don't touch me," Haggerty said, disengaging his arm. "I've got hazardous chemicals on me from the box."

Woyzeck pulled his hand back. "I forgot."

"Wash your hands at one of the M.T. units," Haggerty advised.

Both men turned as sirens whirred close to the stage. Haggerty used the distraction to bend down and pocket the keycard, mindful that having touched it with his glove it was now potentially toxic. The vehicle pulled in almost at their feet, and a moment later its doors extended upward, the BBI logo clearly displayed. Elsa stepped from the driver's side, with Corbin emerging from the passenger door, her uniform half unfastened against the rising heat, revealing more of her ample cleavage than was professional. Woyzeck gave the exposed flesh a fleeting glance, then turned to Haggerty.

"They with you?"

Haggerty nodded. "Give me a second alone with them. The new kid's a little green about procedure."

"Sure thing," Woyzeck said with a wink. "I gotta go wash my hands, remember? But call me later."

They watched Corbin and Elsa trot to the lip of the stage and bound up and onto their level.

"You got it," Haggerty told Woyzeck as the others arrived. Woyzeck nodded to Corbin, then stepped away to the nearest M.T. unit to clean his hands before overseeing the removal of the second body, a teen with a shock of blue hair in a white pleather jacket with CLONE JESUS embroidered in red on the back.

"I want this assignment," Corbin told Haggerty.

"It's my assignment," Haggerty stated flatly.

I tried to stop her from coming, Elsa linked to him. *But she's been cleared by the Director.*

"I've got training in youth counsel," Corbin retorted, turning to survey the stage. "And you don't."

"There aren't any youths to counsel," Haggerty said.

"Maybe not here, but less than twenty minutes ago there was another press—a teenage girl, right in front of the viewscreen as her parents watched. And that's my assignment."

Sounds like a copycat, Haggerty thought. While it was ridiculous for Corbin to assert that the connection justified her taking over the triple press, it was sufficient for Haggerty to let her in on it in a subordinate position.

But Corbin wasn't finished. "I believe your little cryppie's got inside information. Remember this?"

Corbin held up a crumpled piece of paper. Haggerty recognized the Java Joint logo and Regina's hand-drawn timeline of Old Testament names. He tried to mask his surprise as he reached for Regina's discarded napkin.

Corbin pulled it back and folded it into her jacket. "You're not the only one with a taste for the finer things in life," she said.

Haggerty handed Elsa the minthizine case with the girl's unit and told her to retrieve the other two after making sure that the bodies had been moved and the units remained where they'd fallen.

"I don't know what you were doing at the Java Joint or why you swiped that from my table," he told Corbin, "but the person you refer to as my *cryppie* has no connection to what happened here."

"What do you know about her?" Corbin said smugly. Clearly she had information and intended to make him ask for it.

"Not a lot," he said. "We only met a few hours ago. What makes you think she's involved?" Brief as the time he'd spent with her had been, he couldn't believe Regina had anything to do with this tragedy.

Corbin produced a photograph of the protesters Haggerty had encountered that morning outside BBI. There was Regina, standing next to the girl who had moments earlier lain dead on the stage at his feet. Both girls had their arms raised in protest.

"Like it or not I'm in on this one," Corbin stated. "And we'd better get answers off those KV's fast before any more go off. The Dragon's authorized a media conference in one hour."

Elsa stepped up. "Do you want to review here?" she asked Haggerty.

"Yes," Corbin answered.

Elsa ignored her, awaiting Haggerty's instructions. Corbin glared at his assistant.

God bless whoever forgot to remove Elsa's chip, Haggerty thought. Sixty years ago, review agents working with the first androids assigned to BBI discovered that their new assistants were frighteningly narrow in interpreting company policy and frighteningly zealous in enforcing it. After a few "unfortunate accidents," the union demanded the installation of Personal Loyalty Chips to combat the problem. Ultimately, design improvements and continuous upgrades rendered the chips unnecessary and BBI directed that all PLCs be removed. It was hardly Haggerty's fault that a clerical error incorrectly recorded the removal of Elsa's chip.

"I don't want to do the review here," Haggerty said. "We need someplace more private."

"Autodrive. Home. Park," Haggerty called into his car's relay terminal, then watched the vehicle maneuver itself off the field and slot the beltway onramp.

Corbin slid into the driver's seat of the BBI vehicle and popped the doors for Haggerty and Elsa. "Where to?" she asked, looking back over her shoulder.

Haggerty mentally flipped through his options. Going to his place would put Regina at risk. While Corbin's picture proved nothing—it was a public demonstration, and Regina and the girl who had pressed might never have met before—the junior agent would no doubt insist on having Regina taken in for questioning, if not arrested on who knew what charges. Headquarters was also out—too many noses and far too much pressure. Besides, there was no equipment there that could not be remotely accessed by Elsa from the vehicle. Until the kids were identified there were no obvious associates to consult except the band members, and those interviews would take hours to clear. They might as well retrieve the unit from Corbin's case.

"Let's check your supposed copycat while we upload," he said.

Corbin engaged the engine and took the car out on manual.

Elsa ported the first unit and jacked into the small dashboard console. *I assume we're sharing all information with agent Corbin?* she linked.

Haggerty remembered the plasticine keycard in his pocket. He wasn't ready to reveal that tidbit, but under the circumstances, anything Elsa got off the boxes was fair game. *We might as well,* he linked back. *The Dragon would breathe real fire if I didn't cooperate after she gave Corbin the go-ahead.*

Elsa acknowledged his order with a gaze, then said aloud. "Jason, as you retrieved it, I assume you know the name and serial number on the girl's unit were rendered illegible."

"What?" Corbin demanded.

"Yes," Haggerty replied. "Do you know how it was done? Will it be possible to reconstruct them?"

"Uncertain. The numbers appear to have been first effaced with a metal file then exposed to corrosive acid. I don't know if our lab techs will be able to retrieve anything."

"How about the other two units?" he asked.

"Also illegible," she said. "And the units appear to be unregistered. When I attempted to obtain the usual warrants, none of the devices was for a registered client. I had to use an older protocol to obtain the general warrants I sent you."

"So we're dealing with retrofit black market boxes?" Corbin interjected.

"It appears so," Haggerty said.

"How is that possible?" Corbin said. "BBI security is supposed to be the best."

"It is the best," Haggerty said. "I have no idea how this level of tampering is possible."

"Then good luck getting anything off the units," Corbin said sourly, banking into the government-only lane and shifting to overdrive.

"I doubt whoever retrofit them got through all the safeguards," Haggerty said. "The video on the arming mechanism can't be disengaged or the unit won't function, even if the printscan's switched out."

"Jason, this is most curious," Elsa said. "The toxin residue on this unit is not polythinisine based."

"It's one of our units, but it's not our drug?" Corbin said in disbelief.

"That is my analysis," Elsa confirmed. "The administered toxins are not of the same base chemical compositions loaded into KV units."

The situation was getting worse by the moment. Not only had someone stolen the units and figured out how to tamper with them, they'd synthesized a deadly new drug to fill them.

"Play the visual," Haggerty told Elsa.

Elsa ported the visual into the dashboard console screen. The first image was an obtuse angle of roughhewn floor and red cloth, presumably curtains, the audio the raucous chanting of the crowd as Clone Jesus played their encore. Elsa adjusted the image ninety degrees and it was clear the unit was being held in the palm of the girl, waiting backstage to press. The music stopped, the crowd cheered, and the girl rushed out onto the stage. The visual then showed her arm with the box outstretched and button pressed without hesitation.

"There's no prior recording?" Corbin demanded.

"Negative," Elsa replied.

"Let's see the next one," Haggerty said.

Not surprisingly, Elsa informed them that the toxin residue in the second unit was the same poison that had been loaded into the first one. This scene was earlier, as denoted by the embedded timecode. "Dawn, it's me," the boy with the shock of blue hair said. Nude to the waist, with an oriental dragon skinpainting curving around his torso, he was smiling at himself with amusement in what appeared to be a bathroom mirror, holding the black box. "Someday you'll probably see this," he said, "and you're gonna think I'm a grokless idiot, and wonder why I didn't just call you and tell you what I had to say, why I'm doing it this way. But then you'd try to talk me out of it, and I don't want that."

"He looks drugged," Haggerty said. "Maybe SkyWhip?"

Corbin agreed. "And that bathroom's pretty chic. My guess, it's a hotel."

"It's just ... easier if I talk to the box, okay?" the boy continued. "I wanted to let you know that I love you, and I'm sorry that I haven't called in so long. I love my life, but I have no regrets about what I'm doing... . Fuck it!"

The recording halted as the boy disarmed and the unit began prepping for the next installment.

Something seemed off, Haggerty thought. This was not the usual resignation found in most final recordings. It was hard to believe the kid would seriously contemplate pressing if he hadn't been dosed on some drug. The second installment was a repeat performance of the blonde girl's nonchalance, seen from the opposite side of the lead singer, ending as the boy slumped onstage, smiling dead into the box.

"Let's see the third," Haggerty said.

Once again, Elsa confirmed the presence of the unknown toxin. The timecode for this one was several days prior to the press.

"Hey, it says it's recording!" exclaimed the third dead child, whose golden bronze skin hinted of at least one African-American grandparent. The boy was somewhat taller than average, his body lean but well-muscled, as though he had spent time in a gym. A faux diamond stud winked in his ear, and he'd shaved his head. Wide pupils in dark, almond-shaped eyes showed he was clearly elated, possibly dosed. Haggerty found something familiar about his features, as if he'd seen him before but couldn't place where. Could the kid have been an actor in some forgettable viewcast or feature film?

"This could be something," Corbin said. "He's playing with it. And that's definitely a hotel room. I see four, maybe five people on the couches behind him. There's probable narcotic use in progress."

"Elsa, take close-ups of all room occupants and magnify for identification," Haggerty ordered.

Images filed down the side of the screen; Corbin identified several as band members.

"Turn that thing off," came a male voice from across the room.

"Ya wanna kill yourself?"

"Maybe," the boy answered, laughing. His tone changed to mock viewcaster as he addressed the unit's recording device. "I'm standing in this beautiful penthouse suite, partying my ass off with the enlightened, the infamous Clone Jesus. And I'd just like to say, put some hurt on New York, you lame-ass NewVada Bulls—"

"I said, turn the bloody thing off!"

The recording skipped ahead.

"This is about four hours later," Elsa said.

The audio snapped in with pronounced moaning and the unit adjusted light for what appeared to be a darkened closet, revealing the boy, pants around his ankles, hands in the hair of a young brunette on her knees before him.

"Oh God, oh yeah!" the boy moaned as he climaxed.

That should have signaled the end of his encounter with the brunette, but rather than tapering off, the boy's moans intensified. The young girl looked on appreciatively, not stopping her ministrations until the boy finally collapsed, several minutes later.

"Hey," she said, wiping her mouth with the back of her hand. "Where can I get some of that?"

The final installment was another repeat of the onstage press.

"End transmission," Corbin told Elsa as the boy collapsed.

Elsa looked to Haggerty, who nodded without looking up.

"So," Corbin summed up smugly, "All we know is that these kids were living the life and had no fear of pressing."

Haggerty wasn't sure he shared her assessment. Something about the recordings didn't add up. He knew in his bones there was more than was obvious on first viewing. He was about to say as much when Corbin announced that she was preparing to slot, and Haggerty decided to wait.

She steered the car toward the garage system of a dilapidated twelve-story building and docked next to a waiting ambulance. "This part of the investigation is mine," she reminded Haggerty, popping a cube of gum in her mouth and triggering the hatch.

"Stay and coordinate with Detective Woyzeck," Haggerty instructed Elsa. "Tell him the boxes were unregistered and try to identify the people in that hotel room."

"Affirmative, Jason," she said.

He left her opening a comlink to the detective, as he followed Corbin into the garage.

Chapter Four
COBAIN SYNDROME

The DeLongpre residence was typical of most CCs' compartments. Surveying the shabby but neat cramped living room, Haggerty reflected that Regina had been wrong. He didn't live like the other half. The top ten percent, maybe. And the Gen-Ohs couldn't even hope for as much as the little the DeLongpres had. He accepted a glass of water from a young M.T., who pointed out where the press had occurred and the fallen black box before wheeling the copycat's body out the front door.

Since no foul play had been indicated and the girl had been uninsured, neither police investigation nor full review were required. Corbin would watch the final recording to see if any personal messages needed a copy-and-release authorization, but that was unlikely, given that the dead girl had pressed in front of her parents. Presses of persons not yet a legal adult were the most harrowing cases. Haggerty hoped Corbin was up to the task as she sat down with the girl's parents to begin the interview.

"I'm taking the box," he told Corbin.

She nodded agreement.

Discreetly dosing a celtrex, Haggerty gloved up and prepared to assume possession of the discharged unit at the foot of the small viewscreen. As he reached for it, something on the edge of the table caught his attention: a photograph of the DeLongpres with their daughter at Disneyland. Slightly chubby, pimpled, with braces on her teeth, the young girl stood with the aid of a small crutch—one leg being notably shorter than the other. Quite a contrast to the perfect bodies and faces of the teens she'd just emulated. Even with all the DNA screening that preceded the grant of a license to have a child, defects still occurred. Though painful to endure while they lasted, such physical imperfections could be fixed by plastiche once a child's body finished growing. This girl's never would.

Haggerty picked up the unit, relieved to see the serial numbers intact. He cased it, put the gloves in a biohazard bag, and walked down a short hallway to the DeLongpres' tiny washroom to clean his hands. He returned to the living room as Corbin was attempting to wrap up her interview with the parents.

"Mr. and Mrs. DeLongpre, this is my associate, Mr. Haggerty," she said.

The mother extended her hand limply. Haggerty returned the pressure of her fingers firmly.

"I'm sorry for your loss," he said.

She nodded, tears glistening on her cheeks.

"Their daughter, Pamela, was in possession of a unit after successful petition under Kevorkian Act 516," Corbin said flatly, simply stating facts. "It was a calm decision Pamela made after watching the broadcast. I judge this a clean press."

"A clean press!" the father exploded, his pain obvious to Haggerty.

"Arthur, please calm down," his wife said quietly.

"Calm down! These people don't know the ridicule our baby suffered!"

"Sir, I assure you—" Corbin began.

"Assure me of what?" DeLongpre snarled. "That you understand our loss? Have you lost a child?"

"No sir, I haven't. But—"

"Do you know how long we waited for permission? Thirty goddamned *years*. Pamela was everything to us! You might as well hand us our own fucking boxes right now!"

He stormed out of the room, smashing a lamp as he went.

Haggerty understood what the father had not spoken. When couples lost a child they could apply for permission to have another and usually get approval. But when the lost child had congenital defects, permission was denied.

"I'm so sorry," Mrs. DeLongpre said contritely, ineffectually dabbing her eyes with a crumpled handkerchief.

"It's totally understandable, ma'am," Haggerty said gently. "Do you mind if I ask you a question? Did Pamela listen regularly to this band, Clone Jesus?"

"Not that I know of," she said. "She keeps to herself mostly. She doesn't have many friends. She really likes—" Mrs. DeLongpre gave a choked sob, pulled herself together. "Pamela really *liked* to listen to music over the Indranet after school."

"Could we please see her room?" Haggerty asked.

Corbin looked at him aslant, the gears turning in her head.

They'd interviewed the parents and retrieved the unit. What could they possibly learn from the girl's room?

If Corbin didn't want to come along, that was fine by Haggerty. He turned to follow the mother. Corbin joined them, not about to let him gain control of the case.

Pamela DeLongpre's room was smaller than the walk-in closet in Haggerty's master bedroom. Haggerty looked at the unmade bed, the outdated computer terminal, the bare white walls.

"Ma'am, would you excuse us for a minute?" he asked politely.

Mrs. DeLongpre withdrew from the doorway where she'd been standing and returned to the living room. Haggerty closed the bedroom door behind her.

"What is it?" Corbin asked him. It was more a challenge than a question.

"I've never seen a teenager's room this empty and organized," Haggerty said. "Not even a poster on the wall."

He went to the terminal and powered it on. The Indranet default page was dedicated to Clone Jesus—no surprise there. The glow from the screen bathed Haggerty's face in soft purple as music surged out at the two agents, a soft ballad, presumably one of the band's.

"Turn out the lights," Haggerty said over his shoulder.

Corbin dialed the lights off.

Immediately glowfitti covered the walls, the desk, the ceiling, even the bed sheets—a haphazard collage of hearts, poetry, and song lyrics generated by the site. Haggerty powered down the terminal and the room went dark.

Back in the living room, Haggerty retrieved his com from an outer pocket, ignoring his uneasiness as his fingers brushed against the keycard secreted in the sealed inner pocket beneath it. He flipped the com open and punched in a recall code, detaching the plasticine strip the com produced. Without grief counseling, the DeLongpres would probably end up divorced. And then it would only be a matter of time before their lives consisted of too much dosing, too much self-indulgence, and too little attachment to anything or anyone. Arthur DeLongpre's grief could turn him into a clone of Mitch Tanner. Haggerty hoped Mrs. DeLongpre wouldn't let that happen.

"Thank you for your time, ma'am," he said, offering her the strip. "I know what you and your husband are going through. This is the contact info for a grief counselor I've worked with personally."

Her eyes met his as she accepted the strip. "I'm so sorry," she said, understanding what he'd left unsaid.

"Give him a call," Haggerty said gently. "It's a free service."

"I don't know how I lost control in there," Corbin muttered as they made their way back to the vehicle.

"You're welcome," Haggerty said ironically.

She glared at him. "Thanks for handling it," she finally responded, the words clipped, tight.

Haggerty was tempted to leave it at that, but someone had to take Corbin in hand, if only for the sake of the next of kin she would deal with in the future.

"Believe it or not, your *loss of control* had less to do with control than with experience," he told her. "There are things they can't teach you in training. You can only learn them in the field."

Corbin looked unconvinced.

"What have you got for us?" he asked Elsa as they strapped themselves in place in the car.

Elsa swiveled in the driver's seat. "I've identified the men and women in the hotel room. All are either band members or known associates. Unfortunately, neither local nor national databanks can make positive ident on any of the three children."

"Of course they can't," Corbin snapped. "The only databanks we can legally check are for convicts, missing persons, and government employees. Lax chance of finding them there. The transit and consumer purchase databanks would give us idents in five minutes."

"Those sources are constitutionally protected," Haggerty reminded her. "I'll be happy if we get them in five hours."

"They're already dead," Corbin retorted. "What's the harm in accessing files where we know we'll find records? Who does that hurt?"

"Any number of living people who don't want the government poking around in records showing where they've been and what they've purchased," Haggerty said. "We've got to exhaust all other methods of identifying the bodies and prove the existence of a public danger before any judge will let us anywhere near the other databanks. You know the drill. Or you ought to."

"I think it's stupid," Corbin persisted.

"Tell that to the Founding Fathers," Haggerty said dryly.

He turned his attention to Elsa. "Anything else we should

know?"

"Detective Woyzeck is en route to State Facility Four to interrogate Clone Jesus."

"How long have we got until the Dragon wants me online?"

"Thirty-six minutes."

Haggerty laid his head against the seat cushion, closing his eyes.

"You want to lose me, don't you?" Corbin said, her blue eyes glittering with annoyance.

"Come again?" Haggerty said.

"You want me out of the way so you can go question your subversive girlfriend. You know she can identify that dead girl."

Corbin was partially right, damn her. While he was by no means certain that Regina knew anything that could help them get an ident, it was true that he wanted to talk to her about the situation. It was equally true that he had a keycard in his pocket that might provide the information they needed, but Corbin didn't know that. Because he had removed it from a press scene without proper clearance, she might try to use it to get him thrown off the case or charged with interference in a criminal investigation.

Haggerty didn't like the idea of Corbin coming anywhere near Regina. Who knew what she would accuse her of? He also realized that he had to ask himself why he was protecting Regina. Had their physical intimacy changed the equation between them? Could he trust his own judgment when it came to Regina? Was she actually involved in what had happened? Maybe he needed someone like Corbin—someone pushy and obnoxious and competitive—to get to the bottom of things.

"Take us to my compartment," he told Elsa, resigning himself to the inevitable.

But when they got there, Regina was gone—along with his KV unit.

"That proves she's involved," Corbin said triumphantly as they fired out of the tunnel slot and back onto the BBI offramp.

For reasons he would not share, Haggerty knew that this was not necessarily true. Regina had her own motives for taking his unit, motives that had nothing to do with this case.

Corbin flipped on the comlink for an incoming call.

"This is Corbin."

"Haggerty with you?" Tanner asked.

"I'm here," Haggerty said.

"Protesters are all over the place," Tanner warned. "Better come in through the back entrance. You've also got the parents of one of the kids waiting in reception. The Dragon herself wants to be present when you interview them."

"Thanks for the heads up," Haggerty said.

If he'd pressed that morning, all this would be someone else's problem. Procuring a new unit could prove embarrassing and would take time. But he wasn't going to let this last assignment hinder his plan to press. At least now they'd have a positive ident on one, if not all, of the children.

"Taking us around back," Elsa said.

The usual crowd of protesters that milled about the front steps had more than doubled. They made it from the garage to the viewing room without incident. Elsa took her seat at a console while Corbin went to file her report on Pamela DeLongpre. Haggerty was prevented from handing the keycard to Elsa to pull up its data by the arrival of the Dragon.

"Don't get comfortable," she ordered. "We have to speak with some parents."

Consuela had traded her usual dress suit for her division director uniform, a savvy choice conveying both her authority and respect for the gravity of the situation without a word having to be said.

"Who are the parents and why are they here instead of down at the precinct with Woyzeck?" Haggerty asked, falling into step beside her. "Those kids weren't clients. Their units were black market."

"But they *were* our units, at some point," Consuela said, "and the parents want to know how one of them got into the hands of their son. Frankly, so do I."

"Which boy was their son?" Haggerty said.

"The darker one. His name was Tyler Stelwyn. The only son of Antonio Stelwyn, who owns half this city."

Now Haggerty knew why the image of the beautiful boy with shaved hair and golden bronze skin who liked to experiment with his unit had seemed familiar when he reviewed the press recordings. Stelwyn, the African-American industrialist, known to everyone in the country was a bit taller, more heavily muscled, his skin tone a few shades darker, but the shape of the face, the line of the jaw, and the cast of the mouth were identical to his son's. If a triple press with illegal boxes viewcast around the world hadn't been bad enough, the fact that Antonio Stelwyn's only son was one of the victims increased the gravity of the situation. The Indran's voice sounded mockingly in Haggerty's head: *You have a difficult night coming.*

"Do we have ident on the other two kids?" he asked Consuela.

"Nothing yet from the police. I was hoping you'd have something."

"Unfortunately, I don't." Haggerty scratched the back of his neck.

"Quite unfortunate," the Dragon agreed, reaching for the reception room door.

"Finally," Antonio Stelwyn spat when they stepped inside. A powerfully built man used to giving orders and having them obeyed, faced with the one situation he could not control he lashed out with a vengeance. "Are public triple presses so goddamned common you can take your goddamned time investigating them?"

A woman seated at a small table sobbed softly: Sylvia Marchand, the legendary supermodel who had dominated the annual *Most Beautiful* lists of all the major e-zines and viewcasts for over fifty years. Even before her marriage, she'd been a celebrity in her own right. But at the moment, she was merely a grieving mother with her head buried in her hands as she wept, and Haggerty knew her only by the heartbreaking sobs she couldn't control. He could not help but reflect on the different treatment the Stelwyns would receive, compared to the DeLongpres.

Haggerty was surprised to see Primrose, making ineffectual efforts to comfort the bereaved couple. Of all the adjusters in NewVada, what were the chances of the same one being involved in two back-to-back, unrelated multiple-press cases the same day? One more thing about this case that didn't feel right. Primrose looked up as they entered, whispered a final soothing platitude to Mrs. Stelwyn, and approached Haggerty and Consuela, extending his hand.

"Oliver Primrose, adjusting agent for the insurance firm of Cromwell and Sons," he said as he shook Consuela's hand. "Sorry to be meeting you under these circumstances."

"Mr. Primrose," Consuela acknowledged.

Primrose nodded a greeting to Haggerty, then turned to the Stelwyns and surprised Haggerty again by performing the introductions.

"Mr. and Mrs. Stelwyn, this is Consuela Pitcairn, the director of BBI NewVada, and Jason Haggerty, the agent in charge of the BBI portion of the investigation."

Antonio Stelwyn had no interest in social niceties. "I'm about to sue your company out of existence," he snarled.

"Mr. Stelwyn, I understand both your anger and your grief," the Dragon responded calmly. "You have my deepest sympathies for your loss. However, before we begin, I must remind you that your son's possession of one of our unregistered KV units was not authorized, and as such is not our responsibility."

Mrs. Stelwyn raised her head, her tear-streamed face contorted with anguish. When her career began to take off, her agent had insured her eyes for a billion dollars, stating that they were the main reason for her appeal. Other celebrities had been insuring their body parts for centuries, and Haggerty had never given the matter much thought. It was just the usual celebrity hype. But Sylvia Stelwyn's eyes were indeed the most striking feature in a collection of extraordinarily striking features. And her son Tyler had inherited those eyes.

"Then whose responsibility is it?" she demanded. "It was your unit. How did our son get the damned thing, if not from you?"

"We're working on that," Consuela said.

Antonio raged. "My assistant wakes us up to tell us she thinks she just saw Tyler kill himself on television, prompting me to call that imbecile Woyzeck, who tells me to come to the morgue to identify our son's body, and then you keep me waiting here all this time to tell me *what*? You're *working on it*?"

"My client has every reason to be outraged," Primrose interjected. "As a government agency, BBI is fully accountable for its hardware. If the box was originally in the possession of BBI, some sort of security breach led to its being in the hands of an unauthorized user. And that breach of security, Director Pitcairn, *is* your responsibility."

"I'm well aware of that, Mr. Primrose," the Dragon said.

Haggerty finally stepped in.

"Please allow me to explain," he said. "We are doing our best to find out how the boxes came into the possession of these three young people, but there are impediments to our investigation. The serial number on the unit your son used was filed off, then scrubbed with acid. Whoever effaced it was very thorough. If our techs can't raise an image of the original number, it will be difficult to ascertain exactly where the unit came from."

"You mean you might not be able to find out how Tyler got that box?" Sylvia Stelwyn asked.

"I mean it's going to take time," Haggerty said gently, then addressed both parents. "I know you want answers as quickly as we can get them. Believe me, we'll do our best to provide them to you. But we have to explore several avenues to figure out which codes we're looking for. BBI is only responsible for the units in our possession. The box your son used could have belonged to any one of several million duly registered BBI clients, for whose units we are not legally responsible. The investigation might take only a few hours or it could take as much as weeks."

"Are you telling me that no one's responsible for a registered box that gets lost or sold on the black market?" Stelwyn seethed.

"No, sir, I'm not," Haggerty assured him. "Registered clients sign an agreement to notify us if a box is stolen or misplaced. The boxes themselves can be globally tracked on our systems. Possession of an unauthorized box is a felony. Incidents in which a box is either lost or stolen and goes missing for more than a few hours are rare, but they do occur. For that very reason, there are safeguards to prevent anyone but the registered owner from discharging a KV unit. Even if an unauthorized user manages to figure out a way around those safeguards, the toxin in the unit is matched to the body chemistry of the registered user. Rarely is it fatal to anyone else."

"It proved fatal enough to my son!"

"Actually, the situation is more complex," Haggerty began, keeping his voice soothing and deferential. No matter the power Stelwyn wielded outside this room, he was still a father grieving a terrible loss. Haggerty was keenly aware of the pain the man must be in, and that what he was going to say next would only make it worse. "Whoever tampered with that unit found a way around the toxin specificity issue. With the serial number obliterated, it's going to take time to track it down, but we *will* identify where it came from. And once we've done that, I give you my word that we will do everything in our power to find out who tampered with it and gave it to your son."

"And we wish you every success in that investigation," Primrose said. "But what you said doesn't change the fact that BBI can't deny its responsibility in this."

"That remains to be seen," Haggerty said. "It's one thing if the unit was taken directly from BBI, and another if it was taken from a registered client. In either event, a preliminary analysis indicates that the toxin in the unit was not our serum—"

"Your gun, but not your bullets?" Primrose sneered.

"Mr. Primrose," the Dragon cut in. "I assume your presence here means there's an insurance policy involved, but I doubt that it was against an illegal form of suicide."

Pressing a KV unit was a legal option entitling the survivors to whatever insurance benefits had been arranged, provided that the press wasn't performed until at least six months after the policy was issued. It was probable that Tyler Stelwyn had been insured from birth and the statutory limitation was not a problem. But killing yourself in any way other than with a properly registered KV unit voided most insurance claims. Unless Tyler had registered for a unit and it could be proved that someone had switched it for another without his knowledge, his actions had voided whatever policy his parents had purchased. Haggerty chose not to think about the pressing-as-public-entertainment aspect. Not until he had to.

Stelwyn probably didn't care if the policy ever paid out. No amount of money could make up for the loss of his son. He'd likely considered it an investment for his future grandchildren and never imagined he'd find himself in a position to collect. Cromwell and Sons, however, would be pleased if the boy's suicide was illegal, thus saving them from having to pay out a huge number of credits.

"Tyler wouldn't do that to himself," Stelwyn insisted. "If anything, he was coerced by that band and those other kids."

In which case, the courts might find the policy valid. It was easy to understand why Primrose was here. Haggerty braced himself for what he had to say next, knowing the devastating blow he was about to deliver.

"I've reviewed the recording, Mr. Stelwyn. I'm very sorry, but your son appears to have been a willing participant."

"Impossible!" Stelwyn bellowed.

"There's a recording?" his wife asked, her voice breaking.

"I want to see it now," Stelwyn demanded.

"I'm afraid that's not possible at this point without a legal warrant," Consuela said. "It's part of a state criminal investigation that, I might add, could become federal at any moment."

"You viewed that recording without an adjuster present," Primrose snapped.

"Don't be ridiculous," Consuela said tiredly. "An adjuster for an unregistered unit in what appears, for the present, to be an illegal suicide? You know you have no standing in such a case. In any event, I assure you we used proper procedure and had the required warrants."

She eyed Haggerty for confirmation. He nodded. Except for the keycard, he'd followed protocol every step of the way after Woyzeck gave him permission to remove the boxes before certification.

"Since no identity had been confirmed," Consuela continued, "and the device was judged to be stolen property, viewing the recording was a necessary measure to assist the police in identifying the victim."

"Forgive me if I challenge that all the way to the Supreme Court," Primrose said.

"Be my guest," Consuela retorted. "Now I must ask the Stelwyns: Do either of you have any information on the other two children? Were they friends of Tyler's? Had you seen either of them before?"

Stelwyn and his wife indicated they had no such knowledge.

"In that case, I extend my condolences, Mr. and Mrs. Stelwyn. As Mr. Haggerty promised, BBI will do everything in our power to find out how that unit got into your son's hands and bring those responsible to justice. But he and I are now required by law to attend another meeting."

"Of course," Stelwyn said bitterly. "We wouldn't want to let a probable murder interfere with the bureaucracy, would we?"

"There's no evidence of murder," the Dragon said, her ire finally roused. "Criminal conspiracy, perhaps. But while you prepare to sue us *out of existence,* as I believe you put it, let me offer a final thought. Because your son, a minor, was in the willing, illegal possession of one of our units, the courts may find *you* to be at fault here, not us."

"I'll have you dismissed, Director. That's a promise. And I'll have that recording."

"I'm just doing my job, Mr. Stelwyn," Consuela said, attempting to be conciliatory. "I'm a representative of a subsidiary of the United States government. Believe me, we'll get to the bottom of this. Again, please accept my condolences."

She turned to Haggerty. "Let's go."

Outside in the hall, Consuela was less sure of herself. "That man has tremendous power and influence," she told Haggerty. "We may very well be *held* responsible, whether we are or not."

"Scapegoated, you mean," Haggerty said. He'd been aware of the possibility as soon as Tyler Stelwyn's identity had been revealed. Pressure would certainly be brought to blame someone for what had happened, and the BBI agents responsible for the investigation would get it if they couldn't place it elsewhere. "I admired the way you handled that," he told Consuela.

"Duly noted, Mr. Haggerty," she replied. "Now tell me what was on that recording."

"Tyler was with the band for some time, probably taking narcotics," he said. "He recorded himself in some embarrassing acts. We'll want to clean that up, edit it into something for the mother to view down the road. But there's no doubt. He was a willing participant."

"There's something you probably don't know," Consuela said. "While you were out, O'Connell fielded three more copycats, all minors with black market boxes."

Haggerty thought he should be shocked; instead he felt numb.

"Here's what I want you to do," Consuela continued, her confidence restored. "Speak with your friend Woyzeck and get him to allow you access to the band members and their manager."

"They're out of our jurisdiction now," Haggerty responded. "Their testimony is part of the police investigation. You just told the parents—"

"Jason," she said, stopping him. "How long have we worked together?"

"Nearly sixty years," he said, bewildered at her first use of his given name since she welcomed him into the agency.

"In all that time, have you ever known me to break with procedure?"

Haggerty shook his head no.

"Well, then," she said, "you can judge that this matter is of singular importance. The motives behind the presses in this case are secondary to me. We need to know where those kids got their hands on those black boxes before this thing spins out of control. Or this agency's days may be numbered. Are you on board?"

How simple it would be to say no and walk away, but a lifetime of loyalty to the agency, an agency that not long ago had bent over backward on his own behalf, coupled with his deepseated desire to know the truth, wouldn't let him.

"Count me in," he told her.

"Thank you, Jason," Consuela said. "Your efforts will be well rewarded."

The promise was moot. "We'd better get ready to meet the media," he reminded her.

"I'll handle that," she said, to Haggerty's relief. "You have more important tasks to tend to."

Haggerty found Elsa sitting at her console. Now would be a good time to give her the keycard.

"You're needed in psych right away," she said, looking up from her viewscreen. "Corbin is already there. Dr. Zabrowski wanted a word with her following her report on the copycat press. There have been three more—"

"Consuela told me," Haggerty said flatly. Once again, the keycard would have to wait. "Have the lab techs got anything off those boxes yet?" he asked Elsa as they tubed down to Doug's office.

"Nothing," Elsa said. "And they're not hopeful. The damage was too complete."

The news wasn't unexpected. Rounding a corner, Haggerty saw Doug and Corbin saying their good-byes.

"I'll be speaking to you later," Corbin called to Haggerty as she hurried off, hopefully to badger O'Connell about the new copycats, leaving Haggerty to pursue without interference the interviews the Dragon wanted.

Doug perched on the edge of his desk and reached for a cigalite. "I'm glad you're on this assignment," he told Haggerty, who had seated himself in the chair opposite.

"Not sure I can add much to Corbin's report," he said.

"I don't expect you to. O'Connell and Corbin told me about the copycats. I'm damned worried."

"We all are," Haggerty said.

"Yeah, but I'm not sure it's about the same things." Doug took a drag of the cigalite. "The Dragon and everyone else are thinking in terms of lawsuits, trying to figure out how those kids got the boxes and how to minimize the damage if BBI is found culpable in any way."

"You're not worried about that?"

"I'll tell you what I'm worried about. Are you familiar with Cobain Syndrome?"

"Can't say I am," Haggerty said.

"It's named for Kurt Cobain, the lead vocalist of the late-twentieth-century musical group Nirvana. He committed suicide in nineteen-ninety-four."

"That was more than one hundred fifty years ago," Haggerty said. "What's the relevance?"

"The relevance is that a few hundred teens followed his example. It's called suicide contagion. Two girls in France left a note that they could not live without their idol and shot themselves, as he had. Four teens locked themselves in a car to die from exhaust inhalation while playing Cobain's music on the radio. Teens played his songs on their personal music devices as they threw themselves off bridges. Some even vid-recorded themselves suiciding while listening. Luckily it was contained, but those were much different times, sociologically speaking."

"How so?" Haggerty asked, growing anxious.

"Kids in high-risk groups for suicide contagion fit a certain profile. They feel isolated, depressed, outcast. They have poor family relationships and seek acceptance in fringe groups or cults. Too often, the only person they can relate to is their musical idol. They over-identify with the artist and develop non-reality-based relationships, memorizing the words to all his songs and believing he wrote the lyrics specifically for them. When the idol kills himself, they romanticize the death and see it as their chance to take control of the direction in their own lives."

"But this was not a band member who killed himself," Haggerty objected.

"It was three fans just like them," Doug said. "Kids who were living out their fantasy of being accepted by the band. The lead singer maybe knew they were going to press. Maybe he didn't. It certainly looked like he knew in the clip of the viewcast—and *approved*. That's what counts."

Doug took another drag of the cigalite.

"My fear is that the kids who pressed onstage are going to be revered as heroes among an urban population that harbors much less hope of control in their lives than children a century, even half a century ago. Our Cobain Syndrome copycats are no longer a rarity. Their profile fits the standard psycheval for three quarters of the under-age-twenty-five population. And with the band in police custody, their fans will be outraged. The displaced animosity could reach epic proportions. I'm talking more than dozens of kids. If this thing gets out of control ..."

He snubbed out his cigalite.

"This is just speculation, Doug," Haggerty said, trying to convince himself that things weren't as bad as his friend believed.

"I hope you're right." Zabrowski pinched the bridge of his nose. "But bear in mind that there have already been four copycats and the media coverage is only beginning, with more outlets than at any time in recorded history. Contagious suicides increase dramatically with reports of other suicides, especially when a particular suicide is treated prominently. If the suicide is described in detail, copycats mount exponentially—and our first three were viewcast to millions of fans worldwide."

"What can be done?" Haggerty asked, dismayed.

"I'm drafting a memo to the Surgeon General urging him to control the media. This is dangerous ground and I'm gonna need your support."

"I'll do whatever I can," Haggerty said. "Let me start by giving you some news that may help. I don't think the Dragon wants this known generally, but I'm on my way to try and interview the band members."

"See if you can get them to publicly decry the presses," Doug said urgently. "That could go a long way to heading off disaster."

"Count on me, Doug," Haggerty said, grimly determining that, one way or another, Clone Jesus would do just as his friend had asked.

Chapter Five
FALSE IDENT

Haggerty considered stopping downstairs to order a new black box—it wouldn't take long, as his requiem was on file—but the Dragon had sent word that he was to get himself to State with no further delays. And the more he thought about it, the more inappropriate registering a lost box seemed right now. How would he explain it?

A huge mass of people overflowed the quad in front of State Facility Four. From the ramp, Haggerty could detect Clone Jesus fans holding burning candles, and heard the band's music blaring from hundreds of coms set at maximum audio. A cadre of what Haggerty guessed to be angry parents milled about on one side beneath a SAVE OUR CHILDREN FROM CLONE JESUS! banner. Nearby, another group gathered under a banner proclaiming INDIVISIBLE!—The term niggled at Haggerty's mind for a moment until a connection was made. Haggerty remembered that the Indivisibles were the back-to-nature cult founded by Svoboda, the character Tanner had mentioned that morning. Nice to know the Religious Right weren't the only extremists represented in the somber crowd. Interspersed throughout were what appeared to be ordinary Conscientious Citizens who likely were neither parents, Clone Jesus fans, nor political extremists—people with the dazed look of accident victims driven from their climate-controlled compartments into the torpid streets in search of fellow witnesses of the tragedy to share their grief with.

Yet most of the country was still asleep. Haggerty recalled Doug's words uneasily. If throngs this size and variety were forming in the middle of this stifling night, what would morning bring, when another forty-one million NewVadans awoke to endless repeats of the triple press—to say nothing of the rest of the country, the rest of the world? As the review agent assigned to those presses, it was his responsibility to find answers and prevent disorder.

Elsa gained clearance and slotted into the parking structure adjacent to precinct headquarters. Since there was no direct access to the building, they were forced to find the street entrance. They made their way through the crowd to where soldiers in riot gear ringed the facility's perimeter. Haggerty displayed his BBI identiplate to a harried sergeant, who waved him and Elsa through to the lobby.

The hypersteel walls, once gleaming silver, were now gray, pitted, and scored. Police departments had been consolidated into statewide agencies in the middle of the twenty-first century, and there was little money for noncritical expenses. Although the state and federal governments both contributed funds, there were too many cities with similar claims and not enough credits to go around. Consequently, police were dependent on local taxes for their operating budgets. Credits were tightly allocated, resulting in massive layoffs and the freezing of police wages and benefits. Forensic labs had been closed and precincts consolidated. The NewVada precinct façade had gone uncleaned for decades, while carpeting inside was threadbare and the waiting rooms all had broken furniture not likely to be fixed or replaced soon.

But the city's police force boasted state-of-the-art security equipment, weapons, and surveillance, and the guard on duty was protected by a permaglass partition that could stop a rocket.

"What can I do for you?" she asked briskly as Haggerty and Elsa approached.

"Review agent Haggerty, BBI," he told her. "Here to meet Detective Woyzeck."

"He's expecting you," the guard said. She was about to buzz them through the security gate when her attention riveted on the lobby viewscreen.

"Oh, no," she said. "Not another one."

Haggerty and Elsa followed her gaze.

A boy stood on a rooftop, scattered lights from hypersteel towers glimmering behind him in the black night, a beatific smile on his face and an earset just visible beneath his shaggy brown hair. He couldn't be more than twelve years old. "But I understand," he said dreamily. "Maybe someday you will, too." He stretched his arms wide, closed his eyes, leaned backward, and tumbled off the roof to the beltway below.

"We believe this footage was somehow sent directly to Channel 115 from the victim's com," a voice droned as a smiling picture of the boy filled the screen. "Timothy was a sixth-grader at

NewVada Primary Education Facility 29. He had recently been approved for a full athletic scholarship with complete bio-enhancement, to the Mid-level Education Facility of his choice." The screen split to include a live shot of the boy's body splayed against the beltway, blood pooling around him.

"Don't know how the kid got the roof door access code," the guard said, returning her attention to Haggerty and Elsa. "Or the other jumpers, either."

"There were more?" Haggerty asked with growing dread.

"Half a dozen so far," the guard said grimly.

Doug's worst-case scenario had started. The sooner Haggerty could talk to the band, the sooner he could get them to stop what was happening.

The guard pulled herself together. "Your assistant a 'droid?"

Haggerty nodded confirmation.

"You can enter through the security archway to the left," she instructed him. "But your assistant's powerpack will raise hell with the scanners. I'll open the gate for her."

The guard depressed several buttons on her station console and Haggerty passed through the archway, peering at the elaborate sensory display that was capable of identifying and, if necessary, detaining or stunning him. The guard then drew the gate aside just enough for Elsa to squeeze through, and manually searched her for weapons before clearing her to join Haggerty and returning to the viewcast.

Detective Woyzeck met them, moving sluggishly like someone who'd downed too many bottles of KeepAwake in too short a time.

"We gotta stop meeting like this," he greeted Haggerty. "Wanna guess who I just had to fend off?"

"Antonio Stelwyn and our new buddy Primrose."

"You got it in one. What do you say the two of us retire right now and get the hell out of here?"

"Where do I turn in my identiplate?" Haggerty deadpanned. "Have you gotten a lead on the other two kids?" he asked.

"They were carrying false ident and there's nothing to tag them with yet," Woyzeck said, leading them toward one of the unoccupied interview rooms. "That's the problem with kids—no priors, and if they haven't applied for licenses or work visas, they slip through the cracks. Sure the Feds can break the Privacy Act and order a warrant for a DNA trace, but so far they've denied our requests. No idents off the boxes?"

"They were black market units, serial numbers thoroughly effaced."

Haggerty took a seat in one of the room's mismatched chairs.

"Why am I not surprised?" Woyzeck sighed, seating himself on the opposite side of the scarred wooden table.

"At least four JCs committed copycat presses after the viewcast," Haggerty said, "and I hear you've had reports of a half dozen illegal suicides. BBI's nervous it's going to get worse."

Haggerty explained contagion theory briefly to Woyzeck, then asked. "What charges are you holding the band members on?"

"Band and their manager, Shintag Lake," Woyzeck corrected. "Who's a real shithead. Has his lawyers all over us threatening illegal detainment suits. Chief gave him the main conference room upstairs and a couple of phone lines. They're currently being held on three felony-two manslaughter counts of assisting an illegal suicide and a violation of the ordinance making it illegal to conduct a suicide for entertainment purposes or to host or promote such events." He grimaced. "But the charges may not hold up, because although they seemed to condone the presses they did not assist them, and the language of the ordinance is weak and has never been tested before—as their lawyers rudely pointed out."

"What do the band members say?" Haggerty asked.

"The lead singer, Zephyr, pled the Fifth—right after he told me to fuck off. Wiseass. Then the rest of the band did the same. Except the bass player, kid named Cherub who actually seems like he gives a crap. Lake claims they knew the kids but had no prior knowledge of their intentions."

"How long can you hold them?"

"Not long with the amount of pull they have," Woyzeck said in disgust. "It's gonna be out of our hands soon, anyway. Feds are on their way. Should be here within the hour."

"I'd like to talk to the bass player and the manager," Haggerty said.

Woyzeck chuckled. "Mind telling me how I broach that to my boss?"

"What if I offered you a few more charges, like that the minors were using illegal narcotics while partying with the band. Think that'd get me in?"

"You have recorded evidence?"

Haggerty nodded.

"When could we have it?"

Instantly, Haggerty thought, scratching the back of his neck. They just needed to show Elsa to the appropriate interface. But right now, the recordings were his only leverage.

"I'll have BBI send it over the minute I complete my interviews," he said. "I realize the time to build your case is limited."

Woyzeck scrutinized Haggerty's face with the skill of an accomplished poker player, his expression giving away nothing. Whatever he was looking for, he seemed satisfied he'd found it.

"All right," he said. "I'll go talk to the chief."

"Thanks," Haggerty said. "Tell him I'm just interested in learning if they knew how the kids came into possession of the black boxes."

Once Woyzeck had left the room, Elsa turned to Haggerty.

Keep it private, Elsa, he linked. *The interview rooms are probably under full surveillance.*

Then you do realize that those recordings are still uploaded in my storage banks.

Of course, but I don't want Woyzeck to know yet.

Haggerty fingered the dead girl's keycard through his pocket. He needed to get the damned thing decontaminated, investigate its info, and make sure he gave it to Woyzeck in a way that wouldn't land him in trouble.

The conference room they were shown into was a far cry from the cubicle with mismatched chairs and ancient table they'd just left. Haggerty guessed they reserved it for interrogating celebrities and other detainees with the power to make things difficult for the chief of police. Apparently one of the critical uses for the police budget was to provide the chief with a private suite the size of the average CC living compartment. There were two men in this room. The band's bassist sipped what looked to be an imported carbonated beverage while taking in whatever the extremely agitated man standing next to him was whispering in his ear. Haggerty pegged the man as a lawyer. Despite having been called out of bed in the middle of the night to represent his client, he was immaculately dressed in an expensive, conservative suit with an equally expensive com visible in the breast pocket. The lawyer straightened as they entered the room, gave the bassist a stern glance, and turned his attention to the newcomers.

Woyzeck performed the introductions. Haggerty recognized the lawyer's firm as the proprietary counsel to the rich and celebrated. Gregory, Mendell and Finkelstein had a reputation for winning cases even when their clients' guilt was widely accepted. He wanted very much to excuse himself to pop a celtrex, but decided against it.

Woyzeck futilely raised his empty KeepAwake bottle to his lips. Finally he gave up and poured himself a mug of coffee from the carafe on the counter beside a sizable refrigerator. The counter was also equipped with an antique espresso machine and an assortment of refreshments including a bowl of real dried fruit.

Haggerty and the lawyer shook hands and took seats at the polished mahogany conference table, with Haggerty opposite the lawyer and his client.

"Mr. Haggerty," Ryerson began in his best courtroom voice, "you will please limit your questions to your company's hardware. I warn you that I will veto any question pertaining to the criminal investigation."

"Understood," Haggerty said as Elsa poured coffee into a porcelain mug and handed it to him. "My assistant will be recording, if that's acceptable."

"That's acceptable, on the condition that such recordings will be used solely by BBI and not made part of the criminal investigation. But understand that I'm only allowing this to show that my clients are willing to cooperate." He tapped the com in his pocket. "I'll make my own recording, as well."

Haggerty glanced at Woyzeck, who nodded agreement. If anything pertinent to the detective's investigation was said, he wasn't apt to forget it. Client-attorney privilege protected whatever Ryerson recorded, and Haggerty's recording wouldn't make or break this case.

"Your condition is noted," Haggerty said, sipping his coffee, and turned his attention to the bassist.

Elsa began recording.

"Let's dive right in. I assume that Cherub is your legal name. Is that correct?"

"Right, had it changed," the bassist answered.

Had Haggerty not recognized Cherub from the viewcast, the blisterbrandings he and his bandmates favored would have given him away. Cherub couldn't be more than twenty-two years old, Haggerty surmised. His hair was cropped and spiked and tinged with the popular gold and silver. Blisterbrandings were visible from the top of his tunic to the base of his neck and also adorned his palms. He seemed slightly high and, as was to be expected, somewhat nervous.

"Did you know the JCs who pressed had black boxes in their possession?"

"Yeah," he said.

"Did you know they were illegally obtained?"

"I figured."

"Do you know how the kids came into possession of them?"

"Not exactly."

"How do you think they got them?" Haggerty said.

Cherub looked to Ryerson.

"My client has stated that he does not know. Whatever he would answer is pure conjecture and speculation, and not admissible in court," the lawyer told Haggerty. "You know that."

"And we've agreed that this interview is not part of the criminal investigation," Haggerty reminded him. "But anything your client can tell me might help us clear up this matter."

Ryerson told Cherub to answer.

"I guess they got them the same way we get whatever we want—through Shintag or one of his assistants."

Ryerson winced.

Haggerty swooped in. "Did you know the kids were going to use the boxes onstage during the concert?"

"Don't answer that," Ryerson instructed his client.

But he was too late.

"I didn't know she was going to kill herself," Cherub blurted. "She was a good kid and she seemed happy."

Woyzeck smiled at Haggerty.

"That pertains to the criminal investigation, Mr. Haggerty," Ryerson said, trying to regain control. "I insist that it be removed from the recording."

He turned to Cherub.

"I must caution you not to answer questions against my advice. As your lawyer, I am experienced in how certain lines of questioning can lead to an appearance of wrongdoing *even if you've done nothing wrong.*"

He glared at Haggerty. "Pull a stunt like that again, and this interview is over right now."

Haggerty nodded. "But since your client brought up the girl, let's talk about her," he suggested. Before Ryerson could object, he said, "She had an unregistered unit, and we can't ascertain her identity."

"That was a global viewcast," Ryerson said. "Surely someone

recognized her. No one's come forward with information?"

"No one," Haggerty confirmed. "And we're not in a position to wait around for leads to drop in our laps."

If Ryerson wanted to prove his client was being cooperative and gain leverage in the criminal investigation, he'd have to cave on this point.

"All right, Mr. Haggerty," he said tightly. "Ask your questions."

"Do you know who the girl was, Cherub?"

"She called herself Teardrop," he said. "Never assumed it was her real name. I told the police that."

Haggerty recalled the blisterbrand on the girl's cheek as Woyzeck nodded.

"And Tyler Stelwyn. You knew who he was?"

"We all knew who Tyler was."

"What about the other boy?"

"Never caught his name," Cherub said. "He was a quiet one."

"You hung out in hotels with them for weeks and you never asked him his name?"

"That's the end of this line of questioning, Mr. Haggerty," Ryerson said.

Haggerty tried a different tack. "Are you a believer in the product my company dispenses and the services we provide?" he asked Cherub.

"Don't answer that," Ryerson said forcefully.

Cherub ignored him.

"I don't think the government should have any say in the matter," he told Haggerty, looking him directly in the eyes. "I believe in a person's right to die as they see fit."

"Do all your band's members feel that way?"

"I insist that we end this interview," Ryerson said.

Cherub reclined in his chair, put his boots up on the table, and took a long pull on his bottle. "Ever listened to any of Zephyr's lyrics, Mr. Haggerty? I can't speak for anyone but myself, but it's pretty much all there out in the open," he said.

"Would you be willing to publicly decry the act?" Haggerty asked. "We have grave concerns regarding copycats among your fans. Some have already pressed or found other ways to suicide. Your cooperation could prevent further tragedies."

"That's very sad," Cherub said. "But I would not decry it, if that's what they chose to do." He gave Haggerty a pitying look. "You don't grok, do you? We're no longer one nation indivisible, with liberty and justice for all. We're divided by age, by privilege.

The average age for first jobs, legal ones anyway, is rising every year. The Gen-Ohs aren't going to begin their careers until they're in their sixties. Who the hell wants to wait that long for life to start? They can't afford to live. So every day, underage citizens file petitions under the Kevorkian Act. And every day, the courts approve those petitions and the government puts Killswitches into their hands. What's the difference if someone doesn't bother with the formalities? Isn't the choice already made? Hasn't society already said it's okay to make that choice? Who the fuck am I to *decry* what's going on?"

"This interview is over," Ryerson interrupted, pulling his client to his feet.

"Wait," Cherub stopped him. "Do you happen to know when the funerals are planned?" he asked Haggerty. "I'd like to attend them, if I'm free."

"The Stelwyns haven't informed us of their arrangements. If we can't find next of kin, I don't know how long the bodies of the other two will be held before the State inters them."

"We're out of here," Ryerson stated firmly.

"Thank you, Cherub," Haggerty told the bassist. "I wish you the best of luck with your case and your career."

Woyzeck led Ryerson and Cherub from the room.

Polygraphic analysis? Haggerty linked to Elsa. The old term had stuck for a vastly more sophisticated analysis of human physiologic reactions, such as pupil dilation, than had been available with the ancient polygraph machines of past centuries.

Elsa considered her analysis. *He grew extremely agitated when you asked about the boxes. He knew they had them, and that they were going to use them onstage. However, when cross-analyzed with his admission that he had no prior knowledge of the girl's intent to die, I calculate a ninety-seven percent certainty that he was telling the truth.*

Haggerty considered, sipped his coffee. *He knew they were going to use the units, but not that they would die? That doesn't make sense. Did he think they were just making a political statement?*

Elsa reviewed the data. *His indication of the girl specifically, not the three collectively, suggests her death in particular brought emotions of remorse.*

I caught that, Haggerty sent through the link. *I'd bet they were sleeping together.*

That is my analysis, as well, Elsa agreed.

Think there's any connection to that cult, the Indivisibles?
Haggerty asked.

His response to your inquiry on right-to-die issues was markedly hostile, but he does not appear to believe in the right to die. His comments about the Kevorkian petitions and reference to the Indivisibles indicate disapproval, but perhaps also resignation. I don't believe he's a member of the Indivisibles, merely that he's acquainted with their philosophies and finds merit in them. Overall, he doesn't think that they will effect any change in society, and he is resigned to things as they are. Cross reference of full interview suggests that he was well rehearsed, knew to some degree that the incident was planned, and strongly disapproves of what actually occurred. It came as a shock to him.

"You don't grok, do you?" Cherub's challenge sounded in Haggerty's mind, echoed by the boy Timothy's words before he threw himself off the roof: "Maybe someday you'll understand." Haggerty doubted that he ever would.

Thank you, Elsa, he linked. *I'll want a full briefing on the Indivisibles later. They seem to keep popping up. Now let's see what we can get from the band's manager.*

Shintag Lake had turned the room where he was being held into the temporary nerve center of his global entertainment corporation. To Haggerty it seemed like security measures were keeping out undesirables rather than restraining the occupant. The conference table had been moved against one wall, and most of the chairs that usually surrounded it stacked to the side. The few kept in use were scattered throughout the room and the center of the floor was piled with large cushions covered in costly hand-painted silk—certainly not part of the original decor. Lake's clothes were even more expensive, with one element predominating. His vest, flared pants, and boots were all black suede. He hadn't bothered with a shirt; his smooth, hairless chest was visible under the open vest. If Haggerty had thought the leather jacket on the rich kid in the Orphanage men's room was a statement of contempt, Lake's fabric choices were beyond that: CCs who might find his wardrobe deplorable were less than dirt to him.

"If one person suggests we cancel a single tour date, I'll cancel them all. Do you understand!" Lake barked, his com's earset half buried beneath thick, braided hair.

Two female assistants, of Asian descent like Lake and clad

in red suede sheath dresses with mandarin collars and hems slit to the thigh—suede seemed to be required wear for his employees, as well—made notes on their coms as he paced the floor. The four-foot-seven mogul barely acknowledged the new arrivals, dismissing them with a hand wave. Finally he disconnected his call and turned to one of the women.

"Pasha, get me a drink. Then get someone on the line from the appellate court who can make a decision."

He muted the viewscreen.

"Just the collector," he ordered Woyzeck. "You and the android remain outside. And close the door! You're letting the air-conditioning out."

Haggerty looked at Woyzeck, who nodded that the break in procedure was all right. It bothered Haggerty that Elsa would not be present to polygraph, but he would take what he could get.

Lake motioned his assistants to leave; they hurriedly retreated to a smaller room off the main conference room, rather than into the corridor with Elsa and Woyzeck. Acknowledging Haggerty with a bob of the head, Lake waved him into a chair as he himself sank onto the pile of cushions.

"My name is Shintag Lake," he said. "No doubt you know who I am, just as I know who you are, Mr. Haggerty."

"Sorry to meet you under such harsh conditions," Haggerty said ironically.

"Don't waste my time with your attempt at amusement. Ask your questions."

"All right, then. Did you get those kids their stolen units?"

"I authorized it. Whatever the band or their select entourage requests—drugs, women, bloody farm animals if they feel like it—I see that it is obtained for them. Why they want something is of no consequence. I keep them happy because they make me money—a very considerable amount of money."

"Are you saying that you had no direct knowledge of what you were supplying, or the purpose for which it was intended?"

"Your hearing is good, at least," Lake said dryly.

"Do you know who supplied the boxes?"

"I employ over four hundred men and women to do my bidding, Mr. Haggerty. I have as little knowledge of where things come from as I do of which delivery service prepared the band's last meal."

"Can you find out?"

Pasha returned and knelt at Lake's side, offering him a snifter of brandy. Lake took the snifter and dismissed her to search for an amenable judge.

"I suppose it is possible," he said. He sipped his brandy. "But why should I?"

"The recordings off those units provide damning evidence against the members of your band."

"Clone Jesus is only one of my bands, Mr. Haggerty. In my hundred and two years I've had scores of them, and I'll have scores more before I'm through."

"But Clone Jesus is the one that will go down in history, and like it or not my findings will be part of how that history is written. I don't think you want your role in it tarnished by my proving you a willing participant in the corruption of minors through narcotics and a rash of suicides used as a promotional device."

Lake searched Haggerty's expression for any trace of bluffing.

"You think you have power over me, Mr. Haggerty. You haven't the slightest notion of what power is. If you held it for a moment, it would slip through your fingers like sand."

"Maybe," Haggerty said. "But Antonio Stelwyn does, and he will probably hold you responsible for the death of his only son. You don't want that hanging over your head."

Lake took another sip of brandy. "You have finally managed to impress me, Mr. Haggerty." He inclined his torso in a half bow.

Haggerty bowed back. "You'll contact me with the name of the provider as soon as you have it?"

"And you offer in return?"

"What do you want?"

"The recordings," Lake replied.

"Learn anything?" Woyzeck asked Haggerty as they strolled with Elsa toward the security station at the precinct entrance.

"A few lessons on the music industry," Haggerty said.

"Thought so," Woyzeck responded. "How soon can we get the evidence that convinced the chief to clear those interviews?"

Before Haggerty could answer, Woyzeck stopped abruptly. "What the fuck—that's you on the viewcast," he said.

Haggerty followed the detective's gaze to the viewscreen, where a holographic image of him turned by degrees to reveal his full face and both profiles.

"... Code Six for review agent Jason P. Haggerty, the chief suspect in the murder of BBI psychiatrist Dr. Douglas Zabrowski," the commentator intoned the unthinkable. "Agent Haggerty had access to the storage facility where the discharged units were kept, as well as direct control over the investigation. Haggerty has been certified suicidal and is believed to pose an immediate threat to himself and others... ."

The security guard sprang to attention. Woyzeck cursed fluently, unclipping his holster and gripping his sidearm.

"I don't know what's going on here, Haggerty, but—"

Haggerty yanked the chair from under the guard, dumping her onto the floor, and flung it at Woyzeck, knocking him backward. Grabbing Elsa by the shoulders, he directed her through the security arch. The relays blew and the entire system shorted, showering them with sparks. Haggerty quickly guided her by the arm out the front entrance, into the stifling night, past the first ring of riot squad, and down the steps into the milling throng. The crowd had grown larger during the time they'd been inside, which would make it easier to conceal themselves but harder to get to safety.

Woyzeck was out the door seconds behind them, stungun drawn and shouting orders to the sergeant which the sergeant relayed into his helmet mike.

Haggerty pulled Elsa along firmly. He couldn't afford to let the crowd separate them.

Jason, what are we doing? Elsa linked.

Trying to figure a way out of here. It's a setup, he told her. It could be nothing else. Doug was dead and he'd been named the chief suspect, not only in Doug's murder but in the black market sale of the stolen KV units used in the triple press. Woyzeck hadn't been wearing a stungun when Haggerty arrived at the precinct. What were the odds he'd be standing within Woyzeck's reach at the precise moment it was revealed that he was wanted? And who had sent Haggerty to State in the first place? *Well rewarded* indeed.

They kept low, weaving through the crowd, but Haggerty knew there was little chance of clearing the outer edge of the quad, which was now also ringed by riot police. He scanned the area; those budget-driven layoffs might just come back to haunt the administration, he thought grimly. The police line was thin in some places, particularly behind the group of parents shouting "Save Our Kids! Save Our Kids! SaveOurKids!" who were probably deemed less likely to go out of control than Clone Jesus's young fans. The streets behind them seemed clear of traffic. If he and Elsa could make it that far, they might be able to reach one of the nearby beltways to the Vegas District and maybe buy enough time for Haggerty to find out who was behind this. They ducked and dodged through the angry throng, who were too absorbed in their own protest to notice them.

A rifleman appeared suddenly ahead. "Halt!" he shouted. "You're under arrest!"

The CCs nearest to Haggerty pulled away, making him an easy target.

Defend! Haggerty linked, and Elsa stepped before him. The two of them determinedly moved forward.

"Stop, or I'll fire," the policeman warned, priming his stungun.

Elsa stretched her arms and weapon-proof shielding sprouted from her wrists down to her waist.

The startled policeman fired. The stun bounded off Elsa's midriff, leaving only a small tear in her tunic.

But a second policeman had got through the crowd and was raising his weapon. "Switch to detonator," he ordered.

As he was taking aim, the BBI vehicle tore to a screeching halt between Haggerty and his pursuers. The canopy door snapped open.

"Hurry, get in!" Corbin shouted from inside.

The vehicle careened out of the quad and slotted onto the minor beltway.

"I need to get myself an assistant like Elsa," Corbin quipped. "Does she have any brothers? Not that I'm likely to have a job much longer."

"That makes two of us," Haggerty said.

"Three of us," Elsa added, in an unusual attempt at levity. "Though I suppose I can be repurposed as a vending machine."

In fact, if BBI caught them and did a thorough analysis, they'd find Elsa's overlooked loyalty chip, along with all the periodic modifications and upgrades she'd performed herself. They'd simply remove the chip and reprogram Elsa, deleting unwanted abilities and appropriating what they found useful, then assign her to another agent. Elsa had to know that as well as he did.

But Elsa's fate was mild compared to the probable fates of Haggerty and Corbin. If they couldn't get evidence to clear him of the charges, he and Corbin would face exile to one of the backwaters where the technology for stem-cell therapies didn't exist. Instead of enjoying long, disease-free lives of perpetual youth, they would be vulnerable to whatever infections and plagues they encountered. Even if they survived, they would ultimately face old age and breakdown of their own flesh and bones. For Haggerty, deprivation of the geno-therapeutic celtrex would accelerate the effects of time. His real age would catch up with him in a matter of months and he'd be dead in a few years. Intent on suicide, this did not concern him much, though he'd prefer to go down with a clear record. But Corbin was young enough that she could go on for decades, albeit in an utterly alien society with none of the comforts she took for granted each day.

Haggerty had to admit that she was putting herself at incredible risk to help him. Given their history, he wondered why.

"Are you committing career suicide out of compassion?" he asked, pulling down the rotoscope screens and scanning for pursuers.

"The Dragon told me to assist you," Corbin said.

"Was that before or after Doug's murder?" Haggerty asked.

"Before it," Corbin said. "I saw that last viewcast on my way to the precinct. There were Feds all over BBI when I left. It looks to me like Consuela framed you, to save her own neck." For once she wasn't smirking.

Haggerty was surprised that Corbin agreed with his suspicions. If the Dragon thought heads would roll if she couldn't find someone to blame for the triple press, framing him made sense, however unscrupulous the logic. But she needn't have mixed Doug's murder into the bargain. Or was it Doug's death that had pushed her into framing Haggerty? If so, wouldn't that let the real killer go free? And if she didn't know the motive for Doug's murder, might not her own safety be at risk? *Did* she know the motive? Haggerty's head was spinning.

"I'm sorry about Zabrowski," Corbin said. "I know you two were friends. I'm presuming your innocence, based on how he talked about you."

"Thanks," Haggerty said. "I've known Doug almost as long as I've been at the agency. He was as good-natured as they come. I don't understand why someone would hurt him. What could anyone possibly gain by his death? He wasn't part of the investigation. Why would Consuela pin it on me rather than find the real killer—two birds with one stone?"

Unless the Dragon killed Doug. But why would she want him

dead?

"What sort of evidence has she fabricated?" he asked Corbin.

"For Zabrowski's murder? No idea. For the triple press? How about three blank boxes for starters—Which I quickly realized put me at potential risk, since I happened to have seen what was on them."

"Thank God," Haggerty said, meeting her eyes. "I was having trouble believing your assistance was simply altruistic."

"I'm really not amused when my ass is on the line, Haggerty. So do me a favor and tell me that Elsa still has copies of those reviews in her databank."

"She does—shit, here they come!"

Two armored vehicles, lights flashing, had fallen into position behind them.

"I anticipate more of them ahead," Elsa offered. "They'll use the emergency lanes coming toward us."

"Next offramp?" Haggerty asked.

"Downtown Six," she calculated. "The shoppingplex."

"Then buckle in and get ready to commit some major traffic violations," Corbin said as two more armored cars appeared up ahead.

Corbin slammed the vehicle over the yellow rails, into the emergency lane. "Chicken they used to call it in your day, right?"

"Before my time," Haggerty called, strapping in and holding his palms flat against the car roof. "But I get the idea."

"It's going to be close, agent Corbin," Elsa warned, having calculated the rate of speed of the vehicles rushing toward them against the distance required to make the offramp without collision. "You'll need to increase speed by forty miles per hour in the next several seconds"—which was impossible, as Corbin and Haggerty both knew—"if you plan for us to survive this. I'm disengaging the governor now."

Elsa slotted her fingers into the vehicle's control panel. Palms mashed against the wheel, Corbin floored the accelerator, her teeth grinding and beads of sweat streaming down her face.

Haggerty braced for impact. The oncoming armored vehicle could withstand the collision; he could see the determined look on the driver's crash-helmeted face. Haggerty had wanted to terminate, but not quite like this.

"We're not going to make it," Elsa said calmly.

"The hell we're not," Corbin responded.

She flipped an overhead switch that brought their vehicle's sirens to life, causing the oncoming driver to reflexively lighten up on his throttle. Their car broke right, into the offramp, with tremendous force; the left front side panel sheered away in a torrent of grated steel sparks. The car was damaged but continued forward under Corbin's control. She *yehawwed* in triumph like an old-time cowboy.

Haggerty checked the rotoscope. The other vehicles had narrowly escaped impact but were immobile, blocking the offramp and impeding further pursuit from the slotway.

"Everybody in one piece?" Corbin inquired.

"Thanks for asking," Haggerty said. "Slot us into the shoppingplex. We need to lose this car."

Corbin decelerated. They docked and quickly stepped onto the deserted platform that was usually swarming with customers, its beltways inactive because of the hour.

"Elsa, is it possible to block the tracking chips in our coms?"

"I can block them from passing or receiving ping transmissions, but if you use them to make outgoing calls, your location can be traced. Sorry about that."

"I just don't want them to know we've left the vehicle." Haggerty said.

He and Corbin passed Elsa their coms; a flash of infrared light passed from Elsa's left iris to each com as she held it up in turn.

"Ping transmissions blocked," she said, handing back the coms.

"Autopilot," Haggerty ordered, reaching into the car. "Fastest possible route, Nevada state line."

The vehicle departed.

Haggerty scanned the darkened storefronts with his eyes. "There," he said. "Men's and women's apparel."

He extracted his identiplate and banged hard on the thick glass door. Within moments an irate security guard, looking as though he'd been jolted from sleep, lumbered into view.

"What can I do for you?" he growled from inside.

"We've got a warrant," Haggerty said, holding up the plate. "We've reason to believe there's been a press on your premises."

"You're smooth as silk," Corbin whispered as the guard fumbled for his keycard.

Restrain him, Elsa, Haggerty linked when the door opened.

Elsa grasped the guard and held him in place, locking his arms with one hand and covering his mouth with the other.

"Don't try to speak," Haggerty warned him. "I know you must

have an alarm word. If you open your mouth, she'll break both your wrists."

Secure him, Elsa, somewhere comfortable where they'll be sure to find him. Then deactivate the surveillance.

Elsa rejoined them as they removed clothes from racks in the minimal off-hours lighting of the Casual Wear department.

"Discard your grays and find a pedestrian outfit that won't attract attention," Haggerty told her.

Corbin selected a bronze duratine shirt and a pair of jeans. "I'll be right back," she said, draping her BBI coat over her arm and moving toward the changing rooms.

Haggerty stripped off his grays, moving quickly and nearly stumbling as he pulled on a pair of retro khaki cargo pants. The cold floor soothed his bare feet. An undershirt and hooded black sweatshirt completed his transformation into what he hoped would be an inconspicuous CC.

Elsa returned in a beige sheath dress about a size larger than she normally wore that gave no hint of her perfect figure, with most of her perfect blonde hair hidden beneath a cheap print scarf. Haggerty nodded approval. He pocketed the identiplate, pillcase, and keycards from his uniform in the sweatshirt.

Use one of the minthizine bags in your storage compartments to open the inner breast pocket of my grays, he linked to Elsa. *You'll find a keycard there. It's from the dead girl, Teardrop. Extract it and run a decontamination protocol. See if you can get her address.*

Elsa slid the card into one of her hidden ports.

Corbin emerged from the changing room tugging a turquoise wig into a more comfortable fit on her head. "I found it next to the hats by the changing room," she answered Haggerty's inquiring expression.

"Good thinking," he said, grinning. "You have your identiplate?"

Corbin patted her pocket. "Not that I'll ever use it again in an official capacity," she said. "Now what?"

Haggerty looked to Elsa. She nodded.

"I have a possible address on the dead girl," he said.

"You found something the police didn't know was lost."

Haggerty bit back his anger at her assumption, since it was correct. He considered telling Corbin that the photo of Regina with Teardrop led him to think the dead girl might be one of

Regina's roommates. But in comparison to their illegal acts during the past twenty minutes, removing the keycard from a press scene seemed of little consequence.

"Yes," he acknowledged.

"Possession of stolen evidence is a felony," Corbin said.

"Add it to the list," he said. "You want out? You could still come away from this in reasonable shape."

"I doubt that," Corbin said. "Count me in. As long as we're sharing, you should know that your girlfriend's a fugitive of the State of Indiana. I took a glass from your place with her fingerprints and DNA samples all over it, had it analyzed."

"What else did you learn?" he asked tightly. Trusting Corbin was going to be very difficult.

"Her full name is Regina Dawn Sokolov, and she's wanted for questioning with regard to a fire set at a women's clinic. On top of that, she's a registered gender offender."

Haggerty was struck speechless, realizing what that implied. Regina had refused compulsory contraception, was capable of birthing unlicensed children.

"Her family were immigrants," Corbin continued. "They were denied refugee status when they fled from some war in the hinterlands of Eastern Europe. Smuggled themselves across the Canadian border."

What Corbin was telling him about Regina's background screamed true from the ideals she had professed. Still, Haggerty did not believe she was nefariously involved in the triple press. He believed with every instinct he owned that she did not, could not have faked her response to the triple press viewcast.

"All right," he told Corbin. "Let's see what we find at that address."

Chapter Six
A NEW FACE ON THINGS

Elsa led them through the underground and up onto the street, into the oppressive heat. The infocrawl on a nearby building read two o'clock. Their civilian clothing didn't cool as well as BBI grays, and sweat gathered instantly between Haggerty's shoulder blades and down his spine. Corbin wasn't doing much better; he didn't envy her the wig.

The Westside was almost as busy in the predawn hours as Vegas had been earlier that evening. Few CCs lived here. The Westside had long functioned as a kind of holding cell for immigrants awaiting Provisional Citizenship, but few of them got far along that path anymore and their population was dwindling. Sanctions had been tightening for years, until it was almost impossible to gain legal entry to the country. Even CCs who ventured beyond its borders weren't guaranteed permission to return. Increasingly, NewVada's least desirable neighborhood had become home to disaffected JCs too restless to continue living with their parents and too young to be hired for anything but part-time, low-level work. They crowded three and four to compartments meant for no more than dual occupancy, pooling meager resources to scrape by.

The Westside was also home to another, unsavory element, as Haggerty had pointed out to Regina: betting boards, shoot-up galleries, sex parlors, and individuals that preyed upon the less fortunate in quasi-legal or outright illegal ways. A group of such undesirables observed them as they passed the recessed alcove where they were sharing a bottle. The rough young men with painted faces unleashed catcalls and sexual gestures at the two beautiful CC women, giving Haggerty dark, calculating looks.

Corbin and Haggerty quickened their pace.

Elsa led them past gaily lit ten-credit stores thronged with immigrants, some of whom clearly had availed themselves of the relatively inexpensive plastiche parlors. But without geno-immunization and telemor, there was only so much plastiche could do. For Westsiders, flesh was not always flawless and unmarked by the passage of time or disease. A woman emerged from a storefront, purchases dangling from a bag carried awkwardly in her left hand, her withered right arm held close to her side. A few blocks farther, they encountered an old man, back bent, pock-marked, nearly bald, walking unsteadily toward them. The old man glanced up at Haggerty as they came abreast of each other, and Haggerty intuited that the old man must be truly as old as Haggerty himself. To be confronted by the reality of his actual age unmediated by technology was unsettling.

"Oldster got a good look at you," Corbin said, turning to watch the man shuffle away. "We should hurry, in case he sounds the alarm."

"Not that kind of neighborhood," Haggerty said.

He pointed out the broken surveillance cams. In this district, Big Brother turned a blind eye. Only marginally reassured, Corbin kept skittishly glancing around.

The buildings surrounding them were older, decrepit, and barely habitable if they weren't already abandoned or condemned. A billboard for BBI towered above the street, depicting an elderly woman—her true age, like that of the old man they'd just encountered, was apparent—happily displaying her unit above the slogan *They care enough to let me make my own decision.* Haggerty found it deeply disturbing. In this place, who needed a KV unit? The Westside immigrants were already dying of the old evils that had beset the industrialized world before the stem had been cracked, evils that continued to plague the rest of the planet. As for the JCs ... Cherub's taunt sounded in his mind: *What's the difference if someone doesn't bother with the formalities?*

"This is the building," Elsa said, stopping before a courtyard alcove strewn with stinking refuse baking in the heat.

The building's façade had fallen into such disrepair that the seams and dried adhesive were visible in the simulacrum slate designed to look like brickwork. The upper floors were dark. Corbin grimaced and plunged after Elsa through the refuse to the entrance. Haggerty followed slowly, holding his breath and peering into the shadows to make sure they weren't walking into an ambush. He felt the need for a celtrex, but it would have to wait.

They made it to the entrance without incident, then down a

narrow hallway only marginally less filthy than the alcove out-side. Both of the building's tubes were inoperable; they had to walk five flights up damaged stairways. Elsa looked at each door carefully; a third of the way down the corridor she stopped.

"That one," she said.

"Do we knock or just break and enter?" Corbin asked dryly.

"We knock," Haggerty said.

Corbin pounded on the door. "Open up!" she shouted. "Police business."

No response—and no one stirred from the other compartments. Haggerty knocked. More silence.

"Try the card, Elsa."

Elsa inserted the plasticine keycard in the locking mechanism. The bolt slid back with a snick. Haggerty gently pushed the door open and stepped into the dark, windowless pairplex.

"Lights on," Corbin called, to no effect.

Haggerty reached his hand inside of the door frame and flicked a switch, and the lights came on.

"These old buildings are still on manual," he explained to Corbin.

Immediately visible in the tiny room were bunk beds, a flowmat, a sink full of dishes, and multiple darkglow posters of Clone Jesus aiming their instruments at the viewer. Climate control was nonfunctional. A small makeshift desk housed an ancient desktop computer plugged into an electric socket. Beside it lay an old-style spiral bound notebook filled with scribbled diagrams and technical jargon Haggerty could not fathom. Then a holographic photo frame on the desk caught his attention. He lifted it for a better look—and felt like he'd taken a body blow.

The holograph showed five young people—four girls and a boy—in front of a small cottage somewhere in the desert, sunlight glinting off a power grid in the distance. There was Teardrop, her platinum hair skinpainted with streaks of black, and beside her stood Regina, looking no older than she did now, laughing at the camera. Behind them, one arm thrown casually around each girl, was the blue-haired boy who had pressed, grinning. The thin girl Regina had talked to at the Orphanage reclined on a flowmat at their feet like a vamp from a bygone film era, long red curls draping her narrow face and blisterbrands on both arms. Hovering beside Regina, dressed in a black skinsuit, her hair skinpainted purple, fuchsia, and magenta, was a girl Haggerty did not recognize.

"Looks like we're in the right place," Corbin said, inspecting the holograph over his shoulder.

Haggerty was forced to admit that Regina was involved with Teardrop and the boy. How and why had yet to be determined.

"Your girlfriend—" Corbin continued.

Elsa broke in. "Jason, I'm picking up erratic breathing."

The agents turned their attention to the bathroom door, which stood ajar. Corbin lunged forward, slamming the door open.

Collapsed on the bathroom floor was the last girl in the picture, wearing only a simple camipant underskin. Her hair was dark now. She moaned softly, her back arching and her hips twisting, her fingers clutching the bathroom rug as paroxysms gripped her body.

"Looks like she's on some kind of euphoric," Haggerty said.

"Most likely one that produces sexual stimuli," Elsa elaborated.

Corbin stared in disgust. "Is there something we can do to bring her down?"

"Check the cabinet over the sink," said Haggerty. "See if there's any SoberUp or Qwik-D-Tox."

Corbin stepped over the writhing girl to open the cabinet. None of the commercial preparations for counteracting the effects of alcohol and most recreational drugs were on hand.

"We'll just have to wait until she comes out of it," Haggerty said. "Elsa, watch the girl while agent Corbin and I look around."

Five kids in one small space produced a lot of clutter. Haggerty scrounged through unlaundered girls' clothing, papers and leaflets, empty bottles of alcohol and spent poppers, and bags of makeup. Cabinet shelves held personal care products. A box of SoberUp gave him brief hope they'd be able to get the girl back to normal quickly, but it was empty.

"We've got an illegal black box," Corbin called, extracting it from the kitchen cabinet. "The tabs are sealed but the name and serial numbers have been scraped."

She handed the unit to Haggerty. He wondered if it was his. There was no way of telling unless he activated it, and reviewing an undischarged box was a Federal offense that Elsa would not override without authorization.

"Jason, the girl is reviving," Elsa informed them from the bathroom.

"It's about time," Corbin muttered, moving straight to the girl. "What's your name?" she demanded, pulling her up by the shoulders.

"Sharyn," the girl said, staring emptily at Corbin, apparently too high to be alarmed. She giggled. "What's yours?"

"I'll ask the questions," Corbin said, roughly moving the girl to the flowmat. "You're in serious trouble, Sharyn."

"I'm already past trouble," the girl said, sobering for a moment, a look of despair replacing the drug-induced euphoria.

"Who gave you this?" Haggerty said, indicating the black box and then pocketing it.

Sharyn laughed abruptly. "It must be Traci's. She must've nicked it from someone at work."

Haggerty grabbed the holograph and indicated the thin, dramatically posed girl with copper curls and blisterbranded arms. "Is this Traci?"

"That's her all right," Sharyn said.

"And where exactly does she work?" Haggerty asked.

"It's a secret." Sharyn placed a thin finger to her lips and shook her head—then burst into hysterical laughter and doubled up on the floor, clutching her stomach.

"What are you dosing?" Corbin demanded.

She was laughing so hard they could barely make out her words.

"Happy Sticks?" Haggerty said.

"That's right," she giggled, which started another laughing fit.

Haggerty looked to Corbin, who shrugged.

"Elsa?" he inquired.

"I have nothing on it in my data banks."

Haggerty leaned over Sharyn. "Who are the other people in this holograph?"

The girl glanced at the picture again. "That's me," she said, her finger hovering over her own image. "God, I look like shit. That's Traci, Teardrop, Regina, and Sunset."

"The boy's name is Sunset?" Haggerty said. "Do you know his surname? Do you know Teardrop's?"

"Do you know they're both dead?" Corbin added coldly.

"What?" Sharyn stared at the other woman in horror.

"You heard me. They're both dead. And if you don't help us you're going to spend the rest of your life in a cell—if you're lucky. Otherwise, you'll get shipped off to exile. No more drugs. Just disease, poverty, and early old age."

The girl retreated on the flowmat, terrified, until her back hit the wall.

"Take it easy," Haggerty told Corbin.

"What was Teardrop's real name?" Corbin persisted. "Who was she with the last time you saw her?"

"I thought that was her real name," Sharyn whimpered. "It's the only one she ever used. She hasn't been home in over a week. She went with Sunset to meet people who worked with Clone Jesus. Last I heard she was making it with Cherub."

"The bass player?" Corbin demanded.

"They got the total hook-up."

"And where are Regina and Traci now?" Corbin asked.

Sharyn shook her head.

"Tell us or we're turning you over to the police!"

Tears flowed down Sharyn's cheeks. "I don't know where anybody is! Traci should be at work. She won't be home until morning. Regina went looking for her brother."

"Who's her brother?" Haggerty snapped.

"Sunset's her brother," Sharyn answered desperately. "But—"

Haggerty winced, recalling Regina's shrieks that woke him into this nightmare. She had watched her brother commit suicide and been unable to tell him. He didn't know anyone who actually had a true brother or sister—birth applications had been so tightly controlled for the past century—and couldn't imagine the bond that must exist between them. But he was familiar with grief, and he couldn't help aching for her.

"We need you to tell us where Traci works," he told Sharyn.

"I don't know," Sharyn insisted.

"Polygraph analysis indicates she's lying," Elsa said plainly.

Haggerty turned stern. "You work with her?"

Sharyn's face contorted. "I'm just a delivery girl."

"Delivery girl for whom?" Haggerty demanded.

Sharyn shook her head rapidly, alarm escalating to fear. "Are Teardrop and Sunset really dead?"

"Yes," Haggerty told her softly. "And we're trying to keep more people from dying. But to do that, we need to find Traci and whoever gave her the box."

"I'm dead if I tell you where we work," she whispered. "And if you go there then Traci's dead too."

Haggerty took her gently by the shoulders. "I promise we'll get you into protective custody and arrest everyone involved," he said. "We'll go there with a squad of police and Federal agents and get Traci out before anything bad can happen to her. Just tell me where you work and the place will be out of business come morning."

Corbin was pacing with agitation. The girl watched her with mounting anxiety.

Confident that he could get Sharyn to answer if Corbin would leave them alone, Haggerty stood and motioned Corbin to step away with him, to tell her.

Corbin shrugged him aside. "All right, that's it!" she shouted, advancing on the girl and slapping her hard across the face.

Sharyn curled herself into a ball and wailed. Haggerty moved to her side.

"Why the hell did you do that?" he snarled at Corbin.

"She's lucky I don't kick the shit out of her."

Corbin extracted the com from her hip pocket and flipped it open. She clipped her earpiece and began pressing in a call code.

"What are you doing?" Haggerty barked, his hackles rising. "They'll trace us!"

"That's what I want," Corbin said. "Let Woyzeck get it out of her. Once she tells him that Traci gave her the box we're in the clear."

Could it be that simple? Under normal circumstances, letting the police handle the investigation now was the right thing to do. But these were hardly normal circumstances. Corbin could establish that Regina had been the one to accost Haggerty. The holo established Regina's connection to the triple press. Sharyn could confirm that Traci had supplied the box and Woyzeck would find out who was really behind this. But Haggerty wondered if Sharyn truly held the answers, and he still didn't know if he could trust Corbin.

He knelt beside the sobbing girl as Corbin's call went through.

"Detective Woyzeck," Corbin said into her earset, "this is Nia Corbin. I'm with Haggerty on the Westside. We found a witness that can clear us of any criminal charges regarding those stolen units." There was a pause, then, "Yes, his assistant is with us. Yes, she has the recordings uploaded." Another, shorter pause. "Understood."

Corbin switched off and raised her autostun.

"What the hell are you doing?" Haggerty shouted, angrily getting to his feet. "She's in no condition to make a run for it."

Sharyn covered her face, her sobs graduating to keening moans.

Corbin smiled tightly. "Sorry, Haggerty," she said.

As Haggerty realized the drawn weapon wasn't for Sharyn, the room went black.

Corbin fired. The shot went wide in the dark. Sharyn screamed.

Then nothing.

The lights came on again. Elsa stood over Corbin's crumpled, unconscious form.

"I judged agent Corbin's actions to be dangerous to your well-being, and incapacitated her," Elsa told him. "Forgive me for taking so long. I should have begun polygraphing her the moment she hit the girl; however, I am only capable of testing one subject at a time."

Haggerty thanked God for the loyalty chip.

"Your actions were quite appropriate, Elsa," he said. "Take Corbin's stunner, her com, and everything in her pockets. And find something to bind her hands and feet."

He turned to Sharyn, who was pressed against the wall as if trying to burrow into the plaster.

"It's okay," he told her calmly. "You'll be safe now. I'm sorry agent Corbin hurt you. As you can see, she's no friend of ours either."

"Jason, look at this," Elsa called.

Haggerty moved to where Elsa knelt over Corbin. The junior agent's shirt was undone, exposing blisterbrandings etched into one shoulder and a blisterbrand design on the opposite hip, above the waistband of her pants.

"This is truly fucked up," he said.

He returned to Sharyn.

"Please let me go," the girl begged him.

"I plan to," Haggerty said, squeezing her arm comfortingly, "as soon as you tell me what you know. But first we have to get out of here, before the police arrive."

Sharyn quickly rummaged through her clothes, dressed, and threw some personal items into a small travel bag. Either she had sobered up or Happy Sticks left her clear-minded enough to know where her best interests lay—more likely the former, Haggerty surmised. He lifted the notebook off the desk.

"Is this Regina's?" he asked Sharyn.

"It's all her crackware and computer shit."

Haggerty took the notebook and the holograph, then hurried

Elsa and Sharyn out of the tiny pairplex shrine to Clone Jesus, past the bound and unconscious Corbin.

The Westside denizens paid little heed to the trio as they sped along the streets. They finally stopped at a dimly lit dive where they could refresh themselves briefly and talk.

"I need you to help me help your friends, Sharyn," Haggerty said, quietly but intently, once they were settled. "Please tell me where you and Traci work."

Her anguished expression told Haggerty she was truly terrified.

"Think of Traci," he implored. "Think of what they did to Teardrop and Sunset. Help me!"

"All right," she finally said. "I don't want to see anyone else die. We work for the Society of the Last Supper. It's an after-hours club run by the Triads."

The Triads were the only organized crime leagues remaining in NewVada. The understaffed police generally left them to their own devices because they ensured that no petty crimes or offenses to tourists were committed on their turf. What could be going on at this club that merited their involvement?

Haggerty asked Sharyn.

"I don't know," she said. "Traci says it's a members-only restaurant. I've never been inside. I just deliver invitations."

Haggerty looked to Elsa, who nodded that Sharyn was telling the truth.

"How do you get the invitations?" he asked.

"I pick them up from a guy, an ex-footballer, at the Orphanage."

"I've been there," Haggerty said.

Sharyn lowered her head and dug a fingernail into the pad of her thumb. "He hands me the invites," she continued, "and the list telling me where to deliver them. And my credits for working the last run. I destroy the list afterward, so there's nothing to tie me to what's going on."

And nothing to tie the club's owners to Sharyn, Haggerty thought.

"I'd need one of these invitations to get inside?" Haggerty asked. "They won't know how I got there," he reassured her, responding to her obvious alarm. "And you'll be safely on your way. I promise, Sharyn."

"I made my last run before I dosed. I don't have any left."

Elsa again confirmed she was telling the truth.

"Do you remember where you went tonight? Can you give me any names, addresses?"

Sharyn retrieved a lipstick case from her bag. She swiveled it up, unlatched a small compartment, and pried out a thin scrap of paper.

"I was gonna burn this after I dosed," she said, offering it to Haggerty.

He ran his eyes down the list.

"Thank you, Sharyn," Haggerty said. "Tell me, is Traci also a delivery girl?"

"Until a couple weeks ago. She got promoted inside. You'll have to ask her about it—if you find her."

"All right then. Where is this Society of the Last Supper club?"

"Sinatra and Main," she whispered.

Vegas District, of course. "What time do they open?"

"Three o'clock."

"You've been very helpful, Sharyn," Haggerty said. "Now let's get you out of here." He extracted several hundred credits from his wallet and handed them to the girl. "That's enough to get you out of NewVada, over the California border into Ridgecrest or Porterville." He smiled at Sharyn.

"Thank you!" she said.

Haggerty and Elsa watched Sharyn leave the dive and flag down a taxi. As the cab jetted off, Haggerty looked around to see if they were being observed. Satisfied that they were not, he turned to Elsa.

We need to remain inconspicuous, he linked, and handed her the list. *Run a search on these people. Find someone male who isn't likely to be already on his way to the club.*

Haggerty knew from his once-over that there were about twenty names on the list, each with an address and a time.

"So we're going to this Society of the Last Supper?" Elsa asked him as she processed.

Haggerty nodded. "What do you have?"

"There are five names for male individuals not scheduled to arrive at the club for at least another hour."

"Whose address is closest?"

"Edward Stevens."

"We need to know if he's at home."

Elsa returned to linking. *Jason, I must remind you that I am not authorized to access public surveillance systems.*

I know, Elsa, he linked back.

And you wish me to proceed anyway?

Like all androids, Elsa had an ethics program preventing her from breaking the law. How much of that programming was negated by Elsa's loyalty chip? She might already have overridden the hierarchy directive deterring an android from purposefully harming a human being, when she'd downed Corbin. But Haggerty had no way of knowing how far he could push her boundaries. Until he tried and failed.

He nodded.

May I request an explanation of why this is necessary, Jason?

Haggerty couldn't help feeling pleased with her hesitation, having honored and followed the law himself for a lifetime—which Elsa knew from having worked with him a good part of it. He'd forbidden Elsa ever to polygraph him, and to his knowledge she had never disobeyed that command. He instructed her to polygraph him now, just this once, then proceeded to remind her that she had been with him when Regina first accosted them on the BBI quad and he had provided the keycard that led them to the pairplex, where Corbin had turned against him after seemingly rescuing them before. *And why save us from Woyzeck only to turn us over to him again?* Unless both Corbin and the detective had reason to keep something from the Feds that Haggerty knew or had in his possession—something damning to their own careers: the triple press recordings. Hadn't Corbin confirmed that Elsa still had them uploaded before calling Woyzeck and producing the stungun? Did Elsa doubt that they were probably the only copies left? Moreover, Zabrowski had been alive when they'd left for precinct headquarters, and Consuela had told the world that Haggerty had killed him just before Corbin showed up—to save them, she claimed, but more likely to prevent them from evading Woyzeck and find out what she needed to know before taking them back into custody. And just what did Corbin's blisterbrands imply? Their only chance was to find out the truth, and they could only do it if Elsa continued to help him.

Elsa cocked her head, computing Haggerty knew not what. He waited tensely, hoping her loyalty chip could withstand the strain.

"Edward Stevens is not at home," she finally said. "But Sasha DeAngelo is."

Haggerty wasn't sure if he was relieved or chagrined that the PLC seemed to trump Elsa's ethics program, and that she had circumvented the security codes protecting sensitive data in less than five minutes.

The trip to the Northside was relatively quick. Whereas accessing the whereabouts of private citizens without a warrant was illegal, having public transportation systems alert the police when a known fugitive entered was not. Elsa stood before Haggerty at the belt entrance, pressing her thumb to the turnstile reader like any ordinary citizen. She had no prints for it to read, but was capable of transmitting information to the scanners. The turnstile opened.

As with everything else in the Westside, the belt entrance was as busy during the middle of the night as most stations were during the day. But Westsiders minded their own business. No one looked closely at anyone else, and Haggerty felt fairly certain he and Elsa went unrecognized. Still, he kept the hood of his sweatshirt forward, covering his hair and casting his features in shadow, and was relieved that the crowds thinned as they left the environs of the Westside.

Still, it would take only one person with a comlink to make the connection and notify the police. Elsa had proved she would defend him, but she had her own limits.

You weren't able to recharge tonight. How much longer will your power supply last? Haggerty linked as they belted north.

If I am not called upon to make unusual expenditures of energy, I believe I can remain at optimum function for another twenty hours.

Could you jack in to a station and recharge? Haggerty hoped against hope that she had some other extraordinary ability he didn't know about. He didn't know how long it would take them to prove his innocence. Maybe hours, maybe days. If Elsa shut down before she could upload the recordings, the reviews would be lost.

I'm sorry, Jason. My signature would be traceable.

We should have enough time before your need to recharge becomes critical. Let's hope Traci gives us the answers we need.

The difference between the Westside slum they'd started from and the enclave in which DeAngelo resided was profound. DeAngelo's compartment tower was a sleek monolith of black permaglass, its lobby clean and well-lit. There were doubtless security cameras, but this surveillance was not hooked in to law enforcement systems, though such measures were under review.

They tubed up to the ninetieth floor.

Polygraph and follow my lead, Haggerty linked, reaching for his BBI identiplate at Sasha DeAngelo's compartment. *Alert me immediately if he recognizes me or doubts my authority.*

He knocked on the door. They heard footsteps approaching slowly.

"Yes?" came a voice from the other side.

"Police business, Mr. DeAngelo," Haggerty said, flashing his identiplate at the peephole, knowing it couldn't be seen clearly. "Please open the door. We have some questions for you."

He hoped DeAngelo's guilt at his own illegal activities would work in his favor.

The bolts unlocked and the door slowly opened, revealing a gaunt, weary-looking man in a white tuxedo. Strains of classical music played somewhere behind him.

"What is this about?" Sasha DeAngelo asked nervously.

Haggerty lifted his BBI plate again, but not long enough for the man to get a clear look at it. "I'm Detective Woyzeck, Precinct Four," he said, slipping the plate back into his pocket, "working undercover with Detective Smith, here. I believe you can help us with our investigation of the Society of the Last Supper. May we come in?"

DeAngelo stepped backward into the compartment. Haggerty followed as if he'd been invited, with Elsa close on his heels. She closed the door behind them. When DeAngelo stopped, Haggerty pushed past him through the malachite simustone foyer and into the living room.

The rug on the floor was no doubt a very good replica of an eighteenth-century oriental, given how little wear it showed. The art deco mirror on the wall behind them was probably real. DeAngelo's telemonitor was larger and clearly more expensive than Haggerty's. Fortunately, it wasn't turned to viewcast, but to display, the screen showing an operatic production selected from DeAngelo's personal media library. Haggerty recognized Bellini's *Norma*. No guarantee that the man hadn't been watching a viewcast earlier, but Elsa would quickly confirm if he recognized him, and Haggerty had Corbin's autostun in his pocket. For the moment, DeAngelo was too busy trying to cover his own illicit activity, whatever it was, to be overly suspicious of the supposed undercover detectives.

"I've done nothing wrong," DeAngelo said, shifting from foot to foot. His voice lacked conviction. "I don't understand what you would want with me. I'm a Conscientious Citizen. I pay taxes."

"You were given an invitation tonight to the Society of the Last Supper. You're expected there at four. Is that not true, Mr. DeAngelo?"

"Please, you must understand," the man said. "It's a difficult decision."

"Of course it is," Haggerty said sympathetically, playing along.

"I thought I was sure," DeAngelo said. "But then I thought maybe I should cancel the reservation."

"But you didn't," Haggerty guessed.

DeAngelo looked distressed. "Please, detective, I've committed no crime."

"But you were about to, weren't you?" Haggerty baited.

The man began sobbing. He slumped against the wall for support.

"They promised me complete secrecy," he choked. "They said no police even knew this place existed. Don't I have enough to deal with?"

"Easy," Haggerty said, wondering why DeAngelo was in such a state. Happy Sticks—whatever they might be—were illegal, but the penalty for the user would be a misdemeanor fine the man obviously could afford. Most people didn't find the decision to dose at all difficult. "It's clear that you don't really want to do this, Mr. DeAngelo. If you'll cooperate, we won't pursue charges."

"You can do that?" the man said.

"If you help us now, no one will ever find out you were involved."

"What do you want from me?" DeAngelo asked, his relief palpable.

"Do you have the invitation?"

DeAngelo handed Haggerty an envelope from his breast pocket. "Take it," he said. "It's all arranged and prepaid. I don't care if it's nonrefundable. I promise not to do this again."

"A good decision, Mr. DeAngelo. Now tell me, how did you learn about the club?"

"I found it on an Indranet holochatroom. They made me prove I was serious and could pay."

"Do you know who runs it?"

"I didn't care. They guaranteed they were safe from the police and it's clear they lied."

"They're in for a surprise. We're taking them down tonight. Seeing as you've realized your mistake, I'm going to let you off with a warning. But I need this invitation for internal evidence, and your I.D. for my private file. Get yourself new I.D. tomorrow."

"Whatever you say, detective." DeAngelo gave Haggerty his card.

"Now remove that tuxedo and let me take it. I don't want you in any more trouble tonight."

"Yes, yes, of course. Please have a seat while I change."

He rushed off to remove the offending clothing.

Haggerty sat down on a superb imitation Louis XIV chair and studied the three-dimensional image of DeAngelo's face on the I.D. card. He estimated that they were close enough.

Polygraph analysis, Elsa?

He doesn't recognize you.

Good. I need a plastiche parlor that's open, one that's been cited for possible criminal conspiracy but is careful enough that the police can't prove anything. Or that's paid off the police. I don't care which.

You need a parlor that abets identity theft.

That's correct, Elsa. Preferably in the Vegas District. Someplace that won't question my desire to turn myself into another CC for an hour or two.

Elsa processed for a moment.

I've got one not far from the coordinates Sharyn provided.

DeAngelo, now in a bathrobe, returned with a garment bag.

"Thank you for overlooking my foolishness, detective," he said, thrusting the bag at Haggerty. "I'm sorry I ever got mixed up with these people. If I can be of any further assistance ..."

The man was on the verge of hysterics.

"You've been a great help, Mr. DeAngelo. I can see that this has been very stressful for you. Go to bed now and get some sleep, and consider yourself under house arrest until I contact you tomorrow. This will soon be behind you."

DeAngelo hurried to open the door for them.

"Thank you again, detective."

"Good night, Mr. DeAngelo."

Haggerty and Elsa moved quietly down the hall toward the tube.

He believed everything you said, Elsa assured him.

Good. Does DeAngelo have a car?

I'll access the Department of Motor Vehicles. Confirmed. He owns a 2156 Jetstream Corvair.

Haggerty whistled. DeAngelo's vehicle was well out of his own price range. He pressed the button marked Garage.

You mind driving, Elsa? We're short on time and I think we had better stay clear of platform scanners from here on.

The small waiting room was mirrored floor to ceiling on all sides and illuminated with harsh fluorescent light, tricks of the trade designed to fill prospective customers with as much self-revulsion as possible, to keep them from changing their minds. A small mirror-framed plaque above a bench read: "The world will change for the better when people decide they are sick and tired of being sick and tired of the way the world is, and decide to change themselves." The convoluted statement was attributed to Sidney Madwed, a twentieth-century American philosopher who probably never would have imagined it would one day be used for such a purpose as promoting plastiche.

A mirrored panel slid open. A cream-skinned brunette in an enclosed booth regarded Haggerty and Elsa with gold-flecked, half-awake eyes.

"How can I help you?" she said, stifling a yawn.

"I want some work done on my face," Haggerty said.

She looked closer. Haggerty tensed, wondering if she'd recognize him from the newscast, and if it mattered if she did. He didn't see any monitors, but that was no assurance. He'd wanted someplace that wasn't too scrupulous about legalities, but he couldn't be sure they'd found one. He moved his hand to the stunner concealed beneath his jacket.

"You've got a nice face," she said. "I'd hate to change it."

Haggerty relaxed his hand at his side. "I doubt your employer would enjoy hearing you say that," he told her. "Besides, everyone can use a change once in a while."

She shrugged. "It's your face. You want temp or perm?"

"Depends on how long it takes."

"Perm takes a few hours and I may need to do bonework, depending on the level of change. You'd be heavily sedated. Temp's a synthaderm overlay I build and burn onto you. It's much easier, just a topical painkiller. I recommend temp if recovery time's a factor. It's also easier to fix if you change your mind later."

"Temp it is then," Haggerty said.

"Good choice." She winked at him and quoted the fee. "Payment is due up front."

Haggerty extracted a roll of thin plastic notes from his pocket and passed several of the larger denominations across the counter. Giving Sharyn the means to get out of NewVada had taken almost everything he had on him, and as a fugitive his bank accounts would be flagged. He'd had Elsa short the circuits on an automated teller machine, causing it to spit out a thousand credits without debiting any account. By now Elsa's ethics program must be in shambles, although she said nothing about it and never demurred from his increasing illicit requests.

"Keep the change as a rush charge and we won't bother with a receipt," he said. He'd rounded the fee up by a hundred credits.

The technician smiled. "Your friend will have to wait here," she said.

Haggerty looked at Elsa, dismissing her grievance before she could voice it. A buzzer sounded him through the door. The technician led him to the procedure room, positioned him on a high-tech recliner, and powered it on.

"There are questions I'm required by law to ask you," she said as the chair lowered to horizontal.

Haggerty wasn't surprised. The parlor had at least to pretend to comply with statutes. The technician seated herself on a stool and brought down a lamp whose light stung Haggerty's eyes.

"Are you involved in any criminal activities that would prevent me from legally altering your appearance?"

"No." Haggerty scratched his neck.

"Have you undergone any plastiche procedures within the past year?"

"No."

She scooted back to power on a machine snaked with clear plastic tubing. Haggerty watched the tubes fill with a viscous, skin-colored fluid, followed a moment later by fluid of a different color meant to bring the mixture closer to his own skin shade. She fired on a twin set of burners and set her pallet above them.

"Are you currently using any medications, prescribed or otherwise?"

"Only celtrex."

The technician ran a hand through his hair, the corners of her lips rising. "Is the blonde your wife or your girlfriend?" she asked playfully.

"Just a friend," he said lightly, smiling back.

She tested the elasticity of the flesh beneath his eye with an instrument Haggerty could not identify.

"All right then. I assume you have something in mind?"

Haggerty fished DeAngelo's I.D. card from his cargo pants pocket.

"I want to look just like him."

The technician studied the holorep image. Whatever doubts Haggerty might have had about Elsa's choosing this place evaporated. Any legitimate parlor would demand to see a signed waiver from DeAngelo.

"Bone structure's close enough. Need to build the nose a bit, bloat your cheeks. Skin tone'll have to be darkened a few shades. I'll want to do a color wash on your hands and anything else you think will be exposed. You look much younger than this guy—and you're a lot handsomer." She flashed another smile. "Glad you're only going temp."

Haggerty grinned.

She produced a syringe from some shelf beyond Haggerty's vision and tapped it off.

"This will make you doze a bit," she explained, and plunged the needle into the side of his neck. "Just relax and enjoy the ride."

Chapter Seven
THE SOCIETY OF THE LAST SUPPER

Main Street was dark and deserted: no signs, no cars, no people in sight. The sleek Jetstream Corvair pulled up a couple of blocks before Sinatra, hoping to avoid Triad surveillance. If someone was watching, they would identify DeAngelo's car. Haggerty had taken the precaution of switching to the driver's seat at the slotway, just in case, and hoped that Triad technology did not include night vision.

We've got ten minutes before DeAngelo is scheduled to arrive, Haggerty linked to Elsa as he emptied his identiplate, com, the defaced black box, and anything else that could identify him as Jason Haggerty into a storage bin beneath his seat.

Jason, I'm worried about you going in alone.

We need evidence regarding the origin of those stolen boxes, and I'm praying it's in there. I'll be out as soon as possible. He handed the stunner to Elsa. *If anything happens, defend yourself. Then turn yourself in to the Feds and show them the recordings and the unit we confiscated at the pairplex.*

Elsa accepted the stun warily. *Please be careful, Jason.*

"I will," he said aloud. *Meanwhile, go through that notebook and see if it offers any clues to Regina's whereabouts. People. Places. Anything.*

Haggerty dosed a celtrex and handed Elsa the pillcase, then got out of the driver's side of the car in DeAngelo's tuxedo and headed toward Sinatra. They'd agreed that Elsa would linger long enough for him to get safely inside the club, and then drive down Main a few blocks in the opposite direction to a factory where she could park and wait for his return.

At Sinatra, Haggerty stopped before a battered warehouse with a smallish, peeling reproduction of DaVinci's famous mural on the deteriorating wall. He was still alone, but had no doubt that he was being observed now and was glad that the dim lighting revealed DeAngelo's face and not his own. The plastiche technician had done an excellent job; he felt confident at least about his appearance as he calmly entered the building.

He descended a staircase to a gleaming, expensive, well-maintained hypersteel door—a stark contrast to the derelict appearance of the rest of the building—and knocked.

"Please slot your invitation into the receptacle," a genderless electronic voice requested.

Haggerty inserted the plasticine card engraved with Sasha DeAngelo's name in flowing script. Scanners whizzed. A small light above the reader switched from red to green and the door slid back, revealing a huge doorman who looked more like an ape than a human.

"Welcome to the Last Supper Club, Mr. DeAngelo," he said. His manner was soothing but he projected brute strength. Haggerty thought he must be an ex-footballer, perhaps the one Sharyn had mentioned. His face seemed somehow familiar. Haggerty pitied the young man; normal people couldn't develop like that and the enhancements made to footballers came at a heavy price. With all the permutations lavished on his DNA since childhood, he wouldn't live much past fifty. Telemor treatments had yet to solve the damage to the individual's cell-replication cycle.

Haggerty stepped onto plush red carpet. "I hope I'm not late," he told the doorman.

The ape indicated a small security arch. "If you wouldn't mind passing through the scanner?"

Haggerty made it through without setting off the alarms Corbin's autostun would have triggered. His stomach growled; too much celtrex on too little food. It was just as well that his best lead had brought him to a restaurant.

"This way, sir."

The ape led him to the hostess station. The hostess was one of the most beautiful creatures Haggerty had ever seen. Lithe and dark, she looked to be of Cambodian or Thai descent, her shimmering blue-black tresses fell to the waist of her bolero-type garment and sheer trousers. She regarded Haggerty calmly with large, liquid sapphire eyes. Haggerty's suspicion was confirmed as she extended her hand and he felt the weight differential. She was too perfect to be human.

"Good evening, Mr. DeAngelo," she said, her well-tuned mezzo-soprano tinged with vibrato. "Your table will be ready soon. I'm here to answer any questions and explain the rules."

"Thank you," he said.

"The first rule is, once you enter the club you may have anything that you like."

"Anything?"

"Anything. Your courses will proceed as you wish, when you wish. If you see a performer you'd like to pair with, simply ask and it will be scheduled, as long as it does not interfere with the wishes of other guests. You'll know who they are. They'll be wearing white roses, like this one."

She pinned a white rose to his shirt front—a *real* rose.

"The second rule is that you dose as instructed."

Haggerty's interior alarms went off. "Happy Sticks?" he guessed, then cursed himself for saying anything.

"You are well informed. Most guests don't know what drug we use." If he'd aroused her suspicions, she didn't show it. "Do you also know the procedure?"

"I don't," he admitted smoothly.

Though Sharyn had seemed to come down from the drug's high relatively quickly and appeared clear-headed by the time she'd got into the cab, Haggerty preferred not to compromise his ability to reason even temporarily. But he might have no choice.

"You dose at regular intervals," the hostess continued. "It keeps you level and enhances the pleasure."

From behind her station she produced a small box and placed it in his hand. It looked like a slightly smaller KV unit, only it was white with a bright amber button and half as heavy, no doubt due to its lack of armswitch and recording apparatus. It occurred to him that the thing might be loaded with the same toxin used in the triple presses. But no doubt killing customers would have an adverse effect on return business.

As he followed her into the club, Haggerty searched for an acceptable way to protest. Surely some customers changed their minds when confronted by the reality Haggerty now faced. Then again, the club was run by the Triads. It was likely that patrons knew beforehand that drugs were involved, and still likelier that the android and the ape directly behind him—each far stronger than a normal human—were there in part to dissuade procrastination, by whatever means necessary. And even if they allowed him to leave the club, that meant the end of his investigation and probably any chance to clear his name. On the other hand, he was expected to dose more than once. Could he withstand the effects enough to keep his wits about him?

They halted at a curtained doorway. The hostess pulled aside the curtain, revealing a small alcove containing a very good replica of a nineteenth-century chaise lounge. "One press equals one dose," she said. "We find it is best if you are seated, or even reclined, for the initial press."

The hostess and the ape regarded him intently as he settled onto the chaise. She handed him the white box.

There was no turning back. Haggerty pressed.

The number "1" registered on the unit display as the button clicked down and a dozen microfibers injected the drug through the pores of his thumb, a cool, tingly sensation. A few seconds later, warmth emanated from a glowing ball in his chest and sang along his veins—not unlike celtrex but better, more intense. Celtrex dulled emotional and physical pain. This stuff banished it completely. Pleasure flooded his body, suffusing every nerve. He lay on the chaise moaning, a wide grin on his face.

Then pain clenched his vitals. He convulsed and began retching the minimal contents of his stomach into a silver basin the hostess had ready for him.

"This is natural on your first dose," she said reassuringly. "It won't happen again." She mopped his brow with a cool cloth fragrant with rose water.

"In a few minutes it will be as if this hadn't happened at all," she murmured soothingly. "You'll find your second dose even more pleasurable, with no aftereffects whatsoever."

At length, Haggerty's convulsions subsided. The basin was nowhere in sight. "I hope so," he said, exhausted.

The hostess smiled. "I assure you, Mr. DeAngelo, you won't be disappointed." She turned to the ape. "Brian, please escort our guest to the washroom and help him clean up, then see him to his table."

She turned to Haggerty. "Enjoy your stay with us, Mr. DeAngelo. I will let you know when it is time to dose again."

Once Haggerty was cleaned up, Brian showed him how to clip the white unit to his waistband to keep it within reach and led him to the dining hall. Haggerty's table, one of a half dozen forming a semicircle around a barren platform stage, was set with sterling cutlery, assorted crystal for drinks, and opulent porcelain dishes upon crisp white linen. His plush chair was made of real, elegantly carved wood, atop a floor of veined Italian marble that matched the walls of the large room, upon which were hung large mirrors in gilded baroque frames. A huge crystal chandelier floating at the center of the ceiling cast soft illumination to supplement the dim light from ornate silver candlesticks on each table.

The hostess had been right about the return of his euphoria. And the Happy Sticks had an interesting effect: Haggerty felt both languid and oddly clear-headed, mesmerized by his surroundings but aware of every absorbing detail. It was as though he were making love, his body everywhere caressed, but in no hurry to climax; the journey itself was the object. At a nearby table the lone occupant, a bearded male with a white rose in his lapel, sipped from a wineglass. The man nodded at Haggerty and raised his glass. Haggerty grinned back, the outside world forgotten.

"Your waitress will be with you soon," the ape said politely, and left.

Haggerty sat transfixed by how the candle on his table reflected rainbow colors off a crystal goblet. He felt parched. Lifting the goblet, he took a sip of the purest water imaginable.

"Good evening, Mr. DeAngelo."

The soft tektronic voice belonged to another exquisite android. She was dressed in the tightly laced corset and waspwaisted gown of the Belle Epoque. Haggerty studied her splendidly sculptured face, the high cheekbones accentuated by long jet hair piled into what once had been called a Gibson Girl style.

"I'm Polly and I'll be your waitress. You have an amazing meal ahead of you." She presented a bottle for his inspection. "It's over one hundred years old," she said, her smile promising delight to come.

Haggerty frowned reflexively.

"This is the wine you ordered, isn't it?" she asked anxiously.

Haggerty eyed the label; the French inscription was meaningless to him. He had sworn off alcohol long ago, but seeing how far he already had come tonight, he decided it was not worth refusing. He nodded that it was acceptable.

"Pity you're an android," he said as the beaming waitress uncorked the bottle with white-gloved hands and poured him a glass of ruby liquid. "I'd invite you to share a drink." He lifted the glass to his lips. The wine was smooth on the tongue and utterly delicious, the best thing he'd ever tasted. He giggled like a child.

"There's more coming," she promised. "Do you prefer black or red caviar?"

"Is it real?" he asked.

"Of course," she said. "Everything here is real."

"Then I'll have both red and black," Haggerty said, and laughed, not only at the absurdity that caviar was accessible in this day and age but that the android found no irony in her statement that everything in the club was real.

"I'll be right back," she said, and swished her hips in the tight gown back toward what Haggerty supposed was the kitchen.

The wine certainly was real, he had to admit as he sipped it guiltily. At the far side of the stage, another lone man wearing a white rose was eating what looked to be a turkey leg. A large, heavy signet ring glinted with candlelight as he lifted the leg in his hand. Turkeys had been extinct since Vertibrate Spongiform Encephalopathy—what did they call it then? *Mad Animal Disease*—laid waste to America's food supply and decimated its pet population long ago.

"That's cloniform turkey he's eating, right?" he asked Polly when she returned to the table.

"No, Mr. DeAngelo, it's not. As I told you, everything here is real. We have access to genetic materials and the technology required to clone entire animals. We actually breed the most requested varieties. Turkey is a popular item. That particular guest is having an authentic, historically accurate Thanksgiving dinner. Cows are very much in demand but we can also accommodate more exotic requests like yours."

She placed his appetizer tray before him, a small dish of black and red caviar, bread and *petit-gris* snails. He looked at them quizzically, torn by conflicting claims on his consciousness: a voracious appetite to devour every morsel set before him and the knowledge of the vast expense to clone an extinct breed for the sole purpose of his doing so—or DeAngelo's as it were, and the club's other patrons. The audacity of it, the cost of their illegal access to the genetic material alone, were obscene—and irresistible.

"Is this not what you ordered?" the waitress hazarded.

"It's just that I've never actually eaten them before," Haggerty offered lamely, his mouth salivating.

"I'll show you how," she said, bending across to gather the appropriate utensil and extracting a snail from its shell with a deft twist of the wrist.

Haggerty opened his mouth and let her place it on his tongue. He chewed it hesitantly, groaning in delight. The snails had been cooked in a buttery sauce ever so lightly infused with garlic. He marveled at the taste of real meat from a real animal with its own distinctive flavor and texture, not the bland flesh produced in nutrient tanks everyone else in the country had to settle for. Delicious could not begin to describe it. Haggerty sighed with pleasure.

Polly beamed at him. "I'll give your compliments to the chef." She fed him another snail, her delicate movements as entrancing to Haggerty as the sublime ambrosia she delivered to his lips.

He closed his eyes, ecstatic. When he opened them again he glimpsed a cloche hat rising from beneath the tablecloth of the man across the way, followed by the head of a woman then revealed to be dressed as a flapper from the Roaring Twenties, dabbing her lips in apparent enjoyment. The man seemed equally pleased as he lowered the tablecloth back over his lap and smiled at Haggerty.

Appalled and aroused, Haggerty gagged just as Polly offered him another snail. Noticing his state, Polly followed his gaze.

She put down her utensil. "If you like, I'd be happy to perform that service."

It took Haggerty a moment to recall that he avoided sex with androids on principle, even if the principle seemed questionable under the circumstances. He was here on serious business. Lives were at stake. It was hard enough to concentrate without an android's sexual ministrations further clouding his mind.

"Maybe later," he said. "I'm a little overstimulated at the moment."

"As you wish," she replied, refilling his wineglass. "The entertainment is about to begin. I'll be back with your next course after the opening act."

Haggerty reclined in his chair and turned his attention to the stage.

A large portion of the platform had descended and was gradually replaced by a rising twelve-man orchestra outfitted in white tuxedos. The dimly lit room went black, save for the candlelight on the tables, as the conductor lifted his wand. The band softly played a rhythmic, repetitive motif. A spotlight targeted the ceiling above the stage.

A skinsuit-clad girl floated downward on a swing, executing graceful gymnastic movements with supple flexibility and athletic strength. When the swing reached the stage, a young man emerged from the wings to help the girl alight and led her into a sinuous, sensual dance. Other dancers—eight of the most beautifully sculpted men and women Haggerty had ever seen—joined them from the wings, the floor, the ceiling, balancing on swings and hidden pulleys as the tempo escalated from the sensual to the erotic. Haggerty recognized a holostar whose image had appeared on magazine covers displayed at the newsstand in the BBI lobby. All the while the music increased by infinitesimal degrees in speed and volume. The performers' beautiful bodies swirled and mingled, their movements progressing seamlessly from ballet to jazz to burlesque and culminating with the full strip of clothes and every imaginable sexual activity as the orchestra reached its crescendo.

Haggerty looked over at the man at the Thanksgiving table, who absently stroked the silk-stockinged leg of the waitress seated on his lap. Beyond him at the farthest table, a dark-haired woman sporting a white rose laughed giddily as her handsome male waiter poured wine for her. She might be thirty or a hundred thirty and was clearly enjoying the show. Haggerty was fully aroused when the music climaxed and the stage went dark.

"You can have any of the performers you like," Polly murmured into his ear.

Her words, combined with her sudden materialization at his side, had a visceral impact, intensifying his arousal to the point of pain. Haggerty closed his eyes.

"Watching was enough," he said through gritted teeth.

Polly smiled knowingly. "Saving yourself for your guest?"

He noticed with alarm the second setting at the table. Who the hell had DeAngelo invited? Would this *guest* blow Haggerty's cover? His Happy Sticks glow faded. Haggerty found himself extremely annoyed.

"In that case, please come with me," Polly said. "The club's owner would like you to make a decision regarding your meal."

Haggerty followed her. The floor was like air beneath his feet.

"She's famous, isn't she?" he asked Polly, indicating the holostar entangled with the bearded man and two of the other performers.

"Yes, she is," Polly told him. "We provide nothing but the best for our guests." She led him down a dim, marble-lined corridor.

"Is Traci working tonight?" he asked recklessly.

"She's in the next number," Polly said evenly. "Do you know

her?"

"We have mutual friends."

"I see. Will you require her services?"

"I'd like to meet with her as soon as possible," Haggerty said eagerly.

"I'll inform scheduling."

The marble surface terminated at a smooth, transparent aquarium in which large, dim shapes moved through the confined water. The waitress halted, indicating that Haggerty should observe the contents. She ordered lights on; it took a moment for Haggerty's eyes to adjust to the sudden illumination that filled the tank.

"Dolphins," he said in awe.

"Your main course was difficult," Polly said. "It took months, so they made more than one."

Whoever was behind this place had performed a miracle. Dolphins had been one of the first species to exhibit VSE and become extinct. He had never hoped to see one alive, and here there were two of them. A dorsal bumped hard against the glass.

"That's the male," the android said. "I'd never heard of them before I came here. I watch them sometimes. They seem really smart."

Haggerty recalled from textbooks that they were indeed highly intelligent, some claimed more so than humans. He watched them circle the tank just large enough to hold them, bobbing helplessly. His waning euphoria evaporated completely as he realized with horror that he was looking at his dinner. What a sick individual DeAngelo must be to have made such a request. Why on earth would he do it? Tears streamed down Haggerty's face.

"Which one will it be?" Polly requested brightly, mistaking his emotion for joy.

Haggerty knew he must sacrifice one of these splendid creatures in order to save countless humans. But he could not bring himself to choose.

"I trust you are enjoying your experience thus far, Mr. DeAngelo," came the hostess's soft mezzo-soprano like a dream. She stood beside him, beautiful and dispassionate, his white unit extended in her hand. "It's time for your second dose."

He hadn't even noticed that she'd unclipped it from his waistband. The counter turned over to "2" as he pressed. And then the hostess was gone, along with her unsettling gaze, and somehow the unit was back at his waist.

"Your choice, Mr. DeAngelo?" Polly asked again, her soft voice soothing, caressing.

Haggerty turned to the tank. How beautiful they were. A moment ago he'd been horrified. But the horror was muted now by pleasure. The female was near the bottom, barely moving. The male bobbed above her. It seemed to Haggerty the dolphin took note of him, making the decision for him.

"The male," he said, the regret in his voice so dim that Polly did not hear it. "I'll have the male."

DeAngelo's guest was seated at the table when Polly led him back, his mind hazy with pleasure. The dark-haired Asian girl smiled as he approached. Her right arm was missing and the right side of her face was a mass of red, blistered scar tissue. Her deformities would have been unsettling even in a culture familiar with disease and illness. To someone used to the bland perfection of plastiche-smoothed good looks and geno-immunized healthy bodies, seeing a human being so physically ruined was a nauseating experience—or would have been were Haggerty not in the grip of drug-induced euphoria. Instead he was fascinated. What would it feel like to touch that cruelly disfigured skin? Did her wounds retain the heat of the fire that had scarred her? Would those crimson ridges of hardened tissue burn his fingers?

Polly introduced the girl as Suniko. He offered her his hand.

"Welcome, my dear," he said.

"It is a great honor to meet you, Mr. DeAngelo," the girl said timidly.

Haggerty resumed his seat, relieved to discover that she did not know DeAngelo. "Would you like a glass of wine?" he asked her.

"Thank you," she replied.

Haggerty studied her as she watched Polly fill her glass. Suniko's damaged skin extended from the base of her neck downward, past the intricate straps of her gown. From the shape of her, it seemed likely her right breast had been removed.

"Most people turn their gaze away from me," she said softly as his eyes returned to her face.

"I am not most people," he said.

"No, you are a great and powerful man," she said. "I could not believe it when they invited me to join you."

"May I ask what happened to you?"

"I was caught in a chemical fire at the care center where my parents worked," she told him. "I was twelve. They lost their jobs and could not afford to have my arm replaced."

The longer she spoke, the lovelier she seemed to Haggerty. He realized she must have been striking once.

"That's why I'm so thankful. I hope that you will find me pleasing. I have never paired with a man. But after tonight, I may have a chance for a new arm."

Then Haggerty understood: DeAngelo had requested a deformed virgin to have sex with, a notion that, even drugged, Haggerty found appalling. What drove a man to be sexually aroused by a stranger with a deformity? The fact that Suniko's sacrificing herself to DeAngelo might earn her the chance for reconstruction only muddied his feelings further.

"I'm glad I could help," he said, placing his hand on hers.

A waiter in a kilt making the rounds stopped at the table with a cart holding canisters of every illicit drug Haggerty could think of except celtrex. Polly asked Suniko if she wanted to dose. Haggerty suggested SkyWhip, and was happy when she agreed; it would be best if she were drugged as well. Polly brought the inhaler to her mouth and popped for her. Suniko slumped in her chair, eyes glazed.

"One for you, Mr. DeAngelo?" Polly asked.

"No, thanks," Haggerty replied. "Is Traci available yet?"

"She's having cocktails with another guest in one of the private suites before she goes onstage. You and your guest are not scheduled for a suite until after your main course."

"Can I reschedule?" he asked.

"I'll go and see what can be arranged."

A short time later, a young man strode to the table. With shock, Haggerty recognized the boy with the silk handkerchiefs from the Orphanage.

"Greetings, Mr. DeAngelo," he said, offering his hand. "I'm Max. May I join you?" Without waiting for a response, he pulled a chair from another table and sat down. "I trust you're enjoying my club." His eyes pierced Haggerty.

The boy's looks were extraordinary; he could easily have been a holostar. Haggerty was taken aback that someone so young could be the owner of this establishment. Maybe Max was another Tanner, only better at pulling off the illusion of youth—or with access to better plastiche. Haggerty had the unsettling feeling it wasn't so.

"Everything's wonderful," he said.

"I pride myself on delivering whatever my guests request," Max said, flicking his gaze at Suniko but otherwise ignoring her.

"Worth every credit," Haggerty said, regarding the slumped girl, who refused to look at Max. "I congratulate you on the drug. It's quite an accomplishment."

"I'm pleased you like it." Max's smile seemed genuine. "I created it."

"I'm impressed," Haggerty said.

Max accepted the compliment as if it were his due. "I understand you'd like to change your scheduling, Mr. DeAngelo."

"If possible," Haggerty answered.

"I can make anything possible," Max stated matter-of-factly. "I must admit, I thought you'd be in worse shape, given your condition. I'm impressed by your doctors. You're one-forty-three, if I remember correctly?"

"I've been kicking around a long time," Haggerty parried, sensing a trap. The drug kept him from panicking, but had not yet eradicated his ability to think. Best to say as little as possible.

"And a sports fan?"

Haggerty nodded noncommittally.

"I like football myself," Max offered. "Funny you chose tonight to dine with us, what with the big game tomorrow."

Was he being tested? Haggerty felt he had to respond. It was probably unwise to say football was not his sport of choice. "I assume you have a telemonitor with full access, should I find myself still in your company come game time?"

Max sat forward, his chair legs grating on the marble floor. "I pride myself on being able to meet the needs of any and all of my guests," he said smoothly. Haggerty relaxed, sensing that the test was over. Brian hadn't been called to forcibly eject him from the premises—or do whatever it was they did to gate crashers in this place—so he must have passed. "If you are still with us when the game is viewcast," Max continued, "I promise you an unforgettable experience. I myself will be at the game in style."

He signaled the orchestra.

"The floor show is about to begin again," Max told Haggerty. "Have a nice rendezvous in your suite. I'm sure Suniko will see that you enjoy yourself."

He gave the girl a meaningful glance. Suniko nodded, her eyes contracting slightly. Haggerty felt like he'd been slapped.

"I'll leave you now. Perhaps I'll join you for dessert. Be sure to dose again before you dine, Mr. DeAngelo."

A line of young women entered from stage left, a line of young men from stage right. The boys wore 1930s finery complete with spats, top hats, and swallow-tailed coats; the girls were dressed in beaded satin gowns of the same era cut on the bias, their hair in period chignons. At center stage the lines reassembled into couples who waltzed in a circle and swept back into the wings—revealing Traci and her partner posed in a passionate embrace.

Traci was thinner than she'd been in the holophoto, too thin to be truly attractive. At first Haggerty wondered why the Last Supper Club, which prided itself on only serving the best, had hired her. Then she and her partner began dancing.

Traci wrapped herself around her partner with fluid grace. The young man supported her with skill, but it was Traci who turned a simple ballroom dance into an expression of intimate desire. Her beautifully executed arabesques, the quality of her leg extensions and pirouettes bespoke rigorous training she wouldn't be able to use for decades, if ever. Centuries ago, a ballerina's career was over by the time she reached forty, when her body could no longer sustain the demands of her art. But that was no longer the case. A prima ballerina could dance until she was past the century mark, her skill undiminished and her appearance still youthful. By the time today's dance stars retired, decades hence, those who'd spent their lives denied opportunities while the *grandes dames* hogged the spotlight would be passed over in favor of younger talent. So it was not surprising that Traci poured all her energy and ability into this titillating dance in an illegal club with an adequate but uninspiring partner. It was as close as she was ever likely to come to a starring role.

Her partner released the closures of her gown and she spun away from him, left in a glittering skinsuit. The gown discarded, he pulled her back into his arms. Haggerty leaned forward, eager to see if Traci could sustain the atmosphere of sensuous grace when the *pas de deux* turned blatantly erotic.

Then Polly returned. "Your private suite is ready for you now, Mr. DeAngelo," she said.

Haggerty could hardly tear his gaze from the stage. He nodded to Polly, reminding himself that lives were at stake, and rose from the table, taking Suniko's single hand to help her stand. They followed Polly along an endless corridor, past ornate doors affixed with colorful carved representations of jungle palms, an antique Japanese pagoda, the Mad Hatter from *Alice in Wonderland*. Haggerty was amazed at the vastness of the restaurant grounds. Finally they stopped before a door with a carving of two whips crossed in an X, which Polly opened.

The hard stone floor inside was strewn with archaic torture devices: a bed of nails, a stock with spaces for a victim's head and wrists, and instruments Haggerty did not recognize but had no doubt DeAngelo would. One wall held whips and chains and other objects whose purpose he couldn't guess and didn't want to. Suniko stood nervously observing a small metal cage.

Polly indicated a rope pull hanging inside the door. "Ring the bell and I'll come and collect you," she told Haggerty, and turned to leave.

"What about Traci?" he asked.

"She said she didn't recognize your name."

The clock was ticking down to morning and Haggerty needed to get out of there before dosing again. He'd only dosed twice and sensed that the drug was impairing his judgment. But he couldn't leave without first speaking to Traci.

"I was told I could have anything or any*one* I wanted," he shouted.

"All right," Polly said.

Haggerty could not tell if she was acquiescing to the club's policy or merely trying to make him quiet. He scratched the back of his neck.

"If you must know, I'm an associate of Shintag Lake's. Tell Traci I have a message regarding a common friend of theirs."

Polly nodded.

"And before you go, give me another canister or two of Sky."

Polly smiled. She handed him three additional canisters and left, closing the door behind her.

Haggerty turned his attention to Suniko. The poor girl was shaking.

"There's not even a bed," she said, her normally timid voice reduced to a near inaudible whisper. She gestured to the cage. "Do you want me to get in?"

"Don't worry, Suniko," Haggerty said gently. "I'm not going to use any of these things on you. Here, this will calm you down."

He held a Sky canister to her quivering mouth and dispensed

the contents. Within moments she was barely conscious. Haggerty guided her into a chair equipped with iron leg and wrist straps. He tucked the other canisters of Sky into his cummerbund for easy access, next to the white box—he didn't want Suniko to overhear the conversation once Traci arrived.

Ten nerve-wracking minutes later the door opened and there was Traci, all ninety pounds of her. She'd taken her hair down; her long red curls seemed to bounce at her shoulders. She was dressed in a gown from a later era than the one she'd worn onstage. A bodice of boned green satin molded her breasts and cinched her waist; a skirt of a lighter green chiffon billowed from the waistline, supported beneath by stiff crinolines reminiscent of a costume from a classical ballet; he wondered if it was coincidence. If not, the choice was unfortunate in Traci's current state. The color might have been good on her once, but her complexion was pallid now and the green made her look sickly. While the 1950s gown appeared to have been altered to fit her body, this clearly had been done when her figure was fuller. The scrap of green chiffon draped over her arms like a shawl couldn't disguise how thin they'd become or camouflage her prominent collarbone. The vintage dress didn't hang off her frame, but it was loose enough to suggest what it should have looked like when properly filled out.

She leaned back against the door to close it, one hand on her thin waist while the other toyed with the pendant at her breast.

"You told Polly you're a friend of Lake's?"

"We've met. But the message isn't from him."

"Whatever." Traci glanced at the limp form of the girl in the chair, examining Suniko's deformity and wrinkling her nose. "Are you planning a threeway? Because I have to say—she makes me uncomfortable. I mean, I will if you want ..."

"I'm not here for that," he said.

She stepped closer; Haggerty could smell she was recently perfumed. She fingered the rose on his shirt, looked down at his waist, and noted the white unit. She ran her tongue across her lips. "All right, I'll play along." She stepped away and walked around the room, staring at the cage and the bed of nails. "So what's this message you have that isn't from Shintag Lake?"

"I'm friends with Regina and Sharyn. I'm trying to find out the truth behind what happened to Teardrop and Sunset."

Traci stared at him, her face a storm of suppressed emotion.

"You're on H, right?"

"Happy Sticks?"

She nodded.

"Yes."

"Wish I was," she said dreamily, rubbing her right thumb against her pendant. "Isn't it fabulous? I don't suppose you'd be willing to let me have a press?"

"Sharyn told me you dosed," he said.

"Whatever. She's a bagbite."

Traci went to examine the wall of ancient instruments. Haggerty came up behind her.

"She also told me you brought home an unregistered black button unit. That's a Federal offense."

She stiffened. "I don't have any idea what you're talking about. I'm outta here."

Haggerty grabbed her roughly as she made to leave. "You're not going anywhere until you tell me how you got that stolen box," he said. "I've been blamed for giving Teardrop and Sunset those units."

"Bites to be you then," she snarled, struggling to pull away.

"I'll have you locked up for a long time," he said.

She shrugged off his grip, then rubbed her arm where he'd held it. "Like that scares me," she said. "I'm under the protection of—"

"Max and the Triads," he finished for her. "They'll be happy to know you're stealing from them. Employees aren't allowed to dose on Happy Sticks. It gets in the way of their doing their jobs."

Traci threw back her head and laughed hysterically. "Max won't be happy with me if he finds out I'm dosing, but I think he'll be even less happy if I answer your questions."

"He's not your main concern now, I am. And he'll be safely tucked away in a cell soon as well."

"I doubt it. He has the police in his pocket."

"But not the Feds. And they're involved now. So you'll tell me what I want to know if you plan to come out of this without a jail stretch—or worse, an order for deportation and exile. Did Max supply those black boxes?"

"I'm not telling you anything," she said tightly, crossing her thin arms over her breasts.

"He already admitted to me he invented Happy Sticks," Haggerty said. "That's enough to indict him. You can't protect him now and he sure as hell won't be in a position to protect you later."

"He only told you because he knows you won't have a chance to tell anyone else."

"I plan to as soon as I leave here," Haggerty said.

Again that unsettling, hysterical laugh. "The only way you're leaving here is in a bag. Haven't you worked it out yet?" She flicked her gaze at the unit on his belt. "You're already dying."

"What?"

"It's not *sticks*, like twigs," Traci said. "It's Styx like the river of death in the Underworld. Once you're dosing, you're dying. H is the most addictive drug ever invented. When the fix starts to wear off, you'll do anything to get it back, including die—which is exactly what happens, because your seventh dose kills. You're here to die, man, going out in style after one helluva last meal."

Shock pumped adrenaline through Haggerty's system, flushing the drugs and leaving him cold sober. He recalled DeAngelo's indecision about coming, his complaint that he was already in enough pain, Max's reference to the man's doctors and his condition. This wasn't simply an exclusive club offering customers exotic, illegal dishes and drugs. The Society of the Last Supper was an illegal suicide parlor, a snuff house.

Had NewVada's elite grown so jaded that even in death they had to satisfy hidden desires, no matter how heinous? And how could the disappearance of such wealthy CCs go unnoticed by local law enforcement? Traci must be right. Police were on the take. Woyzeck might be one of them. Given the extravagance and expense of the operation, the club's profit margin must be astronomical. No wonder Max had placed himself under the Triads' protection. And of course they would take their cut.

How was all this connected to the triple press? Max couldn't possibly want publicity. His success depended on keeping the club secret.

"Is the seventh dose a different drug, a higher concentrate?" he demanded.

"It's the same. It builds up in your system."

"And the seventh dose always kills."

"It does if it comes within a week of your first dose. If you wait long enough between presses, it can't build up enough in your system to be lethal. But it's incredibly hard to go a week without seven. The craving is like nothing I've ever felt before." She laughed hollowly. "I thought I could beat it. A couple of SoberUps and I wouldn't have to worry. But I was wrong. The detox pills get enough of the shit out of my system that I can survive seven doses but it's harder and harder to keep track of how often I've pressed. Or to care ..." She shuddered.

"How long have you been on it?

"Two months ... I think. How many times have you dosed so far?"

"Two," he told her.

"I'd stick at six as long as you can," she said. Her eyes wandered back to the unit; she wet her lips again. "I'm planning to hang at five this week, myself."

"Listen, Traci," Haggerty pleaded, "I need your help. It's not just my neck on the line. Don't you care that your friends are dead because of those boxes?"

"Of course I care, I loved Teardrop," she said.

"Then help me stop the people who hurt her from hurting anyone else."

"Why do *you* care?" Traci demanded. "What's it to *you* if the box is from the street instead of a government issue killswitch? We're all dying."

"But you don't have to be," Haggerty said. "You have a choice."

"Like Teardrop did?" Traci asked bitterly.

"Your choice doesn't have to be hers."

Traci broke down, weeping. "Why did she do it? She never took drugs the way I did," she choked out. "She was studying art, planned on exhibiting soon as she was old enough to license a show."

Haggerty took her in his arms. "I don't know why she pressed," he said honestly. "But I'm a button collector. That's why I care about what's happening here. I want to find out why Teardrop did it. How she did it."

That seemed to get through to her. Traci lifted her head from his shoulder and stared at him. "A button collector?"

"Yes. And part of what I do is to make sure that no one gets tricked or coerced into pressing. If that's what happened to Teardrop, it's my job to stop it from happening to anyone else."

"Okay," she sniffled after a moment. "What do you want to know?"

"Have you ever seen Max with Lake, or with Clone Jesus?"

"Zephyr was here with Max during the day once, scoping the place. He invited me to a party."

So the lead singer had been there. What did that mean? Too many questions, not enough information.

"The band got involved with Max and you got your friends involved with the band, and then they killed themselves while Zephyr stood by and watched," he said. "But why? Now there are kids out there killing themselves."

"Like Teardrop," Traci whispered.

"Like Teardrop," Haggerty agreed. "We need to stop it," he said. "And we might be able to if you'll testify that Max provided those units."

Traci's fear of Max was stronger than any guilt she might feel over her friend's death. She backed toward the door, shaking her head in denial. "He'd kill me. And not with Happy Styx."

"He can't hurt you if I get you out of here."

"There's no getting out of here for you," she cried. "No guests leave here alive. You leave in trash bins, for God's sake."

"There must be some way," he said, maneuvering her against the door. "You must know this place inside out."

"There's no place safe out there. They'll take me into a room like this, only the instruments won't be toys." She shuddered. "The people he works with—"

"I can guarantee your safety," he said desperately, hoping he wasn't lying. "I have powerful people on my side too. You know that Tyler Stelwyn died with Teardrop. His father's the most powerful man in NewVada."

"I don't know how to get you out!" she cried, scraping her thumb raw with her middle finger.

"Think, Traci. There has to be a way for us to leave. You'll be safe, protected, your system cleaned out!"

She shook her head desperately, biting down on her thumb like a child, her face wet with tears, too selfish and scared to help him escape. What was one oldster's life to her? She would doom hundreds, perhaps thousands of kids to save herself. But if Traci embodied the hopelessness and lack of responsibility ascribed to her generation, Haggerty had to admit he embodied the despair and disenchantment of his own. And if she didn't care, then why should he? He could dispatch himself tonight, right now, just by pressing the white unit multiple times. He'd planned to kill himself anyway and now he could do it ecstatically. He looked at the unit at his waist. Traci followed his gaze.

"Maybe you're right," he said tiredly, reaching for the unit. "We're all dying, and we might as well enjoy the ride. Maybe that's all Teardrop was doing."

Traci's head snapped up at the mention of her friend, but

before she could speak, someone knocked on the door. "It is time for your next dose, Mr. DeAngelo," came the voice of the hostess.

"Just a second," Traci called.

She ripped Haggerty's white box from his belt and pressed, gasping as the drug hit her system. She pointed to Suniko, who thankfully remained in a stupor.

"Quick! Bind her in the chair," she hissed, forcing herself under control.

Haggerty snapped on one wristlet and both ankle straps. Was Traci's press a noble act or merely the desperation for a fix? It didn't matter. He'd make sure something good came of it. Her choice had renewed his own determination to see this through to the end.

Traci shoved the unit back into his hands and stripped off her gown and frothy crinolines. Her thin nude frame was silhouetted in the doorway as she opened the door to the hostess.

"He already dosed," Traci said. "I watched him."

"Show me your unit please, Mr. DeAngelo," the hostess requested.

Haggerty held up the unit so she could see the number "3" on the readout, giving the hostess a dazed smile and swaying slightly on his feet, trying to mimic the effects of the drug just as Traci tried to mimic sobriety despite the fine trembling of her limbs.

But the hostess's attention was fixed on him. The android nodded as he reclipped the unit to his waist. She observed the girl in the chair and the nude performer. "Sorry to disturb you, sir."

Traci closed the door as she departed and fell back against it, her eyes glazed, her chest heaving in bursts.

"Down ... through the orchestra pit ... cremation room ... a vent ... into the sewers ... go to your table first ... pretend ..."

"How fast can you meet me?"

She shook her head, spasmed. "I think ... I miscounted."

Haggerty welled with pain and shame. He took her in his arms. She shuddered.

"You're ... gonna stop ... them ... right?" she gasped. "For Teardrop?"

"For Teardrop, and for you," he whispered. "I promise."

"Who'da thought ... anything I'd ever do ... would make ... a difference ..." She began to convulse; the spasms lasted several minutes. Traci's face was transfigured by joy. "It feels so... good," she moaned. The breath went out of her.

Haggerty sobbed. "Thank you," he said, lowering Traci's body gently to the floor.

It took him several moments to compose himself. He looked at Suniko unconscious in the chair and prayed that the Triads would honor whatever promises Max had made her, then slipped out of the room and moved quickly down the corridor.

Haggerty peered from behind one of the curtains at the left wing of the stage. The orchestra pit was shut. How was he going to get down there? Footsteps approached; his heart pounded in his chest. Any of the android servers could overpower him and Brian could crush him with one blow.

Someone was on the other side of the curtain, mere inches from him. He saw a long fall of sable hair. He reached out and grabbed her, locking his arm around her throat and dragging her behind the curtain. The holostar from the first floor show choked as she struggled to break his hold.

"You're hurting—"

"Quiet or I'll crack you neck!" he hissed. "Tell me how to open the orchestra pit."

"There's a lever ... on the other side of the stage."

The only route was directly across the stage, in full view of the dining hall.

"Follow my lead or I'll kill you," he whispered.

He spun her to face him and put his mouth against hers, forcing her body to his, and backed her onto the stage; with luck they'd think the holostar was fulfilling a guest's request. She used her dramatic training well to counterfeit passion, wantonly gyrating and running her hands through his hair, their mouths fused tightly as they progressed to the right wing and out of view.

"Where's the lever?" he demanded, spinning her back into a chokehold.

"There," she gasped, indicating a handle attached to a system of pulleys.

The guests would probably believe the next floor show was starting once he pulled it but management would realize something was wrong. He needed to know who was out there. He risked a peek through the curtains. The man with the beard was not at his table; the remaining tables were occupied by diners wearing white roses. Haggerty scanned farther back. Bile rose to his throat as he saw Corbin enter the hall with Max.

It made sense. A BBI agent with access to the mausoleum and an endless supply of discharged units tied to an illegal nightclub run by the Triads. Corbin had fought to get charge of the triple press review. If she'd succeeded, she would have judged the presses clean despite the use of black market boxes. The recordings somehow proved her culpable; hence the need to secure and erase them. Corbin had caught things Haggerty missed, things that would blow the lid off whatever was going on between herself, Max, Clone Jesus, and God knew who else— Woyzeck or whomever had been on the other end of her com call and freed her. Was Consuela involved? Haggerty was on the verge of fitting it all together.

If his death warrant weren't sealed before, surely it was sealed now. Max had figured out he wasn't the real DeAngelo and left it alone because he expected the impostor would end up in the crematorium anyway, along with all the other guests. Corbin's presence meant Max now knew that Sharyn had revealed the existence of the Last Supper Club and it was Haggerty pretending to be DeAngelo. Max had to find Haggerty and eliminate him quickly.

The holostar seized on Haggerty's distraction a moment too late, not quite getting the air into her lungs to scream for help before Haggerty covered her mouth with his palm.

"Don't try my patience," he growled. He pulled the second canister of Sky from his cummerbund and held it up before her. "Open your mouth," he said.

She tried to struggle. He yanked her arm behind her back and double-dosed her as her mouth spread in agony. She went slack in his arms.

He set her down behind the curtains and looked out again. Brian was with Max and Corbin, nodding incessantly; his mammoth figure dwarfed them.

Haggerty was wasting precious time. Any moment he could be discovered. He pulled the lever.

He gauged the orchestra platform's slow descent, observing the counterbalance of the pulley system. When the pit was open halfway, he jerked the lever back to reverse the process. The gears groaned loudly. Haggerty dove for the opening, praying he'd make it in time.

"That's him!" Max shouted.

Brian charged forward like an enraged bull; the dark-haired

woman shrieked as he overturned her table in his rush to the stage. The other guests looked about with mounting confusion.

Haggerty hit the rising platform and rolled towards the edge and under, barely clearing the gap, then hung from the edge by both hands preparing to release. The ape gripped one of his hands. Instinctively Haggerty pulled the other hand away from Brian's reach and twisted his body hard. The lip of the closing platform scraped painfully against the back of his trapped hand. Haggerty wrenched himself free as the platform reknit with the stage, dropping several feet as Brian bellowed above him, his fury or pain muffled by Haggerty's abrupt landing. Something wet dripped onto the shoulder of his tux; Haggerty saw three enormous bloody fingers on the floor. Sounds of screaming, stomping feet, and Max's shouting penetrated the stage above him. He guessed he had under a minute to find what he needed.

He hurried from room to room, past a man in a sooty apron who shouted, "Hey, no guests down here!" Haggerty grabbed him in a chokehold and slammed him against a wall.

"Tell me where the incinerator is or I'll crush your fucking throat!"

The terrified man pointed to a room at the end of the carpeted corridor. Haggerty released him and ran for it, past an empty hospital gurney and a rack of oversized pots and pans. He slammed open the door and rushed in. The roar of the burners was deafening; the smell of burnt flesh nearly overpowered him. It had to be over a hundred fifty degrees there. Within seconds Haggerty's tuxedo was glued to his skin by sweat.

A second gurney stood near the incinerator, its occupant thankfully shrouded. Haggerty shoved it in front of the door as a barricade. An arm slipped from beneath the shroud and dangled limply, the signet ring on the hand identifying the owner as the man who'd ordered Thanksgiving dinner. Forcing back his gorge, Haggerty searched the walls frantically for the vent and panicked briefly when he could not locate it. He got down on the floor and saw an opening under the incinerator. The heat from the burners seared him even at that distance. There was no way he could survive under the burners. He had to find a means to put them out.

He stood up. Beside the incinerator was a cast iron control wheel. Haggerty spat on it; his saliva evaporated with a sizzle. He tore off the tuxedo jacket, wrapped it around his hands, and gripped the wheel. It refused to turn. Heat scorched him through the material.

Pounding and kicking hammered at the door. Haggerty yanked the wheel with all his might. Finally it gave way, cutting off the gas and extinguishing the flames. The Thanksgiving guest's body fell from the gurney as the door began to open. Haggerty dropped to the floor. He could still see waves of radiating heat. The door burst inward.

Haggerty covered his face with the jacket and rolled under the incinerator. Instantly his eyes went dry and started to ache. He breathed in fire, certain his lungs would explode, and dropped downward head first through the vent.

He plunged into a pool of foul water. Resurfacing in darkness, he took a breath of blessedly cool air and spat out a mouthful of sewage. Dripping wet, Haggerty pushed the rusted grate from a drainage hatch and pulled himself up to street level, immediately thankful for the warm night air. He checked to see that the white unit was still clipped to his waist, then made his way to the factory where he'd instructed Elsa to wait for him.

"Get us the hell out of here," he told her, climbing into the Corvair. "Head for the beltwheel at Carson."

Elsa entered the slotway, speeding them in the opposite direction from the Last Supper Club. "Are you all right, Jason?" she asked.

"No, I'm not. How long was I gone?"

"Approximately eighty-seven minutes."

There might still be time to save some of the guests, though Haggerty wondered if he should intervene. Duty indicated that he must, as they were attempting to perform illegal acts of suicide.

"Jason, how did you get all wet?" Elsa asked.

"I'll explain later," he said. He retrieved his com from beneath his seat.

"You know they'll triangulate on us if you make a call," Elsa reminded him.

"It's necessary," he told her.

He punched in the code for the Dragon's extension at BBI and listened to the line patch, click, and connect.

Silence. "I'm sure everyone's listening," he said. "I need to speak to whoever's in charge."

"This is Federal agent Keenan, Mr. Haggerty," a voice said after a pause. "You're in a great deal of trouble."

"Tell me something I don't know," Haggerty said. "Since you're tracking me I'll be brief—"

"I must warn you, Mr. Haggerty, that everything you say is being recorded and may be used against you in a court of law."

"Then I'll start by saying I'm not responsible for any of this."

"Come in and we'll talk about it," Keenan offered.

"Not until I have enough evidence to prove my innocence," Haggerty said. "There are forces working diligently inside BBI and the police to ensure that I take the blame. I know for certain agent Corbin is an accessory to the triple press."

"That's funny," Keenan responded. "Corbin said the same thing about you when she gave me a glass from your compartment with fingerprints of someone in league with the dead JC girl."

"I'm not saying I didn't know her, agent Keenan. I'm just telling you that I'm not responsible for any wrongdoing. I'm trying my best to stop more JC suicides."

"Why should I believe you?" Keenan said.

"I wouldn't if I were you," Haggerty admitted as Elsa slotted them onto the Carson Street beltwheel. "But you might convince yourself if you get over to the Society of the Last Supper right now and arrest everyone you can. Corner of Sinatra and Main, mural on the wall at the entrance."

"And what exactly will I find at this church?"

"It's no church," Hagerty barked. "It's a snuff house. If you hurry you'll find the real perpetrators there, including agent Corbin, along with evidence of conspiracy to promulgate illegal suicide. If you wait, you'll find nothing."

Haggerty cut the call, pulled off the earset, and hurled the com out the passenger window.

"Where are we headed, Jason?" Elsa queried.

Haggerty wasn't sure. His thoughts were on the contents of the white unit clipped to his belt, on Regina's friend Traci's insistence on dosing, on her final exhalation in his arms.

"What did you learn from Regina's notebook?" Haggerty asked. "Anything that will help us track her down?"

"I received quite an education," Elsa replied. "Regarding an antiquated technology called Personal Electricity."

"Which is?"

"Personal electricity, or PE, is an advanced form of utility allocation that was abandoned in the mid-twenty-first century," she explained. "Basically it was a way of taking existing power supply stations, simple outlets like you have in your compartment, and allocating electricity based on the unique signature of your registered appliances, billing you accordingly regardless of where you plugged them in. It was abandoned when the first fusion plants began operation and appliance makers decided that free electricity would spur product consumption."

"And Regina was using this how?" he asked, yawning.

"I have difficulty believing this was the work of a Junior Citizen," Elsa said. "It's quite revolutionary. But from what I've read so far it appears that our computer systems are vulnerable through their electrical lines."

"That seems ridiculous," Haggerty said, as he dug a filthy fingernail against the tingling pad of his thumb. "Data doesn't stream through a power supply."

"She seems to disagree," Elsa replied. "And I did note her work station had no form of cellular modem. It was merely plugged in to a wall."

"I think you're telling me," Haggerty said groggily, "and pardon me for being inept, that our computer systems can be cracked by some sort of program running piggyback on the electricity we plug into."

"Yes," Elsa acknowledged, "Put simply. PE is the penetration protocol, but the actual data allocation appears to be made using echo technology. It's quite elegant and extremely ingenious."

"And this helps us find Regina how, exactly?"

"I'm not sure it does, Jason," she answered. "But I am exploring several options. Shall I make this my primary concern?"

No, Haggerty thought. While he did harbor an immediate, perhaps unwarranted emotional drive to find Regina, to talk to her, to be with her—her whereabouts seemed only of secondary concern to the case. He needed someplace he could rest and review the recordings everyone so desperately wanted erased, with full projection. Someplace not likely to be staked out, where they would not be disturbed.

It occurred to him that only one place fit the bill, and he chuckled when he realized that he had only the crazy Indran woman, from the Java Joint, to thank for supplying it.

Chapter Eight
THE KILLSWITCH REVIEW

"It's a cemetery," Elsa stated flatly as she powered the Corvair down a dilapidated section of deserted beltway.

"My family's final resting place," Haggerty said. "Pull up to the gate."

She drove alongside a security fence lined with laserwire to an autoterminal. Haggerty told her his code. She entered it on a keypad and the gate swung wide.

The place was deserted, as Haggerty hoped it would be; at this early hour few patrons ventured out to visit the departed. Haggerty assumed android groundskeepers had monitored their arrival but unless he summoned one via a call button or committed some act of vandalism, he doubted they would hinder him and Elsa.

They stopped at a restroom. "Keep watch while I change out of these filthy clothes and clean up," Haggerty told his assistant.

He stood shaking on weak legs, his skin burning over spastic muscles, staring at his awful reflection in the restroom mirror. The tuxedo reeked of sewage. He clutched the white box in his hands, staring at the numeral "3."

It took seven doses to kill and Traci had used one, rendering the unit nonlethal. There was no danger if he dosed again. He needed a clear head and right now he didn't have one. His skin itched, his mouth was dry, his limbs trembled. He couldn't concentrate, couldn't think. And he needed to think. He needed to calm the craving and concentrate on gathering the evidence required to prove him innocent. He hesitated a moment, then pressed. The unit ticked up to "4."

With a moan he resisted the orgasm threatening to engulf him. The effort brought him to his knees. It was several moments before he was able to force himself to his feet and strip.

The sink provided as much of a shower as he was going to get. It was a long way from what he needed but Haggerty was satisfied he'd washed away enough of the stench to not draw undue attention in public. He dressed in the stolen cargo pants and sweatshirt, concealing the white box beneath it. He stuffed the ruined tux into a garbage bin and rejoined Elsa, who waited by the car.

"Is everything all right, Jason?" she asked. "You were in there longer than I expected."

"I'm fine," Haggerty said, and wasn't lying. The Happy Styx infusing his system had stabilized his body, leaving him certain that he could do what needed to be done.

They walked along a path, their steps activating pinlights every few feet ahead as they proceeded. Moonlight reflected on the slick gravestones around them. The mere mention of this place had horrified Haggerty as a child. The trip here two years ago with his father had devastated them both; returning alone the following year had drained what little spirit Haggerty had left. Now the place felt welcoming, oddly comforting. They halted before the structure with his surname engraved above the entrance.

"Please see if you can open the lock without breaking it, Elsa," Haggerty said.

She placed a palm against the ancient key-style lock and in moments the door opened. The vault self-illuminated as they entered, triggering climate control. Haggerty had planned on arriving here today but not on his feet. The irony didn't escape him; he felt strange anyway.

"Elsa, give me a moment to pay my respects to my family."

He ran his hand along his mother's engraved stone. "It's me, Mom," he said quietly. "I miss you." He touched another shelf. "I'm sorry I haven't come by as often as I should, Dad. I know exactly how you felt now and I forgive you."

"They were both very nice people," Elsa said.

Haggerty knew it was a programmed response but he appreciated the gesture. He guessed that he mattered to Elsa in some mysterious way, although surely his biological parents did not.

"They had me when my father was sixty," he told her. "That was late for those times. I was one of the last children born in NewVada before people needed to register to have kids. They were approved later but they felt one was enough. They were doing their part to keep the population in check."

"Conscientious Citizens," Elsa said.

"*Model* citizens," Haggerty corrected. "But yes, when CC status was formally instituted they were among the first in our cityblock to seek it."

He moved to the simple silver plaque adorning the next tomb. "Oh Lorraine," he said softly. "If only you didn't act so quickly. I understood and forgave you. If only I knew that you'd forgiven me."

Elsa said nothing this time. Did she understand that respectful silence was what Haggerty would appreciate most? He took two more steps, the most difficult of all. The final stone bore the name of his son. Haggerty had no words left.

"I'm sorry for your loss," Elsa said quietly. It seemed she might say more but Haggerty forestalled her by moving to an empty shelf.

He ran his palms across the shelf with morbid fascination. "This is where they'll put me when I'm done."

Elsa came and placed a hand on his shoulder. "I hope that won't be for a long time to come, Jason."

He turned to look at her. Elsa was so childlike, her motives pure, her mind unable to grasp the emotional aspect of the facts he'd just given her about the weight of his loss, the erosion of his will to continue.

"Hopefully," he said, not wishing to alarm her. He wondered if she knew he was lying. "Now let's review those recordings and find out what everyone's so eager to erase."

Haggerty took a seat on the stone floor, draping an arm across his upturned knee.

"Play Teardrop's first. Full room projection."

Elsa's irises whirled into motion.

They were backstage at the concert. Haggerty could see the audience straining against barricades beyond the wings. He reviewed the girl's death and found nothing new.

"Play Sunset's recording," he told Elsa.

The small mausoleum grew notably smaller. Sunset stood bare-chested before the hotel bathroom mirror. "Dawn, it's me," he began, confirming Corbin's revelation that Dawn was part of Regina's given name; the boy's final message had been directed to her. "Someday you'll probably see this," Sunset continued, "and you're gonna think I'm a grokless idiot ..." The transmission ended with the boy pressing onstage.

Haggerty rubbed his eyes. If anything, the recording proved Sunset was a willing participant, leaving a last testament to his sister. But something about the message didn't feel right.

Haggerty told Elsa to run it again.

The scene played out once more. "But I love my life ..." the boy was saying.

"That's it, Elsa," Haggerty said. "Pause the recording."

"What did you see, Jason?"

"Sunset said *love*, not *loved*."

"I do not understand the significance."

"The significance is that Sunset used the present tense. He didn't say his life was over and he loved it for what it had been. He hadn't stopped loving it—and he hadn't decided to end it. People who still love their lives don't press, Elsa. I don't think Sunset knew he was going to die."

"I understand how that interpretation can be placed on his words, Jason. But it makes no sense. He was holding an armed black box that was recording. What else could he have expected to happen when he pressed?"

"That's what we need to find out, Elsa." Haggerty dug at his thumb pad. "Let's see if Tyler Stelwyn's recording has anything useful."

They were in another hotel room. Haggerty recognized Cherub on the couch behind Tyler.

"Hey, it says it's recording!" the boy said as he played with the box.

"Turn that thing off," an unidentified male voice ordered from across the room. "Ya wanna kill yourself?"

"Maybe," Tyler answered, laughing, then told the recording device about partying with "the enlightened, the infamous Clone Jesus."

The transmission ended abruptly when the voice demanded that Tyler "turn the bloody thing off!"

The next installment began with the armed unit adjusting for light inside the closet, presumably in the same hotel. As Tyler moaned in prolonged sexual ecstasy, his envious fellator inquired where she could get whatever he was dosing.

"Do you think he was using the same drug as Sharyn?" Elsa said.

"I'm sure of it," Haggerty said.

He briefed Elsa on what had happened at the Last Supper Club, omitting the fact that he'd been forced to dose himself and was currently under the drug's influence. She might decide to protect him from himself and remove the drug from his possession. He couldn't allow that and he wasn't sure he'd be able to stop her.

"And you believe the boxes used in the triple press were also loaded with the drug?" Elsa asked.

"Yes, but I need to prove it. Skip back to when Tyler climaxes. Slow the action to half time and magnify. Bring up the contrast and brighten the room."

Haggerty walked slowly around the image, moving closer for a better angle and kneeling beside the brunette, studying her as she serviced Tyler Stelwyn. The boy's hand was on the unit as he thrust his hips. "There it is," he said under his breath. "Elsa, review and enhance visual on the button hand and isolate for the sound."

As it replayed, it was revealed in all certainty; the visual of the boy's thumb pressing, the audible pop of the delivery mechanism.

"There's our evidence, Elsa. Tyler pressed and lived. That box had been reloaded with Happy Styx and Tyler knew it. But he didn't know the drug could be lethal."

"You said Traci understood it would kill her, Jason."

"What if Tyler and Teardrop and Sunset believed Happy Styx was harmless?"

"How could someone control the number of doses to make sure the lethal dose was taken onstage?"

"Perhaps the units were only made available at specific times, so they couldn't press too often. Sharyn said Teardrop and Sunset had only been gone two weeks, and according to Traci you can detox as long as you don't overuse. Whoever is behind things could have managed it so the kids thought it was part of the show, that they were making a statement. Remember Tyler's calling Clone Jesus 'the enlightened.'"

Onstage, Zephyr strutted before the frenzied audience. The kids ran to his side and dosed. Tyler fell along with the others, his face ecstatic. The crowd screamed. This was the point where Corbin had halted their first review. Haggerty watched now as Tyler spasmed, moving in close and trying to read the boy's mind through his eyes. The crowd kept screaming. Haggerty silently counted out the predictable physiological shutdown he'd witnessed in thousands of recorded deaths. Something was wrong. Did Tyler's eyes register shock? The unit continued recording, going on and on for what seemed like eternity. At length the projection showed Elsa's hand reaching for the unit on the stage. The transmission finally went black as the box entered the minthizine case.

"It appears that Tyler Stelwyn was still alive when I retrieved his unit," Elsa said.

"There was no one at the press site to certify that vital signs had ceased before the bodies were removed," Haggerty said, sitting back against his vault. "It troubled me at the time but I attributed it to crowd control and unusual circumstances."

"Tyler Stelwyn may not be dead," Elsa suggested.

Haggerty felt a surge of hope, immediately dashed. "His parents identified Tyler's body at the morgue. Whoever staged this made sure the boy died." Reluctantly, he retrieved the white box hidden beneath his sweatshirt and handed it to Elsa. "This is from the club. Analyze the contents, compare it to the drug you found at the scene, and return the unit to me."

Elsa dealt with the closures of a dress not designed for her unique needs and ported the unit. As Haggerty expected, the drugs matched. He clipped the unit to his waistband as Elsa rearranged her dress, then laid his head against the shelf and closed his eyes.

"Now we know why those involved want the recordings erased, Elsa. We're dealing with murder. Not merely of the son of the wealthiest man in NewVada but of Teardrop and Sunset, and accessory to murder of every copycat. The recordings prove it. But who can we show them to? We don't know who to trust."

"Have you considered enlisting the aid of Detective Woyzeck?"

"Woyzeck broke procedure at the triple press and had his gun ready to arrest me before the viewcast aired naming me as the chief suspect. Help me to figure this out, Elsa, if you can. Your logic boards may work better than my reasoning right now. Let's go through what we know or have cause to believe."

Elsa nodded consent.

"Max invented the drug, so he's involved. Corbin's arrival at the club proves she's involved with Max. So was the lead singer of Clone Jesus, who came to the club and invited Traci to a party. Traci involved Teardrop and Regina's brother, which seems to implicate Regina, although it's clear from Sunset's recording she had no idea he planned to press. And if I had any doubt about that, her reaction to the viewcast of the concert removes it completely. We've deduced that none of the kids knew that pressing at the concert would kill them, although we can't be sure yet what Zephyr knew."

"We haven't accounted for Tyler Stelwyn, Jason. Why was he

there? Was someone as wealthy as he likely to be involved with Teardrop and Sunset?"

"We don't know that he was, Elsa. Neither of them was in his recording before the concert. He may have met them there for the first time. Probably he was involved with Clone Jesus for the high life—the drugs, the celebrity, the hotels, God knows what else. And we know from Regina's pairplex that the other kids were fans of the group. Their manager, Shintag Lake, is probably involved. He told me he provides whatever the band members request, no questions asked. Woyzeck's boss did his best to accommodate Lake's demands when he had him in custody. He may also be involved.

"But who is big enough—or stupid enough—to risk incurring the wrath of Tyler's father?" Haggerty wondered aloud.

"The Triads? We know that they protect Max's club."

"The Triads have worked out their arrangements with law enforcement to everyone's satisfaction. I can't believe they'd risk bringing the entire establishment down on them. Who would profit from that? It's likelier that Antonio Stelwyn is in league with the Triads, and if they were even distantly responsible for his only child's death, he would stop at nothing to extinguish them. No, everyone in his right mind fears Antonio Stelwyn. The only person I can think of who might not is Consuela. She didn't bat an eye at the pain the Stelwyns revealed in her presence."

"It was Consuela who told the media you killed Dr. Zabrowski."

"Correct. And it was Consuela who hired Corbin and according to Corbin sent her after us, supposedly to save us."

"Do you think Dr. Zabrowski's death is connected to the triple press, Jason?"

"We can't rule it out. But if so, what was the link? He hadn't seen the recordings. He'd had no direct contact with any of the witnesses or victims. But he told me he was going to ask the Surgeon General to control the media's reporting in order to prevent an explosion of copycats. That was before Consuela sent me off to interview the band members."

"Who could possibly argue with his request for media restraint, Jason?"

"Someone who wanted the media coverage to be as extensive as possible, Elsa. Someone with something to gain if Doug's scenario of a contagion of suicides played out. Or something to lose if it didn't!"

Haggerty went pale. "It's too absurd," he said. "It's grotesque."

"What, Jason?"

"Think about it, Elsa. Doug would have required authorization from his direct superior to contact the Surgeon General. After Consuela sent me to the precinct, Doug would have told her about Cobain Syndrome and his intention to try to stop a wave of suicides. Was Doug killed to prevent him from going to the Surgeon General?"

"Do you believe that Consuela engineered the triple press?" Elsa asked.

"Can you think of another explanation for Doug's death?"

Elsa considered what had been said and answered no. "But why would Consuela want children to kill themselves, Jason?"

"Maybe it wasn't Consuela's design," Haggerty said. "What if she was carrying out orders? BBI is a subsidiary of the State Department of Public Health. Could the State itself want a rash of youth suicides as some bizarre means of population control?"

"Then why send agent Keenan to investigate?"

"It wouldn't be the first time one branch of the government didn't know what the other was doing."

"If we present him the information we have retrieved thus far, he could clear you."

"If Consuela and her superiors at BBI are involved, agent Keenan will be given false information against me. And whatever they come up with will be very convincing. This unit loaded with Happy Styx isn't enough to prove my innocence. If anything, it could have the opposite effect."

"But coupled with Tyler Stelwyn's review—"

"You don't understand the circumstantial evidence, Elsa. I had access to the units. They know I was with Regina and that she knew Teardrop. I stole a piece of evidence from the triple press site and withheld your copies of the recordings that suggest it was murder. We have to assume that those boxes have been erased. I've eluded the police and failed to turn myself in despite a Federal demand to do so. The fact the media was told I was responsible means someone in power wants to guarantee all this gets pinned on me. And the only way for them to ensure that is to have me dead. I'm even in possession of a dispenser of the same illegal drug that killed them."

"But if you are in the custody of the Federal Bureau—"

"Then whoever is wielding this power can get to me and clean up their tracks after I'm out of the way. I can't take that chance.

There's still something missing. We don't know why Clone Jesus was involved or what Max has to gain. Let's get out of here, Elsa. I'm not giving up until I've found out and exposed the monsters who think murdering children is sound social engineering."

The chances were good that the bodies would still be in chemical freeze at the Central Morgue, where Antonio Stelwyn and his wife had gone to identify their son. Haggerty had spent more than his share of time there and knew all the examiners by name, since his presence was required whenever a press under his jurisdiction had been judged unclean and he'd requested an autopsy.

As Elsa pulled the Corvair back onto the beltway, Haggerty popped another celtrex, reached into the storage compartment, and retrieved the com they'd taken from Corbin. "I've reconsidered your suggestion to contact agent Keenan," he responded to Elsa's questioning look. "We need to at least pretend to trust someone." He punched in the code for Consuela's office at BBI.

Keenan picked up at the first tone. "Haggerty?" he asked.

"What did you find at the Last Supper Club?"

"A dolphin in a tank and a dead girl in a dungeon with your DNA on her," he answered. "You aren't doing yourself any favors staying out there, Haggerty. Come in, tell me what you have, and I promise we'll use all our resources to get to the bottom of this."

"I'd love to, agent Keenan, but I'm as suspicious of my superiors at BBI as you are of me. I don't know if I can trust anyone, you included."

"I understand your concern," Keenan said. "But it's my job to—"

"My only concern is staying free long enough to prove the triple press was staged with criminal intent and prevent more copycats. So why don't you help me by doing your job? Find the club's owners and investigate everyone at BBI, especially Consuela. And run an autopsy on that girl with full toxicology. Because unless you or someone else cracks this case, I'm going to keep trying to."

"Damn it, Haggerty, if you don't—"

Haggerty disconnected the com and threw it out the window. "This is getting to be a habit," he said. He laced his fingers together, extended his arms, and cracked his knuckles. The celtrex did little to dissuade what felt like a squadron of ants climbing all over his skin, but he couldn't afford to indulge them just yet.

"That went well," Elsa said.

"We'll see," Haggerty replied. "If Keenan comes up with anything I requested, he just might be trustworthy. Until then ..."

The car's control panel went dark. The engine seized. The car barreled powerless down the belt. Realizing the steering column was no longer under her control, Elsa reached for the emergency brake. Haggerty gripped the roll bar and braced his knees against the dashboard as the Corvair's state-of-the-art manual braking mechanism engaged, thrusting the vehicle into a screeching fishtail. It jostled and jumped three slots, narrowly avoiding a collision with another car, then came to a jarring halt in the center lane. Smoke from the radials engulfed the interior and the surrounding beltway.

"Get out," Haggerty shouted. "Before the emergency lane sweeps us!"

Warm clean air rushed into his lungs as they dashed across the belt to a slim maintenance walkway. He bent low, hands to his knees, taking long, deep breaths as the belt section beneath the Corvair broke free and slammed the car into the emergency lane amid a shower of safety foam.

"So much for trust," he told Elsa. "They must have found DeAngelo and run the VIN number. Damn!" They had only a few minutes before the com call gave Keenan a fix.

Haggerty looked over the side of the walkway. A smaller pedestrian belt ran some sixty feet below. He'd never survive that steep a drop.

"Jason, there." Elsa said. He turned and saw that she was scanning the edge of the beltway in the direction they'd come from. Her optical scanning systems must have picked up something his human eyes hadn't noticed.

"What is it?"

"A crude maintenance ladder connecting the belts. It is less than half a mile back."

The dim wail of sirens approached from a distance. Haggerty and Elsa ran for it. Haggerty's lungs were in perfect condition but his determination faltered. Before they were halfway to the ladder he wanted to stop and dose. He reached for the unit clipped to his belt and clutched it tight as they pounded their way down the walkway. The sirens grew louder.

"We're not gonna make it," Haggerty spat.

"The hell we're not," Elsa said, gripping his shoulder and elbow and urging him forward.

Three police cruisers came into view as they reached the ladder. Elsa went over the rail and began to descend. As Haggerty followed he realized he'd left the stolen black box in the Corvair's storage unit.

They rushed along the belt toward a switchpoint, encountering a half-dozen citizens, none of them wary. But it wouldn't take long for platform scanners to find their trail once they were identified.

"The Code Six fugitive has changed his face with plastiche," a female anchor on graveyard shift at Global Networks NewVada reported on an infocrawl as they jumped the rail at Mandalay Junction. Haggerty's new face flashed across the screen. He pulled his hood forward. "Jason P. Haggerty is considered very dangerous. If you see him, do not attempt to apprehend him. Instead, please call—"

Two male JCs on airboards sat across from each other, their backs to the rails on the swiftly running belt, oblivious beneath Indranet telecast visors. Haggerty and Elsa moved ahead of them unnoticed.

"I see the morgue allows my kind," Elsa said as they stood watching lowtech android attendants in blue overalls move past two armed and armored policemen through the doorless entrance of the lonely gray building.

"Not without an I.D. wristlet," Haggerty told her. "Let's look at the docks around back."

They moved quietly down an alleyway to a loading dock currently in use, hiding behind a waste disposal unit while two male attendants lifted a coffin off a conveyor belt into a waiting limousine. Haggerty hoped it was not Tyler Stelwyn's body, as the macabre solution to gain entry occurred to him. Again he might have the Indran woman to thank.

We need to get you one of those wristlets and a set of overalls, Elsa, he linked.

Before he could protest, she was walking toward the attendants. She stopped one of them, communicating via infrared transfer. Haggerty was startled to observe him unclasp his wristlet and hand it to Elsa, then sit motionless on a nearby bench. The second attendant continued loading as if nothing unusual had occurred.

Elsa secured the wristlet on her arm and returned to Haggerty. *I'll be able to obtain a uniform in the storage shed a meter to the left of the gate*, she informed him.

How did you manage that? Haggerty asked.

He's a Descartes model. They're simple to override with the proper protocol.

Clearly Elsa's ethics program was now subject to her PLC and she was comfortable operating outside the law. The damage an android with her capabilities might cause were she to act with malicious intent would be formidable. Haggerty had to proceed carefully—and hope that his own motives remained honest.

Nightworkers paid no attention to Elsa as, minutes later, she wheeled a casket toward the room Haggerty called the Freezer, opened the steel portal, and rolled the casket through. The wristlet merely *bleeped* to register her entry. She scanned the room to make sure it was unoccupied by workers, then locked the door behind her.

Inside the coffin, Haggerty had yielded to the demands of his system, telling himself the two doses left should be enough for evidence. Euphoria washed over him as the glowing digital readout clicked to "5."

We're in the Freezer, Elsa linked. *Are there cameras that I should disengage?*

No, they don't allow them in here, Haggerty linked back. *Let me out.*

Haggerty sat up and raised himself by the hands from the casket, his mind clear again. The ants had ceased their Fandango on his nerves. *We don't have much time, Elsa. This building will lock down as soon as someone finds the body you moved.*

In the center of the room a woman was laid out for autopsy. Euphoria overcame Haggerty's usual squeamishness. He glanced at the splayed, cut-open corpse and determined it wasn't Teardrop, although she was young enough to be one of the copycats. Teardrop and Sunset must be here someplace, but every moment was precious.

Find Tyler, Elsa.

She moved along the banks of storage compartments where bodies were kept, scanning coded indexes. In seconds she found Tyler Stelwyn's remains and learned how the control panels worked. With a low *hiss* the drawer slid seamlessly out of the bank.

Tyler Stelwyn's once golden bronze skin had a bluish tint from the chemical freeze. Haggerty noted a half-finished blisterbrand across his naked stomach.

It appears that no autopsy has been performed, Elsa linked.

And there won't ever be one if Consuela is behind this, Haggerty responded. *She'll have Corbin judge the press clean. Record please, Elsa. Check his head for contusions.*

Elsa glided a hand carefully around Tyler's skull and neck. *No contusions, Jason.*

Take samples, he directed.

Elsa detached a coverlet at the center of her palm, revealing a miniature screen. She lifted the hand Tyler had used to press, placed his thumb against the screen, laid his arm down again, and repositioned the coverlet. A needle sprang from her index finger; she injected it into a vein on the boy's arm and retrieved samples, and began scanning Tyler's arms.

Someone attempted to open the door, then knocked loudly. "Is anyone in there?" a disturbed male voice shouted.

Haggerty considered possible exits as Elsa hastily extended her scan to Tyler's naked legs and inner thighs. She moved closer, localizing a patch of skin on the left thigh with her fingers.

Haggerty heard the soft whiz of her eyes shifting focus. The silence outside told him whoever had knocked had gone to get a keycard for the door.

We're out of time, Elsa.

She depressed a sequence of buttons on the drawer's control panel and it began to close. Footsteps were audible beyond the door. Haggerty moved Elsa quickly to the casket and instructed her to lie down inside; he managed to get himself on top of her and close the lid just before the door opened.

"Everything seems fine," the man's voice said, "except ..."

Footsteps approached the casket; someone knocked twice on the wood above his head. Haggerty sweated profusely.

"This coffin was supposed to be brought to the loading dock," the man's exasperated voice continued. "Bring that one in and take this one out."

"Yes, sir," came the automated voice of an android attendant.

Haggerty rested his forehead against Elsa's with relief.

Inside of a hearse, inside of a coffin, Haggerty shivered in the dark, counting the miles they'd been in the vehicle since it pulled away from the morgue, as Elsa cradled him, attempting to keep him calm. She was no match for the claustrophobia assailing him. It was bad enough being in there alone, but two of them left almost no room to breathe. He'd had more than his share of nightmares that ended with him in a coffin following a failed press, alert and aware but unable to free himself.

I can't take it anymore, Elsa. Pass me the stunner and get us out of here.

Elsa forced open the casket lid and handed him the weapon. Haggerty looked through polarized windows at the beltway speeding by. He crawled on the red velveteen carpeting to the cab and banged on the glass.

The startled driver pulled to the side of the slotway and ran to the back of the hearse. He opened the cargo door and found Haggerty aiming the stunner at him. The young-looking man in a black suit stepped backward, hands in the air, as Haggerty and Elsa emerged from the vehicle.

"I don't want any trouble," Haggerty said. "Give me your com."

The man handed it over.

"The body you were supposed to deliver is behind a waste disposal unit at the loading dock," Haggerty said. "Make sure you see to it."

"I will."

You drive, Elsa, Haggerty linked.

They left the driver confused and shaken on the edge of the belt.

"What did you find in Tyler?" Haggerty asked Elsa.

"The pores on his thumb were heavily laced with Happy Styx. Blood analysis confirms he'd had numerous doses. I also detected a known polythinisine-based toxin injected into his left thigh."

"Our drug?" Haggerty asked.

"Yes."

"That's proof that whoever killed Tyler wanted people to believe he died from the press."

"Your logic appears sound, Jason. Now what do we do?"

Haggerty thought for a moment. If he turned himself in he could get medical attention, have his system flushed of the toxins from Max's white box. But there were two doses left, which meant he could keep going for a few more hours and try to find out who was behind this. His gut told him that once he was in custody, whoever was responsible would make sure he took the fall to stop his interference with whatever they were planning.

The question was what clues remained to follow up. He'd exhausted all his resources. But there was someone definitely not involved in the triple press who would be interested in his evidence. Someone with inexhaustible resources. Haggerty merely had to convince him he was innocent before he killed Haggerty himself.

Chapter Nine
GHOSTS IN THE MACHINE

Antonio Stelwyn probably wanted him dead but Haggerty had no one else to turn to. Ten hours had passed since the triple press, ten hours in which copycats had to have been escalating. Anyone in another time zone who had been asleep when it happened had woken to a media barrage that, with nothing to counter it, was going to bring about Doug's worst-case scenario.

The hearse off-looped at the Northside terminus and parked in a public garage. Haggerty and Elsa walked briskly along a blue slate footpath bordered by carefully manicured grass and intermittent wrought-iron benches beneath lush palm trees—all real. If Haggerty was wealthy and Sasha DeAngelo a rung above him on NewVada's economic ladder, Antonio Stelwyn was in the top one percent worldwide.

At the end of the path the SDS tower soared into the pre-dawn sky. Home to the wealthiest citizens of NewVada, the building was a monument to man's triumph over Sensory Deprivation Syndrome, the last major medical epidemic of the twenty-first century, and the eradication of all human disease. Haggerty pushed a button on the automated system at the entrance, hoping the Stelwyns would not call the police before he could plead his case.

"Stelwyn residence," a male voice responded smoothly.

"I need to speak with Mr. Stelwyn," Haggerty said. "It's a matter of grave importance. I'm the man who saw the recording of his son."

The door released. *Do nothing if we encounter hostility, Elsa,* Haggerty linked as they crossed the lobby. *Let me handle it.* The tube doors were open and waiting. They shot upward a hundred stories to the penthouse. A soft chime announced their arrival as the doors opened.

"Proceed carefully, Mr. Haggerty." Antonio Stelwyn greeted them with an antique revolver clutched ready in his right hand. "I know how to use this."

Obviously Stelwyn had seen the last viewcast. He was dressed in a bathrobe over nightclothes, mouth pinched and thin, his face ashen and unshaved.

"I'm sorry if I seemed rude to you earlier," Haggerty said. "I was doing my job."

"And now you're a fugitive."

"I'm trying to continue my investigation, Mr. Stelwyn, and I need your help."

Stelwyn did nothing to hide his astonishment.

"You said you believe Tyler was coerced into pressing."

"I still believe it."

"I have evidence that proves you're right."

"I want to believe you, Mr. Haggerty," Stelwyn said, his face a mixture of conflicting emotions. "But how can I when you're the prime suspect?"

"I'm a prime suspect because of what I know and the evidence I have. Would I come here if I didn't have proof, knowing I could never escape if you didn't want me to?"

"Let's see what you have," Stelwyn said, lowering the gun. "Come into my study."

Stelwyn led them through the polished-granite foyer large as Haggerty's entire compartment past a small, cascading waterfall with a pool teaming with live koi at its base. The shelves in Stelwyn's study were real wood and packed with leather-bound volumes—an extravagant display of wealth. Trees were sacred, the oxygen they produced too precious, to allow them to be turned into paper, and the only surviving paper books were registered antiques. Haggerty caught part of a gilded title, *Do Androids Dream*, and wished he were here for purely social reasons. He was reasonably proud of his own library; his slim replitext contained hundreds of classic and modern works he'd loaded into it over his lifetime. But what was a digital library compared to actual books, each volume dedicated to a single work? What would it feel like to hold one in his hands? He wasn't going to find out today.

Exhaustion made Stelwyn's tempramassage couch vastly more enticing than the prospects of handling an antique. Haggerty sank onto it without waiting to be invited and popped his last celtrex, hoping to keep the ants at bay a while longer. Stelwyn sat in a chair across from him and waited.

"I must warn you, Mr. Selwyn," Haggerty began. "It's clear that Tyler didn't think you would ever view his recording. He was engaged in behavior that may be difficult for you to see."

"If it will help me find out who was responsible for my son's death, I want to see it," Stelwyn said flatly.

Haggerty instructed Elsa to play the recording at half room projection, same speed and coding as their last viewing, and walked Stelwyn through it.

"As you can see, Tyler presses but the drug isn't lethal. It simply enhances sexual pleasure," Haggerty said gently.

Stelwyn's expression was grim as he viewed the rush to the stage, the screaming crowd, the press. "Why is it still recording?" he asked, choking back a sob, bewildered as the recording went on and on. Finally Elsa's hand retrieved the box and the projection ended.

"I want you to know how deeply sorry I am for what I'm about to say," Haggerty warned. "The recording continued because Tyler was still alive, though unconscious. The press didn't kill him. Someone injected him with the toxins used by BBI *after* his body was collected and sent on to the morgue. Your son was murdered."

Stelwyn groaned in pain. He buried his head in his hands. "Who did it? Who murdered my boy?" he asked softly.

"I'm trying to find out," Haggerty answered. "The likely suspects are all people who want to see this recording erased. That's why I brought it to you. I deeply regret your son's death, Mr. Stelwyn. I lost my son two years ago in a car crash."

Stelwyn raised his tear-streaked face from his hands and for a moment they were two grieving fathers. "How did you go on?" he asked Haggerty.

"To be honest, I'm not sure I did. My son's death pretty much ruined me and my family. But I hope now that you know what I've learned—"

The study door opened abruptly. Stelwyn's wife, dressed in bedclothes, hurried to her husband's side. Her face was etched with sorrow, her beautiful raven hair unbraiding.

"Antonio, what's going on? Harold said someone was here to see you about Tyler." She looked up and saw Haggerty. "*You!* You've changed your face but they showed the images. You're the one they're looking for. You killed my son!"

Stelwyn stood up. "Mr. Haggerty's not responsible, Sylvia," he said gently. "He has information for me."

"What kind of information? Why doesn't he take it to the police?"

"I don't have enough evidence yet, ma'am. I was hoping your

husband could help me get to the bottom of what happened. For Tyler's sake."

Sylvia Stelwyn glared at him. "Don't you dare speak my baby's name." She turned to her husband. "Don't you see? If he had real evidence, he would have turned himself in and let the authorities handle things. But he doesn't. He's desperate and he's trying to use you, use your pain. He'll get away with giving Tyler that filthy box if you let him."

"That's enough, Sylvia." Stelwyn took his distraught wife in his arms. "I promise you, I'm not being used. Mr. Haggerty has shown me very convincing proof of what happened to our son."

"Show it to me!"

Stelwyn and Haggerty exchanged a look.

"It's too disturbing, darling. Trust me that I know what I'm doing. Please?"

Sylvia closed her eyes in pain. "I always trust you, Antonio," she said tiredly. "Haven't I trusted you for the past sixty years?"

"Go to bed and I promise to explain everything in the morning."

She drew away from his embrace. "Of course, darling." She gave him a thin, watery smile. "Do what you need to do."

"Thank you, beloved."

Stelwyn kissed her forehead tenderly. He led her to the door of the study. They exchanged a few words too low for Haggerty to hear. Sylvia laid her palm on her husband's cheek; Stelwyn kissed the palm. Sylvia smiled sadly. Standing on tiptoe, she kissed her husband's cheek and turned away. Stelwyn closed the door behind her.

Haggerty wondered if he'd have been able to bear Josh's death better if Lorraine had remained with him to share the loss and pain. "If I may offer some advice," he began delicately, "have someone keep an eye on her. The suicide of an only child frequently leads to the suicide of a parent."

Stelwyn nodded grimly. He headed toward the com on his desk and placed a call, speaking in low, urgent tones, then returned to Haggerty and Elsa.

"If something happens to her ... I want revenge, Mr. Haggerty. Now tell me, who is trying to stop you from releasing this recording?"

"I'm not clear how deep the conspiracy runs," Haggerty said. "It might be my own people trying to set off a contagion of suicides among young people as some kind of unholy population control. Whoever is behind this left little to chance—and that includes the choice of your son. Do you know of anyone who would want to strike at you?"

"I have many enemies, Mr. Haggerty."

"Do you have a listing of all of your corporations, Mr. Stelwyn?" Elsa requested. "I may be able to correlate data and find something that connects to all of this."

Stelwyn offered Elsa a chair at his computer and began clicking keys.

Haggerty stood, arms crossed, anxiously digging his fingers into his biceps. "Do you have any celtrex you can spare, Mr. Stelwyn?" he asked.

"In the bathroom down the hall, medicine cabinet," Stelwyn called over his shoulder.

Haggerty made his way quickly to a garish bathroom larger than a public restroom. He was sweating as he opened the cabinet, found the celtrex cannister, and transferred a few to his pillcase. He pulled out the white box. If he pressed again there would be only one dose left as evidence. The battalion of ants gnawed at his nerves. This isn't about you, he told his reflection in the mirror. Swear on Josh's memory that this is the last time.

The digital reader clicked to "6"; Haggerty contained a moan as bliss coursed through his system. Weak-kneed, he returned to the study, pleasantly dazed as he retook a seat on the couch.

Stelwyn and Elsa scanned data silently. "Find what you needed?" Stelwyn asked.

"Thanks," Haggerty said.

He forced himself to focus. While the drug enabled him to continue his investigation, it made it increasingly difficult for him to care.

"I see that you own a pharmaceutical company that manufactures the serum BBI uses in its KV units, as well as the KV units themselves," Elsa said.

"North American Health Initiatives," Stelwyn confirmed.

"This whole thing's about drugs that kill," Haggerty said. He gave Stelwyn an abbreviated account of what went on at the Last Supper Club. Stelwyn was clearly disgusted. "The club is run by a young man who calls himself Max," Haggerty said. "He's in league with a BBI junior review agent named Corbin. I sent the FBI there but Max was prepared. By the time they showed up, nothing was left of the club but one piece of evidence that implicates me."

Stelwyn frowned. "Tyler had a friend named Max. He was an Indivisible, as I recall. Ban the Box crowd, part of the Religious Right."

"That must be how Tyler came into contact with the other kids who pressed," Haggerty said. "But they hate BBI. And Max doesn't oppose death now, he deals it."

"Maybe you do have enough evidence," Stelwyn said. "I can pull strings at the mayor's office."

"No offense, Mr. Stelwyn, but I doubt even you could help me turn my evidence into freedom," Haggerty responded. "I still need to find out how the band fits into the picture and the motivation behind this."

"If you need to find that boy Max's motivation, go to the man who molded him."

"If we knew who his father was ..."

"Not his father," Stelwyn said. "We hope and pray it will be us, but it rarely is. I'm talking about Yosif Svoboda, the man who founded the Indivisibles. He's been on both sides of picket lines at any number of my firms. He's a retired NASA scientist with a stunning command of technology. He can argue technical points beyond the comprehension of most protesters. I've heard him speak. Joe Svoboda is a very charismatic man."

Joe, Haggerty thought. The Anglicized version of Yosif. Regina had spoken of her friend Joe who jacked the Indranet and built bulletproof tek. Could she have meant Yosif Svoboda? And if so, would she have flown to his side?

"How can I find him?" he asked Stelwyn.

"That's a good question. I'm sure the FBI would like to know the answer. He's just below you on their most wanted list. Top of mine."

A knock at the study door. "Come in," Stelwyn said.

A man in the formal attire of a butler poked in his head. "Sir, there are several members of the police downstairs, led by a Detective Woyzeck. They're demanding to have a word with you."

"Show them into the morning room, Harold," Stelwyn said calmly. "Tell them I'll be with them directly. Offer them whatever they like to keep them occupied, but avoid answering questions until I get there."

"Very good, sir."

"Damn it, Sylvia," Stelwyn swore quietly when they were alone again. He gave Haggerty a hard look. "If anything you've told me is rigged ..."

"I've told you the truth, nothing was rigged," Haggerty said.

"Can your assistant fly a Jetpod 786?"

"I can," Elsa said.

Stelwyn extracted a keycard from a desk drawer and passed it to Haggerty. "It's on the roof," Stelwyn said. "Take it and contact me when you know more. I'll hold them off as long as I can. Of course, I have to tell the police you forced it from me."

"Of course," Haggerty said. "Be careful. Woyzeck may be in on this."

"I'm a sensible man, Mr. Haggerty. Get more evidence."

Stelwyn moved to the door and left.

"Jason, do you believe Regina may be with this man, Yosif Svoboda," Elsa asked as soon as they were alone.

"There's a very good chance," Haggerty replied. "What've you got?"

"From reading Regina's notes, I understand she doesn't trust the com system, Jason. She thinks it's too vulnerable to cracking. She uses her personal electricity protocol for communication through her handheld. If I access the main electrical power supply system terminals, I think I can now cross correlate for her PE signature and determine her location. But this will alert BBI to our whereabouts."

"They know we were here anyway," he said. He glanced at a grandfather clock in the corner. "Do it fast, Elsa."

Her android fingers blurred at the computer terminal's holographic keypanel. Holoscreens came and went faster than Haggerty could follow. "She gained access in your compartment," Elsa said. "That's one address. We can assume she accessed often from her own address. There, I've isolated the signature of her handheld. Let's hope the power company updates continuously." More screens flashed past. "I've got her signature, Jason. Used less than half an hour ago."

"Then clear your trail and let's go find her."

They scrambled up to the roof and into the hangar. Elsa keyed the ignition; thrusters fired the small craft off the SDS complex into open sky.

Haggerty looked beneath his feet through the pod's viewer and saw Detective Woyzeck standing below them—red-faced, fists in the air, middle fingers jabbing upward. His curses were muffled by the sound of the jetpod engines.

They wove between stalks of NewVada skyline toward the

rising sun. Haggerty leaned his head back against the panel and closed his eyes. He'd gone a long time without sleep. He popped a celtrex while Elsa threaded them between the monolithic skyscrapers of the Kubrick district past the city demarcation line and over the desert.

"Where is she, Elsa?" he asked.

"The geographical coordinates of her last signature place her approximately twelve minutes out," Elsa replied. "But scanners indicate there's nothing there but a power grid."

Haggerty cracked his knuckles. Twelve minutes was a long time in the air; they might be tracked via satellite or, worse, shot down. Mile after mile of desolation sped by in the viewer and miraculously no weapons lock was detected. Either they were incredibly lucky or somebody was on their side.

"We should be coming up on visual range of the grid now," Elsa said.

The protruding hypersteel dome of the grid shimmered into existence atop the sand—and nothing else.

"Could she be in there, Elsa?"

"It's possible," Elsa replied. "But we're talking very small maintenance shafts and her signature registered outside the grid."

She directed Haggerty's attention to an empty patch of sand and rock and began dropping altitude to circle. The pod pitched forward, throwing him hard against his seatbelt.

"Initiating emergency procedure," Elsa said calmly, adjusting the aircraft's trim and retracting the steering mechanism full back, bringing the nose of the pod suddenly skyward.

Haggerty caught his breath as Elsa's fingers blurred into motion on the thruster controls.

"We impacted with something beneath us and sustained damage," she said. "I'll bring us down as slowly as possible. Cross your fingers."

Haggerty watched the ground rush up to meet them. He was painfully jolted again as the landing gear struck prematurely and Elsa quickly disengaged the thrust.

"We're down," she said, "although the altimeter readings state otherwise."

Haggerty rubbed at the base of his spine. Someone wearing goggles and a loose, enveloping robe—male or female was impossible to tell—appeared out of nowhere and headed across the sand toward them.

Haggerty drew the stunner and popped the hatch, confused

as he stepped down; it didn't feel like sand beneath his shoes. "Hands in the air!" he warned.

The approaching figure complied instantly and cautiously continued in their direction, stopping about two yards from Haggerty and Elsa.

"Pull down your face mask," Haggerty said. "Slowly."

The goggles and face mask came away, revealing a man with dark eyes, a reddish beard, and heavily tanned skin. He looked like someone in the prime of a vigorous, active middle age.

"Who are you?" Haggerty demanded.

"I'm Joe Svoboda, Mr. Haggerty. It's a pleasure to meet you. I'm sure Regina will be happy to see you. If you'll put that stunner away, I'll bring you to her and answer all of your questions."

He's telling the truth, Jason, Elsa linked.

Haggerty pocketed the weapon.

"Thank you, Mr. Haggerty," Svoboda said. "Come inside and meet your fans."

Haggerty looked bewildered. "Inside?" he asked, indicating the miles of empty desert around them.

"You crash landed on top of our mess hall. I'm hoping you didn't cause too much damage to our projection cells."

"We are standing atop a projected image?" Elsa asked.

"A bit of holographic technology," Svoboda said proudly. "Hundreds of tiny cameras continuously capture images of the desert and project them across the surface of our little town."

"Making it virtually invisible," Elsa said.

"Precisely," Svoboda responded. "Follow me. Be careful on the glass."

He led them toward the place where he'd first appeared out of the sand and retracted a small hatch, abruptly ending the illusion. Before them was an old-style electrolift. Dozens of people shouted up at them excitedly from below.

"They're cheering for you, Mr. Haggerty," Svoboda explained, stepping onto the lift and activating a control. "We've all been following your investigation and we're very impressed."

Haggerty looked up at the underside of the massive screen of projection cells as they descended. "I'll be damned," he muttered.

Svoboda smiled.

The hidden town was comprised of several dozen double-decker cabins, a few buildings that appeared to be made of desert rock, a huge water tower, and at least fifty antiquated mobile homes. When they reached the ground, a young man attired similarly to Svoboda stepped over to him.

"Ricardo, please get up there with some men and tarp their vehicle before it gets noticed," Svoboda said.

"Sure thing, Joe. Nice going, Haggerty!"

Haggerty was bemused. A Code Six fugitive, they treated him like a conquering hero. People rushed up to him yelling his name, reaching out and touching and demanding that he shake their hands, which he did to the best of his ability. Too many names and remarks for him to make sense of anything being said.

He was startled to realize that most of them had never been to a plastiche parlor. Many appeared too young for the standard geno-immunization treatments Conscientious Citizens underwent at age thirty. All were dressed in loose robes. The majority of them were women.

Svoboda held up his arms. "Everyone, please," he said in the voice of someone used to making himself heard above large, noisy crowds. "Mr. Haggerty has had a long night and we have a lot to discuss. I'm sure he'll make time for you later. Everyone get back to work."

The crowd dispersed with shouts and waves and grumbles.

Svoboda, Haggerty, and Elsa passed a lean-to where two women with prominent bellies smiled and waved excitedly at him. Haggerty waved back good-naturedly. "How many people live here?" he asked Svoboda.

"A little over three hundred at present."

"I notice your population is predominantly female."

"The organization's pretty equally divided," Svoboda said. "But you're right, the majority who live here are women."

"Pregnant women," Haggerty said as another strolled by, one hand on her protruding stomach and the other leading a small child.

Svoboda grinned. "Yes, Mr. Haggerty, we're gender offenders. I don't hold with the government interfering in an issue as personal as choosing to bear a child. These are all applicationless, unapproved pregnancies, and mostly unregistered children you're seeing."

Fertility was illegal but unregistered birth was punishable by exile. "I'm not a policeman," Haggerty said. "Although I admit that yesterday I'd have reported you and had you arrested."

"Yesterday you were an obedient cog in a dreadful machine, Mr. Haggerty. As we all were once. Today that system will be taken to task."

They were passing through a makeshift square where a few dozen women and toddlers milled around a viewscreen powered by exposed electrical groundwire. Haggerty looked at the screen and saw himself looking at the screen with Svoboda beside him. He turned to Elsa, who was drawing the same conclusion.

"You cracked Elsa?" he said.

Svoboda nodded. "She's an amazing piece of work."

"You did this utilizing PE technology?" Elsa asked. She stared at her transmission; the monitor displayed a video feedback loop repeating to infinity.

"I do hope you'll forgive me. I cracked you while you were in hibernation mode two nights ago. Had you begin transmitting to us on secured channels over Indra and blocked your awareness that I'd done so. Not bad for tek running on rusty wire, huh? I'll assume that's how you found us, a reverse trace? It's quite fortunate that Regina left her notebook for you to find."

Haggerty was astounded. If his personal information were that vulnerable, all stored information was vulnerable. And his assistant had been used as a surveillance cam.

"Make it stop, Svoboda," Haggerty demanded angrily.

"As you wish, Mr. Haggerty." Svoboda went to the door of a stone building. "Please join me. My receiver is just inside."

Haggerty stepped into the dwelling ahead of Svoboda.

"Jason!" Regina cried and rushed to him. Instinctively his arms reached to hold her.

"I'm so glad you're alive," she said. She laughed through her tears. "Although I wish you'd found a better disguise." Her hand rested lightly on his plastiched cheek.

"Regina," he said, staring down at her tearstained face. It felt so good to hold her again. She looked the same as when he'd seen her last—the same clothes, including his shirt. But so much had happened to him since then. "I'm so sorry about your brother."

She placed a finger gently against his lips. Haggerty pulled her close.

"Your friend Traci is—"

"We know," Svoboda said. "You've been blamed. We know you're innocent. We know everything you've learned, from watching your investigation through Elsa. And I have information you don't have that you'll find useful. That's why you're here. Let's go into my sitting room, shall we?"

"Come to me after, Jason?" Regina pleaded.

"Count on it," Haggerty told her.

She went to Svoboda, clasped his hands, and stood on tiptoe to kiss his cheeks. With a tremulous smile to Haggerty and a sidelong glance at Elsa, she exited the room.

"Our meeting was no coincidence, was it?" Haggerty asked Svoboda.

Svoboda smiled. "I sent her to spend the night with you. Don't look so hurt, Mr. Haggerty. It was completely her choice to seduce you. I sent her to keep you from pressing."

"How could you possibly know I was going to press?"

Svoboda placed a hand on his shoulder. Haggerty winced.

"I could tell you about deviations in your normal routine, graph the downslope of your psychevals I've pilfered from your company. But I won't. I knew you were suicidal because your assistant knew it." He glanced at Elsa, who stood to the side surveying the device that transmitted her audiovisual signal. "That red button on top will cut the connection and end transmission," Svoboda told her. Before Haggerty could speak, Svoboda prodded, "Again I apologize. Please, come inside and make yourself comfortable."

The adjoining chamber felt like a retro-Moroccan sensual hashish dream: wine-colored draperies, fire in a large pit, pushpillows for seating. A pitcher of water had been placed on a circular table of beaten brass, along with a pair of tall plastic cups. Svoboda poured water into one of them for Haggerty.

Haggerty used it to down three celtrex, covertly inserting them beneath his tongue while his host poured himself a cup of water. Elsa sat beside him expressionless.

"Clean water must be a luxury out here," Haggerty said, extending his cup for a refill.

"I've got it pretty well rigged," Svoboda said. "I'm glad you appreciate it." He refilled Haggerty's cup. "You may wonder why I'm skilled at these antiquated technologies."

Haggerty took the bait. "Tell me."

"I invented most of them or oversaw their implementation," he said. "Including the one that's kept you gainfully employed for the past six decades."

"That's not possible. The Kevorkian unit was invented by T. J. Sovereign."

"At that time I was still using the Anglicized version adopted by my grandfather when he came to this country. My full name is Tomas Yosif Svoboda."

Haggerty scrutinized the man before him, comparing the dark eyes, the reddish hair to his memory of the portrait he'd passed daily going to and from his office at BBI. The skin was now deeply tanned, but it was easy to imagine how pale it had been before decades of exposure to the sun. He calculated the English equivalents of his present ethnic name.

"Thomas Joseph Sovereign," he said.

"That is the name my father gave me," Svoboda acknowledged. "I used it until I realized my great mistake, my terrible sin, and rejected what I'd done."

"You invented the box and then had some grand religious conversion?"

"Not a religious conversion," Svoboda told him. "I merely came to my senses. Please allow me to explain.

"Before the stem was cracked, my mother was diagnosed with cancer. She went through endless surgeries, chemotherapies, radiation treatments. Her disease would retreat for a while and come back more aggressive than ever. Eventually, the fight was useless. But it took a long, long time and her suffering was terrible. Our doctors were compassionate—they gave her more pain medication than was legally allowed—but she was begging for death long before she finally succumbed. Her story wasn't uncommon. I vowed to do everything possible to see that others didn't go through that kind of suffering.

"I had studied engineering at MIT, courtesy of the United States, and when I got out Uncle Sam expected a lot back from me. Before I knew it I was heading the think tank that oversaw all new technology directives for everyone from the Department of Energy to the CDC to the North American Aerospace Defense Command. Endless funds were put at my disposal. I invented the Kevorkian unit to provide a more humane way for the terminally ill to end their lives. I fought for the legislation to make its use legal and then sat on the board of directors at BBI. I didn't foresee what would happen once stem therapy eradicated all terminal illness. KV units were like a drug waiting for a new disease. Soon the laws were changed to allow anyone who could pass a minimal psycheval to press when they saw fit, just to escape periods of treatable depression or boredom. And BBI evolved to accommodate these changes."

"So you retired to the desert and founded the Indivisibles," Haggerty said.

"Again, that came later. Initially I thought I could fight the system from within. I moved to another agency and continued to invent the best tek I could. Which I did well and prolifically until the satellite defense grids went up and we sealed ourselves off from the world."

"You say that like you think it was a mistake," Haggerty said. An ant nibbled his thumb.

"I do," Svoboda said, folding his arms across his robe. "Sealing our borders was the worst decision the American government ever made. Our insularity was bound to hurt us eventually."

"You blame the government for what's happening now?"

"It could have been avoided with foresight. I curse myself every day for not getting involved earlier in protesting the system."

"How old are you?" Haggerty asked.

"One-hundred-fifty-six." Svoboda smiled at Haggerty's astonishment. "I can remember what it was like to pump my own gas and I rather miss it," he said. "It can be difficult watching everything transform around you while you continue relatively unchanged, but it gives you perspective. I have a deeper understanding of what's happening and why. In a way I've played a role in recent events."

"You're part of the conspiracy?" Haggerty said, startled.

"Mostly I'm an observer," Svoboda answered calmly. "But I may be responsible for Max Jennings, who is responsible for this *conspiracy*, as you call it. I first met him when I was demonstrating against one of Antonio Stelwyn's companies, North American Health Initiatives. Young Max was a rising star in their chemtech division."

"I would swear he's under thirty," Haggerty asserted. "That's too young to be legally employed."

"There have been exceptions to child labor laws almost as long as those laws have existed, Mr. Haggerty. It is rare, but corporations pick off the best and the brightest from our top universities from time to time, offering them full-time work for a fraction of what they pay legal adults. Max impressed the right people while he was still in school, and the required exemptions were duly processed."

"It couldn't have been Stelwyn. I don't think he knows Max worked for him," Haggerty said.

"You're probably right," Svoboda said. "There was no need

to involve him in a routine business transaction. Max developed a competing drug, which he refused to abandon and refused to give to his employers. So he was terminated. It's doubtful Antonio Stelwyn even knew about it.

"Young Max was the breadwinner in his family. His parents put everything they had into Max's education, and as a result of his success they were living well above their means. Their savings quickly dried up, and they used my damned invention to end their lives—the same invention manufactured by Stelwyn's company."

There was the connection between Stelwyn and BBI. "Was there no insurance?" Haggerty asked.

"If there was, it can't have been much," Svoboda said. "Max came to me with nothing but the clothes on his back."

"And Max blames Stelwyn," Haggerty concluded.

"Very good, Mr. Haggerty."

"Max became part of your colony?"

"I took him in and mentored him," Svoboda acknowledged. "It seemed the perfect opportunity to save someone like myself from the mistakes I'd made."

"And you failed miserably," Haggerty pointed out harshly.

"I did not know the whole story at that point, Mr. Haggerty. Max presented himself to me as wanting to make a difference in the world. I realized too late that his goals were actually vengeance and personal gain. I provided him refuge until he could find the means to achieve them. Then he perverted my teachings against the system and used them for his own ends.

"The philosophy of the Indivisibles is that the system has gone against the natural order and our nation has divided itself. We have therapies to extend our lives indefinitely but not the resources to support the population our longer lifespans create. Our young have been relegated to second-class citizenship with no hope of meaningful employment or purpose to their lives. Black boxes provide a too-easy solution. I offer the young an alternative. I'm training them to be productive members of society."

"Productive or destructive?"

"As part of the present system in America, you might well call it destructive, Mr. Haggerty. But I'm training them to be of service to the world and to the future, teaching them the technology that can transform society here and around the globe. Some of them will achieve positions in this country eventually, and promote the sanctity of life. Those who choose to refuse infertility can come here, as you've seen. Many go to the third world, to bring others the hope of transformation and ultimately reversing the devastation our predecessors wrought."

"You send them into exile, to grow old, risk illness, and die?"

"It's the only place where they are granted permission to be productive *now*, Mr. Haggerty. The only place they can find fulfillment and meaning. And it is their choice."

"Meanwhile you remain here and continue your telemor treatments, living off the fruits of their labor?"

"My purpose is to help as many as I can, and for now that requires that I live as long as possible. That's my penance for creating the black box. I used to believe that everyone should live forever if we could make it possible, and where has that gotten us? Regina told me that she explained to you the decline in mankind's lifespan as recorded in the Bible. But telemor treatments do not naturally regenerate the body. Stop the treatments and the aging process reasserts itself. My goal is to make the world livable for everyone, so that ultimately the planet is no longer divided and all people are truly equal. That will probably take longer than I already have lived or am likely to survive, but that is my destiny now. And the first step is to change the system as it now exists."

"So Max engineered a staged suicide to inspire hundreds or thousands more to bring down BBI?"

"It seems that is the method he chose," Svoboda said, "and unfortunately his plan is already succeeding. Over eight hundred young people in Asia and Europe alone have taken their lives."

Haggerty felt like he'd been struck. "Because of the media coverage?" he said weakly.

"The news media has been quite responsible," Svoboda said. "They instituted a blackout, due in great part to your late friend's eloquent plea to the Surgeon General."

"Doug got word to the Surgeon General?" That might clear Consuela, Haggerty thought.

"He did. But nothing hides from the Net. Recordings were uploaded to the Indranet almost as fast as the presses were broadcast. The most horrific act involved the president of the Clone Jesus fan club in Tokyo, who rallied nearly fifty children to death by drug overdose after he pressed an illegally acquired black box. The reports have been accelerating since sunrise on the East Coast, three hours ago. There are four hundred confirmed suicides here in the States."

"The census bureau reports an average of two-hundred-twenty-six suicides per day in the U.S.," Elsa stated. "This number, although significantly elevated, is not in line with your projections."

"Those numbers relate to the elderly," Svoboda said. "Not to children. The numbers we are seeing now are cumulative and instantly available on the Indranet to any user. Media coverage is irrelevant. One suicide sparks another."

"Suicide contagion," Haggerty said.

"Precisely," Svoboda said.

"But why is Max doing this?" Haggerty asked.

"I taught Max that BBI must fall, and he realized that bringing them down would not only give him his revenge but enrich him far, far more than the Last Supper Club ever could. He's got truckloads of Happy Styx all over the country, ready to supply the demand for a fast, easy, *pleasurable* way to die. And you will be blamed for all the deaths."

"Why me?"

"Max decided you were his best bet to take the fall, and began to study you in depth. If you had pressed last night as he predicted, prior to the concert, things would have gone quite smoothly for him. Instead, you took over the investigation."

"And how exactly do you know all this?" Haggerty demanded, digging at his thumb to quash the ants.

"I have been following Max's activities since I became aware of his true character. I discovered that he was profiling you and realized that I should find out why he was so interested. The best way to do that was to crack Elsa. You know the rest."

The rest being that Haggerty had this man—and Regina—to thank for saving his life and enabling him to figure out what was happening.

"How the hell did he engineer all this?" Haggerty asked. "He's just a kid."

"He created the most addictive euphoric drug I know of. But he needed capital to get started. I understand that he approached the Triads first. They laughed at him. What use was an addictive drug that eliminated the potential for repeat customers? Finally he found someone—I still don't know who it was—and set up the Last Supper Club. The Triads had no objection to offering protection after that, and Max's association with them provided access to celebrities. At which point he hatched his master plan."

"And chose the number one band on the charts to help deliver," Haggerty added, "then used them to befriend Stelwyn's son." He rubbed his right thumb against the knuckle of his index finger compulsively. "Can I have more water?" he asked Svoboda, the cup trembling in his hand.

Elsa looked at him intently as he downed the refill. Time was passing and he needed more answers.

"Do you know how agent Corbin's involved?"

"Nia Corbin was here for a time as well. She and Max were classmates. She's twenty-three years old."

That explained the blisterbrands on her body. Plastiche could work both ways, but Haggerty was surprised at how completely he'd been fooled. Whoever had aged her was a master. If Doug had discovered her true age during psycheval, it supplied a plausible motive for his murder.

"So they both know about this place?" he said.

Svoboda nodded.

"You don't see that as a threat?"

"They know that I won't move directly against them. When the system falls and they rise to take its place, they know I'll be there peacefully protesting."

"Are you in league with Max and Corbin?" Haggerty demanded. "Have you purposely engineered *any* of this?"

Svoboda met his gaze unflinchingly. "No," he said.

Haggerty looked to Elsa. "He is telling the truth as he knows it," she said.

"What are you planning to do to help stop Max?" he asked Svoboda.

"Nothing," Svoboda said calmly.

Haggerty stared in disbelief. "You can't just let thousands of children die!"

"More like tens of thousands, Mr. Haggerty," Svoboda said. "But there is nothing that can be done. You misunderstand what's happening. This isn't merely a reaction—it's a correction."

The ants danced fire over Haggerty's skin. "What the hell are you talking about?" he said.

"In the sixth century B.C. the Chinese philosopher Confucius came down from his mountain retreat at the request of the Emperor to bless the kingdom. At the end of a meal with the royal family, Confucius offered the following blessing: 'Grandfather die, father die, son die.' Interpreting this as a curse, the Emperor had Confucius imprisoned. After many months, a follower of

Confucius risked his own life by telling the Emperor that he had misunderstood what Confucius had said, that it is indeed a blessing when the natural order of death is upheld. When the grandfather dies first, the father second, and the son third, all is as it should be. If the order is changed, some unnatural tragedy has occurred."

"And what is the relevance here?"

"The relevance is that we as a society have been breaking the natural order for over a century. The grandfathers and fathers *aren't* dying, and the sons basically are being raised as a slave class. CC status gets harder and harder to come by, and soon the Gen-Ohs won't be able to procreate at all. It's an affront to nature that can only end in genocide. But Nature will have her way. Max is just a catalyst that was bound to come along at some point, if not now then ten or twenty years from now. I doubt he fully understands his part in all of this. We're about to witness an event that has never occurred before in human history."

"You're one of the grandfathers who refuses to die," Haggerty snarled. "You say it's for a greater purpose, but these kids are copycatting a triple homicide. What greater purpose can that possibly serve?"

"Simply this, Mr. Haggerty. The old refuse to die in a country short on space and resources, and the young people—responding to some deep-seated drive that holds racial survival over personal survival—are going to die for them. And when the parents of those young people find that their only child is dead, the child they waited years and years for permission to have, what do you think will happen? Elsa, please give us statistics on parental suicides in the U.S. following the deaths of only children."

Elsa looked to Haggerty, who nodded, dreading what he was about to hear.

"Two out of five parents of one child commit suicide when that child suffers accidental death," Elsa stated. "When the child commits suicide, the rate rises to four out of five parents within two years after the child's death."

Haggerty's own experience told him this was true. He closed his eyes in pain.

"Grieving parents will start pressing your little black buttons in droves, Mr. Haggerty," Svoboda continued relentlessly. "And when it's over, the population will be corrected. The chinks in the system will be revealed, and that system will finally be abolished."

"Enough!" Haggerty cried. "You're as insane as Max is, willing to sacrifice generations for your own ends."

"Not true, Mr. Haggerty. It grieves me profoundly that this is going to happen. But it will happen. I couldn't stop it if I tried."

"Why do you insist that this *will* happen?"

"For the simple reason that Generation Zero *wants* to die, Mr. Haggerty." Svoboda took a small hypersteel box from a cabinet and extracted two gleaming metal disks from it. "Let me send you to my source—the Indranet."

"A prophecy off the Net is what's causing your reluctance to stop this?"

"Surely you're not such a neophobe," Svoboda said. "The Net embodies the collective consciousness of millions of people and in turn provides acute intuition. Find out for yourself why I believe what I do."

He offered the disks to Haggerty.

Haggerty grimaced. He had no desire to interface with the Indranet, but understanding the Indran "prophecy" was his best hope for finding something that would persuade Svoboda to help him stop the looming disaster.

"Is it like Regina's rig? The one we used—"

"That was nerve impulse transfer. This is EEG."

"Will it impair my thinking?"

"No," Svoboda said. "It's like linking, with the addition of visual." He adhered the cold metal disks to Haggerty's temples. "Close your eyes. It will be too confusing if they're open."

A jolt of connectivity, an explosion of cognition. Haggerty entered a realm of light. He was sitting on the jutting lip of a stone fountain in a crowded plaza amid thousands of dark-skinned Indrans, their tektronic implants flashing as they scuttled past him. Haggerty assumed it was a simulation of somewhere in India. He ran his finger against the crude stone; the rough surface abraded his skin. He examined his thumb, pleased that the ants had abated. This was beyond virtual reality, unlike any Net interface he'd ever experienced. This was total immersion.

A young boy scampered barefoot across the dusty ground to him, his dark eyes fixing Haggerty with a haunted stare. Haggerty took in the ragged shorts held up by a belt of frayed rope and the boy's thin frame and scabbed knees, the cyberoptic pulsations in his transparent skullcap.

"Parsing," the boy said. "New User detected. Do you grant and accept full reciprocal access?"

"Yes," Haggerty said.

"Authenticating ... initiating feed."

The world shimmered. Haggerty was sitting on a rock in the desert, the sky a predawn array of vibrant color. The boy was gone, though Haggerty sensed his presence. A group of extraordinary beings materialized in a semicircle before him.

"Choose your avatar," the boy's voice said.

Avatars—guides and searchers manifesting as religious icons. Haggerty considered them one by one. He recognized Jesus, Buddha, and Mohammed. Some seemed familiar but he couldn't quite name them. A matronly woman in voluminous robes smiled gently and revealed wordlessly, *I am the Great Mother. Ganesh*, roared a giant with an elephant's head. A green-skinned woman with a half-dozen arms whispered *Tara*.

"Please choose your avatar," the boy's voice repeated.

Haggerty extended a hand to Jesus.

"Scanning ... ," the boy's voice came again. "You are not authorized to interface with Christ consciousness."

Haggerty was surprised. One of his great-grandfathers had been an Episcopalian minister. What would he have made of Christ's rejection of his great-grandson?

The boy intuited Haggerty's thoughts. "Not rejection. This is a matter of linguistic symbolism, not theology. May we determine a compatible avatar?"

"Anything to move things along," Haggerty said.

"Scanning ... initiating interface ..."

All but one of the figures dissolved, an emaciated, sienna-skinned man in a loincloth and toga-like sash and sandals, who walked with the aid of a staff. Haggerty recognized his wide toothless smile, steel-rimmed spectacles, mustache, and bald forehead from numerous holoreps.

"Greetings, Mr. Haggerty," he said jovially. "My name is Mohandas Gandhi. I'll be your guide."

"A pleasure," Haggerty said.

Gandhi sat down on a nearby rock and regarded him. "You appear to be suffering grave chemical addiction," he said.

"How can you tell?" Haggerty asked.

"You granted full access," Gandhi said. "I see not only your current physical feedback but your entire data history as well. Every log-on, keystroke, purchase, or report you have ever made.

Any entry made regarding you, on any database, throughout your life."

Gandhi blinked rapidly; Haggerty's eyes allowed in a slit of light from the real world and for a moment the desert sky became translucent. He thought he saw his data-life flashing by in coded bytes. He tightened his eyelids and the illusion regained solidity.

"I see you have had many traumas," Gandhi continued, "witnessed many disturbing things but have carried on well. You are wondering why I was chosen to guide you."

Haggerty nodded.

"In grade school, you did a research report on passive resistance. Even as a young man you understood that the nonviolent activist, while willing to die for his cause, is never willing to kill. That is why you have chosen the path you now follow."

"But I'm an investigator, not an activist," Haggerty said.

"Are you? From my vantage it appears that although in your career you pose as an advocate for self-destruction, your innermost voice cries out against it. That is the crux of your dilemma."

Haggerty's stomach twisted. "You disapprove of me, of my work."

Gandhi spread his arms lovingly. "I disapprove of violence, whether committed upon oneself or against others. About what do you seek knowledge?"

"I wish to find out if the claim made by Joseph Svoboda that thousands of Generation Zero children are predetermined fatalities is true. Do they indeed *want* to die?"

"Scanning ... ," Gandhi said. "There are 274,403,856 young people between the ages of ten and twenty-five currently accessible online who fit the median definition of Generation Zero. I shall initiate a poll through available media, translate, sort, and buffer the results for you. This may take several moments."

The idea that it might be possible to extrapolate the course of action of an entire generation dizzied Haggerty. At last, Gandhi spoke.

"They are despondent, there is much despair, they are indeed collectively suicidal, but they are awaiting instructions," he said sadly.

"Instructions from whom? The lead singer of Clone Jesus?"

Gandhi blinked twice. "There is a divergence. Two possible outcomes. One comes from him. The other comes from you."

"That's impossible," Haggerty said.

"Nonetheless it is true."

Haggerty stared intently at the wrinkled old prophet and saw bytes of data stream across his spectacles.

"Warning," Gandhi said. "Your chemical addiction is about to sever this connection."

"Wait!" Haggerty pleaded. "Tell me what happens, about Max—
"

"There is a stage like a traffic intersection," Gandhi said. His body shimmered. "Max is like an enraged driver speeding toward that intersection, intent on causing an accident. You will discover yourself as a source of that rage."

"Can I stop him?" Haggerty asked. Silverfish leaped from the sand.

"At great personal cost," Gandhi answered. "And even as you do, you find the speeding car is now driven by another, with even darker designs. You find yourself detained but not restrained by a man on a leash, a man you trust but cannot trust."

"But I can stop this ... this *accident* Max wants to cause?" Haggerty cried.

"Perhaps ..." Gandhi's image flickered in and out. His final words were digital wind: "The Indranet honors the part you shall play... ."

Haggerty opened his eyes and vomited his stomach contents onto the sand floor of Svoboda's quarters. Elsa was immediately beside him, peeling the disks from his temples.

"Jason, what's wrong?"

Svoboda stood above him. "Do you believe me now, Mr. Haggerty?"

"It doesn't have to happen as you say it will," Haggerty spat.

"History and the future disagree with you," Svoboda said. "A phoenix cannot rise except from its own ashes."

Get me out of here, Elsa, Haggerty linked. *Now!*

Chapter Ten
PURGING THE SYSTEM

Regina broke away from the group of people she was talking to as Elsa half carried Haggerty out of Svoboda's quarters. He collapsed against a nearby mobile home. Moments later Regina was kneeling at his side.

"What's wrong with him?" she asked Elsa.

"I'm not sure," Elsa replied. "He began to throw up as he was accessing the Indranet. He appears feverish."

"Did you uplink with full immersion, Jason?" Regina asked.

Haggerty nodded weakly.

"He must be suffering system separation," she told Elsa. "It hits some people harder than others."

Older people, Haggerty guessed she meant. The ants were massing for an all-out assault.

"Come to my room."

He held out his hand, motioning Regina back as wave after wave of nausea passed over him. He tried to stagger to his feet. Elsa and Regina helped him stand. He concentrated on breathing, suppressing his need to vomit. He finally regained his footing as they passed through the makeshift square where a dozen or so people sat watching the viewscreen.

"It's a live feed off Indra," Regina explained.

The split screen held two images. On one side was a teenage boy with tears streaming down his face. Beside it was a picture of a pretty young girl holding a violin. "'I can offer nothing but my death,'" the boy read from a sheet of notepaper. "'I choose to represent the muse in the music and the dead in the dedication. Love, Samantha.' Those were my girlfriend's last words. I was holding her hand while she pressed. The media doesn't think she's important, but I want everyone to know. She died for the cause."

Haggerty's stomach knotted painfully. Ants dug trenches through his neural pathways. "Let's keep moving," he said.

Regina shifted to accept more of his weight. She stopped

before a small wooden cabin and pulled back a curtain of strung shells at the entrance. The cabin was smaller than the pairplex she shared in the city, its one modest room divided by curtains into smaller spaces with bare walls and a sand floor. She set him down on her small foam cot.

"Rest here while I make some tea. Then I want to hear all about what you experienced online."

Haggerty sent Elsa to keep watch outside. He glanced around the room. A makeshift nightstand that looked like it was made from antique auto parts held an airboard, a remote access terminal—and a flute, of all things. How little he knew about this girl who had insinuated herself so easily into his life.

Regina ignited a burner in a partially curtained-off alcove. "It's Valerian Root," she said over her shoulder. "Best thing for system separation. Sedates your overstimulated neural network."

Haggerty began to shiver. The ants were closing in for the kill. "Where's your bathroom?" he asked.

"Behind that other curtain," she answered. "It's just a hole in the ground—be forewarned."

The few short feet felt like yards. He managed to drag himself through the curtain. His stomach wrenched at the sight of the hole in the floor. He leaned back, watching Regina prepare his tea through the curtain. He reached in his cargo pants for the white unit, staring at it. If he pressed again, the unit would empty, perhaps leaving only traces of evidence behind. Would it be enough to make the case? Could he justify leaving nothing but trace evidence when he had a full sample, far more useful, far more persuasive, in his hands?

But could he risk the erosion of his own ability to concentrate, to reason, that craving the drug would bring?

Haggerty watched in dull horror as his trembling finger reached for the button. He'd sworn to himself he wouldn't. He'd sworn on his son's grave. But he couldn't seem to stop himself. How many lives were at stake if he failed to make his case because of insufficient evidence? Or would the failure to clear his mind be what put them at risk?

And then it didn't matter, because his finger was on the button and even though he told himself he wouldn't, couldn't, even as he recoiled at the betrayal ... he pressed. The reader clicked up to "7" as the box emptied.

Ecstasy rocketed through his system; he bit his hand to stifle a scream. The pleasure went on and on, sweeping away the ants.

"Jason, are you all right in there?" Regina's voice called from a great distance.

A jangle of strung shells as the curtain jerked back. Haggerty reached out with the hand that held the white unit, his eyes glazed and pupils enlarged, his slack mouth contorted in a foolish grin.

Regina slapped it away. "How could you!" she said fiercely. "And here in my space!" She flung herself onto the cot.

"You don't understand. I was forced to take it and now I'm sick and weak. I can't concentrate without it. I held out as long as I could but I need it to function."

"What's in that box killed my brother," she sobbed. "Now you're going to die too. Why do I have to lose everybody?"

Haggerty sat beside her and took her hands. "Listen, Regina ... *Dawn*. I know what it's like to lose someone you love."

"But it's my fault. If I hadn't brought Sunset here, he'd never have met Max. He never would have pressed."

"You have survivor's guilt, Regina," he said.

She wiped the tears roughly from her face. "What are you, some kind of psychologist?"

"I'm a fellow survivor," he whispered. "Because of me my son, my mother, and my wife are dead." The drug sent him reeling off the cot onto the floor.

Regina knelt by his side, concern written on her face.

"Two years ago I was promoted to the highest rank and got a sizable raise," he said. "I bought Lorraine the new suite of furniture she'd been wanting and a week at a spa resort, bought my son that huge viewscreen, got myself an expensive sportscar. Figured I'd earned it. I thought I'd take my mom and son out for a spin. Lorraine wasn't getting back from the spa until later that afternoon. Dad was golfing. It didn't matter. I could show off for them later. Mom didn't want to go but I insisted. I'd had a few drinks and a dose of Sky, and flipped the controls over to manual. I bragged about buying another one for Dad but Mom said he didn't need it.

" 'Buy one for me!' Josh said, and we all laughed.

" 'Don't think so, sport,' I told him. 'Do you want to give her a spin?'

"Mom thought it was a bad idea. I reminded her that Josh had his license and we changed places. Autodrive would have handled it fine but I was so wasted, I let my son have manual control.

"Josh breezed around a slotted car that was moving too slow for his taste. He swerved a hair, maybe an inch or so, over the line and into the opposite lane of traffic. The car's internal warning sounded—scaring Josh. He jerked the yoke, sending the car reeling across the lane to the guardrail. Then the car leaped and flipped ..."

The sounds of broken glass and grating steel reverberated in his overstimulated head.

"When I told Lorraine, she just walked into our bedroom. By the time I got there, she'd already pressed. Dad said it was an accident but he couldn't live without Mom. I watched him try for a year—until the anniversary. He couldn't pretend anymore. He went out into the desert and killed himself with an antique shotgun. He'd come to despise the black box as the easy way out. I found him at our cabin. BBI helped me cover up his illegal suicide. In the end I'd killed them all."

"Oh, Jason," she said softly, "I'm so sorry. That's why you wanted to press, isn't it?"

"You still think I don't grok what you're going through?" Hot tears coated his cheeks.

She took his face in her hands and kissed him softly, deeply.

Haggerty began shaking. He pulled back, his face ashen. His heart pounded in his chest. His throat went dry. His stomach spasmed. He began heaving.

"Jason, what's wrong?" Regina asked.

He gripped his shoulders, tumbled backward, and convulsed in the sand.

"Elsa!" Regina yelled frantically. "We've got to get Jason to the infirmary!"

"It's a pleasure to meet you in person, young man," the woman said, shining a laserlight into Haggerty's eyes. "I'm Annette, Joe's wife."

Haggerty was lying on a makeshift examination table with an old-style IV tube in his arm. The infirmary was larger and much better equipped than he would have expected in a wilderness outpost. His spasms had quelled although his dose hand continued to twitch. The cramps had subsided. "Nice to meet you too, ma'am," he said hoarsely, his throat raw.

Like her husband, Annette Svoboda appeared to be in her prime. A handsome woman with dark blonde hair, she was dressed in one of the ubiquitous robes the colony favored, though hers was embellished with colorful embroidery at the neck, hem, and sleeves. Haggerty couldn't resist asking if she were anywhere near her husband's age.

"Lord, no! Joe's a baby. I was a hundred-sixty-three last month." She took a blood sample, put a few drops into a tube, and watched the reaction. "But let's not worry about my age right now. I don't like what I see in this tube. What have you been doing to yourself?"

Regina spared Haggerty the necessity of explaining.

"If you need a sample of the drug," Elsa told the doctor, "I have one."

"No," Haggerty said weakly. "It's evidence."

"What's it gonna be, son?" Annette asked him. "You want me to keep you going or not?"

Haggerty covered his face with a hand and nodded.

Elsa produced a tube from one of her ports. "Is it enough?" she asked Annette.

"Should be," Annette replied.

She pipetted drops into tubes of her own, frowning as she watched the reaction. She moved to the machine displays, then correlated data at her computer.

"If that stuff isn't the devil's work, there's no devil," she pronounced. "I won't go into the whole array of effects, but, basically, this drug works selectively on nerve cells, stimulating pleasurable sensations."

"I'd noticed," Haggerty said.

"Trouble is, the nerve cells become overloaded, leading to violent convulsions and death. I think I can fix you up, at least for a day or two. But you are going to have a full system flush the moment this crisis is over, is that understood, young man?"

"Yes, ma'am," Haggerty whispered.

"Never seen such a high concentration of celtrex before. You've got a whole pharmacy load in there fighting for you. I'm sure it helped prolong the interval between doses and probably saved your life, but it wasn't nearly enough on its own. We need to help it out, and I have something that might do the trick."

The smile with which she graced Haggerty was even more intimidating than her scowl. Haggerty could not help wondering what Doug would have thought to hear this.

"Shall we get rid of that temp plastiche job while we're at it?" she said.

"Please do," Regina answered for him.

Haggerty nodded consent.

"Your new face is all over the newscasts, so it's useless as a disguise," Annette said. "It's starting to peel, anyway."

Annette withdrew two steel containers and two syringes from a cabinet and returned to Haggerty's side. "All right, then," she said. "After the therapy we take care of the plastiche." She flipped open the first container, extracted a vial, and filled a syringe.

Haggerty eyed it uneasily. "And the therapy is ... ?"

"Two things," she said matter-of-factly, rolling up his shirt sleeve and swabbing his biceps with antiseptic. "The first is something to counter the stimulation causing the damage. It'll stop the convulsions, slow your heart, allow your system to get back to equilibrium. Once we get you to that stage, we use the second thing to make sure your heart doesn't get so slow it stops beating, among other things. The second thing's nothing to worry about, just a highly effective, highly specific antivenin. Your geno-immunizations should provide all the protection you need from the first thing until I can use the second."

Haggerty looked at her warily as she stuck the needle into his arm. "And the first thing is ... ?"

"Rattlesnake venom," she said dryly, pushing the plunger.

Annette had given Haggerty a healthy dose of painkillers once she'd satisfied herself that the venom and the antivenin had done their work. The ants were gone but Haggerty felt lousy. All things considered he preferred the ants. At least he was wearing his own face again, though his skin was still patchy and felt raw. He'd taken a few minutes to shower, after which he dressed in retro-denims and a T-shirt Regina scrounged together from the colonists. He was in desperate need of sleep he wasn't going to get and was cleaner rather than truly clean, but he was in far better shape than he'd been when he arrived at the settlement.

"Take these," Annette said, handing him a container of pills as he readied to leave the infirmary. "They're maximum-dose celtrex. Take one every half hour until you can get yourself flushed."

Haggerty wouldn't complain about that. He poured the tablets into his pillcase and popped it closed.

Svoboda entered the infirmary with a burly blond associate and kissed Annette. "It appears Mr. Haggerty has been tracked," he said. "Antonio Stelwyn is on his way here as we speak. I'm debating full evacuation of this camp."

"It's all right," Haggerty said. "He's on my side."

"But not on *my* side," Svoboda snapped. "I can't have this location known to him. I have people to protect."

Haggerty bit back his irritation. Whatever his feelings about Svoboda and his decision not to act, he wished the colonists no harm.

"I'm sorry," he said. "The pod must be rigged with a trace." He gave a short bark of laughter.

"You find the situation funny?" Svoboda said.

"I'm imagining you giving Stelwyn the scenario you gave me— and how he'll react to it."

Annette placed a supportive hand on her husband's shoulder. He didn't have much choice if Stelwyn already had the camp coordinates.

Svoboda turned to his burly blond subordinate. "Contact Stelwyn. Scramble the satellite relays and bring him in cloaked. Put everyone on evacuation standby."

The man nodded and left.

Svoboda turned to Haggerty. "You've put us at great risk."

"Welcome to the party," Haggerty said. "If the rest of the country is in half the peril you predict, why should you be insulated? What's the situation out there?"

"The news blackout has failed. Word of the triple press and the suicides that followed has saturated the Net. Governor Benfield has bowed to the inevitable, lifting the blackout and allowing news coverage, using spin as damage control. It's not working, of course. The copycats are increasing. We're trying to get hard numbers but we're having difficulty."

"Maybe Elsa can help with that," Haggerty said.

Haggerty, Elsa, and Regina followed Svoboda to the square. On the viewscreen throngs of angry protesters demanded that BBI give up those responsible for supplying the Junior Citizens with the units and suspend its activities during the course of the Federal investigation.

"How's it coming, Ricardo?" Svoboda asked the young man busy at a remote-access terminal hardwired into the exposed groundwire.

"It's hard to sort through the data," Ricardo answered. "So much of it is clutter and repeats of the same incidents."

"Can you use this terminal to access the nationwide BBI boards?" Haggerty asked Elsa.

"I'm not sure," she said. "My log-in would give central control my coordinates."

"Not if you're using PE," Svoboda said. "We can leapfrog your access all over our network."

"How shall I interface?" she asked.

"Let me see your prongs," Svoboda said.

Elsa raised her left hand and extended her two middle fingers; twin prongs snapped upward from the tips.

"Those are RJ," Svoboda said. "We'll need an adapter to convert her from masscapture down to sinewave."

"Whatcha got under the hood, darlin'?" Ricardo asked Elsa.

She looked at him quizzically.

"What model are you?" he rephrased. "Archimedes or Descartes?"

"I'm a Marcus," she replied, almost proudly.

Ricardo whistled appreciatively. "Hot rod," he said. "I think I've got an adapter in my shop that will work." He went to check on it.

Onscreen the viewcaster reported, "Federal agent Keenan has issued warrants for the arrest of Jason P. Haggerty, the BBI employee suspected—"

The transmission broke up. A grainy image of a young man appeared. "We interrupt the latest government propaganda to bring you the *real* news," he said. "Here's why you don't want a Killswitch, folks."

"Pirate broadcast," Svoboda explained.

The boy's image was replaced by that of a pretty girl no more than fifteen standing in what looked like a wooded area, holding an armed KV unit. She was clearly distraught. The transmission kept breaking up, making it difficult to hear what she said.

"... what does any of it ... too much ... showed me the way. Is this my answer?" The girl stared at the box, tears brimming over. "Is this what I—" A coughing spasm shook her; her finger convulsed on the button.

Her eyes widened as she dropped the box, which kept recording from where it fell to the ground, a dizzying angle.

"I didn't mean to!" she cried as she collapsed face to face beside the box; the lens focused on her wide brown eyes glazing over as the toxin took effect. "I'm so sorry—"

The transmission cut off. The grainy image of the young man reappeared briefly before the "legitimate" viewcast reasserted itself.

"We apologize for these continued interruptions," the

viewcaster said. "Federal officials are taking steps to locate the source of the illegal broadcasts. Representatives from BBI assure us the recording is not authentic but was likely engineered by one of the so-called Ban the Box groups who oppose the use of the Kevorkian unit. So far no one has claimed responsibility. In other news ..."

"Why would BBI assume that the recording is not authentic?" Elsa said.

"Because it's in their interest to say that it isn't. Clearly it's real," Haggerty said.

"Instructions on how to crack the boxes and retrieve the recordings are circulating the Net," Svoboda said.

"Whoever gave the order to cover things up will probably claim it's to keep a lid on the panic," Haggerty said bitterly. He'd come across such things from time to time in his career. The presses were always judged accidental and were so rare as to be acceptable, however tragic. This was different. This child's death was not an isolated, regrettable incident but part of a much larger picture purposely shrouded from public view.

Haggerty felt ashamed. For decades he had accepted the use of a device that made suicide easy. He was part of what was going on. The idea that more young people might get caught up in the suicide contagion, regret their decision, and be unable to reverse it appalled him.

"What's the usual time frame for copycats after a publicized suicide?" he asked Elsa.

"It varies," she said. "The statistical majority occur within the first day, usually within the first few hours, depending on commitment level and access to means of expiration. It tapers off considerably after that, the percentages decreasing over twenty percent per hour, seventy-five percent per day, corresponding in most cases to level of media saturation."

Ricardo jogged back. "Try this," he said, catching his breath and handing a palm-sized electronic device to Elsa. "And we'll pray you don't fry out the terminal." He offered her a stool to sit on.

Elsa fitted the device onto her finger prongs and slid the end into the requisite port. "I shall need instruction," she said.

"Get a feel for it first," Svoboda said. "See how the bit rate comes through at irregular intervals?"

"Highly compressed packets of data unfolding in waveform as they decode."

"Beautifully put," Svoboda said. "Try to create a packet yourself, reversing the process."

"I understand," she said, surprising him. The BBI gateway appeared on the monitor and requested authorization. "Inferior to standard modes of encryption but quite admirable considering you are piggybacking on preexisting technology not designed for this purpose." The terminal began synching and taking in data. "We're inside," she said.

"Get us reports on all national pressage from the moment of the live broadcast until now," Haggerty ordered.

"Processing," she said.

Regina gripped Haggerty's shirt sleeve.

"Fourteen presses overnight across all zones and forty-six presses nationwide since nine a.m. Eastern Standard Time, eighty-nine percent of them from geographical locations in the Eastern time zone."

"You said we were already seeing deaths in the hundreds," Haggerty accused Svoboda.

"I'll be more than happy to be proven wrong," Svoboda said. "But those are only the East Coast numbers, and only the suicides that utilized BBI equipment. It's a Sunday afternoon. Kids are inventive and that type of data is slow to report.

"Aside from utilizing BBI equipment, all other methods of suicide combined average two to seven hundred against termination by press," Elsa said. "Based on that fact I find your predictions unsound."

"Be that as it may, it's been seventeen hours since the press," Svoboda went on. "Twelve hours since the first cracks began appearing in the news blackout, five hours since the news went viral. I believe you will see an exponential increase in those numbers by this evening."

Haggerty winced. "Keep monitoring, Elsa," he said. "Let us know if there's any spike."

"Affirmative, Jason," she said.

"I'll teach her a few tricks to access what we need on the Net," Ricardo offered.

Svoboda walked Haggerty out of earshot. "I'm concerned about Stelwyn," he said, crossing his arms. "I'm also concerned about you knowing what's going on here." He indicated a woman leading a toddler with one hand, an infant strapped to her chest, who crossed nearby and flashed them a timid smile. "I have it on good authority that you'll be interacting with Federal agents when you leave here."

"Trust me," Haggerty said. "Even if your predictions are wrong, I won't be trotting back to my old post."

"What if I offered you a place in my colony?"

"This is a bit different from the lifestyle I'm accustomed to."

"There are benefits," Svoboda said. "Have you thought about having more children? I know that can't make up for the loss you've endured, but it can help you to heal, give you new purpose. There are dozens of beautiful women here who want to be mothers. I'm sure Regina would be more than willing to conceive by you."

"An interesting offer," Haggerty said. "But I'm infertile."

"Annette has an excellent track record of reversing the procedure," Svoboda said.

"I don't think producing a family is the most responsible thing I could do right now."

"It's not irresponsible either," Svoboda said. "We've simply taken back the rights this government denied us: control over our own bodies and how we live our lives. Not all of us live in the compound and not everyone in our organization chooses parenthood. But we are capable of providing for every child born here."

"I'll keep your offer in mind," Haggerty said. "Whatever I decide, I don't plan on turning you in."

"Not today," Svoboda said. "What about tomorrow?"

"Svoboda!" a voice shouted angrily.

Antonio Stelwyn strode across the sand toward them with two dark-suited giants flanking him on either side. Svoboda tentatively extended his hand in greeting. Stelwyn slugged him in the face, sending Svoboda sprawling. Once he was down, Stelwyn kicked Svoboda in the stomach.

"That's for introducing that sycophant to my son, you sonofabitch!"

Haggerty stepped back, unwilling to intervene. A dozen women rushed to see what the commotion was about. The guards closed ranks to enable Stelwyn to beat Svoboda without interference.

Stelwyn hoisted Svoboda roughly to his feet, only to floor him again with punches to the stomach and kidneys. "It's about time you took responsibility for your actions," he shouted.

"You don't know the first thing about taking responsibility,"

Svoboda spat back through bloodied lips. "Not with the companies you own, and not with your only son."

Stelwyn kicked him in the face but Svoboda recovered.

"You think you're so powerful but you're as much a pawn of the system as Haggerty. You could have had a dozen children and you only had one. Now you've lost him to one of your own disgruntled workers."

Stelwyn pulled out the antique revolver and aimed it at Svoboda. "Who the fuck do you think you are?"

"Hold on, hold on," Haggerty begged.

"How dare he imply that I'm responsible for Tyler's death," Stelwyn shouted.

"The truth hurts," Svoboda said. He coughed blood. "But before you shoot me, ask yourself if you're angry because you lost your son or because someone took something away from you."

Stelwyn ground his jaw; the veins of his temple pulsed. His knuckle went white on the trigger.

"Killing Svoboda won't bring Tyler back," Haggerty urged.

Stelwyn fired point blank into the sand beside Svoboda's face. Svoboda screamed.

"I want Max," Stelwyn seethed.

"Then put the gun away and help us work out where he is," Haggerty said.

Stelwyn holstered the ancient firearm. His bodyguards stepped back. Regina helped Svoboda to his feet.

"All right," Haggerty said. "Let's put our differences aside and see if we can get a handle on the situation."

Ricardo joined them. "You'll want to see this," he said, directing their attention to the viewscreen.

A viewcaster stood before the NewVada Central Stadium as crowds of people weaved in all directions behind him, assembling for the Superbowl. "Younger fans are desperately trying to buy scalped tickets since the announcement that the musical band Clone Jesus has petitioned to appear as scheduled in the halftime show."

The live feed cut to a media conference taped earlier, in some location Haggerty did not recognize. Shintag Lake, extravagant in black leather and red silk, sat with his attorney as half a dozen coms were thrust toward him by disembodied hands.

"I know I speak for the entire band when I say we are deeply saddened by the events that took place onstage last night, and for any of the young fans out there who would injure themselves because of it."

"Mister Lake," a viewcaster shouted, "your lead singer, Zephyr, seemed to condone the act last night!"

"Appearances are often deceiving," Lake stated calmly. "That is why Zephyr and the other band members wish so strongly to make this appearance today. They want to decry the violence and implore other children to stop hurting themselves."

"Mister Lake, who are you betting on?" another viewcaster yelled.

Lake smiled. "NewVada, of course."

The broadcast cut to a roped-off area outside the stadium where reporters pushed their coms toward Zephyr as dozens of JCs stood on the sidelines screaming his name. He looked tranquil, as if the events transpiring made no impression on him.

"I'm very sorry that some of our fans took such extreme actions last night," he said mechanically. "If you're listening, please stop and think before you act." His lack of conviction was palpable.

The transmission cut from the tape back to the live feed. "With the reported blessings of the Surgeon General himself," the viewcaster said, "Clone Jesus *will perform* in today's halftime show."

Haggerty turned away in disgust. Cherub had told him he would not decry the act, and now Lake had used that very word. Could the band truly just apologize and walk away from this unscathed?

"I don't care what they say," Regina told Haggerty. "They're part of the reason my brother and my friends are dead."

Haggerty pulled her close. She rested her head on his shoulder, glad for the silent support.

"In related news," the viewcaster continued, "there has not been a single reported suicide since it was announced that Clone Jesus would be granted permission to play."

Haggerty looked to Elsa; she ported back into the BBI system.

"It's true," she said. "There has not been a single light on board."

"They're waiting to hear from the band," Svoboda said.

"I'm going to stop this," Stelwyn said, pulling out his earset.

"Hold on," Haggerty said, noting the tension on Svoboda's face. If Stelwyn called from here, the settlement would be traceable. To what lengths would Svoboda go to avoid that? "Let's exercise that predictive mind of yours, Joe," he said. "What would you do in Max's situation, if your message wasn't heard loud enough to reach your goal?"

"I'm not culpable here, Mr. Haggerty," Svoboda said.

"I think it's safe to assume that Max, if he's still pulling the band's strings, would institute your methods," Haggerty responded. "So please indulge me."

"I'd reinforce the message in some peaceful manner," Svoboda said calmly.

"Last night at a JC dance club, someone was giving away tickets to the game. I thought they must be counterfeit. Now I'm not sure. I think Max wants to guarantee that the audience is filled with Clone Jesus fans at today's game. But not for any *peaceful* reason."

Svoboda lowered his head into his hands. "You're right," he said softly. "Both of you. I am responsible for this. I can see how Max's mind is working. He'll do it again. But harder, much more harshly. The children are waiting for further instructions."

"Can you get us into the Superbowl?" Haggerty asked Stelwyn.

"With no difficulty at all," Stelwyn answered. "I own the stadium."

"Are you coming, Joe?" Haggerty asked.

Svoboda shook his head sadly, stifling tears.

Haggerty had no sympathy for him. "I sincerely hope you'll reconsider getting involved," he said.

"I'm coming with you," Regina said firmly.

Haggerty opened his mouth to protest, then realized she needed to do something to strike a blow against the people who had taken her brother and her friends from her.

"I wouldn't dream of trying to stop you," he said, smiling crookedly.

Chapter Eleven
SUPERBOWL CXC

Regina reached for Haggerty's hand as the turbines kicked in and the multimillion-dollar stealth jetcraft fired off. Stelwyn was at the yoke, his bodyguards seated on either side of him. Haggerty watched the receding compound turn to sand beneath the floorview window. He needed to ascertain the situation at headquarters but had to wait until they were far enough away not to lead the authorities to Svoboda's door.

"How long until we can touch down at the stadium?" he asked Elsa.

"Approximately fourteen minutes, Jason, provided we can land at the coordinates Mr. Stelwyn suggests."

"We'll land all right," Stelwyn promised.

Regina handed Haggerty a small bottle of water and he dosed a celtrex. "Patch me through to the office," he told Elsa. "Tanner's line, visual on."

Elsa punched her codes into the small display comlink above her. Tanner looked like he had not slept and was none too pleased about it. Seeing Haggerty on his display, he spilled his coffee on his disheveled suit.

"Holy shit, Haggerty, do you have any idea—"

"Save it, Tanner. I'm not guilty. What's Corbin's status?"

"AWOL, same as you. Heard you tried to pin this on her."

There was no time to make his case to Tanner. "Are the Dragon and agent Keenan there?" he asked.

"In the boardroom. It's now the Federal command post dedicated to hanging your ass in a sling."

"I'll need you to transfer me, but first I'm calling in favors, Mitch."

"I'm all ears," Tanner said.

"I need whatever information you can give me on a double press for a couple named Jennings."

"Jenkins, double press?" Tanner said, tapping keys.

"Jennings, not Jenkins!"

"Don't get your panties in a wad. Jennings not Jenkins it is."
Tanner continued to tap keys. "Here it is. Uh-oh, it's a red flag."

"Criminal violation?" Haggerty said, surprised.

"Looks like," Tanner confirmed.

"No time for the full report. Just read me the epitaph."

"There's two," Tanner said. "First one's Mr. Brent Jennings, 98, and Mrs. Katherine Jennings, 95. Consecutive presses. Eulogic proceedings convened on September 12, 2152 by BBI agent William O'Connell. Both presses judged clean. Life insurance settlement to be placed in trust and paid in installments to surviving child, Maximilian Jennings."

Max's parents, Haggerty assumed. "Who was the insurance underwriter?" he asked.

"Cromwell and Sons."

Haggerty frowned. Cromwell and Sons was the biggest insurance firm in NewVada. They handled a large percentage of the cases Haggerty reviewed. Still, what were the odds they would be the agency in all three cases he'd become involved with in the past twenty-four hours: Nyuga-Rosenberg, Tyler Stelwyn, and now the Jennings double press?

"The second epitaph is from you," Tanner said.

The hair rose on the back of Haggerty's neck. He dug his fingernail into his thumb.

Tanner continued. "KV units exhumed for post-press revisit by senior agent Jason P. Haggerty due to suspicious stamp from the coroner. Mr. and Mrs. Brent Jennings. Consecutive presses judged clean. Date of death corrected to August 12th, 2152. Insurance policy voided. Jesus, Haggerty, you're a real bloodhound."

Haggerty remembered now. He'd reviewed the recordings multiple times, acting on a hunch. The parents had pressed legally but the dates reported were false. The original audio timestamp had been altered. Haggerty had caught it and correlated the actual press date with a pair of banshee lights on the board—one of the rare events where a circuit malfunction lit up a box that hadn't been used (BBI workers joked that such lights showed who was planning to press next). The Jennings couple's legal suicides had occurred before the allotted waiting period expired and Max, who had worked for the company that made the KV units, had rigged both the boxes and BBI's light boards. He'd also found a way to crack the coroner's records and cover his tracks. Haggerty's discovery had cost Max the proceeds of his parents' insurance policy.

"There was a criminal investigation pending but no follow-up here," Tanner said. "What's this got to do with anything?"

Haggerty recalled the avatar's words: *You will discover yourself as a source of that rage.* "I'll explain later," he told Tanner. "One more favor before you connect me to the boardroom. I need to know if these five individuals registered for boxes."

"Haggerty, this could be my ass... ."

"You owe me, Mitch."

"All right," Tanner grunted. "Gimme the first one."

"Elsa, read us the birth names of each of the members of Clone Jesus," Haggerty instructed.

"Processing," Elsa said. "Alphabetically by last name, the first is Bin Ibriham, Jaleel, aka Whisper."

"Negative," Tanner said, his fingers dancing over his boards. "Next."

"Howard, Gerard, aka Cherub."

"Uh-uh."

The next two names were also negative. Haggerty began to doubt his line of reasoning.

"Olaffson, Clifford, aka Zephyr," Elsa said.

"Match!" Tanner said. "And guess whose name is on the time and date list, same office? Corbin, Nia. That mean something?"

"Only conspiracy to commit mass murder," Haggerty said grimly. "Thanks, Mitch. Now patch me through to the Dragon."

Consuela stood beside a tall, youthful-looking man with dark blond hair, dressed in the unimaginative suit apparently required for all FBI agents.

"Where are you, Mr. Haggerty?" agent Keenan demanded.

"On my way to the Superbowl," Haggerty said. "You might want to meet me there. I'm convinced the next performance is going to be even more dramatic than the one last night."

"Sonofabitch," Keenan swore. "Any reason why I should think you're not involved?"

"I'm afraid I'm short on hard evidence at the moment, but would I be speaking to you now if I was involved? Listen, agent Keenan, I know who's pulling the band's strings—Corbin and the owner of that club, a kid named Max Jennings."

"The club where the only evidence was your DNA?"

"That's right. Jennings invented the new drug that was loaded into the units at the triple press. He's got a grudge against Stelwyn for firing him over it, and a grudge against me for getting his parents' insurance claim cancelled. Corbin's only twenty-three years old. I'll wager that Doug Zabrowski found out and she killed him for it."

"I'm afraid that's not all you need to clear you, Mr. Haggerty," Consuela said.

"I'll vouch for him," Stelwyn interjected.

"Who is that?" agent Keenan asked.

"Antonio Stelwyn," Consuela answered.

"We're about to touch down at the stadium," Haggerty said. "I believe Max Jennings and Corbin are there. All I ask is that you keep your agents off my back while I try to get at them. Afterwards, I'll surrender to you."

"Touchdown in forty-eight seconds," Elsa warned.

"What if I say no?" Keenan said.

"I can't afford to give you that opportunity."

Haggerty clicked off. Stelwyn pulled the nose up hard and powered down fast, dropping the craft directly into the slot reserved for his car—much to the shock of the thousands of spectators observing the game on giant viewscreens in the acres-long parking lot. He popped the hatch and he and his guards deplaned.

Haggerty unstrapped in his form-fitting plasticine seat.

Elsa turned to him. "Jason, I feel it necessary to inform you that I have less than forty minutes of power reserve left."

Haggerty touched her hand. "What are the options?"

"I can stay with you at full operation or shut down to sleep mode and double my time, or borrow this craft and return to BBI and upload. My primary concern is for your safety. I do not fear reset."

Haggerty weighed her words. If Elsa drained to zero without upload, the recordings she held would be lost, along with everything she'd experienced since the last time she'd uploaded. The evidence contained within her might be the only effective way of clearing his name and, more important, stopping the conspiracy. Losing it would be disastrous.

"Go to BBI and upload, Elsa. If there's time."

"If I leave within the next seven minutes, I should make it," she said.

Stelwyn stuck his head through the hatch, clearly disturbed by the delay. Haggerty explained the situation quickly. Stelwyn handed him the keycard.

"Go, Elsa. Upload, make encrypted copies of the recordings, and put them someplace safe. Then show them to agent Keenan."

Haggerty set one foot out of the jetcraft. Elsa placed a hand on his shoulder.

"I find myself in a quandary, Jason. My concern for your safety has overridden your desire to salvage the evidence stored within me. I cannot leave you."

"There's nothing to worry about," he said, scratching his neck. "The situation is under control and the evidence must not be lost. Now go!"

"I cannot," she said. "You scratched your neck. You do that when you are not telling the truth. There is a great deal to worry about, and I must protect you."

A loud horn sounded the start of the second quarter.

"We've got to get in there!" Stelwyn urged.

"Elsa, I order you to short your PLC. We must save the recordings."

"Jason, I—"

"You're too important to me, Elsa. Command override, two-four-Juliet. Short your PLC now!"

Elsa's eyes fluttered; Haggerty imagined he could smell the electrical burn as she fried her loyalty chip's bioelectric synapse. A small blood clot appeared in the upper corner of her left eye.

"Now go," he said. He joined Stelwyn and Regina on the ground. "Show it all to the Federal agents."

Elsa brought the hatch down and began her preflight preparations.

Haggerty took Regina's hand; they followed Stelwyn and his bodyguards toward the South Gate. He glanced back once to see the ascending jetcraft disappear in the sky. Stelwyn's bodyguards cleared a path to the ticketpoint, through throngs of milling kids calling out for tickets. A young man in a Clone Jesus jacket hawking, "Samples, get your free samples!" shoved a small plastic bag into Regina's hand.

"Try it, you'll like it," he said with a glazed stare.

Regina clutched Haggerty's arm tightly. She held up the small white unit with a trembling hand. Haggerty scanned the crowd. Many of the youngsters carried similar bags. One was on his knees, throwing up.

Stelwyn shouted something as his bodyguards pushed through the turngate past the operator. Alarms clamored as they continued through the security arch, triggering anew as Stelwyn,

Haggerty, and Regina followed them under. The roar of the crowd shook the massive stadium. Stelwyn was yelling into his earpiece, trying to explain the situation to security, but the din from the million-plus attendees made communication nearly impossible.

Two uniformed guards rushed from their post with stunners ready, shouting, "Put your hands in the air." They were immediately confronted by Stelwyn's men.

Haggerty and Regina complied.

Stelwyn stepped between his men and produced his I.D. "If you want to keep your jobs you'll lower those stunners," he said coldly. "If you want to spend the rest of your lives in hellish squalor, keep pointing them at me. This is my damned stadium. Check with the office."

One of the guards spoke into his com. Bullhorns pierced the mayhem, punctuated by the bark of a sportscaster.

"Sorry for the mix-up, Mr. Stelwyn," the man said as he unclipped his earpiece. "Enjoy the game with your guests."

They stepped out onto a first-deck platform amid the raucous crowd in the stands. Haggerty surveyed the two-hundred-yard field below them where the double lineup of gargantuan players in bright-colored body armor faced off as a whistle blew. Even from this distance the genetically enhanced warriors seemed inhuman.

"I can't stand how the players are deformed," Regina said. "Their families are so desperate they sacrifice their children so the rest of the nation can enjoy its blood sport. It's blasphemous."

Years ago, Haggerty would have said the parents' choice to have their children mutated was rational, guaranteeing a short, wealthy life with the best of everything rather than a long subsistence in poverty. Since the car accident, his view had changed: Nothing rational warranted the shortening of a child's life. And parents who might live forever needed their children alive and healthy for at least as long as they planned to live, themselves, or they risked falling prey to despair—and pressing to escape that despair. There were many more arguments to be made against condemning children to an early death in the name of ensuring they lived in material comfort. But right now the players' lives weren't his concern.

A flag dropped, halting the next play. A false start call against NewVada unleashed a riot of derision from the crowd. NewVada trailed 21-19, and was lining up to punt, so the crowd was in no mood for mindless penalties. A two-hundred-foot-long plasma screen replayed the call, which only incited the crowd more. The timeclock at the upper right quadrant of the scoreboard indicated three minutes left in the second quarter, which meant ten to fifteen in real time.

Stelwyn clicked off his earset. "Nothing but backtalk from the office," he told his bodyguards. "You go to the staging area and you to the VIP green room. Use my name and authority. Break legs if you have to. See to it that band does not go onstage. Make sure the stage never rises. Understood?"

The men nodded and left.

"Okay, Haggerty, consider the band stopped. Now help me get my hands on Max. You're the only one who can identify him. Where do we start?"

"My bet is he's somewhere out there, watching the game and calling orders from an earset. He said he'd be here in style. That means the lower-level suites on the hundred-yard line."

Haggerty moved along the rail, scanning the stadium. It was impossible to make out the faces of anyone that far downfield and there was no time physically to check each suite.

"Hey man, you're blockin' my view," a fan shouted at Haggerty.

Haggerty turned to his taunter. "Lend me those," he said, indicating the binoculars at the man's neck with his stunner.

He finessed the finger dials and surveyed the distant lower-level suites. The center suite's occupants came into focus: Max, Corbin, and a single security guard. He handed the binoculars to Stelwyn.

Unfortunately, the fastest way to get there was through the stands and across the first row. Haggerty flicked the binoculars back to their owner. Then he and Regina followed Stelwyn, descending two steps at a time.

The crowd rose with a roar as Johnson, the NewVada kicker, sent the ball hurtling down the field and the linemen took off after it. Haggerty could not help glancing at the action. The players sprinted forward with tremendous speed. Their agility *was* inhuman; the biogenetic enhancements had come on so gradually, he'd never really considered it before. When he was a kid the field had been only a hundred yards long. He recalled the first time he'd attended a game, gripping his father's hand and bursting with excitement. How large the place had seemed then. Eventually the UFL felt the new breed of players warranted doubling the field size. The vastness of this complex was almost beyond comprehension.

"Matheson takes the snap," the sportscaster called. "He drops back, he's looking deep... Nolan has a step... Matheson airs it out

... and Nolan makes a beautiful leaping catch! That ball was nearly a hundred yards in the air, folks. First down!"

Stelwyn reached lower level and cut across the front row with Haggerty and Regina close behind. They dashed along the thirty-foot wall through screaming and swearing fans, toward the New York players' warm-up bench on the field. Haggerty struggled to keep up.

A hush fell over the crowd as Gerald Sohl, a NewVada linebacker, lay motionless on the field after taking a big hit. Young footballers died now and then; it was part of the thrill of the game. If the linebacker were dead, the game would be delayed while he was carted off the field and replaced, then play would resume. A quarterback's death could theoretically stop the game, but this had happened only once before, to a stunning talent named Sturgeon, years ago.

"We're moving too slow," Stelwyn shouted. He broke into a run. Haggerty and Regina ran after him, shoving people out of their way as the downed linebacker got up and the stadium went wild.

Inhuman, Haggerty thought. He sprinted toward stadium midpoint, his shoes hammering against cement, pounding and pounding, his legs about to give out, his lungs threatening to explode.

The buzzer sounded. The sportscaster's voice echoed across the stadium: "We have reached the two minute warning, as NewVada, still trailing, is struggling to move into field goal range. It's been a heartstopping first half of action here in Superbowl One-Hundred-Ninety!"

Two minutes left and over half the stadium still to cover. There was no chance of making it to Max's suite before halftime. When the band did not appear, Max and Corbin would flee— and there was no predicting how many other schemes Max might hatch if this one failed to bring about disaster.

Regina skidded to a halt, breathing hard. "I think I can buy us time," she said, looking over her shoulder at a cadre of kids in Clone Jesus jackets in the first row. She pulled Haggerty's head down for a hard kiss.

"Get outta the way," one of the boys shouted.

"Go nail that fucker!" Regina yelled, ripping a colorful airboard from one of the fans' backpacks and clutching it to her chest. By the time the boy got to his feet Regina had powered it on, leapt over the rail, and was plummeting toward the field with the board stretched beneath her at arm's length. Haggerty felt a surge of pride and admiration as she rolled her foot atop it, balanced on the edge of the wall, pulled up a few feet above the field, and surfed the green toward the center of the game, cannonballing straight for the players.

Haggerty tore off after Stelwyn.

"Hold on a minute, folks," the sportscaster announced. "There seems to be a girl hurtling across the field on an airboard!" Regina appeared on the viewscreen, tacking through the air, gaining speed. The players halted, unsure what to do. "Must be a Clone Jesus fan. Look at her go. There's a flag on the field! They're stopping the clock."

The stands erupted with laughter, disbelief, and outrage.

Haggerty pushed himself to midpoint, a stitching pain in his side. On the giant screen a half-dozen security guards converged behind Regina, unfurling barbed catchwire nets; more guards moved toward her through the players up ahead, stunners held high.

"It looks like we're getting a little extra entertainment for our money," the sportscaster observed merrily.

Stelwyn was far ahead of Haggerty, several yards from the door to the suite. Haggerty willed himself to move faster. Looking out he saw Regina nose right and one-eighty to avoid security. She didn't have long before they either snared her or stunned her down. A fall from that height and speed could be serious. Haggerty ran on—desperate to properly spend the time she was buying him.

Stelwyn pushed through the final throng of fans to the suite. He turned back, saw Haggerty, drew his revolver, and pounded on the door. Haggerty fumbled for the stunner in his pocket, arriving just as Stelwyn grabbed the security guard by the collar, dragged him outside at gunpoint, and shoved him backward down the steps. Haggerty leaped over the flailing guard and rushed into the suite, stunner raised.

Max and Corbin turned from where they leaned against the suite's fully stocked bar, registering surprise and raising their hands.

Max smirked beneath flushed cheeks. "I knew you were too dedicated to miss the game, Mr. Haggerty." He was still wearing his tuxedo.

Corbin laughed under her breath.

"And the game is back on," the sportscaster's voice filled the suite. "As they restart the clock, there's one minute left and it's third down and twelve yards to go for a first. NewVada better move fast."

"You little worm," Stelwyn said contemptuously as he kicked the door closed behind him and stepped beside Haggerty.

"That quaint term is out of date, old man," Max said derisively. "And a bit misleading, seeing that I hold the power here."

A dark shape hurtled from the shadows and tackled Stelwyn to the floor, sending his antique gun spinning into the corner. Haggerty kept his stunner trained on Max, who seemed utterly unconcerned.

"I control Shintag Lake, the band, this show, the police, and I'm this close to taking over NewVada's underground," he said. "And at the moment, Mr. Stelwyn, it would appear I control you."

Brian dragged Stelwyn to his feet. The ape seemed indifferent to his mutilated, gauze-swathed hand.

"Stupid punk," Stelwyn snarled. "Lake is using you, the police will sell you out to the highest bidder, and if you move against the Triads, they'll cut you to pieces."

"I'm a song away from cowing them all," Max said, a nasty grin on his face.

"Why are you doing this?" Haggerty demanded.

The ape's head snapped around; his eyes narrowed on Haggerty. "You're the sonofabitch who ruined my hand!"

Stelwyn butted his head into the ape's Adam's apple. Brian released his hold and Haggerty stunned him. Stelwyn pulled a small revolver from his jacket pocket, blowing a hole in Max's face and showering Corbin in blood. The loud report was muffled by a million screaming fans as NewVada scored with a last-ditch shot. No one screamed louder than Corbin.

Max's body crumpled to the floor. The stadium shook with cheering and jumping and stamping. Stelwyn turned the gun on Corbin.

"Don't let him do it," Corbin pleaded to Haggerty.

"Wait," Haggerty urged Stelwyn. "Think of Tyler. The bitch deserves to die as ruthlessly as she killed him and Zabrowski and the others—and to see it coming. But we need her as a witness to help clear up this mess. Let the Feds take care of her."

"Both of you drop your weapons," a new voice said.

Oliver Wendell Primrose emerged from his hiding place behind the bar, plasma rifle in hand. Haggerty dropped his stunner. Stelwyn tightened his grip on the revolver.

"Took you long enough," Corbin said, lowering her hands and smiling viciously.

"Tell me you'll really miss that bagbite and I'll halve your cut for insincerity," Primrose warned her.

"That's how you financed things, isn't it?" Haggerty said. "You manipulated presses where there were no direct heirs, like Nyuga and Rosenberg yesterday morning. Then what? Did you alter the documents so their funds went to a discretionary account?"

Primrose smiled thinly. "Making a favored charity the beneficiary in lieu of or in conjunction with other surviving heirs is a time-honored practice, Mr. Haggerty. And what better charity to benefit than St. Maximilian's Shelter for Widows and Orphans?"

"I suppose Max was the orphan. Who was the widow?"

"That's a recent development," Corbin said coolly, gazing perfunctorily at Max's corpse.

"Grieving, of course," Primrose mocked.

"Hardly," Corbin said. "You were always a better fuck. But I'm not exactly thrilled he's gone."

"Come on, princess. You've been saying you wanted to kill him since junior year."

"We needed him. He had the formula for the fucking drug."

Haggerty realized they'd been classmates together. Primrose had himself aged to join Cromwell and Sons.

"All right, Stelwyn, enough of this. Drop the gun or go for it," Primrose challenged.

"Don't do it!" Haggerty warned. "How will Sylvia survive losing you, too?"

Stelwyn hesitated but Primrose didn't. Haggerty latched onto Stelwyn's arm and pulled him forward as Primrose fired. The shot missed its target and blasted the wall.

Shards of hypersteel ricocheted through the air. One pierced Stelwyn's shoulder. A second splinter lodged in his throat, abruptly cutting off his screams. Stelwyn was down, bleeding profusely at the neck, his eyes open and staring, beyond help.

"What a rush," Primrose exulted. "I killed Antonio Stelwyn! Don't just stand there, Nia. Lock the damned door."

"Watch where you aim that thing," Corbin said flatly. She dusted herself off, crossed the suite, and engaged the digital lock.

Screams shook the stadium. "What an amazing turnaround at the end of the first half of this Superbowl One-Hundred-Ninety!" boomed the sportscaster.

"It's time we granted your death wish," Primrose said, training the rifle on Haggerty.

"Last request?" Haggerty said.

Primrose paused, cocked a brow.

"Pull the damned trigger," Corbin snapped.

"Go ahead, Haggerty."

"Satisfy my curiosity. Zephyr registered for his unit when Corbin got hers. Was he another classmate?"

Corbin snorted. "The little shit dropped out of high school to form a band. Never studied anything but music and never stopped whining about his art."

"Then how was he persuaded to get involved with you?"

"Never underestimate an artist's ego, Mr. Haggerty." Primrose smirked. "All Nia had to do was play the adoring fan and pretend to admire his philosophy, all the while she was manipulating him into espousing ours. She convinced him there were no more challenges for him, he'd already accomplished everything, and his future was all downhill. But if he had the courage, he could make a lasting impression on the disaffected and disenfranchised youth of the nation."

"He thought he was going to save his generation?"

"He doesn't give a damn about his generation," Corbin said scornfully. "I just promised that he and his music would become immortal."

"We've answered your questions, Mr. Haggerty. Time to say good night."

The door to the suite exploded inward, clipping Corbin's shoulder as it crashed down. Elsa leapt in, armor protracted, arms spread in defensive posture, landing in front of Haggerty.

"Don't!" Corbin screamed as Primrose switched to detonator, his finger tightening on the trigger.

A small explosion flattened Haggerty against the wall. He opened his eyes to find Primrose bloodied and lifeless on the floor—the inevitable result of the backlash from plasma fired at point-blank range against Elsa's hypersteel shielding. Corbin lay nearby, blood staining the carpet beneath her head. He didn't know if she were dead or merely unconscious, and he didn't much care. He turned to Elsa.

The burst had blown her to pieces. What little was left—her legless torso missing one arm—lay twisted on the ground. Haggerty went down on his knees and touched her ruined face, more than half of which was a grotesque mesh of circuitry and burnt synthaderm. She'd overridden his command and come back for him despite her disengaged Personal Loyalty Chip.

"Jason ... ," a garbled, deconstructed voice spoke through broken lips, "are you unharmed?"

Startled, he leaned over her one eye that might see him. "Yes," he choked out. It was painful seeing her like this.

"I have disobeyed you," she said, her voice degrading. "I have not ..." A liquid squelching sound, as of shorting circuitry. "... fulfilled my duties to the investigation. I did not ... want you to terminate. I do not ... care ... about the evidence ... as you do. I have ..." Another circuit sizzled. "... acted selfishly, inhumanely."

Haggerty held her broken torso, fluids draining out of her across his lap. Had the chip left some imprint on all her programming, the imperative to protect him become habit through years of service? Whatever the explanation, he was humbled by the *nobility*—there was no other word—of her actions.

"No, Elsa," he said. "Don't you see? The fact that you care about me means you're capable of caring, and discerning who you care about. That's one of the most confounding elements of the human condition, and I'm so grateful you've achieved it." And while putting one person's life above the lives of millions might not be humane, it was only too human. Haggerty wanted desperately to comfort her. "Thank you," he said. "You saved my life. You're the best assistant anyone ever had."

The lamp behind Elsa's eye brightened. "Do you want to hear ... my conclusion ... regarding suicidal ... tend ... tendencies that arise ... from despair?" More circuits shorted. He didn't know how she managed to keep going.

"Yes, very much," he said.

"Osmosis is a ... process that is capable of ... working both ways."

Haggerty nodded that he understood, tears running down his face. She convulsed in his lap. She reached her arm toward his face and then struggled to turn herself toward the wall where Max's corpse had fallen, her eye fixated there. Her arm reached spasmodically outward.

"What, Elsa? What is it you want?" he asked hopelessly.

Elsa convulsed again, spitting a torrent of coolant. She twisted free from Haggerty and struggled to drag her shattered torso toward the wall.

Haggerty put his arms around her and pulled her to Max. "What is it, Elsa?" he asked again.

A gurgling sound as the coolant choked her into another convulsion, and still she reached, not for Max but for something on the wall behind him—an electric outlet. She upturned her hand feebly and sprung her prongs. Haggerty steadied her wrist and guided her fingers to the socket. Trembling, she turned to face him. Her powerpacks made their final discharge. Haggerty felt the last pulse of energy leave her.

"Please don't—" she said, and powered down, whatever she meant to tell him unfinished, the final piece of evidence lost along with her. He doubted he'd ever know what she'd hoped to accomplish.

Haggerty wept, rocking Elsa tightly in his arms, having no desire to untangle himself from her. Her chestport had come unclasped, revealing something inside. He opened the port and found an unpopped KV unit. It had to be the one they'd taken from Regina's cupboard. He'd thought they lost it in DeAngelo's Corvair.

He slid the unit out and pressed the ARM switch, knowing intuitively that it must be his own. "Recording," said the familiar voice he'd chosen long ago; the light beneath the button flashed pale amber. Regina must have scraped the serial numbers off to protect him. He'd had it with him all along and Elsa had broken the law and reviewed it. What was on it? The dozen or so recordings leading to his failed presses? He flushed with shame. And then he realized she'd never have judged him. It simply was not part of her programming.

Haggerty pinched the bridge of his nose, trying to hold back wrenching sobs. Finally, it was time, he decided. Max and Primrose were beyond the reach of justice, but their threat was eliminated. The evidence was lost, and with Stelwyn dead there was no one who could support Haggerty's version of what had happened. Svoboda would not risk his colony. But none of that mattered now. Haggerty had done his duty. The band had been stopped. Doug and Elsa, the last of his friends who might regret his passing, were gone. And Regina would be better off without him.

Haggerty had his finger on the button. One tiny exertion of pressure and he would know if there was a God. If indeed He damned those who pressed. Or would Saint Peter greet him with a post-press review of his own?

The stadium crowd cheered as a trill of electronic melody washed through the suite. Haggerty looked up. Clone Jesus was onstage, warming up.

Breathing deeply to get himself under control, he reached his thumb along the gunmetal, over the cold onyx button, and pressed the ARM switch again, shutting down the unit. Until he stopped Zephyr, his job wasn't finished. If he was going to die, it would be while seeking to stop an untold number of other deaths.

He slid the unit back into Elsa and sealed her chestport. "Good-bye my dear friend," he whispered, leaning close over Elsa's shattered form.

"What the hell?" a voice above him said.

Haggerty looked up to find agent Keenan staring from the scorched walls to the bodies to himself hunched over a broken android. Several men in dark jumpsuits entered the suite and fanned out, stuns drawn. One of them led Regina, hands bound behind her. She had bruises on her face and her blouse was torn but she was alive. She looked questioningly at Elsa.

"What's going on here, Haggerty?" Keenan demanded, stepping over Brian's body.

"I think the ex-footballer is just stunned. Get him in wristbonds before he wakes up," Haggerty said. "You'll need to wristbond the bitch over there, as well."

Keenan bent to examine one of the bodies. "Tell me this isn't Antonio Stelwyn," he said.

Haggerty pushed off Elsa's limp torso and shakily got to his feet.

"Why aren't you restraining Corbin?" he asked Keenan.

The Federal agent turned his stunner on Haggerty. "I've got dead bodies, unconscious bodies, and the suspect everyone's been hunting the past eighteen hours is the only man left standing, and you want me to arrest *her?*"

Haggerty crossed weakly to the window of the suite. "If you want to prevent the suicides of untold thousands of kids and their parents, we have to stop the lead singer from giving them the idea," he said, pointing to the stage at centerfield where Clone Jesus were playing, magnified on the giant viewscreen behind the goalposts.

"He's going to suicide onstage?" Keenan asked incredulously.

"Not if I can stop it," Haggerty said.

"He's telling the truth!" Regina shouted. "Help him!"

Keenan barked an order to his men to take Corbin and Brian into custody and leave the girl. He disengaged his earpiece and leaned toward Haggerty. "I know what's planned," he said, voice low. "Everything you told me was transmitted to my superiors. Now for the love of God, trust me and follow my lead." Straightening, he produced a pair of wristbonds. "I'm glad you've decided to cooperate," he said loudly. "I'm sure things will go much easier on you because of it." He kept eye contact with Haggerty as he fastened the first bond; Haggerty could feel that the clasp hadn't been engaged. He allowed Keenan to turn him and pretend to fasten the other bond.

Keenan was still reading him his rights when the last of his men cleared Brian and Corbin out of the suite.

Haggerty, Regina and agent Keenan raced onto the green as the crowd swayed together in time to the music. It was a soft, simple ballad Haggerty could almost appreciate. The viewscreen switched back and forth between Zephyr on guitar and Cherub on bass.

"Are you going to tell us what that little act was about?" Haggerty asked.

"I got an executive order to prevent you from stopping the halftime show," Keenan told him. "My superiors paid close attention to what you said, weighed the losses against some fucking theoretical benefit, and decided that a few hundred thousand dead teenagers wasn't too high a price to pay for what they see as social stability. Took them all of twenty seconds. I think they were hoping for it."

"From how high up does this order come?" Haggerty asked.

"At least as high as the Surgeon General," Keenan replied.

"This is the United States of America we're talking about, right?" Regina said acidly.

"So they tell me." Keenan's response was just as bitter.

"And you're disobeying that order for altruistic reasons?"

"Two of them," Keenan said. "My son and my stepson, twelve and fourteen."

"Your career may be as dead as mine," Haggerty said.

"Never mind that now. We've got to stop the singer. How's he going to do it?" Keenan reset his earpiece as they jogged.

"Black button," Haggerty said.

"We can't just walk onstage and arrest him because you say he's going to press."

"Trust me," Haggerty said. "I'll bet my life he's got his KV unit on him now."

Keenan halted, grabbing Haggerty by the arm. "He has a *registered* unit?"

"I got confirmation from BBI just before we spoke earlier," Haggerty said.

"That's grounds for suspicion, but pressing a registered unit isn't a crime, Federal or otherwise."

"It is if it's premeditation to incite minors to suicide, and a NewVada ordinance makes it illegal to conduct a suicide for entertainment purposes."

"You'd better not be making that up," Keenan said. "And he'd better be in possession."

The giant monitor showed Zephyr at the microphone gyrating in time to the syncdrums. The blisterbrandings that covered most of his bare upper body made him look like a Rorschach. He closed his eyes, tilted his buzzed head backward, and began to sing in a soulful tenor.

"I don't believe we'll Clone Jesus,

I don't believe in my band,

I don't believe big brother,

All I trust is the voice in my head,

And the choice, and this Killswitch here in my hand... ."

"Sound like grounds for suspicion?" Haggerty asked Keenan.

A row of bull-faced security guards stood shoulder to shoulder across the perimeter of the stage. Keenan flashed his plate to the person in charge. "Federal business; let us through," he said.

The guard apologized to Keenan: he did not have the authority to give them access.

Keenan pulled his autostun. "We've got lives at stake you'll be liable for, so how about I give you that authority?" he asked mildly.

"Right this way, sir."

Lake stood near the steps at the side of the stage in black leather, his hair pulled taut off his ancient, ageless face. "I'm so glad you could make it, Mister Haggerty," he said smugly.

Haggerty resisted the urge to punch him. "This is Federal

agent Keenan. We have reason to suspect that Zephyr is planning to press onstage."

"Even coming from you that's preposterous," Lake sneered.

"We're stopping the performance to search him nonetheless," Haggerty said. "And everyone else onstage as well."

"You'll need a warrant for that," attorney Ryerson said from behind his boss.

"I can have one in five minutes," Keenan snarled, clipping his earpiece.

"Don't bother," Haggerty said. "I've already taken care of it."

Lake eyed him curiously as Haggerty reached into his pants pocket. He leaned forward to look. Haggerty kneed him in the groin, then pushed the doubled-over Lake into Ryerson's startled arms.

"I'll make sure you receive the maximum penalty for assault, Mr. Haggerty!" he shouted.

Haggerty and Keenan were already ascending the crude insta-stairs with Regina close behind. At stage level Haggerty surveyed the enthralled million-plus audience. The screen cut from musician to musician, simultaneously broadcasting to billions of home viewers. He caught a flash of sunlight on metal: dozens of security guards converging from all sides at the foot of the stage, talking over earsets, autostuns at the ready. Who was really running the show?

Keenan looked at him grimly.

"Regina," Haggerty said, "I need you to stay back in case Zephyr tries to get offstage."

"Okay," she said.

Haggerty and Keenan proceeded onto the stage. Seeing Haggerty, Cherub tipped his chin at Zephyr's guitar. A KV unit was attached to the back, the red light encircling the button lit. The drummer built up to a crescendo; suddenly the shrill notes segued back to the soft ballad.

"I don't believe we'll Clone Jesus,
I don't believe in my band,
I don't believe big brother,
All I trust is the voice in my head,
And the choice, and this Killswitch here in my hand... ."

As Zephyr sang he reached for his unit.

"Stun him!" Haggerty yelled.

Keenan raised the stunner halfway, paralyzed between morality and duty. Haggerty realized the agent would not fire. He threw himself against Keenan, smashing him to the stage and wresting the stunner from him. Half a dozen agents trained their weapons on Haggerty, believing their prisoner had just over-powered a Federal agent.

Zephyr pulled the black box off his guitar and held it aloft. Haggerty raised the stunner, sensing the agents' tracer points all over him. If he didn't act now, Zephyr would finish what Max had started.

Haggerty fired.

Pandemonium engulfed the stadium.

Haggerty lay crumpled on the stage, slowly returning to con-sciousness; no sound, no pain, merely the sensation of floating. He opened his eyes.

Regina knelt over him, crying. He could faintly feel her hands in his hair as she looked down into his face.

"What—?" he choked out.

"Just keep breathing for me and keep your eyes open, all right?" she said, her voice trembling. "They've called an ambu-lance." She smiled broadly. "You stunned him. I got his box."

With an effort, Haggerty turned his head and saw several agents milling chaotically nearby. He dimly heard the clamor of the crowd. Zephyr struggled toward them, hand outstretched.

"Hey man, you've got no fucking business stopping my press!"

"Fuck you, you grokless idiot," Regina said. "This isn't even your idea!"

"You won't be pressing anything until this mess is sorted out," Keenan added, wristbonding Zephyr. "Or didn't you know your little stunt is illegal?"

Detective Woyzeck came into view, his eye black and blue where Haggerty had hit him with the chair. "Nice halftime show you put on, Haggerty," he said, grinning. One of his front teeth was missing. "Don't try to speak," he said. "I figured it out. You thought I was involved, I thought you were. I'll find a way to clear you on this, I promise. Just hang on."

Haggerty doubted Woyzeck would be able to fulfill that prom-ise. All the evidence was lost. His act would be seen as that of a fugitive attempting homicide, a tragic end to a series of mean-ingless acts of violence. Even Keenan, who'd risked his career to stop the slaughter, wouldn't risk it further to clear a dead man. But it was all right. He'd foiled Max's plan. He was content.

"Please Jason, I need you to hang on," Regina said tearfully.

He smiled up at her. "You'll find someone younger and less scarred," he whispered. "I'm old enough to be your great-grand-father."

"Tell that to our great-grandchildren," she said, wiping her eyes.

He felt himself fading. The central nervous system could only take so much disruption before it was unrecoverable and he doubted medical assistance would arrive in time. He regretted that the kids they'd saved would never know the truth, never question the dreadful machine complicit in plans for their destruction and take the system to task. Gandhi was wrong. He had no further instructions to give them.

With a loud burst the viewscreen above Haggerty went black and immediately cut back with the image of himself in his family's tomb, wearing Sasha DeAngelo's face.

The stadium went silent.

"Now let's review those recordings and find out what everyone's so eager to erase," his voice boomed. "Play Teardrop's first... ."

Haggerty looked up in disbelief at the unwinding footage from Elsa. Could she truly have uploaded herself? Or had Joe Svoboda decided to help after all by broadcasting her transmissions of the last day? He doubted he'd live to find out.

A Federal agent headed toward him. Keenan held him back.

"Leave them be," Keenan told him.

"What about that?" The agent indicated the viewscreen.

"Let it play," Keenan said.

Images from the reviewed presses flashed past, then Elsa's voice, "You believe the boxes used in the triple press were loaded with Happy Styx?"

"Yes, but I need to prove it. Review again," Haggerty said onscreen. "Magnify and let's see if we can tell if he presses."

"I'll tell them, Jason," Regina whispered. "I promise I'll tell them everything."

And they were seeing it all for themselves now, Haggerty thought. The world would learn the truth. Zephyr would be revealed as the puppet in someone else's schemes, an object of pity rather than an idol to be adored and emulated. Even if he restaged his suicide and succeeded, it wouldn't have the impact his actions could have had today. Surely questions would follow, and maybe a demand for accountability. Haggerty prayed it would be enough, that the danger was truly past.

He felt so proud of Regina, so thankful that she'd helped him remember how to feel. Ready to die since yesterday morning, maybe for the past two years, he wanted very much to live now.

"Make sure you stick around long enough to watch me," she chided him.

Sounds of sirens approached from the distance. Haggerty dimly felt Regina take his hand. He smiled again, but made no promises he doubted he could keep.

AUTHOR BIOS

Steven-Elliot Altman is a bestselling author, screenwriter, and most recently a successful videogame developer, having won multiple awards for his new online role playing game *9Dragons*. His novels include *Captain America is Dead, Zen in the Art of Slaying Vampires, Batman: Fear Itself, The Irregulars* and *Deprivers*. Steven's also the editor of the anthology *The Touch* and a contributor to *Shadows Over Baker Street*, a collection of Sherlock Holmes meets H.P. Lovecraft Stories. Most recently, Steven penned the screenplay of his novel *Zen in the Art of Slaying Vampires,* soon to be a major motion picture. Once upon a time he also worked the night shift on a suicide prevention hotline.

Diane DeKelb-Rittenhouse spent several years in Manhattan as an actress before marrying her college sweetheart and returning to the Philadelphia area where she had been born. Diane first worked with Steven-Elliot Altman when they created the acclaimed, *Publisher's Weekly* Starred-Review anthology *The Touch: Epidemic of the Millennium,* in which her story "Gifted" appeared. Diane has published a number of other critically acclaimed short stories, most notably in the science fiction, murder, and horror genres. Her young adult fantasy novel, *Faerie Rings: The Book of Forests*, is forthcoming.

ARTIST BIO

Eran Cantrell began illustrating at a very young age, in response to her fascination with storytelling and the imagery it evoked. As a result, stories and art have always been inseparable in her mind, and translating one into the other soon became the focus of her life. Her devotion set her ahead of her peers early on, and motivated her to earn a Bachelor of Design at the Alberta College of Art and Design. Today, she emerges onto the scene as a repeatedly-published illustrator, and intends to continue doing what she loves as long as there are stories at hand.

Eran currently resides in Canada.

Yard Dog Press Titles As Of This Print Date

The Green Women, Laura J. Underwood
The Guardians, Lynn Abbey
Hammer Town, Selina Rosen
The Happiness Box, Beverly A. Hale
The Host Series: The Host, Fright Eater, Gang Approval, Selina
     Rosen
Houston, We've Got Bubbas!, Edited by Selina Rosen
How I Spent the Apocolypse, Selina Rosen
I Didn't Quite Make It To Oz, Edited by Selina Rosen
I Should Have Stayed In Oz, Edited by Selina Rosen
In the Shadows, Bradley H. Sinor
International House of Bubbas, Edited by Selina Rosen
It's the Great Bumpkin, Cletus Brown!, Katherine A. Turski
The Killswitch Review, Steven-Elliot Altman & Diane DeKelb-
     Rittenhouse
The Leopard's Daughter, Lee Killough
The Lightning Horse, John Moore
The Logic of Departure, Mark W. Tiedemann
The Long, Cold Walk To Mars, Jeffrey Turner
Marking the Signs and Other Tales Of Mischief, Laura J.
     Underwood
Material Things, Selina Rosen
Medieval Misfits: Renaissance Rejects, Tracy S. Morris
Mirror Images, Susan Satterfield
Mirror, Mirror and Other Reflections, James K. Burk
More Stories That Won't Make Your Parents Hurl, Edited by
     Selina Rosen
Music for Four Hands, Louis Antonelli & Edward Morris
My Life with Geeks and Freaks, Claudia Christian
The Necronomicrap: A Guide To Your Horoooscope, Tim Frayser
Playing With Secrets, Bradley H & Sue P. Sinor
Redheads In Love, Linda L. Donahue, Rhonda Eudaly, Julia S.
     Mandala, & Dusty Rainbolt
Reruns, Selina Rosen
Rock 'n' Roll Universe, Ken Rand
Shadows In Green, Richard Dansky
Stories That Won't Make Your Parents Hurl, Edited by Selina
     Rosen
Tales from Keltora, Laura J. Underwood
Tales Of the Lucky Nickel Saloon, Second Ave., Laramie, Wyo-
     ming, U S of A, Ken Rand
Tarbox Station, Rhonda Eudaly
Texistani: Indo-Pak Food From A Texas Kitchen, Beverly A. Hale
That's All Folks, J. F. Gonzalez
Through Wyoming Eyes, Ken Rand
Turn Left to Tomorrow, Robin Wayne Bailey

The Twins, Selina Rosen
Wandering Lark, Laura J. Underwood
Wings of Morning, Katharine Eliska Kimbriel
Zombies In Oz and Other Undead Musings, Robin Wayne Bailey

Just Cause
(A YDP Imprint):

The Bitter End
Selina Rosen

Double Dog
(A YDP Imprint):

Death Under the Crescent Moon
Dusty Rainbolt

#1:

The Ghost Writer
Selina Rosen

Of Stars & Shadows, Mark W.
Tiedemann
This Instance Of Me, Jeffrey Turner

*It's Not Rocket Science: Spirituality
for the Working-Class Soul*
Selina Rosen

#2:

Meditations of a Hoarder
Melinda LaFevers

Gods and Other Children, Bill D. Allen
Tranquility, Tracy Morris

Not My Life
Selina Rosen

#3:

Home Is the Hunter, James K. Burk
Farstep Station, Lazette Gifford

The Pit
Selina Rosen

#4:

*Plots and Protagonists: A Refer-
ence Guide for Writers*
Mel. White

Sabre Dance, Melanie Fletcher
The Lunari Mask, Laura J. Underwood

#5:

Vanishing Fame
Selina Rosen

House of Doors, Julia Mandala
Jaguar Moon, Linda A. Donahue

Non-YDP titles we distribute:

Chains of Freedom
Chains of Destruction
Jabone's Sword
Queen of Denial
Recycled
Strange Robby
Sword Masters
Selina Rosen

Three Ways to Order:

1. Write us a letter telling us what you want, then send it along with your check or money order (made payable to Yard Dog Press) to: Yard Dog Press, 710 W. Redbud Lane, Alma, AR 72921-7247

2. Use selinarosen@cox.net or lynnstran@cox.net to contact us and place your order. Then send your check or money order to the address above. *This has the advantage of allowing you to check on the availability of short-stock items such as T-shirts and back-issues of Yard Dog Comics.*

3. Contact us as in #1 or #2 above and pay with a credit card or by debit from your checking account. Either give us the credit card information in your letter/Email/phone call, or go to our website and use our shopping carts. If you send us your information, please include your name as it appears on the card, your credit card number, the expiration date, and the 3 or 4-digit security code after your signature on the back (CVV). Please remember that we will include media rate (minimum $3.00) S/H for mailing in the lower 48 states.

Watch our website at
www.yarddogpress.com
for news of upcoming projects
and new titles!!

A Note to Our Readers

We at Yard Dog Press understand that many people buy used books because they simply can't afford new ones. That said, and understanding that not everyone is made of money, we'd like you to know something that you may not have realized. Writers only make money on new books that sell. At the big houses a writer's entire future can hinge on the number of books they sell. While this isn't the case at Yard Dog Press, the honest truth is that when you sell or trade your book or let many people read it, the writer and the publishing house aren't making any money.

As much as we'd all like to believe that we can exist on love and sweet potato pie, the truth is we all need money to buy the things essential to our daily lives. Writers and publishers are no different.

We realize that these "freebies" and cheap books often turn people on to new writers and books that they wouldn't otherwise read. However we hope that you will reconsider selling your copy, and that if you trade it or let your friends borrow it, you also pass on the information that if they really like the author's work they should consider buying one of their books at full price sometime so that the writer can afford to continue to write work that entertains you.

We appreciate all our readers and *depend* upon their support.

Thanks,
The Editorial Staff
Yard Dog Press

PS – Please note that "used" books without covers have, in most cases, been stolen. Neither the author nor the publisher has made any money on these books because they were supposed to be pulped for lack of sales.

Please do not purchase books without covers.

www.ingramcontent.com/pod-product-compliance
Lightning Source LLC
Chambersburg PA
CBHW020640260626
47157CB00008B/2831